RED CELL

MARK HENSHAW

A TOUCHSTONE BOOK
PUBLISHED BY SIMON & SCHUSTER
NEW YORK   LONDON   TORONTO   SYDNEY   NEW DELHI

Touchstone
A Division of Simon & Schuster, Inc.
1230 Avenue of the Americas
New York, NY 10020

First Touchstone hardcover edition May 2012

TOUCHSTONE and colophon are registered trademarks of Simon & Schuster, Inc.

For information about special discounts for bulk purchases, please contact Simon & Schuster Special Sales at 1-866-506-1949 or business@simonandschuster.com.

The Simon & Schuster Speakers Bureau can bring authors to your live event. For more information or to book an event contact the Simon & Schuster Speakers Bureau at 1-866-248-3049 or visit our website at www.simonspeakers.com.

Designed by Akasha Archer

Manufactured in the United States of America

10   9   8   7   6   5   4   3   2   1

Library of Congress Cataloging-in-Publication Data

Henshaw, Mark, 1970–
  Red cell / Mark Henshaw.—1st Touchstone hardcover ed.
    p. cm.
1. United States. Central Intelligence Agency—Fiction. 2. International relations—Fiction. I. Title.
  PS3608.E586R43 2012
  813'.6—dc23
                                    2011040716

ISBN 978-1-4516-6193-4
ISBN 978-1-4516-6194-1 (ebook)

To Janna,
who got me started;

and

to Russell, Adam, and Natalie,
the reasons I keep going.

For centuries China stood as a leading civilization, outpacing the rest of the world in the arts and sciences, but in the 19th and early 20th centuries, the country was beset by civil unrest, major famines, military defeats, and foreign occupation.

After World War II, the Communists under MAO Zedong established an autocratic socialist system that, while ensuring China's sovereignty, imposed strict controls over everyday life and cost the lives of tens of millions of people . . .

Following the Communist victory on the mainland in 1949, 2 million Nationalists under CHIANG KAI-SHEK fled to Taiwan. Over the next five decades, the ruling authorities gradually democratized. In 2000, Taiwan underwent its first peaceful transfer of power from the Chinese Nationalist Party (Kuomintang or KMT) to the Democratic Progressive Party.

The dominant political issue for both countries continues to be the question of eventual unification.

CIA World Factbook

PROLOGUE

The floods had killed another dozen people this year, all nameless *caraqueños* who lived in the shantytowns that covered the hills around the capital city. The mudslides had cut swaths through the slums a week before and dumped the dead into the concrete channel that cut Caracas in half and barely held the Guaire River in its course. Now the canal swelled to its rim with dirty December water and whatever had lined the Caracas streets between the hills and the city center. Cars driving above sent a constant spray into the river, adding a strange sound to the gurgling rush, like the hand of God tearing paper. The brown water was barely visible in the moonlight under this stretch of the Autopista Francisco Fajardo freeway. The shadows turned the canal graffiti into silent monsters, watching the flood, waiting to laugh at anyone foolish enough to play along the water's edge.

Kyra Stryker trudged along the north side of the river, staying off the dirt embankment and giving herself enough distance that a stumble wouldn't send her in. The canal was too steep and the river's current too strong for anyone who fell in to climb out again. The only question was whether the poor soul would expire from the pollution or drowning on his way to the Caribbean Sea. However she was going to die, she wasn't going to go *that* way, she promised herself.

It would be no trouble for the enemy to come up behind her here. She'd given up trying to identify possible ambush spots, there were too many, and the river would be the perfect tool for killing a CIA officer and disposing of the body in a stroke if the SEBIN, the *Servicio Bolivariano de Inteligencia*, were so inclined. They hadn't been so reckless, yet, but the murder rate in Caracas would make it an easy matter to write off her disappearance. The police, as corrupt as the criminals, would wag their fingers at the embassy officer sent to file the missing persons report. *A woman walking alone at night in a dark barrio? Americans need to be more careful,* they would say.

Her dirty-blond hair, pulled into a braid, was already wet from the evening drizzle, and she shoved her hands into the empty pockets of her jacket to keep them dry. The rain was keeping most of the natives off the street, which left her feeling exposed. Tall, fair-haired, even dressed down in blue jeans and a brown leather jacket, she didn't mix well with the normal street crowds in this city. It could have been worse. More than a few of her Farm classmates had drawn slots in Africa and the Middle East, both murderous places for Americans in their own ways, where her only way to disappear would have been under an *abaya*. Caracas offered civilized living, with natives more friendly to Americans than the government. That made the capital a hostile but not lethal environment in which to hone her craft, at least during the daylight hours.

Working the capital streets at night was another matter.

It would be a simple meeting, or so her chief of station had insisted. But Sam Rigdon was a fool and Kyra wasn't the only one who thought so. Rigdon was letting the asset, a senior SEBIN officer, choose the site and time of the meet. The asset claimed he knew the city better than any American—probably true but beside the point—and Rigdon had accepted the man's logic. Kyra wasn't six months out of the CIA Farm and even she knew conceding that particular power to any asset was plain stupid. In this business, *stupid* was just another word for *dangerous*, which could lead to *dead* very quickly.

"This man has brought us good intel," Rigdon said. That was questionable at best. The asset's cigars and Caribbean rum were better than the intel he'd delivered. Kyra tried to talk reason to Rigdon, which was a bold move for someone as junior as she was. CIA chiefs of station were little kings, with the power to eject any junior officer from the country. The mercurial ones were known to do so for the most arbitrary reasons, but Rigdon was more arrogant than erratic, and that was the greater sin. At least the erratic ones could see their mistakes. Some of the other senior officers had stood behind her, and Kyra had heard more than one shouting match erupt behind Rigdon's closed door while she sat outside. But the station chief just dismissed all worries with an impatient wave. "The asset," he said, "is still on our side, still working for us. His loyalty will guarantee your safety."

Kyra was sure that she'd never heard a more stupid thing in her life.

So she was on the street, unarmed. There was no explaining away a Glock to the SEBIN. Caution was her only defense, but the rumble of *autopista* traffic and the sound of the rushing water assaulted her ears, and the staggered street lighting destroyed her night vision. Every possible route to the meeting site was a surveillance detection nightmare.

Kyra cursed herself for being a coward and refusing to disobey Rigdon's order.

The footbridge finally appeared after an hour's walk. It was more a scaffolding than a bridge, barely half-built by the look of it, with a metal grate for a floor. It was twenty meters long, maybe two meters wide, all dark metal, probably rusted over from years of neglect and floodwaters rising and falling over the rails and crawlspace under the walkway. Kyra half expected to see it shored up by vine ropes.

At ten meters from the bridge, Kyra finally saw the asset's silhouette at the midpoint through the trees but could make out no other details. The lights on the bridge were out, whether from neglected bulbs or shoddy wiring she didn't know. She saw the burning end of a *cigarro* rise to meet the asset's mouth, glow brighter for a short second; then the small light fell into the water and disappeared as he tossed the stub away.

A streetlamp marked where the sidewalk ended at the bridge. Kyra reached the spot, stopped, and put herself in front of the light cone so the illumination was behind her. The asset would only see her silhouette, not her face.

Her chest tightened as she scanned the space in front of her. The streetlamp lit up the line of trees in front of her but the light didn't go far beyond. No movement, no sound beyond the water and the freeway.

It felt wrong. She couldn't explain it better than that.

The asset saw her and turned. No question now, she had his full attention. He raised another *cigarro* and Kyra finally saw his face for a short second as he flicked on a torch lighter and set the tobacco on fire. He frowned as he replaced the unit in his pocket. He could make out her shape in the dark. She was in the right place at the right time, but he was expecting to meet a man, Kyra was sure, not a woman.

Then he did exactly the wrong thing.

He waved her toward him.

Kyra clenched her fists to give the nervous energy somewhere to go. She held her poker face and she cocked her head at him a bit as her mind tore the situation down. It took a bare fraction of a second.

You don't know me, she thought. They had never met. She wasn't the asset's handler. A paranoid asset, worried for his safety, should have been skeptical of a stranger arriving at an isolated meeting site. She could be a random tourist, however unlikely that was at this hour in this dark place, or, more likely, Venezuelan security, so the proper response was to act like he was ignoring her as he would any random person he met on the street. The burden should be hers to give him a prearranged signal to confirm both her identity and that she was clean of surveillance. He should then respond with a signal of his own. The asset had violated that simple protocol.

Nervous? It was the only logical reason to have done what he did. The man was an experienced SEBIN officer, a trained professional. But he'd forgotten his training.

Why are you nervous? There were two possibilities. He suspected surveillance, in which case he knew to give her a signal. Or he had confirmed surveillance, in which case he shouldn't have even come. Both assumed he really was a traitor in danger of prison or execution if he was caught.

Of course, if he wasn't in danger, then he would be nervous for a different reason entirely.

You're here, amigo. No signal. Nervous.

SEBIN was here. But he still wanted her to walk onto the bridge.

He wasn't afraid he would be caught. He was afraid she wouldn't be. Afraid that the endgame of an operation in which he had a stake would fail.

Then Kyra saw it all, as clearly as though it had already happened.

El Presidente owned the courts. The conviction of an arrested CIA case officer on charges real and imagined would be a given. The would-be tyrant would use her to extort apologies and concessions from the US. He would make the detention public and drag out the story for weeks, months if he could. Humiliate her, the Agency, the United States. He would claim that her arrest was proof that the US wanted to overthrow him, maybe assassinate him, all to build him up in the eyes of allies here and abroad. He would declare every American at the embassy persona non grata and throw them out of Venezuela as retribution. And when all that was finished, expelling her from the country along with her colleagues would not be a given. He would keep her like a dusty old war trophy on display more to rankle enemies—no, *the* enemy—than for allies to admire.

Like the North Koreans kept the USS *Pueblo* in Wonsan Harbor, SEBIN would keep Kyra Stryker in Los Teques prison.

The asset froze in midwave. He had realized his error.

Six blocks to the nearest safe house.

Kyra ran.

SEBIN raid teams exploded from the dark. Men in black balaclavas, helmets and armor, heavy boots, with sidearms and carbines, all yelling in Spanish. Three teams, maybe six men each, had taken positions at both sides of the bridge in the trees where the darkness gave them almost perfect cover. One fire team erupted up from the bridge midpoint itself, where the soldiers had lain in a space under the dirty grates. There would be more, probably spotters in nearby buildings, maybe on the rooftops. Kyra would have been trapped from the moment she set foot on the bridge.

The first team, the group that had been hiding under the bridge crawlspace, was trying to climb out through the grates. The bridge was narrow and their gear was bulky. It would take them thirty seconds to get to the shore.

The second team was on the other side of the river, twenty meters away. They were already on the bridge, but the team climbing up from the crawlway would block them off. Team two wouldn't be in play for almost a full minute.

The third team on her side of bridge was at the bottom of the embankment, just above the canal and behind the trees only ten meters away, but they had to climb through the brush that covered the earthen wall to reach her. It would take three seconds for the closest soldier to reach the top of the embankment, which was already too late. Kyra would be almost thirty meters away.

She was already running at full speed and no soldier encumbered by a rifle and other gear was going to catch her. She aimed for an alleyway to her left and prayed that another team wasn't waiting in the dark.

She turned the corner and she saw no light at the other end. *No light, no SEBIN*, she realized. *No exit.* Kyra tried to stop, skidded on the slick, dirty concrete, and knew she was going to hit the wall. She put her arms up to soften the impact. Her body hit the wall. She pushed away and made her legs move again.

The second alley was another ten meters away. Kyra covered the distance in three seconds. She reached the opening and then saw the man in black gear standing behind the corner begin to raise his weapon. Kyra was still moving at full speed and couldn't have stopped on his order if she'd wanted to. She raised an arm, put a palm-heel strike into his throat at full speed and the contact sent her tumbling to the wet ground. The soldier got the worst of it. Her momentum and the slick concrete were enough to take him off his feet. He flipped over and landed on his back, breaking ribs on both sides, snapping a collarbone and tearing his rotator cuff. It would be months before he would be able to raise his weapon again.

The sound of several sharp cracks cut through the noise of the *autopista* traffic. *"Idiota!"* someone shouted. Kyra sprinted into the darkness, praying that she didn't trip on garbage or a homeless man or some other detritus.

She heard footfalls behind her, at least a half dozen she thought, but she didn't turn her head to see. Judging by the sound, they were entering the alley as she was leaving it.

Kyra slowed just a bit as she came out of the alleyway. It was past midnight and the sidewalk largely empty of pedestrians. She turned right and kept running, not sure of her next waypoint. El Museo de los Niños was north of her position, maybe two hundred meters. Kyra set course for it and accelerated back to her full speed. Her breathing was now ragged, her heart pounding as hard as she had ever felt it. Only one arm was swinging like it should.

She reached the *museo*. It was an strange building, modern South American architecture, a thousand odd angles surrounded by trees and kiosks and signs. Plenty of places for a fugitive to break visual contact with her pursuers. She sprinted around the building. The footfalls behind her were more distant now, almost getting lost in the street noise of the cars still on the road. A siren sounded somewhere and she wondered whether it was meant for her. The raid teams would be screaming over encrypted radios for support. The target had escaped the net and vehicles were certain to enter the equation at some point if the chase went on long enough. She had to keep them guessing about her direction.

Kyra ran through the complex, obstacles and handrails rushing past so quickly that she was afraid she wouldn't be able to turn fast enough to avoid one if she saw it too late as she came around a corner. She passed the museum proper and raced out onto the street.

Four blocks to the safe house.

She needed to get enough distance between herself and the raid teams so no one would see her enter the safe house, or it wouldn't be safe for long. She turned right onto the Avenida Bolívar. It was an eight-lane freeway lined by trees on both sides with a concrete median running down the center. It was also well lit, which would give away her position once the raid teams came out of the alley. She needed to be on the other side of the street when that happened. Traffic was light at this early hour, in that it wasn't a complete wall of gridlocked cars.

Her hand ached to hold that Glock.

Kyra saw a large break in the traffic. She waited until the cars got closer, then turned suddenly and sprinted onto the street. Crossing the eight lanes took almost three seconds, her timing had been perfect, and the traffic closed up behind her. The raid teams would have to find their own break in the cars to cross without getting hit. Kyra angled right again, then ran north up a side street until she reached the Avenida México intersection. She turned east. Her legs and lungs were both burning now. Her right arm still wouldn't come up higher than her stomach.

Three blocks to the safe house.

The *avenida* curved to the northeast. Kyra followed the bend and saw the Galería de Arte Nacional ahead to her right. She looked behind her and saw no one. The raid teams were probably still looking for a break in the Avenida Bolívar traffic. She ran left in between two large buildings, found a concrete doorway, and leaned against one of the pillars to catch her breath. She didn't want to stop long, but the adrenaline would carry her only so far. Her bad arm was starting to ache a bit and Kyra knew that she was running up against the limits of her endurance. Her chest was heaving and her legs burning. She hadn't paced herself, had probably just run a six-minute mile, and the exertion was catching up to her.

She looked back down the *avenida* and saw no one. Then she listened. In the distance, more than one engine was racing faster than it should, tires screeching. Kyra stumbled back onto the sidewalk and started running again, north this time.

Two blocks to the safe house.

Kyra passed only a few pedestrians over the next hundred meters. She looked back. The SEBIN teams were nowhere she could see and she started to relax. They had been out of visual contact too long. They could find her now only if one of the cars got lucky or if she made a mistake, a favor she didn't intend to grant.

She reached the Avenida Urdaneta and looked west. The high-rise was there. Kyra ran toward the building, half-stumbling now. Her leg muscles were starting to give out. She looked down an alley and saw a car blitzing along on a parallel street far too fast. They were close.

One block to the safe house.

The sounds of the cars were louder now and her endurance was fading quickly, faster than she had expected. She couldn't stay on the street much longer or one of the cars would find her. Her arm ached now, like the pain was deep in the bone, and it was becoming harder to ignore.

Kyra reached the edge of the apartment building and ran up the side street. The safe house was on the fourth floor and the building had a service entrance on the east side. She reached the door, then fumbled in her pants for the key that the deputy chief of station had slipped her before she'd left for the meeting. Her hands were wet from the rain, both shaking hard from the adrenaline rush. She tried to use her right, but it was numb at the fingertips and she had to switch to the left.

She finally jammed the key into the lock, the door opened, and Kyra slammed it open with her body. She closed it behind her, locked it, and leaned back against the entry.

She knew she wasn't safe, not yet. But she was off the street and that was something. Finding her now would involve a door-to-door search of a dozen square blocks or more. Caracas was all skyscrapers and shanty-towns with little in between. There would be tens of thousands of apartments in the search radius. The SEBIN had no picture of her to show the locals and no guarantee that she had stopped running so soon.

Four flights of stairs. Her aching lungs and thigh muscles hurt so much that the thought made her want to cry.

Move. Kyra willed herself forward. She could hardly think at all.

She found the stairwell entry ten feet down the hall. Kyra climbed the four stories, almost pulling herself upward on the handrail the entire distance with her good arm. She managed not to fall into the hallway, then staggered toward the safe house apartment. The hall was empty.

Kyra found the right number, fumbled the keys again, and finally managed to open the door. She stepped inside, closed the door, and threw the dead bolt. Her heartbeat finally slowed a bit. Her lungs still burned, but she was catching her breath, finally. Her legs were weak and she wanted to collapse onto the floor.

Safe. Not really, she knew. But as safe as she could be right now.

The keys fell from her hand onto the wood floor. She left them and searched for the light switch.

The safe house apartment was maybe a thousand feet square, just a single bedroom, a bathroom, a sitting room, and a kitchen, all clean and bare-bones. She found the bed and fell onto it.

Kyra had forgotten about the arm. She felt pain erupt from her right side as she landed on the mattress, and the agony was more intense, more sharp than anything she had ever felt. She cried out, then stifled it, afraid that the neighbors would hear her. She didn't know how thin the walls were. With her good arm she pushed herself back up to sitting and finally looked down at the aching limb.

There was a hole in her leather jacket, midway between her shoulder and elbow. Kyra pulled the jacket off, carefully, but movement was agony now. The dark stain on the back of her arm was surprisingly large. Deep red, almost black where it mixed with her shirt, it ran all the way down to her wrist.

She knew there would be only one way of getting the shirt off without serious pain. She pulled a Leatherman from her pocket, held it in her left hand, and opened the knife blade with her teeth. She slipped the blade under her collar and pulled it to the right, then around the junction where the sleeve met the shoulder. She cut the sleeve loose. It slid off her arm and fell with a wet noise onto the floor.

There was a tear across her triceps, skin and muscle torn loose in a shredded horizontal line. She couldn't see the bone at the bottom of the gory furrow only for the blood. Adrenaline had masked the pain.

When—?

The brain has a gating mechanism that had kept her mind focused on the more immediate pain, and the adrenaline had kept her from feeling the gunshot wound. Her brain got its first look and switched its focus from her tortured lungs and legs. The pain from the laceration detonated across her upper body, cutting off her thoughts, and Kyra had to stifle an open scream.

The first aid kit would be in the bathroom. Kyra stumbled in, trying to keep her arm from moving, and found the large duffel bag under the sink. CIA security, former Boy Scouts she was sure, always came prepared. The trauma kit was designed more for a war zone than a metropolis. Trying to focus through the haze, Kyra found the two items she needed most. The first was a roll of QuikClot gauze. The second was a morphine syringe. She stabbed herself with the needle in the arm, just above the wound and had to suppress another scream as it entered her torn flesh. She depressed the plunger, then pulled the needle out. It was the longest ten seconds of her life.

Her arm began to numb and her body finally began to stop shaking and relax. Kyra felt the pain begin to fade and steeled herself for the next bit of self-surgery. She balled up a wad of QuikClot in her left hand, the only one she could still feel, and packed it into the wound. The cloth stopped the bleeding almost on contact.

The morphine worked fast. She hadn't been able to think when she dosed herself, hadn't checked the amount. Whatever the dosage, it had been enough. Too much, maybe.

She rolled the gauze around her arm to hold in the wad she had stuffed into the tear in the arm. It was an ugly wrap job, but both the drug and the cloth did their job and a pair of butterfly clips finished the task.

Kyra staggered back into the bedroom and almost collapsed before reaching the bed. She pulled herself off her knees onto the mattress and rolled onto her back. She rifled through her jacket and found the encrypted cell phone the deputy chief of station had given her two hours before.

The morphine and stress release were going to knock her unconscious, she knew. She had maybe a minute to call before she passed out in a haze. Her arm was entirely, mercifully numb.

A pair of sirens sounded outside the window. She couldn't judge the distance but they seemed to come from different points.

Not safe here, she thought. She didn't know the last point at which the SEBIN had seen her, and therefore the point that would mark the center of the enemy's search. They could be nearby, going high-rise to high-rise, floor by floor. The SEBIN could come crashing through the safe house door. They could be outside, in the hall, on the stairwell. The walls wouldn't keep them out.

The room seemed to shrink around her. Kyra felt the panic rising inside her chest, the stress of the last few minutes finally catching up. Her good hand started shaking, this time not from shock or pain.

Not safe.

Kyra speed-dialed the only number programmed into the cell phone. The call connected. The voice on the other end was American.

"Operator."

CHAPTER 1

TWO MONTHS LATER

SUNDAY
DAY ONE

Of Beijing's countless parks, Pioneer loved this one alone. Emperors had lived in this retreat a thousand years ago, when the Christians had been losing the Crusades. Its beauty was unique, he thought, and the Tai Ye lake offered comfort even in winter, when the Siberian wind tore through his thin coat and left him shivering on the shoreline. Tonight he had spent a full hour in the cold as he watched the soft waves lap the rocks. It was not the act of pure meditation he would have liked. He had been watching to see if the few people willing to endure the wind lingered near him. The eternal rumors of a mole in the ranks of the Ministry of State Security—the Guojia Anquan Bu—had turned into an internal sweep again. It was always a concern, but the investigations had come before and always passed him by.

Still, Pioneer indulged in the dinner. Coming to the Fangshan restaurant was a persistent mistake but his discipline always failed him in this one way. The show of affluence was a risk. Presidents and prime ministers dined here. The prices were high by local standards, almost three hundred yuan for this evening's supper and it was not the most costly meal he'd ever ordered. It was the one expense he allowed for the funds the CIA had been paying him. The rest was in an account held by the Wells Fargo Bank in the United States and it all meant nothing to him. He would never live long enough to use it. He was sure of that. Traitors received no final meal of their choosing in the People's Republic of China. If he was going to walk into an arrest, and therefore his execution, he would enjoy a meal worthy of an emperor before he went. At least that was the lie he told himself. The truth was that it gave him something to focus on. He was a traitor to his country, not proud of the fact, so he sat at his table before every meeting with his handler and caged his guilt in a private liturgy as routine to him now as drinking the green leaf tea with his meal.

He finished the meal of fried prawns and crabmeat and lifted his teacup. It was almost time to leave and his mind was running like a clock counting down. He always hated this moment. He could never stop counting the minutes until the next meeting. The little timepiece in his head never spoke louder than a whisper, but somehow it always threatened to swallow every other thought. Relentless, quiet torture it was, and had been for twenty-five years. He never lost track of that time even when he was sleeping. It was a miracle that he was still a sane man.

The restaurant was only half-full. The filthy, polluted snowfall had kept most of the tourists away. Pioneer counted three tables of Occidentals, whether Americans or British he couldn't tell. He recognized a table of Koreans, a pair of lovers he thought were Thai, and a small group of . . . Turks? Iranians? He could never tell the Arabs from the Persians.

In the far corner he saw a Chinese face, a man dining alone like himself. He had seen that face . . . when? His memory was eidetic by training but his recall was not instant. He held his own features in a rigid mask as he searched his memory. Time and distance . . . had he seen the man today? Yes, at the lunch market seven hours and two miles from the very table where he now sat—too far away and too long ago. Was it random chance that the man was here in the Fangshan? That was possible but not probable.

"Your bill, sir." The waiter laid a leather folio on the table.

Pioneer nodded, let the waiter leave, placed cash inside, and left the table. He did not turn to see whether the familiar man was standing to follow. The dinner ritual was finished, and he had more subtle ways to see whether the man pursued him.

Pioneer quieted the voices in his mind and walked into the dusk. He walked over the short bridge to the mainland and turned east.

TAIPEI
REPUBLIC OF CHINA (TAIWAN)

The condominium was average in all respects, a space on the third floor of an unremarkable structure in one of Taipei's oldest boroughs. Perhaps forty years old, the exterior was clean with a small lawn, a few hedges, and bare flowerbeds with graying mulch that would wait another few months before filling with weeds and wildflowers. The apartment sat near the building's rear stairwell, so chosen by the occupants so that visitors could not approach easily without notice.

The building presented no tactical challenges for Captain Kuo's team. Such places were not designed for defense against an armed raid, and the variables involved in staging one were minimal. It would be unfortunate for the targets that a safe house remained safe only so long as it was secret.

The sun would break the horizon within the half hour and Kuo wanted the element of surprise that would vanish with the dawn. He looked to the rear of the staging area behind the line of trees. Officers from the National Security Bureau stood there fidgeting and trying to find something to do with their hands. They wanted desperately to smoke cigarettes to ease the tension but the light of burning tobacco could give away his men's positions in the dark and would certainly disturb their night vision, so Kuo had forbidden it. They were an arrogant lot, ordering his men about like they were hired help, so he had enjoyed the exercise of that little bit of authority.

The senior NSB officer had been on an encrypted cell phone for more than an hour. He caught Kuo's look and muttered an impolite phrase into the phone. He finally closed the handset and approached Kuo.

"I say again, you must use the rubber bullets," the NSB officer said.

Idiots, Kuo thought. "Can you guarantee that the targets are unarmed?" Like a good lawyer, he'd known the answer to the question before he had asked it.

The NSB officer gritted his yellow-and-brown teeth. He'd answered that particular question twice already during the night and had no desire to humiliate himself again before this arrogant little policeman. The man was barely one step removed from a street cop. He couldn't have any appreciation for the political sensitivities at stake. "You must bring them out alive and unharmed."

Kuo rolled his eyes and gently ran his gloved finger across the safety on his Heckler & Koch MP7, which act the federal officer couldn't see in the dark. "How they come out depends on how they react once we go in," Kuo said.

"My superiors demand this! Alive! Do you understand me? Even bruises on their faces and hands are unacceptable, much less a corpse."

Kuo studied the other man. The federal was agitated, almost desperate. That meant he was under high-level scrutiny during this operation, and *that* meant the targets were to be bargaining chips for someone very senior. Who the NSB wished to bargain with was the question, and Kuo was sure he didn't want to know. He had demanded the federals' dossiers on the targets, refusing to even accept the raid assignment without access to the intelligence reports. Three were mainland Chinese. Their affiliations had been blacked out. Organized crime was a possibility, but the government wouldn't bargain with the Triads. One target was a Taiwanese American, and Taiwan would not hold hostage a citizen of its largest Western patron. That left one possibility. It was common knowledge that Taiwan was overrun with Chinese spies, and until now the government had been smart enough to leave them alone. The National Security Bureau had never arrested a Chinese spy for fear of the reaction. Apparently that policy had changed . . . or someone was changing it now. Kuo didn't like it, but foreign relations with the Chinese were far beyond the scope of his job.

"Then your superiors can execute the raid," Kuo said.

"You have your orders!" The federal was almost yelling now and drawing attention from the others standing nearby, police and NSB officers alike.

Kuo stepped forward and leaned toward the man's face. "I will not put my men at risk for someone's political agenda," Kuo said, sotto voce. "Whether your suspects come out alive will depend on whether they are armed and resist. If that is unacceptable, then you should rethink this."

The NSB officer took a deep breath and shook his head. "If my superiors are unsatisfied—"

"Given the information you've provided, my decision is correct," Kuo said. "Do we go or not?"

The federal toyed with his phone, thought about making another call, then finally returned his cell phone to his coat pocket. "You go."

Kuo turned away, motioned his men forward with a hand signal, and gave the same order over his encrypted radio to the team on the building's far side. In the back, men in black boots, jumpsuits, hoods, and helmets moved forward in the early morning dark. They reached the building's side and raised portable ladders against the brick wall. Two men quickly climbed to the top rungs, careful to keep their heads below the windowsills, and pulled breaching crowbars out of their backpacks. The men below extracted stun grenades from their vests.

Kuo led his team to the front entrance, then held up a fist, and the line of men stopped on command. The officer behind Kuo stepped around, dropped to a padded knee on the dirty concrete, and slipped a fiber optic line under the door. There was a camera in the tip and the officer held the color monitor where Kuo could see the screen. The officer twisted the line to the right. Kuo saw no one. He heard voices through the door, but his helmet and balaclava dulled his hearing and he couldn't make out the conversation. The kneeling officer twisted the optic line back and the camera looked left. Three men came into view. Kuo nodded and held up three fingers to the men behind him. The officer removed the camera and fell to the back of the line.

Kuo extracted a stun grenade from his vest, pulled the pin, and held down the spoon. He nodded to the breaching officer holding the ten-pound sledge. The camera officer in the rear of the line grasped his radio microphone and whispered. The breacher drew the sledge back and then swung his tool hard, smashing the lock and ripping the dead bolt out of the door frame with the sound of branches snapping in a high wind. Kuo tossed the grenade into the room.

The targets in the front room twisted in their chairs to look toward the broken door as it crashed open. It was an instinctive reaction. The grenade ignited a 6 million candela flash that lit up all the photosensitive cells in their retinas simultaneously. Their vision froze like a film reel stuck on a single frame, sending the same picture to their brains over and over as their eyes struggled to restore their sight. The 180-decibel blast that struck their inner ears a millisecond later was not far below the threshold that would have caused soft tissue damage. Blind, nearly deaf, they reached out and groped for any support within reach.

In the rear, the second team smashed out the windows with expandable batons and threw their own grenades into the back rooms. They had kept the apartment under surveillance for more than a week while Kuo argued with the federals about the raid plan. There were four men inside the apartment, but only three in the front room. Another was somewhere in the rear, where the lights were dimmed. Kuo had hoped that the last target was not inside the windowless bathroom they knew to be in the back.

Kuo heard the grenades in the rear rooms fire. He turned the door's corner into the apartment, his line of officers following behind like a black snake, each man raising his MP7 rifle to eye level. Kuo and the man behind swept the front room while the rest moved to the hall to help the rear entry team secure the back rooms.

There were no armed combatants in Kuo's sight and the men they had come for were helpless. Kuo extracted a baton from his belt, snapped it open, and struck behind the first man's knees hard enough to topple him. The second and third men went down like the first. Kuo and his partner fell on them and bound the men's hands with flex cuffs.

Kuo heard shouts from the back of the apartment and the high *crack* of small arms fire, a 9 mm pistol from the sound. He raised his own weapon to eye level and took a step toward the hall when he heard the faint three-round buzz of an HK like his own. He moved down the hall to the bedroom on the right, staring over the gun barrel as he went.

There were three men in the room. One wore street clothes—the Taiwanese expatriate who worked for the American company and who had been meeting with the Chinese spies in the front room. The other two were Kuo's breaching team. The civilian was prone, motionless, with a bloody stain growing on the front of his shirt. Kuo's men were gagging. There was a hole in a silver metal thermos on the floor and a white aerosol was escaping like steam from a kettle with enough pressure to spin the bottle in a lazy circle. One of Kuo's men had likely mistaken the container for a weapon in the dark and fired a three-shot burst. Two rounds had struck the dead man in center mass. One had penetrated the pressurized thermos.

One of his men let out a strangled gurgle and Kuo reached out a hand. Without thinking he took in a breath to hold. It was a mistake and he realized it as his throat began to burn. He dragged his subordinate back toward the hall by the drag strap that ran across the top of the man's tactical vest.

"Out! Everyone out!" he yelled. It came out as a wet rasp. He felt his throat swelling.

His partner in the front room saw Kuo dragging a body and radioed for medical help. Kuo expelled the contaminated air in his lungs and sucked in a breath of fresh air. It did not stop the burning, which felt like a thousand needles driving into his throat from the inside. He ignored the pain and rushed back down the hall for his second teammate. He would not bother with the civilian. Two of the three rounds had struck near the dead man's heart. The quantity of blood on the floor suggested that a bullet had perforated a major artery, if not the heart itself.

Breathing was becoming difficult, the burning was worse, and Kuo began gasping for air himself. The burning pain and slow asphyxiation collapsed his knees. Certain that he was going into cardiac arrest, he pounded his chest with a fist to keep his heart beating. An officer took him under the shoulder and carried him outside while the others took the prisoners and their incapacitated colleagues. Kuo fell onto the grubby hallway floor and rolled onto his back.

"Evacuate the building," Kuo tried to say. He failed. He tasted blood on his tongue. Lots of blood.

The unexposed officers set up for triage on the lawn and started artificial respiration on their teammates. Kuo doubted they would live. He rolled onto his side and spit blood. Whatever else the aerosol was, it was highly acidic. He could feel it eating his mucus membranes, and the amount he had inhaled had been small compared to the others. Even if the medics rushing to his side had the supplies to treat this— whatever *this* was—the exposure his teammates had suffered would prove too severe.

The federals approached the group and examined the prisoners on the grass. One pulled out a sheet of photographs and compared it to the targets' faces in sequence. All three were bleeding heavily from their noses and ears but the medics assured the officers that no permanent damage had been done. They had been secured without visible injury besides the blood, which could be cleaned up, and they had not breathed in the chemical that had incapacitated Kuo's team. Their identities confirmed, the security officer stood and pulled out his cell phone.

A medic lifted Kuo's head and a second forced a tube down his throat. Kuo's last thought was that the federals would answer to him if they had known about the thermos.ww

CHAPTER 2

MONDAY
DAY TWO

The midnight shift was still young, but Jakob Drescher wasn't and the senior duty officer refused to show weakness to the staff. He was past middle age, older by a decade than anyone else in the Operations Center, and night watches were getting harder by the year. He argued to himself that his subordinates' true advantage came only from coffee's power to keep the brain active in the dead of night. Caffeine addicts staffed the night shift in CIA's Operations Center, and they couldn't imagine how Drescher found the will to resist. One of the perks that made up for a government salary was access to the river of java that ran through Langley, fueled by officers in the field sending back foreign brews that made domestic brands taste like swill. But good Mormons don't drink coffee, Drescher was a Mormon, the son of Cold War East German immigrant converts, and the argument ended there.

The world was quiet tonight. The broadcast news playing on the floor-to-ceiling matrix of plasma televisions was all trivial stories. The cables coming in from CIA field stations were infrequent and blissfully dull by any standard. If the rest of the shift stayed this quiet, he would have nothing to pass over to his day shift counterpart in a few hours. Drescher checked the clock, which was a mistake. The true secret to surviving a night watch was to never mark the time. Drescher couldn't prove it, but he swore that Einstein must have worked night shifts as a patent clerk to come up with the theory that the passage of time was relative. A night during a crisis could pass in a hurry, but tonight the lack of activity was the answer to a prayer. Drescher had plans for his weekend, which fell on a Wednesday and Thursday this week because of the rotating Ops Center staffing schedule. He would miss church on Sunday, which his wife wouldn't appreciate, but he would need the sleep during the day too much. He would always pass on the coffee, but he was too old to give up the Sunday sleep anymore.

"Got something for you." The analyst from the Office of Asian Pacific, Latin American, and African Analysis (APLAA) rose from her desk and maneuvered her way down the aisle without looking, eyes locked on the hard-copy printout in her hand. Drescher couldn't remember the young woman's name. She was a Latina, a pretty girl, newly graduated from some California school, but Drescher had forgotten her name as soon as he'd heard it. He'd given up on trying to learn the names of most of his subordinates, in fact, and had taken to calling them by the names of their home offices. The Ops Center staff changed so often, with all the young officers eager to punch tickets for promotion and staying only a few months at a time.

"Either give me a hundred dead bodies or I don't want to hear about it," Drescher grumbled. "Fifty, if it's Europe. And where's my hot chocolate?"

"You know, under that gruff exterior beats a heart of lead," APLAA remarked.

"Compassion is for the weak," Drescher said. "It's why I'm the boss and you're my peon."

"I live to serve," the analyst replied.

"Don't be facetious, APLAA."

"I've got a name, you know," she said.

"Yeah, it's APLAA. What have you got?"

"NIACT cable from Taipei. One body and a lot of other people getting carried away in paddy wagons and ambulances. The locals just arrested big brother's chief of station." APLAA thrust the paper at Drescher. NIght ACTion cables required immediate attention regardless of when they arrived. That wasn't a problem at headquarters, where there was always someone on duty. Cables going back to field stations were more troublesome. When one of those went to a station overseas, someone, usually the most junior case officer, had to report to work—no matter the obscene hour—to field the request.

Drescher took the paper and scanned it twice before looking up. "Why did they need a hazmat unit—?" He stopped midsentence. None of the answers his tired mind offered were encouraging.

"Yeah. Hazmat got the call in the middle of the raid. NSA labeled it a 'panic' call. Someone walked into a nasty surprise. The Fort is waking up everyone who can understand at least basic Mandarin, but they'll need a few more hours to translate everything." Translators were a scarce resource for the hard languages, and Mandarin Chinese was in the top five on the list.

"Any civilian casualties?" Drescher asked. This was getting good.

"None reported."

The senior duty officer grunted. "Any reaction from the mainland?"

"Nothing yet," the woman told him. "Beijing Station said they're going to work their assets. Wouldn't tell me who they'd be talking to."

"Don't bother asking," Drescher ordered. "You'll just make 'em mad." CIA's National Clandestine Service, the directorate that did the true "spy" work of recruiting foreign traitors, was protective of its sources. Twelve dead Russian assets courtesy of Aldrich Ames had been a string of harsh reminders that intelligence networks could be fragile things. But the APLAA analyst was young, one of the ambitious young officers who didn't yet know not to ask.

"Nothing on the local news or the Internet," APLAA said, ignoring the rebuke. "Taipei probably clamped down on the press. Nothing like a story about a Chinese spy bringing chemical weapons onto the island to scare the locals."

"Don't assume that it was a chemical weapon," Drescher corrected her. "Could've been a gas spill or bystanders downwind of some tear gas. Just report the facts and save the analysis." He kept a map of the world's time zones under glass on his desk. The first cable said the arrests started at 1830 eastern standard time—6:30 p.m. on a civilian clock and six hours ago. A twelve-hour time zone difference meant 1830 in Washington DC was 6:30 a.m. in Beijing and Taipei. The raids went down almost at the crack of the winter dawn. Drescher checked the television. CNN's brunette was talking about yesterday's minuscule drop in the Dow, a nonstory meant to waste a minute of on-air time during a slow news cycle. BBC's blonde was talking about labor protests in Paris, and the other channels were offering stories equally trivial. "It hasn't reached the foreign wire services," he noted. "Does State Department have anything?"

"Their watch desk hadn't even seen the report yet."

Drescher sat back, reread the two cables, and finally allowed himself a smile. He was awake now. Adrenaline was the best stimulant, far better than caffeine. Taiwan had arrested twelve people, several of which were known to work for China's Ministry of State Security, and arresting officers were down. David had poked Goliath in the eye with a sharp stick and Goliath might have poked back.

The senior duty officer reached for the phone and pressed the speed dial without remorse. The CIA director picked up her own secure phone at home on the third ring. "This is the Ops Center," Drescher recited. "Going 'secure voice.'" He pressed the button that encrypted the call.

CIA HEADQUARTERS
ROUTE 123 ENTRANCE

Kyra Stryker turned onto the headquarters compound from Route 123 and slowed her red Ford Ranger as she approached the guard shack. The glass and steel shelter connected with the Visitor Control Building to the right through a dirty concrete arch open to the wind. Kyra dreaded lowering the cab window but there was no choice. The freezing air invaded her truck and she thrust her badge out at the SPO. A second guard was standing on the other side of the two-lane road, this one cradling an M16 with gloved hands. A luckier third was sitting inside the heated shack to the left with a 12 gauge Mossberg shotgun within arm's reach. Doubtless there were more inside the Control Building, all carrying 9 mm Glock sidearms and surely with much heavier guns in reach. Kyra's was the only vehicle coming down the approach and she had their undivided attention. For a brief moment, she had seriously considered running the checkpoint and pressed the brake only when she conceded that the guards wouldn't open fire. They would have just activated the pneumatic barricades that would smash her truck. Then they would have arrested her and spent the rest of the day with her in a detention room, asking repeatedly why a CIA staff officer with a valid blue badge had done such a stupid thing. Not wanting to go to work would have been viewed as a very poor excuse.

The officer gave her the signal to proceed, a lazy military wave. Kyra withdrew her arm, rolled up the window, and turned the heater on full so the cab would recover the warm air it had hemorrhaged to the outside.

Please let the barricades go off, she thought, and she was surprised at how much she meant it. The pneumatic rams had enough power to snap the truck's frame in half, if not flip the vehicle onto its cab on the frozen asphalt. But the thought of a sure trip to the hospital didn't seem any worse to her than where she was going at the moment.

Her Ranger rolled over the closed hydraulic gates, the barricades didn't rise up from the road underneath, and Kyra sighed, not in relief, she realized, but in slight frustration. She hadn't been to headquarters in six months. She shouldn't have been returning for at least six more, but that plan had jumped the rails and nobody was happy about it. Her visit today wasn't by choice, hers or anyone else's, and it galled her to think that she would have to make the same trip every day going forward. Maybe the new assignment would be short. Working at headquarters was not one of her ambitions.

She passed the front of the Old Headquarters Building (OHB), which offered the view most familiar to those who had only seen the facility on the news. She was taking the long way around but she was in no hurry. The George Washington Parkway entrance was ahead and it would have been easy to turn right, leave the compound, and go home. She turned left after sitting at the stop sign for ten full seconds. There were no other cars on the road.

There's my girl.

The A-12 Oxcart loomed over the roadway, sitting at a rolled angle, nose up on three steel pylons, and Kyra smiled for the first time that morning. She loved the plane. She'd never earned that pilot's license despite her childhood ambitions—her parents had never been willing to spend the money—and had been reduced to reading about planes and spending hours in the Smithsonian Air and Space Museum and its annex at Dulles Airport. On her first visit to the Agency compound, she'd climbed the concrete facade surrounding the Oxcart and touched the cold, black wing. It had been the most spiritual experience she had enjoyed in her twenty-five years. Kyra still wondered what it would be like to fly Kelly Johnson's masterpiece at ninety thousand feet, setting the air on fire at Mach 3.

The plane passed behind her and the diversion came to a rude end.

Those with more leave hours to burn, which looked to be almost everyone, had left the parking garage nearly empty. Kyra pulled into a space on the bottom level near the front, killed the engine, and debated starting it again and driving away.

Just do it. Or you'll have to come back and do it just like this tomorrow.

She abandoned the truck before she could talk herself out of it.

The wind brushed up snow from the drifts piled on the grounds and threw it across her path. She hadn't bothered with a hat or gloves and instead thrust her hands into her coat pockets. There was no help for her face. Her cheeks and ears, numb when she reached the glass doors to the New Headquarters Building, tingled painfully as she passed through the heated air curtain. A shot of Scotch would have warmed her stomach faster than coffee, and for a second she wished for a hip flask of anything strong. The urge died quickly. Meeting with the CIA director while smelling of alcohol before lunch would kill whatever career she still had left.

The lobby was a cathedral in miniature, unlit, thirty yards long, and flanked on both sides by dark gray marble pillars that framed bronze sculptures and modular gray vinyl couches along the walls. The grayish-blue carpet, brightened only by the CIA seal in the center, matched the odd gloom that was unusual for the normally bright space. Kyra looked up and saw snow covering the semicircular glass ceiling. It blocked out the sun and washed out the colors in a drab, filtered light. The entrance was abandoned except for a security protective officer manning the guard desk at the lobby's far end. His reading lamp created a small bubble of warm light in the darkness.

She walked the length of the room, ran her badge over the security turnstiles, and entered her code. The restraining arms parted and the SPO didn't look up. Kyra walked around the guard desk to the escalator leading to the lower floors. The windows beyond ran floor to ceiling and Kyra could see the empty courtyard below and the massive Old Headquarters Building a few hundred feet beyond. The dark and quiet combined to make the compound feel deserted, which was an unearthly feeling given the size of the OHB filling the bay windows. The Agency complex covered three hundred acres cut out of the George Washington National Forest along the GW Parkway, barely a stone's throw from the Potomac. Kyra couldn't guess from the view how many people worked there. The exact number was classified anyway, and the building's size made her realize how important she was to the place.

Not at all. A cog in the machine.

The desire to reverse course welled up in her throat again. She beat it down without mercy, never breaking stride, and the craving for a drink surged up to replace it.

The walk to her destination took a long three minutes. The Office of Medical Services lobby on the first floor looked like any doctor's office, which had surprised her the first time she visited. It was a medical facility like any private practice in the outside world, but it seemed out of place in a government building. More so, Kyra thought, given that it was wedged in between the Agency museum and the Old Headquarters lobby.

Kyra signed in. After a short wait, the desk nurse escorted her back to an examination room. Kyra took the usual place on the exam table and the nurse didn't bother to assure her that someone would be in to see her in a few minutes.

The doctor was an old man, she noted, gray hair and his share of weathered skin, though Kyra suspected he'd been a handsome man when he was younger. He said nothing as he studied her chart, and Kyra took the time to study him. She'd been here, just after Caracas, and talked with another doctor about his job. It was relatively simple, with most duties consisting of performing physicals and dispensing vaccinations to clear staff officers to travel overseas. The doctors were usually busiest at Christmas when they had to dole out the free flu shots to all comers. But every so often analysts would call for a consult about theoretical patients they wouldn't identify despite the doctors' own TS/SCI security clearances. They were trying to determine when some particularly unpopular foreign leader was going to drop dead, Kyra supposed, which made for a nice puzzle with no patient to examine.

And sometimes they got to treat patients, like Kyra, with wounds or diseases contracted in places they couldn't always tell him they'd been. She was sure that broke up the monotony.

"Still sore?" the doctor finally asked. He closed up the chart and set it on the nearby counter.

"Yes," Kyra admitted. "It's stiff mostly. Makes driving a little more complicated."

"You drive an automatic or a stick?"

"An automatic," Kyra said, and she was grateful for it. Driving a stick shift would've been torture in Beltway traffic, which was stop-and-go most of the time. "I usually don't feel it until I have to make a hard turn or mess with the radio."

"You probably still have some residual deep tissue bruising," the doctor said. "You lost some triceps and brachialis, and there's scarring across the site and down into the muscle. Scar tissue isn't real pliable, so you're going to suffer some loss of flexibility. Not too much, I think, but you'll notice it. Right- or left-handed?"

"Left."

"That's good news. It won't affect your primary arm," the doctor told her. Kyra was sure it was an attempt to comfort her, but it struck her as weak. "Okay. Let's have a look."

Kyra unbuttoned her shirt and pulled her right arm out of the sleeve, exposing a large, thick medical bandage taped on all four sides across the back of her right upper arm. The doctor pulled the cover back, gently separating the tape from her skin until the gauze came away. She had a lateral laceration running almost three inches across her triceps. The once-ragged edges of the torn skin had been trimmed neat by a surgeon's scalpel and pulled together, and they were still held by two dozen tight stitches.

The doctor stared at the wound, turning her arm slightly from side to side as he studied the wound. "It looks good," he finally said. "No signs of infection. I think the stitches can come out whenever you want, but keep it covered for another couple of weeks to be safe." Kyra nodded, put her arm back inside her shirt, and pulled it down over her waist. "How's the Vicodin working for you?" he asked.

"Pretty good, I guess," Kyra said. "It lets me sleep. Still hurts sometimes, though. Like deep, in the bone."

"I'm not surprised," the doctor replied. "It's probably the bruising. The fracture in the humerus should be healed by now. And if it gets too bad, we can go up on the Vicodin. Do you need a refill?"

"Sure," Kyra said, without enthusiasm.

"I'll write one up." He caught the depression in her voice. She hadn't tried to hide it. "You were lucky," he offered. "You could've lost that arm."

"I don't feel lucky," Kyra told him. She finished straightening her shirt and pushed herself off the exam table onto the floor.

"Getting shot will do that, I guess," he conceded.

Kyra finished rolling up her sleeve as the doctor left the room. One appointment finished. She was far more worried about the second.

Kathryn Cooke's first visit to the Oval Office had been her own inauguration as CIA director. That summer day, the president of the United States had spent two minutes, carefully timed by the White House chief of staff, on small talk and a tour of the room. The national security advisor had administered the oath of office while the White House photographer recorded the event. The White House press corps had been admitted to hear the president deliver a statement of confidence in the job she would do. Cooke made her own brief statement—she'd worked for six hours, revised it a dozen times, and memorized it—expressing the usual gratitude. Five minutes were granted for six questions before the president excused the press corps. Cooke was allowed thirty seconds of small talk and then was politely dismissed. Her few return visits had mostly been social affairs. The job of CIA director was not what it once had been. For fifty-nine years, her predecessors had both run the CIA and managed the intelligence community, as much as it could be managed. But the Agency had suffered too many failures, an angry Congress had created a new office to take over the latter job, and so Cooke answered to the director of national intelligence. The DNI, Michael Rhead, was now the president's intel advisor, and that left little reason for the commander in chief to ever summon the head of the Central Intelligence Agency to the White House.

Cooke had never dwelled on the job's new limitations. It was a higher post than she'd ever expected to hold and she was still an agency director with the usual perquisites—a basement of security personnel and secure communications gear, an armored Chevrolet SUV with a driver, and a chase car of armed guards. She would have preferred to drive her BMW but conceded that the escort gave her time to read instead of fighting perpetually clogged Beltway lanes.

It was a true blessing this morning. The Ops Center call came after three hours of sleep. Coffee, a shower that wasn't as hot as she preferred, and old Navy discipline brought her online. The senior duty officer had sent the raw SIGINT to her secure fax, and a scan of the pages over blueberry yogurt and granola put her in full motion. It had then been her unpleasant task to notify the DNI and the national security advisor. The former had a demeanor that always made phone calls an irritating duty regardless of the hour. The latter took the early call like the gracious gentleman that he was.

The cold Virginia morning chased away the last vestiges of sleepiness as she walked to the armored car. A security officer ran the President's Daily Brief article to the vehicle as she was climbing into the back seat.

In the Last Few Hours . . .

Arrests in Taipei Threaten Cross-Strait Status Quo

Taiwan's arrest of eight Chinese nationals—at least three of whom are PRC Ministry of State Security (MSS) intelligence officers—could sow confusion among the PRC leadership about Taiwanese President Liang's intentions and lead to a confrontation over the "One China" policy. We have no information on how Taiwan's National Security Bureau (NSB) identified the MSS officers or who issued the orders to arrest them.

- The arrests could damage the MSS espionage infrastructure in Taipei in the short term, but the MSS almost certainly has other MSS officers in place who will redeploy to maintain or reconstitute asset networks affected by the arrests.

It is unlikely that Taiwan's NSB would have executed the counterintelligence operation without Liang's knowledge and approval. Tian almost certainly will consider Liang personally responsible for the operation and will demand the release of the detainees.

- Liang likely will resist giving up the detainees without diplomatic concessions from the PRC to avoid appearing even weaker before the March general election.

- Tian likely will offer no concessions given the "One China" position that Taiwan is not a sovereign equal of the PRC.

The arrests could disrupt MSS access to highly placed human sources from which PRC President Tian Kal draws insight into Liang's foreign policy intentions. Tian often relies on MSS reports to settle Politburo debates over diplomatic, economic, and military responses to Liang's frequent nationalist rhetoric.

This article was prepared by CIA with reporting from CIA and NSA.

Cooke's driver pulled the armored car into the executive garage under the Old Headquarters Building a minute after passing through the George Washington Parkway gate. The garage had its own guard post manned by SPOs to keep out the masses. Cooke didn't care for the elitism. Many employees had to walk a good quarter mile from the parking lot's outer limits, but she bowed to the fact that, most days, parking spaces and time on her schedule were too limited.

The cold erased her guilt that this garage had a private elevator that ran to her office. The doors opened onto the Old Headquarters Building seventh floor, where Clark Barron, the director of the National Clandestine Service, stood waiting for her with a cup of hot coffee in hand. Cooke wondered how the man had ever blended into a crowd during his younger days as a case officer. The CIA director was not a short woman, a few inches shy of six feet, and she still strained to look up at the man's face.

"God bless you, Clark," Cooke said. She traded her coat for the mug and drained half the coffee in a single swig.

"I thought you were agnostic," Barron said.

"Just shows how grateful I am," Cooke said. "And this is good brew. How did you know how I like it?"

"I recruited your assistant," Barron said. "She's my most valuable asset now. I've been thinking about assigning her a code-name crypt."

"Scoundrel."

"It's what case officers do," Barron reminded her. "Even the old ones."

"And you do it well. Whatever you want, it's yours," Cooke promised.

"No ulterior motives this time. I knew you were coming and chivalry is dead in this town, so I'm left to play the gentleman," Barron said.

The CIA director's "office" actually was a complex. The door to Cooke's private workspace sat back along the rear wall of the larger area. Her office windows opened to a view of the George Washington National Forest. Her desk sat to the immediate left of the door and she was religious about keeping it clear, mostly out of fear that once the paperwork started to pile up she would never get ahead of it. The walls were home to curiosities under glass, the number evenly split between gifts from foreign peers and trophies smuggled out of countries by case officers. A US flag covered the western wall, shabby and torn, with burns and scorches over its surface. A CIA officer had recovered it from the smoking crater of the World Trade Center and no Agency director would ever remove it. The September 11 flag was the lone permanent artifact in an office that changed occupants and mementos more often than the Oval Office changed presidents.

Barron followed Cooke into the office and closed the door behind her. "The National Weather Service says we've got two days before the temperature climbs up into the teens and more snow inbound from a nor'easter. We should just catch the edge of it, but still," he said. "A shame we can't close the place down and send everyone home."

"Unfortunately, it's not snowing in Taipei," Cooke observed.

"Or Beijing," Barron said. "I renew my request for a CIA Southern Command in Miami."

"Denied," Cooke said. "Again."

"I have allergies to snow, I swear."

"I grew up in Maine. I have no sympathy for you," Cooke said. "Didn't you do a rotation in Moscow?"

"Two actually. Three years as a case officer, four as station chief," Barron said. "And I grew up in Chicago. You can see why I'm looking to spend my remaining years in the sun." The promotion path to Barron's office historically ran through Moscow. Even during the War on Terror, getting that ticket punched without being declared persona non grata by the Russian government never hurt a case officer's career.

"If you can get it past Congress, I'll go for it." Cooke finished the coffee in a single swallow and traded the empty mug for the black binder of intelligence traffic Barron carried under his arm. She opened the book. "Tell me the story."

The first page was a map. "NSA caught most of it from the raid teams' radios and some phone calls made after the fact by federal officers. Some of our people filled in the blanks afterward using our own data about officers the MSS has in country. The raids went down at two different locations in Taipei," Barron said. "There were also raids in Taoyuan to the north and Kaohsiung in the south. Federal officers were present at all four scenes and reported to their superiors by cell phone, which gave us the intel identifying the targets at the first site. Eight Chinese nationals and four Taiwanese detained. One of the Taiwanese is an expatriate, now a naturalized US citizen employed by Lockheed Martin. James Hu. He entered Taiwan on his US passport the day before the raid."

"The raid teams' radios weren't encrypted?" Cooke asked.

"They were, in fact," Barron said.

"Kudos to NSA," Cooke said. "Hu was working for the MSS?"

"Looks that way."

"Have FBI contact Lockheed. Find out what he was working on," Cooke directed.

"I assume the Bureau is already working on that," Barron assured her.

"I try not to assume anything when it comes to the Bureau," Cooke said. "What do we have on the Chinese taken down at that site?"

"Names and bios. They caught a big fish," Barron said. The second page featured photographs of the arrested suspects. Several of the slots were blank, black silhouettes with white question marks inside. Barron pointed at one of the photos. "Li Juangong. We pegged him a year ago as the MSS station chief in Taipei. We think the other two are members of his senior staff."

"He's a piece of work," Cooke noted, skimming the bio.

Barron grunted. "The mean ones always are."

"You would know," Cooke said, smiling.

"You try herding a few thousand case officers," Barron said.

"I'll call your bet and raise you two congressional oversight committees," Cooke joked. "How long can the Chinese keep the story contained on their side?"

"Good odds, not very long," Barron said. "The MSS has a very poor record of keeping state secrets. In Chinese society, family relations are valued so highly that officials don't consider sharing classified information with close relatives a breach of security. State secrets can end up on the streets relatively quickly. And Tian Kai is already trying to get ahead of it." He pointed Cooke toward page three. "Tian convened a meeting of the Politburo Standing Committee within an hour of the arrests. We don't know what was said."

"They were talking damage control most likely," Cooke said. She set her binder on the table. "If you told me that the MSS had rolled up twelve of our assets in China, I'd run you out of town on a rail."

"If the MSS rolled up twelve of our assets, I'd deserve it," Barron agreed. "My guess is that Liang pulled this stunt because of the presidential election next month. He's too far down in the polls to come back without rigging the election or creating a crisis. Nixon had better approval numbers when he resigned in seventy-four. And Liang will face a corruption indictment if the opposition wins, so he's motivated.

He could be setting this up to turn the public's attention to an external threat."

"I'm worried about the Chinese reaction," Cooke said with a frown.

"You think Tian wants to get rowdy?"

"APLAA says no, but I'm not sure I believe it," Cooke said. "Have somebody connect with Pioneer. I want to make sure we've got some advance notice if they're wrong."

Barron bit his lip at the mention of the "Pioneer" crypt, which itself was classified Top Secret NOFORN. NO FOReigNers, not even the friendly ones, had access to it. Some sources and methods were too sensitive to tell even allies that they existed, much less share the information they yielded. "I'll talk to Carl Mitchell," he conceded. "He's the station chief out there."

Cooke saw the hesitation in his face. "You haven't run this by anyone in the Directorate of Intelligence," she realized. The DI was the CIA analytic division.

"No," he admitted.

"Not even Jim Welling?" Cooked asked. Welling was the director of the DI and Barron's equal. The two men even worked out of the same vault on the seventh floor, just down the hall from Cooke's own.

"That's one source I don't want burned," Barron admitted. "It's personal. I don't even want Jim to know about him, much less some DI analyst. They're all a bunch of glorified journalists, just looking for the next big thing to write about in an intel assessment for some politician who can't keep his mouth shut."

"Same team, Clark," Cooke said.

"Mistakes get made," Barron said.

"They do, but your people have blown more ops than DI analysts ever have." She knew that would offend the NCS director's pride, but he knew it was the truth. "I want your people to cooperate," Cooke told him. "If an analyst asks about sources and methods, the one answer your people aren't allowed to give is no. If they don't like that, they've got my phone number."

"I won't let it come to that," Barron promised.

"You know, this clash of civilizations between the DI and the NCS needs to stop," Cooke said. "Analysts and case officers need to be working together, not sitting around in little cliques like kids at the prom."

"If you can manage that, the president should nominate you for secretary of state," Barron replied. "By the way, I saw Stryker sitting out in your waiting room. I've told my people to play dumb if anyone from the DNI's staff asks about her. Have you decided where to stash her?"

"Oh yes." Cooke sounded very satisfied with herself. "A nice safe harbor where nobody will go looking."

"Want to let me in on the secret?" Barron asked.

"You sure you want to know? Mistakes get made, after all," she said. "Touché."

Cooke told him. All Barron could do was shake his head before leaving for his office.

Kyra knew Clark Barron on sight. He'd addressed her class during the graduation ceremony at the Farm the year before. Many of the men who had held his post—there had never yet been a woman chosen for it—had been disliked by the rank and file. Some of his predecessors considered that to be a job qualification. Barron argued in the speech that if charisma was a valuable trait for a case officer, a manager who didn't have enough to connect with his own troops must not have been very good in the field. He left unspoken, though not unnoticed, the insinuation that those unlikables must have climbed to the top using other, less respectable skills. Kyra had liked him instantly.

Barron moved past the door into the hallway without a word. A minute later, Cooke stood in the doorway to the waiting room. "You're Stryker?"

"Yes, ma'am," Kyra answered. She rose and fought the urge to stand at attention.

"Let's take a walk," Cooke said without preamble.

Kyra followed Cooke out to the hallway. The director steered Kyra to the right. The corridor was empty, leaving their conversation as private as if they had been sitting behind the door of Cooke's office. "Have you found a place to live?"

"Yes, ma'am, a condo in Leesburg just off Route Seven."

"Long commute," Cooke remarked. "General George Marshall's house is out there in Leesburg. Dodona Manor. Interesting place if you like military history."

"I was a history major at the University of Virginia," Kyra said. "I prefer the Civil War, though. Shelby Foote and Michael Shaara."

"*The Killer Angels.* A great book, that one," Cooke said with approval. "You couldn't find anything closer to headquarters?"

"Not on a GS-twelve salary, ma'am," Kyra said. "And I don't think a promotion is coming anytime soon."

Cooke cocked her head, nonplussed, and looked at the younger woman. *Bold honesty?* she thought. *Or no sense of self-preservation?* Cooke had read the girl's file. Stryker's sense of self-preservation was just fine, so the former, Cooke decided, probably with a healthy dose of anger and resentment in the mix. "You deserve one, but no," she admitted. "I know it feels like you're getting hostile treatment—"

"Yes, ma'am, it does," Kyra admitted. "I just expected it to come from the enemy and not our own people."

Cooke repressed a sigh. "Have you called the Employee Assistance Program yet?"

"No, ma'am."

"Any reason why?"

Kyra kept walking but said nothing for a few paces, long enough that Cooke looked over. The younger woman finally spoke. "I don't walk to talk to a counselor, ma'am. I'm fine."

"That would surprise me very much," Cooke told her. "Don't make me turn it into an order."

"Yes, ma'am."

"It will help. So will getting a little satisfaction. Sam Rigdon might be a station chief, but he's not one of our people," Cooke said. "Your exposure was his fault and we're not going to let the DNI sacrifice you to save him. But I want you to understand how bad this might get. *Washington Post* headlines and Sunday morning talk shows if it leaks," Cooke advised her.

"Are you trying to scare me, ma'am?"

"No. I just don't want you to drop out on me when the shooting starts," Cooke said. "You've got a chance to do something for the Agency now. Lose the attitude and be patient. I'll get you back into the field. I can't tell you when or where, but I can tell you that Clark will remember that you took the bullet." *In more ways than one,* she thought. "We'll get you right again. You understand me?" Cooke opened a stairwell door and the two women began their descent to the lower floors. The stairs were grubby and dark, and red pipes erupted from the walls, clashing with the yellow cinderblock.

"I think so, ma'am," Kyra answered.

"Either you do or you don't. If you fold on me when the moment comes, then we're both done here. Clark Barron too, and probably a few others."

"I won't resign," Kyra assured her. "But if you're not sending me to the field, where are you sending me?"

"You're going to the Directorate of Intelligence," Cooke said.

"You're hiding me?"

"That's one way of putting it. You have a problem with it?" Cooke asked.

"I'm not an analyst," Kyra replied, dismayed. "I don't know how to do that job. And I've never heard much good about analysts anyway."

"Have you heard of the Red Cell?" Cooke asked.

"No, ma'am, I haven't," Kyra admitted.

"It's an alternative analysis unit . . . not your usual DI shop," Cooke said. "George Tenet created the Red Cell on September thirteenth to make sure the Agency didn't suffer another September eleventh. Their job is to 'think outside the box'—to find the possibilities that other analysts might overlook or dismiss."

"Devil's advocate? War-gaming?" Kyra asked. That, at least, could be interesting.

Cooke steered Kyra to the left. The second floor hallways were claustrophobic and dark, the combination of government-standard yellow paint and fluorescent bulbs that always looked like they were dying. The ceiling was low; Kyra could have touched it with her fingertips. There was no carpet, just dirty tiles that, permanently soiled from over a half century of footsteps, soaked up what little light escaped the ceiling. "They do those occasionally, but it's not their sole mission. And to be honest, the rest of the analysts don't like them. Or I should say 'him.' The Cell is running low on manpower," Cooke said.

"How many?"

"Right now, one." Cooke admitted. "It's not field work, but you'll stay connected with what's going on around, you'll draw a paycheck, and we can pull you back in a hurry."

They turned right down another hallway. Kyra found herself reading wall placards that announced room titles and numbers cut in small white letters on black plastic as she went. Cooke stopped in front of a door on the hallway's left side near a dead end. The vault sign was distinct, not government standard but white letters in sans serif type on a globe bathed in red, all of which was hard to see in the dim light.

CIA RED CELL
THE MOST DANGEROUS IDEAS IN THE WORLD

"Questions?" Cooke asked.

"Why are you walking me down in person?" Kyra asked.

"To make sure he doesn't kick you back out," Cooke told her. She pressed the buzzer set in the wall next to room 2G31 OHB. No one answered. Cooked swiped her badge against the reader and the door opened with a click.

Every government office Kyra had ever seen looked the same. They were all nests of shoulder-high, beige dividers set up to cram as many public servants as possible like cattle into the available space. It was a miracle, she thought, that anyone with claustrophobia could be a bureaucrat, and she had assumed that DI offices would adhere to the norm. Analysts and case officers were different animals, but government-approved floor plans were the same everywhere.

Except here, she thought. The Red Cell had more in common with a newsroom than a government office. The cramped vault was divided into a large bullpen, a smallish conference room, and a manager's office. The far wall was glass, floor to ceiling, giving Kyra a wide view of New Headquarters. The other walls were covered with marker boards, maps of Middle Eastern nations, calendars, political cartoons, and newspaper articles. Stacks of *The Economist, New Republic, Foreign Affairs,* and intelligence reports covered the tables. The east wall was home to a life-sized full-body portrait of Vladimir Ilyich Lenin that some case officer might well have stolen from some abandoned Soviet building. Facing the Russian across the room was a near shrine of smaller black-and-white photographs of a young Ronald Reagan, dressed as a cowboy with six-shooters drawn, and a framed *Economist* cover billing the dead president as "The Man Who Destroyed Communism."

A man stood at the far side of the room, his back to the door, his full attention given to a whiteboard. He held a red marker in one hand and an eraser in the other. He didn't turn to see who had just invaded the room.

"Mr. Burke," Cooke announced. It wasn't a question.

The man turned his head slightly, barely enough to look back over his shoulder for a second before turning back to the board. "Director Cooke." Jonathan Burke was tall, only slightly more so than Cooke, with an average build for his height. His hair had no observable gray and his eyes were an intense green. He wore the standard analyst uniform of brown khakis and a blue oxford shirt.

"What's on the board today?" Cooke asked.

Burke said nothing for a second while he drew connections on a wire diagram with labels so sloppy that Kyra couldn't read them. "I'm trying to develop a structured analytic technique to counter confirmation bias in finished intelligence products."

"Ambitious," Cooke warned him.

"I was bored," Burke said. "I don't handle boredom well."

"I'm aware. Does it work?" Cooke asked.

Burke sighed, capped the marker, and dropped it on the whiteboard tray. He stared at the board for several more seconds before turning around. "Given how much confirmation bias goes on around here, you would think that developing a test for it would be trivial. Not so."

"So that's a 'no,'" Cooke said, smiling.

"A 'not yet,'" Burke corrected her. "I have no shortage of case studies to work with. But I assume you're here to send me on a detour."

"You've always said that you don't have enough warm bodies," Cooke said.

"I have plenty," he said.

"You have one," Cooke observed.

"As I said."

Cranky bugger, Kyra thought. And the man was putting on no airs for a CIA director. That was interesting. *How do you get away with that?*

"Now you have two. Kyra Stryker, meet Jonathan Burke, analytic methodologist."

Jonathan looked at the younger woman only briefly. "What have you heard about the Red Cell?"

"Only that you're not very popular," Kyra said. *Two can play the cranky game,* she thought, and she wasn't in the mood to put on airs herself.

Jonathan lifted his head and studied the younger woman. "True. And irrelevant. Occasional hostility is the acceptable price of doing this business. And you're keeping company with the director, so a lack of likability hasn't slowed you down," he observed.

"At the moment, being liked is not my problem," Kyra said.

"How charming." Jonathan looked to Cooke. "She shows promise. But I assume that you didn't come just to escort this young lady down?"

"You heard about Taipei?" Cooke asked.

"Of course," Jonathan said. "The hazmat unit was the interesting bit."

"'Interesting' is not the word I would choose, but I agree. That's why everything else on the Red Cell's plate is now on hold."

"You disagree with the China analysts on the situation?" Jonathan asked.

"You don't?" Cooke answered.

"Of course I do," Jonathan said. "But I'm disagreeable, so here I sit. What's your issue?"

"My issue is that we've suffered a major intelligence failure every seven years since Pearl Harbor on average," Cooke said. "So when APLAA tells me this is just going to be a little tiff, I want some insurance in case they're wrong. The Red Cell is it. So tell me what you think."

"I think the president should send in the aircraft carriers," Jonathan said.

"You're serious?" Kyra asked. "The Taiwanese arrest a few Chinese and you—"

"The Taiwanese arrested a few Chinese *spies*," Jonathan corrected her. "And that is the prerogative of sovereign nations, so you can imagine why the Chinese might object to the Taiwanese doing that. Before last night, the Taiwanese had never detained an MSS officer in six decades precisely because they didn't want to rile Big Brother. Now that little policy has changed and I suspect the Chinese won't be amused. They'll rattle the saber before this is finished."

"All right," Cooke said. "You have my attention."

The analyst directed the women to a pair of chairs in the small open bullpen space and took a seat across from them. He stared past them out the window as he talked, making no eye contact with either woman. "Chiang Kai-shek and the Nationalists lost the Revolution, then fled to Taiwan and never surrendered. Imagine Jefferson Davis moving the capital of the Confederacy to Cuba in 1865 and never giving up its claim to the southern states. The Chinese see the Taiwanese as descendants of an enemy who should have surrendered, didn't, and now want a consolation prize they don't deserve. So the Chinese established the 'One China' policy and made it the prerequisite for doing business with the mainland. But every so often, the Taiwanese stick their head up, act like a sovereign country, and make the policy look like a farce. That doesn't just humiliate Beijing. The

Communist Party partly justifies its hold on power by arguing that it's the best protector of Chinese interests. That includes bringing Taiwan back into the fold, so the government's legitimacy depends in part on Taiwan keeping its head down. Arresting spies threatens that. Tian will have to act."

"You're talking about military action?" Kyra asked.

"Possibly," Jonathan observed. "Military exercises along the coast opposite Taiwan are always a favorite way to send a message."

"What about an invasion?" Cooke asked.

Jonathan shrugged. "There has always been a debate about whether the PLA has the capability to invade Taiwan proper. But that kind of yes-no argument discourages thinking about scenarios that don't fit neatly at the poles, which is foolish. History proves that there is such a thing as limited war for limited gains. So a few years ago I drafted a Red Cell paper positing a limited war scenario in which the Chinese moved across the strait in stages. It took five years, but the 'incremental moves' view has become accepted now, not that APLAA is happy about it."

"They disagree?" Kyra asked.

"Actually, no," Jonathan responded. "They just dislike the fact that I and not one of their own wrote the paper. That group holds grudges and has long memories."

"I've had to stop them from ordering a hit on you more than once. You're welcome, by the way," Cooke said. "How will Tian play this?"

"Passive-aggressive at first, to see if Liang will cave," Jonathan said. "He'll start with the usual public speeches, editorials in the *People's Daily,* that sort of thing. Keep track of what the *People's Daily* is saying. It's the Chinese *Pravda,* controlled by the party, so the editorials are official announcements. On the diplomatic front, Tian doesn't see Liang as an equal. He'll suggest negotiation in public, but privately he'll expect all the compromises to come from Liang."

"Good enough to start." Cooke stood and nodded at Kyra. "Send me that invasion plan of yours by close of business. And put this young lady to work."

"If I must," he said. He turned to Kyra. "How long will you be staying?"

"Ask her," Kyra said, pointing at the director.

"Undetermined," Cooke said.

"So helpful." Jonathan pulled a pad across the desk and wrote out the titles and publication dates of several intelligence papers, all inked in neat block letters. "The China analysts keep hard copies of past research papers in their vault. Fifth floor." He ripped the paper out and handed it to Kyra.

The titles were boring but the publication dates were not. "Some of these are as old as I am," Kyra said.

"I wasn't going to mention it, but that's true," Jonathan replied. "It's a common error of the young to mistake the recent for the important."

"You're too kind," Kyra said.

"Without question," Jonathan agreed.

"Five bucks says you've got Asperger's," Kyra said.

"You'll have to raise your bribe to find out," Jonathan said.

"What if they won't let me have these?" she asked, holding the paper up.

Jonathan raised an eyebrow. "If you have to ask permission before taking things, you're working for the wrong Agency."

Jonathan waited until the door closed behind Kyra before moving to the manager's office. He threw himself into a chair while Cooke stopped at the doorway and leaned against the metal frame.

"I presume that she's the reason you asked me to come in today?" he asked.

"She is," Cooke answered. "Thanks for doing this."

"I know an order when I hear one."

"Still, you could have made this much more unpleasant," Cooke said.

"The day is still young."

The CIA director allowed herself a smile. "How've you been, Jon?" she asked.

"Well enough," he said. "And you?"

Cooke shrugged. "Well enough," she answered back.

"Are you still smoking Arturo Fuentes?"

"Only at home," Cooke said. "I can't change the no-smoking policy. It's a federal law, after all."

"It was bad enough when George Tenet walked around here chewing those things," Jonathan said. The former director's love for cigars had been so famous that his official portrait in the Agency gallery showed one sticking out of his coat pocket.

"George had impeccable taste in tobacco," Cooke observed. "And he had the king of Jordan slipping him Montecristo Edmundos from Havana. I still have a few in the humidor at home that he gave me. You should come by and light one up with me sometime."

Jonathan either missed the hint or ignored it, and Cooke couldn't tell which. "No, thank you," he said. "I'm on good terms with my lungs and I want to stay that way."

"Your loss," Cooke said. "You seeing anyone?"

Jonathan cocked his head and his mouth twisted into a wry grin. "Hardly. I'm an acquired taste," he said. "You?"

"The job keeps me busy. And there's not much privacy at home with all the SPOs running around."

"No doubt."

"It won't last forever, Jon," Cooke told him. "Tread lightly with Stryker. Sending her up to APLAA by herself was throwing a Christian to the lions."

"I don't believe in teaching analysts to swim in the shallow end of the pool," Jonathan said.

"What do you think of her?"

Jonathan shrugged. "She's too young for me."

"Not what I was asking," Cooke said, her voice taking on a slightly cold edge. "She's a case officer. Her first tour lasted six months. We had to pull her back from the field."

"She blew an op?" Jonathan asked.

Cooke shook her head. "In a manner of speaking. She crossed paths with a station chief who's personal friends with the director of national intelligence. He sent her to meet with an asset who turned out to be a double. She suspected it going in, and so did we, but the station chief ignored her. Gave her a direct order to go. She got burned and was almost picked up by the locals."

Jonathan considered the answer for a second. "Venezuela?"

Cooke nodded. "The DNI was basing his advice to the president on a double agent's reports. He needed someone to blame and was close friends with the station chief, so the hammer wasn't coming down there," she told him. "She needs a safe harbor."

"The rest of the DI doesn't like me, and the NCS doesn't like the DI as a whole. You just put her in the one place where she's guaranteed to be hated by everyone."

"Not your problem. If she's smart, she won't let it become her problem either." Cooke pushed herself away from the doorframe, turning to leave. "By the way, Liang is going to give a statement to his press corps at twenty-thirty. I've told Open Source Center to make sure it runs on the internal network. State Department says that he'll be talking about the arrests."

Jonathan checked the wall clock and corrected for the time zones in his head. "Is that solid or a rumor some junior diplomat heard over drinks?"

Cooke shrugged. "Neither? Both? The arrests are the only thing going on over there worth a press conference. Anything else you need to get started on this?"

"A transcript of that Politburo Standing Committee meeting in Zhongnanhai."

"That's what you call a hard target," Cooke said, smiling. "It would be like trying to plant a bug inside the White House."

"Doesn't mean it can't be done," Jonathan replied. "We should be able to recruit a member of the Standing Committee, right?"

"Couldn't tell you if we had," Cooke said.

OFFICE OF ASIAN PACIFIC, LATIN AMERICAN, AND AFRICAN ANALYSIS (APLAA) CIA HEADQUARTERS

The APLAA vault was everything Kyra had thought the Red Cell would be, ten times the space or more, with enough cubicles that Kyra wondered whether the Agency wasn't violating fire codes. There was a two-level rack of laser printers sitting next to an industrial-sized copier, all of them running. The burn bags were overflowing with classified trash waiting to be thrown into the dump chutes that ran to the basement, where somebody would haul them away to be shredded and burned. It looked and sounded like a hundred people or more were in close quarters, and she could feel their energy. *Not-so-controlled chaos,* she thought. The tension in the vault was like the humidity on a hot Virginia day, nearly tactile and just as pervasive. There was no shortage of noise but an almost complete absence of human voices that Kyra found unnerving. Everyone was working, no one was talking. She wondered whether DI analysts were trained to retreat into their cubicles under stress.

A girl in blue jeans and a black polo shirt—acceptable attire on snow days—stepped forward; a gray badge clipped to her pocket announced her status as a college intern, CIA's version of legal slave labor.

Poor kid, Kyra thought, though there was probably less than five years' difference in their ages. *They should've let the interns stay home instead of dragging them in on a snow day.*

"Can I help you?" the intern asked.

I hope I sound like an analyst. She felt like an idiot. "I'm Kyra Stryker, from the Red Cell. We're writing a piece on the Taiwan raids that went down last night and I wanted to pick up a few research papers."

The intern frowned. "Does our office director know about it?"

Even the temporary help hates the Red Cell. "I don't know," Kyra admitted. "We just got the assignment an hour ago. I'm just doing some research for a backgrounder." Another term that she'd heard analysts use and hoped she was using correctly.

Apparently she had. "What do you need?" the intern said, with attitude. The younger woman was showing a remarkable lack of patience given that she wasn't even a full-time staff member. She, of all the staff in the vault, had the least claim on pressure and analytic burdens to justify a lack of manners.

"I could use your help to find some finished intelligence reports."

"Like I said, we're all busy right now. You should look them up online."

They're busy. You're just here to run interference. Kyra studied the younger woman for a moment. Her instructors at the Farm had uncovered a talent in Kyra for sizing people up at a glance, finding character flaws through nonverbal cues alone. It was a divine gift for a disciple learning the arts of espionage, and her instructors had taught her to harness it with tactical planning. Some case officers didn't know how to turn it on and off, lacking the needed conscience, and so used the skill on everyone. Kyra didn't suffer from that problem. Her inner voice nagged her whenever she considered the idea of "case-officering" fellow Agency employees, but that voice was not inclined at the moment to be blocked by a DI analyst, and a college intern barely qualified for that status anyway.

Hostility was not the best approach at the moment, she decided. The intern was under stress and had shown enough spine to defend her assigned territory against an outsider who outranked her. But that courage was founded on borrowed authority, so a display of anger would just put the woman further on the defensive and possibly drive her to call in reinforcements with real power to say no.

Most people have a natural desire to be helpful, her instructors had told her. *Be nice. Be reasonable. Tell them you need them. Don't give them a reason to dislike you, and their conscience will work in your favor.*

Kyra smiled. "I understand, but we really need APLAA's help on this one. Our paper is going to Director Cooke, so we have to make sure we've got our facts straight."

"Oh." The girl's expression faltered.

"If you could just show me where everything is filed, I could probably find the paper myself. I don't want to take up your people's time."

"Which papers?" The intern sounded unsure.

"I have a list," Kyra said. She looked down at her notebook. "I'd be happy to do the hunting if you'll just show me where you store copies of your finished intel reports since 1990?"

The intern's thought process was visible on her haggard features. "Need-to-know" was a gospel commandment. Just because people asked for information, didn't mean they automatically got it. Mere curiosity wasn't sufficient. The intern had to reason out whether Kyra actually needed to have access to the materials she had requested.

"I guess that would be okay," she said. "Come with me." The intern finally cracked a smile, the sure sign that Kyra had defused her. The girl had gone from an adversary to a willing accomplice in minutes. Kyra followed her through the maze to a pair of government beige filing cabinets only a little shorter than herself. "NIEs, IAs, and Serial Fliers here in the top two racks. PDBs and WIRes with background notes and references filed in chronological order in the bottom two. Anything else?"

"Nope. This'll be fine. And thanks. I really appreciate your help."

"You're welcome," the intern said before she walked away.

Kyra stared at the file cabinet, opened it, and began searching through the papers.

CIA RED CELL

Kyra dropped her pencil on the table and checked the clock on the wall; 2030 hours. *I lost track,* she thought. Jonathan had disappeared for hours at a time, leaving her to the welcome privacy of the bullpen for most of the day. Hunger had finally driven her out of the vault a few hours before, but the cafeteria didn't serve dinner and she couldn't stomach anything the vending machines were serving. She had finally settled for the old doughnuts she had found sitting in a box on the refrigerator. She had thought about asking before eating but decided that Jonathan's earlier rebuke about taking without asking gave her the permission she needed.

"Bored?" Jonathan asked. He stared up at the television mounted near the ceiling in the corner. Liang's press conference was starting late and a pair of British journalists were filling time with inanities that the analyst didn't want to hear, so he left the mute on.

"This is some kind of hazing, right?" She had been reading binders of intel reports since lunchtime and hadn't quit even though her brain had stopped absorbing the words hours before.

"If I wanted to haze you, I'd tell you to streak through the gift shop."

"You can guess what I would tell you to do," she told him. "I don't think the China analysts have missed anything."

"They have," Jonathan said. "It's standard practice."

"I see why they love you so much," Kyra said.

"It would be a mistake to care," Jonathan told her.

"Words to live by?"

He sighed. "Cooke was right when she said that CIA has suffered a major intelligence failure on average once every seven years. Postmortems show that every one of them was a failure of analysis, not collection. We had the information to figure out what was happening. And in every case, the analysts suffered from the same mental mistakes—groupthink and whatnot. Requiring analysts to go through more training doesn't prevent them. More coordination and more review and more editing and every other process we've set up to prevent them doesn't work. In some cases, it even makes them more likely. So when I said it was standard practice, I meant it literally."

"So what does work?" she asked.

"Judging by our track record? Nothing, apparently. But a good Red Cell helps," he answered. "Red Cell analysis isn't about right and wrong, or predicting the future. It's about getting people to think about the overlooked possibilities. Evolution, or God depending on your preference, has left us with brains that latch on to the first explanation that seems to fit the facts and our own mind-sets and biases when we face a puzzle. Even smart analysts develop shallow, comfortable mental ruts.

To get them out, you have to make them uncomfortable, make them consider new ideas, including some that they might not like. And that means you have to be—"

"Unlikable?" Kyra asked.

"I was going to say 'aggressive.' But the two are often the same." He looked up at the television. Liang stood at the podium, waving his arms almost violently. Jonathan lifted the remote and turned on the volume as the Taiwanese president pounded the podium in a steady rhythm with his words. *"Zhonghua minguo she yige zhuquan duli de guojia!"* The translator rendered the English a half second out of sync with Liang's excited voice. *"Taiwan is a sovereign state!"*

"Subtle," Kyra observed. She cracked open a Coke and took a short swig. She was running on caffeine now.

"It'll take some diplomacy to smooth that one over," Jonathan agreed.

It was less a speech than a tirade, and Kyra found herself staring at the screen but hearing nothing. "There was a Beijing native in my masters program at the University of Virginia, son of a professional chef and a state-certified culinary artist himself," she said. "When we graduated, he cooked a four-course meal for some of us that ruined me for American-made Chinese food for years. He asked me once whether I thought Taiwan was a sovereign country or a Chinese province."

Interesting, he thought. She was sharing a personal memory with someone she barely knew. "That's a loaded question. What'd you say?"

"I asked him if Beijing collected taxes from Taipei," Kyra said.

"Old debater's trick," Jonathan said, approving. "Answer a question with a question."

"Yeah. I hate that. But he took it well," she recalled. "He was friendly. He was also a Communist and an atheist. When he graduated, we gave him a tee shirt that said, 'Thank Heaven for Capitalism.' That made him laugh. After I joined the Agency, I started wondering if that dumb joke hadn't gotten him in trouble when he got home—spending some time under the bright lights with some MSS officers trying to figure out just how much we'd corrupted him."

"They have a talk with plenty of students who go home," Jonathan observed. "Partly to collect intel, but mostly to intimidate them."

"It works. We don't get many Chinese walk-ins." Kyra stared out the window into the dark. "I never found out what happened to him, even with all the resources this place has."

Jonathan cocked his head. The young woman seemed hardly aware that he was in the room. He decided to offer her a way out. "You can go home. It doesn't take two people to run this up to Cooke."

Kyra looked up and said nothing, as though she hadn't heard him. Then she hesitated, but only to avoid looking like she was rushing for the door. She had the impulse to ask if he was sure but decided against it. She was quite sure that the question would annoy him, if not diminish his opinion of her intelligence.

"See you tomorrow." Kyra picked up her coat, fled the vault, and didn't look back.

CIA HEADQUARTERS

The New Headquarters Building lobby had eight security gates, four on either side of the security desk. Half had "out of service" signs taped over the keypads. Kyra searched for a working gate, found one on the far right, and held her badge to the reader. The machine did nothing for a moment, then made a rude noise and refused to open its metal arms. She pressed her badge to the scanner a second time to no effect. Irritated, Kyra looked to the guard, who finally lifted his head after the third alarm.

"Just go around." The guard returned his attention to his monitor.

Kyra dropped her head. *The biggest intel agency in the world can't keep the badge readers working.*

In the dark, the guard didn't see her disgust as she obeyed. The automatic doors at the far end waited until the last second to open and the cold air smacked her face as she passed through the air curtain into the wind. The sidewalk lights cut a path in the darkness as she hurried south to the garage. Clouds hid the moon. Kyra couldn't see more than twenty yards into the night in any direction.

With the parking deck nearly empty, her truck was easy to find. She crawled into the frigid cab and started the engine.

"*. . . the existence of such a large spy network puts the lie to President Tian's claim that China is a partner for peace and harbors no unfriendly intentions towards the Taiwanese people. Accordingly, I am suspending Taiwan's participation in the National Unification Council . . .*" Kyra had left her satellite radio tuned to the BBC World Service. The translator's English came in calm, measured tones that stripped out the anger and emotion that Kyra could hear in Liang's voice as he spoke underneath the translation. Kyra wished that she understood Chinese and could hear the original feed without the translator. Hearing dual voices in stereo gave her a headache.

". . . *the mainland and Taiwan are indivisible parts of China. We should seek peaceful and democratic means to achieve the common goal of unification. We are one nation with two governments, equal and sovereign* . . ."

Kyra accelerated out of the parking deck and made her way around the compound until she reached the Route 123 entrance. She passed the guard shack ten miles faster than the posted limit. The guards, she guessed correctly, only cared about vehicles speeding inbound.

Route 123 was empty and Kyra plowed through the snow burying the town of McLean. She took the Dulles Toll Road exit, the lane markers appearing sporadically under the shifting white powder, hidden more often than not. The highway straightened a mile past the toll plaza—the snow plows and salt trucks had made at least one pass over the road—and she put the accelerator to the floor. It was foolish to take the truck up fifteen miles over the speed limit, but she couldn't bring herself to care.

Kyra reached the top of the stairs and kicked three flights of wet snow off her boots. It was still falling and there was no covered parking down on the street. She would spend a half hour of her morning defrosting the truck and scraping the windshield with a credit card before she could even get onto the road. That assumed someone would plow the lot during the night.

The knob was freezing in her hand as she pushed open the door to her home and kicked her feet on the mat again before stepping into the small entryway. She tossed her keys onto the cherry hall storage bench, where they slid across the dark wood and fell onto the floor. Kyra left her boots by them and hung her coat.

The flashing voice mail light leaped out in the low light. She stared at it for several moments. She disliked talking on the phone even when her mood wasn't dark, but the blinking light had triggered a thought that had, in turn, started a debate inside her head that dragged on for a surprisingly long minute.

Kyra leaned against the wall and tried to order her thoughts.

Analysis couldn't be *that* hard.

First step, collection of the facts. She'd lived in this apartment for less than two weeks and Verizon had assigned the phone number even more recently. She'd given it only to her parents, the Agency, and several local pizza parlors and Asian restaurants within the delivery radius. End of collection.

Second step, develop scenarios and assign probabilities. She could eliminate the eateries. They didn't call customers to solicit business. A telemarketer? She'd submitted her number to the National Do-Not-Call Registry within an hour of the phone's activation, but some telemarketers ignored the registry. So that probability was very low, though not zero.

Her parents? A strong possibility, but not one equally split between her mother and father. Her mother might have called, but not her father. Their differences had sparked too many arguments. The professor was too proud of his intellect to tolerate a daughter who could see politics in a different way, particularly one who didn't hate either the butchering military or corrupt intelligence agencies. But her mother was the diplomat of the family, always trying to save the father-daughter bridge that was perpetually burning under Kyra's feet.

The Agency was a lesser possibility. As required, Kyra had given her phone number to the Agency, though only two days ago. It would be in the locator database but she had no close friends at headquarters who could dredge it up. There was a possibility that someone from the director's office might have called. That had happened yesterday, the secretary calling to summon Kyra to the director's office, where she had met Kathy Cooke this morning. So it was unlikely Cooke would be the caller.

Burke was a possibility, but she had been with him less than an hour before. He'd been the one who told her to leave. Barring some emergency, and she couldn't fathom what would constitute an analytic emergency, he had no obvious motivation.

Her mother, the director's office, Burke, and a telemarketer. The probabilities stacked up in that order.

Third step, test the hypothesis, she thought.

Kyra pushed the voice mail button.

"Kyra, this is Reverend Janet Harris, assistant to the rector at Saint James Episcopal Church here in Leesburg. Your father called earlier this morning and asked—"

"Thanks so much, Dad," she said to no one, least of all her father.

Kyra lifted the handset, dropped it back onto the cradle, then flung it onto the living room carpet.

Maybe the old man really did care? Not likely. He would be more worried about his public standing than her soul. One of his two doctorates was in theology and he was a senior warden in the vestry at the Saint Anne's Parish in Scottsville, where her parents lived. Having a daughter living outside the church was probably an embarrassment. She doubted he even talked about her to the other parishioners.

Kyra went for the near-empty refrigerator and pulled out leftover gumbo from some Cajun place she'd found off Market Street. She also took out a beer, not lite, and a Styrofoam box of sticky rice and mango. She ate the leftovers, drained the can, left the garbage on the table, then fell into bed.

CHAPTER 3

TUESDAY
DAY THREE

The surveillance team following Carl Mitchell was neither silent nor subtle. The CIA station chief had seen many during his two years in Beijing, more in Moscow, Kiev, and Hanoi before that. Communist governments were paranoid of Westerners by nature and the Chinese were no exception. The MSS and her sister security agencies could cobble together a surveillance team of a hundred men to follow a single target. Mitchell should never have seen the same face on two different nights unless they wanted to send a message, and the faces tonight were all looking familiar.

His companions made themselves known early when a Chinese man wearing a British-cut suit, probably custom-tailored in Hong Kong, had put a body check on the American case officer, almost knocking him into the street. Mitchell had labeled that man Alpha. The clothing and the fact that he'd stayed ten feet behind Mitchell for six blocks had made him impossible to miss. Mitchell had responded with a passive-aggressive approach, walking slowly so the crowd had to maneuver around them both. Alpha had begun bumping him every block, but Mitchell refused to respond. If Alpha and his partners were trying to provoke him into assaulting the local security to give them an excuse to detain him, they would be disappointed. After a half hour of Mitchell's slow gait and window-shopping, Alpha finally grew self-conscious and bored and dropped back through the crowd.

Maybe Alpha wasn't MSS? A criminal? Chinese prisons were nasty places, hard on the life span, so the criminal life in Beijing was fairly Darwinian and only the quick learners stayed around long enough to bother the tourists. Mitchell discounted the possibility after a second's thought. Alpha was too well dressed for that profession. There was an outside chance the man was Ministry of Public Security, the Gong An Bu, China's equivalent of the FBI, or even People's Armed Police. Mitchell didn't care for any of the possibilities. They all collaborated and a Chinese jail was a Chinese jail regardless of who held the key.

Mitchell made a hard stop at the street crossing. Alpha was far enough behind that he could have kept his distance, but he closed in. The timing was perfect. The stoplight turned green and Alpha took a hard step forward and made contact as he passed. It was a hard hit, no apology, and Mitchell stumbled into a stopped car in the street. The driver honked and cursed in Mandarin at the American. Mitchell swallowed his anger, but both his ability and desire to do it were nearly gone.

Time to go home, he thought. Mitchell didn't like taking a beating for no good reason and he knew the exact limits of his patience. He would have preferred to lead Alpha into a filthy alley and give the man some bruises of his own, but anger was a poor substitute for disciplined tradecraft.

Mitchell rounded the block and worked his way six blocks back to the Laitai Shopping Mall north of the US embassy with Alpha never more than a body length behind. The Chinese officer finally gave up the slow chase when it became apparent where Mitchell was heading. The US Marines standing guard at the gate wouldn't hesitate to throw a non-American to the sidewalk if he tried to break through into the massive complex. Managing embassy security was tedious and getting physical with a native determined to be stupid would be a rare treat for the soldiers. Some rules of the game were never broken. The penalties were immediate and painful.

The Marine corporal checked Mitchell's ID and waved him through, and the CIA officer put his feet down on United States soil. The Marine stared Alpha down until the Chinese officer turned and walked into the dark. Mitchell didn't bother to look back.

Chief of Station was a job that didn't allow for bankers' hours and Mitchell had made peace with that unpleasant fact early on. Espionage relies on schedules but has none fixed and is often plied in the dark. Mitchell was past his prime, and time and his job were catching up with his body. A life in the National Clandestine Service had taught him enough self-discipline to make up for the growing weakness thus far, but soon it wouldn't matter. The chief of station posting in Beijing was a job reserved for the most senior NCS officers. Like a Navy promotion to captain of a carrier, it was an assignment that required so much experience that those who qualified were already nearing the end of their time in the field. A desk job at Langley or the Farm would be his next billet, and Mitchell had not quite made peace with that.

Mitchell closed his door, secured it, and fell into his chair. His back protested and he knew Alpha had left him a healthy bruise on his left side, but there was no help for it at the moment. He took up the secure phone and dialed the States. The time zone differential worked in his favor for once. Clark Barron was just starting his day. "Hey, boss," Mitchell said.

The voice delay between Beijing and Langley was slight but perceptible. At CIA headquarters, Barron checked the world clock on his wall and realized what time it was on the other side of the globe. "You're up late."

"Going home just got dangerous," Mitchell said. "I had a meet scheduled with Pioneer, but our hosts were on me the minute I walked out the door. No subtlety at all."

"You've been burned?" Barron asked. Losing a station chief in Beijing at any time would be more than a minor inconvenience, but losing one at this particular moment would be a significant problem.

"I don't think so," Mitchell said. "From what I'm hearing, they're roughing up everyone. Same thing with the State officers. They're following everybody going out the front gate."

Barron grunted. "I talked to Sir Lawrence at Vauxhall Cross last night. He says his boys are getting the same treatment. The Aussies too. 'Very uncivilized' was how he described it. How close did they ride you?"

"Close. I've got bruises." Mitchell could feel another on his right arm where Alpha had pushed him into a wall. He would need aspirin and an ice pack for it after the call.

"Did you give any back?" Barron asked.

"Nope. I'll find other ways to hurt 'em," Mitchell said. He'd learned that lesson in Moscow when an SVR officer had almost pushed him into a moving bus. Mitchell had a short scar between two knuckles born from the Russian's tooth. The man's friends had given Mitchell three broken ribs and trashed his apartment before he returned from the hospital.

"Is this a response to Taiwan?" Barron asked.

"I don't think so. People started getting roughed up before Liang staged his little raid party. Today was the first time I got touched up, but I haven't really been out on the street much lately."

"Did any of your people give them a reason to set this off?" Barron asked. Such physical harassment was rare except in Moscow, and confrontation had never been China's style.

"If they did, no one's told me. I'll get everyone together in the morning and put the question to them, but I don't think we started this," Mitchell said.

"Well, somebody's chapped their hide. That's a lot of manpower to throw around," Barron said. "And if they're not just unhappy about Liang's stupidity, then something else is going on. The Chinese aren't the Russians. They don't do this kind of thing just for jollies."

"No doubt," Mitchell agreed. "Our hosts out there have a bug up their pants and they want operational activity stopped until they've shaken it out. Or at least they want us to work harder. My bet is they've got a line on somebody's asset but they don't know who he's working for. So they rough up everyone and then throw up a tight net around their target to see who's desperate enough to come through it. If that's right and I were them, I'd cover anyone from a NATO country, and the Koreans and Japanese for good measure. Maybe the Russians too, just on general principles."

"You think it's Pioneer?" Barron asked.

Mitchell frowned. "No way to know without making contact. Catch-twenty-two. The times when you need to meet an asset the most are the times when you're the least free to do it. We'll see if he responds to the next dead drop. If not, we'll go for a sign of life."

"Approved," Barron said. "Just make sure that you're taking smart risks, not dumb ones."

"Always. Call you in the morning." Mitchell replaced the handset on the cradle and settled into his leather chair to think tactics. *They want to smother us,* he thought. His people had done nothing to provoke the local security services. The streets were quiet. The population was restless because of the Taiwan events, but they weren't taking their anger out on Westerners. Beijing was always a dangerous environment, more so in recent years, but not unworkable by any stretch. Still, the MSS had changed tactics and Mitchell would have to reevaluate. The security services had started getting physical with his people before the Taiwanese had launched their raids. *Maybe the MSS knew that was coming?* he thought. *If so, why not extract their officers in Taipei before the arrests? If so, why rough up Westerners in Beijing?* He shook his head to clear the nonsensical thoughts from his mind. It was a puzzle without an obvious answer and he knew he lacked the information to solve it.

But digging up information is what you do for a living, isn't it? he thought.

A dead drop attempt with Pioneer was not optional but he might have to suspend other, less critical operations. The MSS wouldn't hesitate to arrest a US case officer. They had jailed two for almost twenty years during the Cold War. A handsome young American man in custody, or, even better, a pretty young woman, would make a fine diplomatic bargaining chip, and the Chinese knew how to drag out negotiations.

The story was different for the assets, natives working for a foreign power. Chinese citizens arrested for espionage were to be shot, of course, and it was no urban myth that the family would get a bill for the bullet. The trials were always short and private, and there would be no negotiations.

CHAPTER 4

WEDNESDAY
DAY FOUR

The evening was warmer than average for a Beijing winter, ten degrees Celsius, which had brought the tourists and lovers out in force. Crowds were always expected on such pleasant nights in the Shichahai neighborhood north of Beihai, where the bars and lakes clustered. Pioneer welcomed them. The crush of foreigners would stress the surveillance teams. If the MSS were following him, they would be looking for actions out of the ordinary, which became problematic as the mobs of alien visitors grew in size, with every person looking and acting far out of the Chinese view of ordinary. They engaged in innocent behaviors that drove paranoid security officers mad—taking photographs of government buildings, talking with PLA soldiers and bartering for pieces of their uniforms, wandering down little-used side streets and alleyways outside the usual tourist lanes. In this locality, the MSS would have to ignore those who appeared ordinary, and Pioneer had never harbored any illusions that his appearance was more than that. It was nature's one blessing in support of his true profession. So he sat on his park bench, content to watch the water and bore anyone watching him. His operational act for the night was finished. There would be nothing for them to see now and it was always an easy thing for Pioneer to lose himself in his own thoughts.

Some nights he wished that they would come for him. It was a miserable thing, being a traitor to one's country for ideological reasons. Such men were found in every country, he suspected, and they all had the same idea in common, that they were fighting their own private revolutions against those who were the real traitors to the countries they loved.

A political revolution is a living animal, he thought, conceived in outrage, fed with anger, and born in blood more often than not. In its early life, there comes a moment when its parents must decide what kind of animal their child will be. Some are allowed to run free and become wild predators that can only be killed by rising tyrants. Others are restrained to become loyal guardians who protect their children's lives and liberties until those children can protect themselves. Washington,

Lenin, Mao, Gandhi, Castro, and Khomeini each raised their own, and those revolutions, like all things in nature, looked and behaved like their parents.

Pioneer had watched as the Second Chinese Revolution was killed during delivery by its grandparents on June 4, 1989, in the streets around an open ground called Heaven's Gate—Tiananmen Square.

Pioneer had been a student then. In the spring of 1989, the Iron Curtain in Europe was crumbling, rusted out from the inside by corruption and a half century of oppression. The Soviet Union, having built the Warsaw Pact through violence, was forced to watch its handiwork come apart at the political welds and economic rivets. The Chinese leaders in Zhongnanhai were determined to avoid the Russians' mistakes.

The students had to come mourn Hu Yaobang, a reformer purged by the Party two years before his death. On the eve of his funeral in April, a hundred thousand people came to the square and many never went home. When Gorbachev came to China that May to discuss his programs of perestroika and glasnost, the student leaders anxious for democracy saw a singular opportunity to push their cause on the party elders. For his part, Deng Xiaoping wanted the world to see a summit where the two great Communist powers were going to close ranks. He opened Beijing to the foreign media and they came with their portable satellite dishes and microwave links by the hundreds. It was a mistake. The student leaders began a hunger strike before Gorbachev's arrival. They made their way to Tiananmen Square and before the day was over the number of strikers had grown to three thousand. Within days, over one hundred fifty thousand people filled the square, some protesting, some there only to see the protests, but even that was an act of courage.

Pioneer was one of the latter at first. He was not one of the true believers in the beginning. At first he came and went, not staying in the square but going home to his soft bed each night. But he did come back. The more he saw and heard, the more he began to believe. By the end, Pioneer was sleeping on the ground with the rest, chanting slogans during the speeches, and wondering whether he could become a leader in the movement. With no resistance from the government, it was easy to cultivate that seed of faith planted as a new convert to the cause.

It went on for weeks and the Politburo began to grow nervous. They knew a revolution when they saw one. Many of them remembered

Mao's revolution. Many of them had helped stage it. If Communism had drilled only one precept into their old, corrupt heads, it was that revolutions were inevitable when the masses were oppressed by the bourgeoisie, which the party leaders had become. Now they were losing control of everything in full view of their own country and the world. Protests were emerging in other cities far from Beijing, and it seemed like the whole world was behind the students. The Politburo's meetings devolved into vitriol and invective.

The crowd in Tiananmen Square surged to over one million.

The party declared martial law in Beijing. The protests in the other cities were smaller and easily handled, but the Tiananmen Square mob refused to disperse. Journalists were banned from the square and forced to stop their broadcasts. The students were ordered to evacuate. The PLA ordered divisions into the city, totaling more than one hundred eighty thousand soldiers.

The students built barricades to stop vehicle traffic around the square. Where they couldn't build barricades, they lay down in the roads. The PLA responded with tear gas. Pioneer still remembered how his own eyes and mouth had burned when a canister had landed near him, a million needles in his throat pushing out. He had picked it up and thrown it back at the soldiers but not before inhaling a full dose of the gas. He had gagged his breakfast onto the concrete. He had wanted to claw his own eyes out of his head as his lungs burned, a feeling that was refreshed every time he drew breath.

His new friends held him on his feet. One, Jianzhu, was a student from Qinghua University like himself, a senior in the school of journalism who thought that facts could change the world. Another, Changfu, was a Foxconn drone who had worked the assembly line and walked out, giving up his job for the revolution. *There will be better jobs when there is a better China,* he said. He had almost no education and no money, but his faith in the future was infectious. A third, Xishi, was a beautiful girl two years younger than Pioneer, a talented calligrapher who taught him a bit during the boring stretches sitting on the Tiananmen cobblestones. It was a strange little group they formed. Pioneer knew they would never have met if not for the protests, and the pressure of Tiananmen began to forge that bond that soldiers built on the battlefield.

The stalemate held. The Politburo and the students each squabbled amongst themselves as to the next move. The threat of military force seemed to fade, and over the long days the number of protesters dwindled. The students finally decided it was time to go home and settled on June 20 as the day to walk away.

The great irony of the Tiananmen Square massacre was that the party decided to use force to break up a protest that was in its waning days.

Mao once said that political power flowed from the barrel of a gun, and the party held that gun. On June 1, it declared that the students were engaged in a counterrevolutionary plot against the state. The order was given: the PLA and the People's Armed Police were to clear Tiananmen Square by any means necessary.

Soldiers began moving through Beijing to the square, and the citizens of Beijing flooded into the streets, throwing rocks and debris at the marching formations. The Twenty-Seventh and Thirty-Eighth Armies fought their way to the square, arresting and killing citizens. Mobs erupted, pulling soldiers into them and tearing them to pieces. Students threw Molotov cocktails, and PLA vehicles burned in the street, filling the air with the smoke and stench of burning rubber, but flaming vodka bottles are a poor match for machine guns. The soldiers turned their weapons on the crowd and fired with abandon.

Pioneer heard later that PLA troops had even fired on other army units that got in their way. With tens of thousands running in all directions, neither the student leaders nor the army commanders had been able to maintain order. The battle raged for three days and it was a slaughter. At least hundreds died, maybe thousands. If the party had ever tallied a count, it hadn't made it public, and Pioneer had never been able to find it even in the secret records.

To his unending shame, Pioneer had fled the chaos. He'd never found comfort in the thought that thousands of others did the same thing.

He remembered the supersonic crack of one bullet that passed close to his head and the wet noise it made as it punched through Xi-shi's soft body. It severed her aorta and spilled the teenager's blood in great gushes onto the cobblestones. A second round took Jianzhu's face and life in the same instant with a gory display that had cost Pioneer at least a year's sleep over the years since he'd seen it. The last time he saw Changfu, the older man was rushing toward PLA soldiers, who raised their guns, and then the mob blocked Pioneer's view. His nerve and faith broke in that instant and he abandoned his friends on their field of battle.

The PLA lines broke and the protesters flooded the streets. Soldiers started firing in self-defense to protect themselves from a mob that was far beyond obeying orders. Pioneer had jumped over the fallen bodies of trampled soldiers and revolutionaries alike, even climbed over a tank to get out.

The protest was broken. The PLA controlled Tiananmen Square and the streets of Beijing.

The authorities never identified Pioneer as being present in Tiananmen Square. The party could never identify everyone who had been a part of the event, but that wasn't considered a problem. It didn't need to punish everyone. True leadership is a rare skill; they only had to punish those who had shown that talent. Many of the student leaders had died in the battle, and the party hunted the rest for years after. The government handed out lengthy sentences to many after trials that lasted only hours.

Unarrested, unmolested, Pioneer's cowardice had bought his life and freedom when his friends' bravery had bought them prison and death.

Two years later, Pioneer earned his Qinghua University degree, and the day before the ceremony, the MSS summoned him to a meeting. At first he had thought that the party had finally connected him to the protests. It took him a moment to realize that had it been so, the People's Armed Police would have dragged him from his apartment instead of issuing him a polite request, really an order, for a private meeting.

The party didn't know about his part in the protests, but it did know about his then-rare skill with computers. Qinghua University was China's MIT. The school offered *guanxi,* personal connections and influence, more potent in China than Harvard could offer graduates in America, and the faculty had connections to people who needed to solve certain military problems. The Americans had just finished a war in Iraq using precision bombs, stealth planes, and other weapons whose efficiency frightened the PLA. The Iraqis had assembled the world's fourth-largest army, supplied it with Soviet equipment, and trained it in Soviet military doctrine, very much like the PLA's own forces. The United States tore that army to shreds in weeks and suffered almost no casualties doing it. Computers had changed warfare to a degree that the PLA and the MSS had not appreciated before. Guns in large numbers weren't enough, and that was a problem that needed rectifying.

Listening to the MSS bureaucrat talking about the glorious career he would have in the service of the party that had gunned down his friends, Pioneer wanted to come across the desk and choke the man. Then, to his shame, the emotion passed, his cowardice reasserted itself, and he agreed to the request he was not free to turn down anyway. The conversation ended and he left the office.

Perhaps his dead friends had talked to him or maybe the unknown God he'd read about in Western books had whispered to his soul. Whatever the source, a thought entered his mind. There would be a better time and way to exact revenge than killing a bureaucrat who could be replaced without a second thought. He had to learn patience and recognize that revenge truly was a dish best served cold.

The first contact had been the most difficult part. Pioneer spent his first years building his career as a model servant, which earned him the party's permission to attend conferences abroad. They were so anxious to learn about new computer technologies coming from the West that it did not require much prodding. On one trip to Tokyo, he slipped away from his handlers and translators during a keynote address attended by a few thousand programmers and made his way unseen from his hotel to the US embassy, where he offered his services to the CIA. They were suspicious of him, of course. "Walk-ins," people motivated by conscience to volunteer themselves as spies to a foreign power, made the best assets. But often they were "dangles," double agents being held out like bait on a hook. However, the chief of station was a bold man willing to gamble. It took them more than an hour to find someone who spoke Mandarin, but the COS needed less than ten minutes to judge that the anger in the young Chinese man suggested he could be authentic. The station chief himself had divorced an adulterous wife the year before and knew that true agony of the soul is not easily faked.

A young CIA case officer named Clark Barron contacted Pioneer on his return to Beijing. The early requests he made were simple and small and Pioneer filled them without question or complaint. Every successful brush pass was a victory, every dead drop or package delivered through a cutout was a knife in the party's back. He learned the use of simple disguises and microfilm, then digital cameras and encryption. He became methodical and never took a stupid gamble.

Barron spent five years teaching him tradecraft, and Pioneer was a brilliant student.

At the same time, the MSS promoted him. The scope of Pioneer's access to the most secure networks increased, which he reported to the case officers who had succeeded Barron. In return, they expanded the scope of their requests to him. When September 11, 2001, came, Pioneer feared that the CIA would forget about him in their zeal to hunt terrorists, but the pace of requests never slackened. His case officers never told Pioneer that CIA considered him their most productive asset in a Communist country since Oleg Penkovsky in the 1960s. The MSS and every other body it touched, including the Politburo Standing Committee itself, was hemorrhaging secrets in a steady gush to the West.

Twenty-five years came and went and he still hadn't found peace. His friends still haunted him. Pioneer hadn't set foot in Tiananmen Square in all that time, but he pressed on for the cause his friends had started there. If he had earned nothing else, the cowardice had been burned out of his soul. So, if he could not have peace, he had decided that his inevitable execution would be well deserved. There was an excellent chance that someday the PLA would stand him before a brick wall and shoot him. So be it. Maybe then his friends would accept him as worthy to stand with them again.

Pioneer stared out at the lake, shaken from his thoughts by a very cold gust of wind that got inside his coat. Time to go home. Time to start watching for surveillance again.

The man from the Fangshan had not reappeared. If he was from the Ministry of State Security, his superiors would have been fools to use him again, and they tolerated very few fools in the ranks; most were in the upper management, where a man's political connections could protect him from his own stupidity and corruption. Pioneer was forced to deal with such people daily.

Last night's aborted meeting nagged at him for reasons he couldn't piece together yet, but missing a single meeting was not a significant problem. He was smart enough to know what information the Americans would request. The CIA would want to know whether the MSS had assembled a list of the men and women detained in Taipei, which were MSS officers and assets, which were not, and what the MSS was doing to protect its other operations in Taiwan. The list hadn't been hard to find and he'd left it in a package at the dead drop site.

Pioneer knew about the Taiwan arrests, of course. *The People's Daily* had dutifully published the official line that the detained Chinese citizens were innocent victims caught in a dragnet of President Liang's personal ambition and corruption and were not working for the security services. It was a lie, of course. He had the truth from internal sources, though even the common citizens without such access knew better. The Chinese mainland natives that the Taiwanese had arrested were exactly what President Tian had denied they were. Aside from the one dead American defense contractor, all the Taiwanese who had been arrested were bureaucrats and politicians, with a member of Taiwan's own security services thrown in for good measure, and all had been considered excellent assets, several trusted as far as the MSS trusted any turncoats. The loss of one, a high-ranking aide to a minister in President Liang's cabinet, was a disaster of the highest magnitude. MSS careers were ending and an unlucky few would be fortunate if they escaped prison terms levied in secret as punishment for incompetence. Losing an asset to the Taiwanese was embarrassing enough. Getting one killed while releasing some toxic chemical that killed locals and required a hazmat unit to clean up was a national humiliation. He didn't know what the asset had been handing over to the MSS, but certainly the CIA would ask.

Tonight's dead drop site was the bathroom of a small market known for its excellent stock of shellfish and superb *mapodofu* recipe. He had never used the location to pass a dead drop before and never would again. He had entered the market, ordered a half pound of prawns wok-seared in black bean garlic sauce with vegetables, and then stepped into the tiny one-stall bathroom and left a USB drive of encrypted files in a sealed plastic bag taped behind the gas heater. The remains of that dinner sat on the bench next to him.

Pioneer waited twenty minutes before standing to leave. He had given the MSS nothing to see. He was a humble government servant who had bought dinner and eaten it in a park where he could enjoy the rare warm sunset in winter. Still, he would run another surveillance detection route on his walk home as he always did. No matter how good the planning and careful the execution, any operation run long enough would suffer mistakes owed to chance. Pioneer had been an asset long enough for bad luck to finally get its turn to play in the game.

• • •

Mitchell was partial to the classier British term "dead letter box," but dead drops were his preferred operation. Trying to intercept one was a counterintelligence nightmare and Pioneer had a talent for choosing good sites that gave his case officers the short time needed to retrieve a package even under surveillance. Beijing's alleys were an embarrassment of riches that gave him time to spare to do his work, especially at night. Figuring out from a distance what a man is doing with his hands at a given moment was almost impossible without the sun's help.

Mitchell gave himself better-than-even odds that someone was behind him tonight. The MSS hadn't played rough this time, but one man had shown himself in two places far enough apart to reduce the chance that it was mere coincidence. Mitchell was tall enough that the crowds didn't give him enough help, so he played with his adversaries, donning a hat, doffing his coat, changing his gross profile from time to time. His overcoat was black, his slacks charcoal gray, and there was no moon, so the shadows cast by buildings and parked cars swallowed him and spit him out every few seconds. Every so often he wandered directly under a streetlight to destroy whatever night vision a surveillance team had managed to preserve.

The little market was not so different from dozens of the stores where he had shopped at home in New York City. Fresh foods sat out on open stands, boxed foods on shelves, cooked meals behind long serving counters. Mitchell made his way through the aisle toward the back. Several men in rumpled clothing sat on bar stools before the counter or a few round tables, eating hot food and reading newspapers. Mitchell couldn't read the Chinese script handwritten on an old chalkboard pinned to a ceiling rafter that published the menu, but he'd been here enough to know the fare and prices.

The cook was an elderly man named Zhang Rusi. The American had gone out of his way to make friends with Rusi, and not for operational reasons. The old man's culinary talents were more worthy of the Fangshan than this ramshackle eatery. Rusi had formal training but had abandoned that career to run the market that his family had owned for three generations. The other men sitting around the counter were childhood friends poor enough that they couldn't afford better than the free food he shared with them. He cared nothing for politics and loved Americans. He had taught Mitchell the game of mahjong, the tuition for which was English lessons, and their matches were still one-sided. Rusi was clever and refused to play below his skill, but the cook appreciated the humility the younger man demonstrated in defeat. Mitchell was improving quickly, and Rusi would be proud when he finally lost a match to the American someday.

"Carl, good evening. How are you?" His accent was harsh but Mitchell had nothing but respect for a man in his seventies who was willing to tackle English as a second language.

Mitchell replied in Mandarin. *"Hai hao. Ni ne?"* I'm well. And you?

"Hai hao. Will you have dinner with us tonight?"

"I regret that I cannot," Mitchell replied, keeping his language simple, slow, and formal. Rusi's comprehension was still lacking. "I would like a bowl of your *mapodofu* to go, please."

Rusi nodded his head. He held up a handful of fingers. "Five minutes. And you come tomorrow and play or it will be ten minutes."

Mitchell smiled and nodded. "I will." Rusi nodded back, his head dipping low, and threw black bean paste and chopped scallions into his wok.

Mitchell walked past the mahjong tables to the tiny restroom hidden behind a high row of stocked shelving. It was a dirty closet that barely offered a tall man room to squat over the toilet without bumping his knees against the wall. The dark space was lit by a dim bulb, for which Mitchell was grateful. He wasn't sure that he wanted to see the room under full light lest he lose his appetite. It was hardly Rusi's fault. The room was as old as the rest of the building, grubby to the point that no amount of scrubbing would ever make the worn concrete and tile floor look clean again.

Mitchell closed the door and reached behind the heater. He felt nothing, suppressed a curse, reached into his coat, pulled out a tiny Maglite and turned the head until it lit. The flashlight had a red lens that dimmed the bulb, though he doubted that anyone outside would have seen any light leaking out from the door. He pointed the Maglite down behind the grating.

Mitchell froze. He swept the beam through the space again and confirmed that he hadn't just missed the expected package in the low light. The space was empty. He killed the Maglite and sat in the near dark to think.

Pioneer had given the signal that he had loaded this dead drop. The chalk mark on the alley wall had been clear and Pioneer wouldn't have drawn it before completing his half of the operation. There had been no miscommunication about which site he'd used, but there was nothing here.

The possible explanations were limited. The first was that someone had removed the package. Either that person worked for Chinese security or they did not. If they did, the MSS could be waiting outside the bathroom to grab Pioneer's handler. If that person did not work for the government, there was an excellent chance they wouldn't know what they had removed, the package wouldn't make its way into government hands, and Mitchell would get to walk out of the market with his dinner in hand. In either case, this site was compromised and Mitchell would never play mahjong with Rusi again, or even see him.

The second possibility, that Pioneer was working for the MSS, was worth a moment of panic. The arrest of a station chief would be embarrassing and end Mitchell's career, but the finest Chinese asset in the Agency's history turning out to be a double agent would be disastrous on a scale that he wasn't paid enough to even consider.

The tiny bathroom suddenly felt smaller and he didn't want to open the door, as though the flimsy wood could protect him from anyone standing outside. He stopped his breathing to listen and did not hear voices of any kind, but that did nothing to reassure him. Had the men playing games outside simply stopped talking, lost in thought over some brilliant lie of the tiles? Could he have heard them anyway? He'd been stupid for not paying attention to that detail the other nights he had come here. Or had Rusi's friends been hushed by the sight of armed soldiers moving into their private little game parlor? Mitchell could not see the shadows of feet through the small crack at the bottom of the door.

He cleared his mind and forced himself to think about nothing. *Lord, help me to accept the things I cannot change,* he thought. Mitchell stood, flushed the unused toilet, and washed his hands anyway. He faced the door and turned the knob. The light flooded in.

There were no soldiers, no plainclothes MSS officers. The old men playing mahjong didn't even look up from their tiles as the bathroom door creaked on its ungreased hinges.

Rusi waved Mitchell over. The *mapodofu* was ready, boxed to go, and the elderly cook held the brown paper bag out to the man.

"Thank you, Rusi." *For everything. I'm sorry, my friend.*

"It is my pleasure, Carl. I look forward to our game tomorrow."

"I will be here," Mitchell lied, and it hurt. *Good-bye, Rusi.* He took his dinner, paid the cashier at the door—Rusi's granddaughter, attractive but a Chinese national and too young for him, both factors preventing her from becoming a temptation—and made his way out to the street. He felt tired. Another friend lost to his job. That list was getting long.

What just happened? he wondered.

TASHAN POWER PLANT
SHUITOU VILLAGE, JINCHENG TOWNSHIP,
KINMEN ISLAND, TAIWAN
2 KILOMETERS FROM THE CHINESE COAST

James Hsueh tossed his cigarette stub onto the gravel, where it glowed briefly in the dark before fading. The engineer slipped his wrench into his toolbelt, then fumbled for the diagnostic laptop that he'd left on the ground after putting another tobacco stick between his lips and lighting it with the last bit of butane in his Zippo. Last night's storm had brought lightning with it and one of the flashes had struck a substation tower. It hadn't worried him at the time. A lightning strike wouldn't damage the equipment while the arresters were working. The surge arresters saved the voltage transformers, but the mainframe insisted that the power flow was now twitchy. He didn't believe it despite what the computers insisted, and so he had to make a trip to the station to see the equipment for himself.

James finally admitted to himself that he really just wanted to be home. He didn't mind the overtime, but there was a young lady in the picture now. He'd met Ju-hsuan at the Taipower human resource office the month before when he'd marched in to argue about a discrepancy in his paycheck. The woman's smile had disarmed his venom in an instant. He hadn't thought about anything else for a week until he finally went back and asked her to dinner.

The engineer stared down at the laptop screen in the darkness. Still with the power fluctuations, it said. He made a rude gesture toward the machine that refused to let him leave for the night and leaned back against the steel pylon behind him. He would finish the cigarette to buy time to think before he made another move.

The high-pitched sound caught his ear for a brief second. He looked around, then up, but could see nothing. The lights of Jincheng washed out virtually all the stars and the moon was absent. The substation lights prevented him from seeing most anything beyond the chain-link perimeter fence. Still, he looked back to the street beyond, trying to identify the sound. Nothing was moving inside the perimeter. He was quite sure that he was alone.

The explosion erupted fifty meters behind him at the other end of the substation, far enough that the structures between James and the compression wave gave some protection, but not enough. The wall of air was supersonic for an instant, then slowed and began breaking up as it passed through the now-crumbling obstacles presented by the sub-station. The part of the remaining wave that struck James blew out his eardrums before it picked up his body and threw him against the chain-link fence along with the shrapnel created from the now-shredded metal parts of the station. His larger bones shattered and his eyes were saved only because he was facing away from the blast.

The fence collapsed in a fraction of a second, and the engineer re-sumed his own tumble along the ground for another half-dozen meters. The largest of the flying razors had missed him while he was pinned off the ground, but a few dozen smaller pieces tore into his back and legs. Surgeons would remove them in a few hours in a failed effort to save his life. The pieces that would kill him were the six that punctured his lungs. He was fortunate that he wasn't conscious to feel them ripping into the soft tissues in his chest cavity.

The heat came next, hot enough to curl the paint off the few sub-station signs that were bolted to the pieces of metal infrastructure still holding together. The exposed edges of the shredded pylons and equip-ment casings closer to the expanding crater glowed brilliant in a second as they turned white hot. The fireball, cooling as it rushed through the air, had dropped in temperature enough that the engineer didn't catch fire when it reached his prone body. It was hot enough only to blister his skin and burn off the exposed hair on his head. It also cruelly pre-served his life by fusing the cloth of his overalls into the open holes in his back, cauterizing the exterior wounds and saving him from bleeding out.

James Hsueh opened his eyes a moment later for the last time. He could hear nothing. He had just enough time to notice that the Kin-men skyline was entirely dark before the merciful pain knocked him unconscious again for the last time.

CHAPTER 5

THURSDAY
DAY FIVE

Ambassador Aidan Dunne sat with his legs crossed, wishing, as he had daily for three years, that he could read the organized scrawl of a Chinese newspaper. It was absurd, he thought, that a Harvard PhD should feel illiterate. He'd spent exorbitant amounts of time and money on his education, and it galled him that he couldn't read a local tabloid. As a boy, one of the sisters teaching at the Maryland Catholic school decided that he had "the gift of tongues" and had promised it wouldn't go well for him on Judgment Day if he couldn't answer the Judge's final questions in at least three languages, including Latin. The nun had been right about his gift for languages, but the ones he'd studied used Roman and Cyrillic alphabets. Chinese pictographs were incomprehensible, and the humiliation had finally driven Dunne to admit that, at age sixty-five, his mind wasn't up to that particular task. He dropped the *People's Daily* on the hand-carved cherrywood end table and held his poker face. His hosts knew he couldn't read their language, but they didn't need to know that it bothered him.

Dunne was a career diplomat, having spent the better part of thirty years living outside the United States and more than a few in some of the most underdeveloped, if not godforsaken, countries on the planet. His reward for it had been the deputy ambassador post in Beijing, after which tour he'd expected to retire. Ambassador Extraordinary and Plenipotentiary to the People's Republic of China was a prized post in the State Department usually given to some favored donor to the sitting president's political party, so Dunne's nomination for the ambassadorship had come as a shock to everyone. But President Harrison "Harry" Stuart was in his second term and wouldn't be trolling for campaign contributions again, which afforded him the luxury of picking people for their skills and experience instead of their largesse. The *Washington Post* and *New York Times* editorial pages had praised the pick as a tribute to the way the process should work, which had sucked what little wind there was out of the opposition. The Senate

Foreign Relations Committee failed to dredge up any defensible reason to kill his nomination, and few senators were ready to vote against a man who was so obviously qualified and deserving. It was too good a chance to earn some political capital of their own, so they praised him on C-SPAN and confirmed him. The only senator who hadn't voted for him had been out of town when the vote was taken. The only critics had been those offended that they didn't get the job, and none were willing to say so in public. The job afforded Dunne and his wife a comfortable last assignment in a modern city and would guarantee a nice stream of moderate speaking fees during his retirement.

Dealing with the Chinese wasn't always pleasant, but he couldn't complain with their preferred venue. West of the Forbidden City, Zhongnanhai was a brilliant estate of lakes, gardens, villas, and office buildings that housed the highest levels of the Chinese government. *Their version of the White House . . . or the Kremlin*, Kathryn Cooke had once told him during his intelligence briefing before assuming the post. Mao had built up the place after the Revolution in '49. It was a massive complex and, in true government fashion, was off-limits to the average citizen. More than a few of the commoners who were "called to Zhongnanhai" during Mao's reign never walked out again. Dunne had no doubts that the security services watched him when he came inside, which was fine. He was not an intelligence officer, and whoever was watching for him to plant a microphone was wasting their time. He'd never been declared persona non grata before and he wasn't going to end his career that way now.

Dunne heard footsteps, the sound of hard-sole shoes beating on the stone tiles in the hallway. He waited for several seconds before turning his head, giving no impression of anxiousness. It would have been undiplomatic to say, and so Dunne would never say it, but the aide looked in no way remarkable. The man's attire was straight from the universal bureaucrat dress code. The clothes belied the man. Zeng Qinglin was *mishu* to President Tian Kai, the personal aide to the chief of state of the People's Republic of China, a civilization a few thousand years older than the United States. His position gave him powerful *guanxi*, the network of personal connections to other leaders in the party who would one day ensure his own rise in the ranks, possibly even to full member status in the Central Committee if he didn't fall out of favor with the wrong people. *The great truth of bureaucracy*, Dunne thought. *The gatekeeper is almost as powerful as the person behind the gate. More, in some ways.*

"Ambassador Dunne, the president will see you now." Zeng's English was grammatically correct and spoken with a hint of an English accent. *Oxford.* Dunne had read the CIA's file on the man before meeting him for the first time. The Communist Party wouldn't send its most promising sons and daughters abroad and risk their defection for the sake of a third-rate education.

"Thank you," Dunne replied.

Dunne stood and rested his weight on his cane, less an affectation and more a needed crutch every year. But the walk was a short one before Zeng stopped and opened one of a pair of dark hardwood doors. He stood aside like a proper doorman, and Dunne walked into the office of President Tian Kai.

Tian—Chinese surnames precede first names—stood beside his desk, an ornate piece of furniture that reminded Dunne of the *Resolute* desk in the Oval Office. The rest of Tian's office was comfortable, though not to excess, and some of the furniture looked like it was drawn from the Victorian era.

The other men in the room were an impressive group in their own right.

Dunne's memory for Chinese characters was weak but his memory for faces was excellent. He had spent time studying the leadership biographies provided by both CIA and State Department. He'd never seen so many members of the Politburo Central Committee and Central Military Committee in one place outside the Great Hall of the People.

They're not here for tea, Dunne told himself. *And they wanted me to see them. You could have cleared the room before letting me in,* he thought. Such things didn't happen at this level by chance. So many men of this stature wouldn't convene at Zhongnanhai for social reasons, and protocol would have dictated that he not be admitted until they had left. Racking his memory, he couldn't remember even seeing these men together at a state dinner, much less for business. If Dunne were suddenly dismissed from the office, what he'd already seen would be worth a cable to Washington.

"Mr. Ambassador, thank you for coming." President Tian's English was excellent, which always frustrated Dunne. It gave the Chinese head of state a significant advantage. Tian stepped forward and offered his hand with a kind smile.

"Mr. President, it is my honor to come," Dunne said, accepting the handshake.

Tian turned to the other men and spoke to them in Mandarin. Dunne interpreted it as a polite request for privacy—*or "message sent"?*—and the group filed out of the room, Zeng leaving last and closing the door behind.

Tian slowly lowered himself into his chair behind the desk. "These are dangerous times," he said without preamble. He was younger than Dunne by less than a decade, shorter by a head, and had a deeper voice than most Chinese men the ambassador talked to. Like Zeng's, his accent was an odd combination of Oxford English mixed with Mandarin tones. "You are, of course, aware of the recent speech made by President Liang, accusing us of espionage in Taiwan."

"I am, sir."

"I will not insult your intelligence by denying that our arrested citizens were officers of our Ministry of State Security. We both understand the necessity of intelligence operations." Tian paused, sipped his tea, and then resumed. "But the facts must be clear now. The Taiwanese citizens were not working for us. Perhaps they were political enemies of President Liang and he seized the opportunity to remove them from his path. Such an act would hardly be beneath him."

Dunne straightened his back in surprise without thinking. *You outed MSS officers. Why?* As one part of his brain worked that puzzle, the part handling the diplomacy arranged his response. "One was an American citizen," Dunne corrected him to buy time.

"Yes, but I honestly do not know why he was in the room with our officers," Tian conceded. Dunne studied his face carefully. If the Chinese president was lying, he was covering it with great skill. "And given his unfortunate death, we will not know until Liang returns our officers to Beijing. Another reason that perhaps your country might persuade Taiwan to cooperate with us in this matter."

Dunne stifled his first response and managed to just raise an eyebrow instead. The intel that Mitchell had reviewed with him that morning told a different story. Dunne hadn't expected the gospel truth out of Tian, but this account was a different lie than the one he had been expecting. "So you don't deny that the Ministry of State Security was conducting espionage against Taiwan?"

"No. Of course, we will publicly deny it."

"Of course."

Tian went on after imbibing more tea. "I tell you this because the presence of our officers in Taipei was legal, and to illustrate the lengths to which President Liang will go to preserve his position. He often seeks to arouse public sentiment favoring independence. My concern is that those efforts could encourage our own native dissident elements. Surely you can see that such political unrest would not be in the interest of either of our countries."

"The United States has always advocated a peaceful resolution of the reunification issue. My country does not support a unilateral move by either side to alter the status quo."

"I regret that Liang may not allow us to resolve our differences in a more civilized way." Dunne noted that Tian hadn't bothered to refer to Liang by the formal title of *President*. Tian set the teacup on the desk, his hand steady as the porcelain landed on the saucer without a sound. "A careful review of his recent speech suggests that Liang might be preparing to declare Taiwan's independence."

The Chinese president locked eyes with the US ambassador and the two men stared at each other for several seconds. Dunne's mind raced back over the sentence, hoping that he had heard it wrong, but there was no ambiguity in the phrasing. Tian certainly had chosen the wording before summoning Dunne to Zhongnanhai.

Dunne picked his own words cautiously. "The United States does not share that conclusion, Mr. President. We hope that your government will allow President Liang the opportunity to clarify his words, lest there be a misunderstanding."

"If Liang were to offer a public apology, we would listen. However, we think it unlikely that he will do so." Dunne stared at Tian, looking for any crack in the performance. He found none. "He is in danger of losing reelection," Tian explained. "History teaches that desperate men often deflect scrutiny from their own deficiencies by turning the public attention to an external threat. And Liang likely believes that the United States will intervene on Taiwan's behalf should we respond with more than words. I hope that your country's past encouragement of Taiwan's rebellious attitudes does not now drag us all into an unpleasant confrontation."

"We have not encouraged independence," Dunne said. "Our position has been to have both sides treat each other with respect."

"And yet you have sold them weapons," Tian countered.

"For self-defense only," Dunne said. It was a weak protest, he thought. A gun was a gun. *Two years to retirement and I get to head off a war*. He knew his next suggestion would be futile. "We would hope

that you would refer the matter to the UN Security Council for delib-
erations."

Tian shook his head. "The Security Council has no place in resolv-
ing internal disputes."

Tian's meaning was quite clear. *China has a permanent seat on the
Council and a veto. You know a Security Council resolution won't pass.
Why waste time playing that game?*

Dunne suppressed an inappropriate smile. He'd been speaking the
subtle language of diplomats for decades and he was good at it. Better than good, in fact. It made him feel young to engage in the back-
and-forth of subtle meanings hidden in delicate phrases. It was why
he stayed on the job at an age when almost all his peers were retired.
"Some would dispute that this is an internal affair, despite Taiwan's
size and proximity to your coast," he said. *To* buy *time. You don't want a
shooting war with Taiwan to get dragged out. Big country, small island—
no one likes a bully.*

"I hope that your nation would not be one of those. We have the
right to maintain order within our borders." *Is the United States prepared
to recognize a declaration of independence by Taiwan? Don't intervene.*

"Maintaining order can be a delicate task, as you know, where a
soft hand is often required." *Let's not see another Tiananmen Square, or
worse.*

"Indeed. Both determination and a firm hand are often needed to
manage such events." *We'll do it.*

"Force is not the only tool that can secure peace. We would hope
that an offer to mediate would be accepted by both sides." *Taiwan will
accept our help, especially if it's backed up by the US Navy.*

"Your offer is appreciated, but the United States could best help
us keep the peace by abstaining." Tian took his time before speaking
again. "Ambassador Dunne, if I may be blunt . . . ?"

Dunne nodded. Straightforward talk was a diplomat's knife—useful
but dangerous if misused. Still, there was no polite way to reject it. "Of
course."

"In 1995, there was an unpleasant confrontation with the province.
Your President Clinton sent an aircraft carrier into the Strait—the
Nimitz, I believe. General Xiong Guangkai answered by saying that
'you care more about Los Angeles than you do about Taipei.'"

What? Dunne lost his composure for a moment. He would have
realized that it was the first time in his recent memory, had he been

thinking about it. Instead his thoughts turned to fighting his urge to come out of his chair. "Are you—"

Tian held up his hand and Dunne stopped midquestion. "I enjoy the history of your country very much," Tian said. "I have enjoyed studying the confrontation over Cuba with the Soviet Union in 1962. President Kennedy was quite masterful, I think. Still, the opportunity for miscommunication was so great. The world has never been so close to nuclear war."

"It was Kennedy's finest hour," Dunne agreed. Tian had twisted the conversation and the American had lost his sense of direction. He suddenly felt like he was blind.

"Yes. His death was a great loss. He might have gone on to do great things." Tian's admiration for America's youngest president seemed genuine. The Chinese president paused, whether to gather his thoughts or for dramatic emphasis Dunne couldn't tell. "My own generals can be bellicose when their passions are aroused, and Taiwan is a passionate issue for us. Should your president choose to send your navy into our Strait, I want no miscommunication. We are reasonable men, unlike the stupid, selfish man in Taipei who is causing us both so much trouble."

"I appreciate your candor," Dunne said.

"If there is to be a confrontation, a good leader must consider the peace that is to come after the war, something I'm afraid your country has often failed to do. But if we do find ourselves at odds, your president certainly must care more for your navy than for Taipei."

Dunne sat silent long enough for the silence to feel uncomfortable. He felt off-balance, inadequate, like his old skills in assembling diplomatic answers had abandoned him. He turned Tian's last words around in his head over and over. "That would not be my decision to make," he said finally. "I'm sure that President Stuart would be willing to discuss the matter." It was the best answer he could find, but it was still weak.

"Of course." Tian placed both hands on the table. "I wish to share with you a copy of the speech that I will give in response to President Liang's remarks," he said, taking the conversation down another path again. Tian took a leather portfolio from the small table sitting between their chairs and handed it to Dunne. "I will reaffirm our commitment to reunification and propose the immediate commencement of talks with Taiwan to that end. Please deliver this to President Stuart and extend my compliments."

I didn't hear the word peaceful *anywhere in there.* "I will, sir. And on behalf of the United States, I thank you for the advance copy of your pending remarks," Dunne said. He looked down at the speech in his hands. *So much for diplomacy*, he thought.

LEESBURG, VIRGINIA

The hard sound of the truck's plow grinding on asphalt woke Kyra a good hour before the alarm had the chance. For a few happy moments she couldn't remember where she was, and then the ache in her arm reminded her. Last night's dinner tasted foul in her mouth. Beer at night didn't agree with her, gumbo even less. She'd known that, had finished both anyway, and she prayed that she had some mouthwash somewhere in the bathroom cabinet. She honestly couldn't remember.

Kyra opened her eyes and realized she couldn't see straight yet either. She pushed herself up with the wrong arm and the pain sharpened enough to wake her up. She kneaded the muscle for a minute, more in fascination over the scarred depression running in a horizontal line over her triceps than over the relief the movement didn't really offer. Well, there was something for that. She still had plenty of Vicodin, even though she was taking more than the dosage on the bottle allowed.

Kyra rolled over, put her feet on the floor, and pulled the curtains apart. It was still snowing. She forced her eyes to focus and turned on the small television on her dresser.

The Office of Personnel Management had again not closed the government, instead offering liberal leave to those with enough leave hours stored up to take it. Kyra couldn't muster the strength to curse the OPM director. She promised herself she would get around to it after the shower.

The phone on her nightstand rang. Kyra let it sound off three times to help wake herself up before she answered the call. "Hello?"

"You might want to come in sooner rather than later," Jonathan said. "Somebody took out a power station in Taiwan. Cooke wants us in her office."

In twenty minutes, Kyra was in her truck, driving east far too fast to be safe.

CIA DIRECTOR'S OFFICE

"We're still not sure how the Chinese did it," Cooke said without preamble. As a general rule, she didn't call analysts to her office like this, but yesterday's conversation with Jonathan had left her wanting to see him again even if she couldn't talk about what was really on her mind. It was a selfish impulse, unprofessional, but she'd caved anyway.

Cooke laid the satellite imagery on the table and Kyra picked up one of the photographs. The picture, high-resolution infrared, showed a large crater in fine detail with fires still burning around the perimeter. Severed electrical lines arced on the ground.

"You're assuming it was the PLA," Jonathan said.

"Is there any chance it was an industrial accident?" Kyra asked.

"I wish," Cooke said. "We've got some SCADA experts coming in, but I'm pretty sure there's nothing in a power plant that would produce a blast pattern like that. And it would be one amazing coincidence, given the timing."

"It's just the one location?" Jonathan asked.

"NSA hasn't reported any other attacks on the electrical grid," Cooke confirmed. "And one was enough. I'm told that the Tashan Power Plant was the big one. When Taipower brought that one online, they shut down smaller plants at Tai-Wu, Luguang, and Chuangjiang to cut costs. I bet they're regretting that now."

"No doubt," Jonathan observed.

"That's a big hole," Kyra said. "Airstrike?"

"The Office of Naval Intelligence says the radar track for Chinese military aircraft and ballistic missiles was negative," Cooke said. "The only aircraft in the area were Taiwanese commercial and Air Force. All of the PLA MIGs were way outside the missile envelope."

"It could have been the work of a sapper team," Jonathan suggested. "Only God and Tian know how many infiltrators the Chinese have in Taipei. Semtex or C-four maybe, but they'd need plenty of it to make a hole that size. That crater must be ten feet deep. Too much material to carry in by hand."

"Car bomb?" Cooke asked.

Jonathan shrugged. "Doesn't seem like something a SpecOps team would do, does it? Maybe if it was fifth columnists. Amateurs tend to overestimate explosive yields. The question is whether the PLA would trust this kind of job to fifth columnists alone." His expression suggested he didn't believe that particular option. "Anything else?"

"Cable from State Department," Cooke said. The CIA director extracted a report from a manila folder. "The ambassador met with the Chinese president."

```
FM AMEMBASSY BEIJING
TO SECSTATE WASHDC IMMEDIATE

TEXT

SUBJECT: MEETING OF US AMBASSADOR WITH PRC
PRESIDENT TIAN KAI REGARDING ARRESTS OF PRC
NATIONALS IN TAIPEI

CLASSIFIED BY: AIDAN DUNNE, AMBASSADOR PRC

1. (S//NF) PRIOR TO MEETING WITH PRC PRESI-
DENT TIAN KAI, AMBASSADOR WITNESSED SEVERAL
PRESENT AND FORMER PRC OFFICIALS FINISH A
CONSULTATION WITH TIAN, INCLUDING:

HU JINTAO, FORMER PRC PRESIDENT, FORMER CMC
   CHAIRMAN
XI JIABAO, CHAIRMAN, STANDING COMMITTEE, NA-
   TIONAL PEOPLE'S CONGRESS
ZHANG DEMING, CMC VICE CHAIRMAN, MINISTER OF
   NATIONAL DEFENSE
WU SHAOSHI, DIRECTOR, COMMISSION ON SCIENCE,
   TECHNOLOGY, AND INDUSTRY FOR NATIONAL DE-
   FENSE (COSTIND)
```

The list of names went on for a half page. "The guy's got a good memory," Kyra said.

"Who'd've thought diplomats could be so observant?" Cooke said. "I guess it helps with the job. Check out the last few paragraphs. Good stuff in there."

Kyra turned the page.

7. (S//NF) TIAN ADMITTED THAT THE PRC NA-
TIONALS DETAINED BY TAIWAN'S NATIONAL SECU-
RITY BUREAU ARE MSS OFFICERS, BUT DECLINED
TO IDENTIFY ANY BY NAME. HE ALSO STATED THAT
BECAUSE TAIWAN IS A PRC TERRITORY UNDER THE
"ONE CHINA" DOCTRINE, THE MSS OFFICERS WERE
OPERATING LEGALLY IN TAIPEI. TIAN ALSO DE-
NIES THAT ANY ARRESTED CIVILIANS WERE MSS
ASSETS.

8. (S//NF) TIAN ANNOUNCED THAT HE WOULD DE-
LIVER A TELEVISED SPEECH WITHIN TWENTY-FOUR
HOURS TO DENOUNCE THE ARRESTS AND DEMAND THE
EXTRADITION OF PRC NATIONALS AND TO CALL FOR
RENEWED NEGOTIATIONS TO RESOLVE THE FINAL
STATUS OF TAIWAN.

9. (S//NF) AMBASSADOR OFFERED U.S. ASSIS-
TANCE IN NEGOTIATING A DIPLOMATIC RESOLU-
TION. TIAN DECLINED AND SAID THAT POTUS
COULD BE HELPFUL BY NOT DEPLOYING USN ASSETS
TO INTERVENE, STATING, "YOU CERTAINLY MUST
CARE MORE FOR YOUR AIRCRAFT CARRIERS THAN
FOR TAIPEI." TIAN DELIVERED HIS PREPARED RE-
MARKS (ATTACHED) TO AMBASSADOR FOR REVIEW.

Kyra handed the stapled sheets to Jonathan. "Only a diplomat can make a threat sound like he's actually worried for the enemy."

"Heads of state don't make jokes about sinking another country's ships," Jonathan said. He stared at the sheet for a moment, then dropped it and moved to Cooke's classified computer and began typing.

"It could be a psychological game," Kyra observed. She rubbed her forehead. The Vicodin had done its job with admirable efficiency. "Would the president refuse to send in a carrier battle group if he thought the PLA could sink it?"

Cooke considered the question for a few moments, tapping her finger on the table. "I played in a war game at the Naval War College a few years ago, when I was still in the service," she finally said. "The red team's first move was to launch every cruise missile they had at the Navy blue team's carrier. The computer judged that they sank the ship. Control stopped the game, restarted the match, resurrected the carrier, and refused to give the red team their missiles back. They said the game wasn't worth playing if the carrier wasn't present. Draw your own conclusions."

"Were you trying to embarrass the game masters?" Kyra asked.

"Ask him," Cooke said, nodding her head at Burke.

"I might have suggested that tactic," Jonathan said. "Hoping that we never lose a carrier is poor strategy."

"Wait," Kyra said. "The two of you—"

"First time we met," Cooke confirmed. "Jon here was an observer, sitting in with the red team. At least he was supposed to just be observing."

"Observing is boring," Jonathan said. "I don't handle boredom well."

"I can believe that," Kyra said. "What would it take to replace a lost carrier?"

"Five years and thirteen billion dollars, minimum," Jonathan told her. "And a dead president liked by the Navy to name it after."

"Cute," Kyra replied. "So how are the Chinese going to kill a carrier?"

"*Shashoujian,*" Jonathan said, pronouncing each syllable slowly.

"What?" Both women asked the question at the same time.

"*Shashoujian,*" he said again. "The closest English translation is 'assassin's mace.' In Chinese lore, it's a small weapon that a soldier in ancient times could hide in his robes to mortally strike an enemy to end a fight before it started. It's also an umbrella label for a series of PLA weapons projects, most of which haven't produced anything. The technologies have been pretty exotic—laser guns, high-power microwaves, real Star Wars–type stuff. Some of it sounds more like propaganda than serious weapons research."

Kyra studied Jonathan's face. "You already have a link," she realized.

Jonathan held out the State cable. "The people listed as being in Tian's office are all members of the Nine Nine Eight State Security Project Leading Group, which is one of the groups overseeing Assassin's Mace research. And there's no record of any other committee with the same membership."

"You memorize the membership rolls of foreign committees?" Cooke asked, slightly stunned.

"Would it impress you if I said yes?" he asked.

"Frighten more than impress," the CIA director told him.

Kyra stared at him until a slight twitch at the corner of his mouth gave away the game. "You ran a search on their names as a group," she said, accusing.

Jonathan looked sideways at the young woman. "You have no sense of humor whatsoever."

Gotcha. "When did the Chinese start the program?" she asked.

"Nineteen ninety-five. Taiwanese President Lee Teng-hui took some not-so-subtle shots in public at the Chinese government during a visit to the US that the Chinese opposed. Jiang Zemin took it badly and the PLA made some threatening moves," Jonathan said. "Bill Clinton sent the *Nimitz* into the Taiwan Strait to calm everyone down. Jiang asked his military advisors what they could do about it and the short answer they gave him was 'nothing.' Jiang pounded the table and ordered the PLA to develop 'an assassin's mace to use against the Americans.'"

"Nice bit of history, but that doesn't help me," Cooke said.

Jonathan raised an eyebrow. "I just gave you a logically defensible bit of strategic warning that the Chinese might have a carrier killer."

"Strategic warning gets me into the Oval Office," Cooke said. "Tactical warning keeps me from getting thrown out. Telling the president that the Chinese have a black program targeting our carriers isn't exactly going to rock his world. But telling him exactly what it is will get his attention."

"The curse of genius is that people begin to expect it on demand," Jonathan deadpanned. "I can tell you what it's not. There are five major classes of strategic weapons that can hit a carrier at sea. Submarines, ships, missiles, aircraft, and weapons of mass destruction. It won't be a submarine or a ship because the PLA Navy is still buying last-generation Kilos and Sovremennys from the Russians. The Russians built the one carrier they do have, and the PLA Navy is still trying to figure out how to use the thing. It won't be a weapon of mass destruction because the Chinese aren't stupid enough to set off a nuke that close to their own coastline, and carriers are hardened against biological and chemical weapons. That leaves missiles and aircraft."

"Missiles worked for you in that war game," Kyra noted.

"They did," Jonathan agreed. "The Dongfeng missile can hit a carrier from nine hundred miles away in theory, but the tracking systems are iffy. The Chinese bought Shkvals from the Russians a few years back. It's a rocket-propelled torpedo that creates a layer of air bubbles from the nose and skin to eliminate drag and friction in the water. Top speed is around two hundred knots but the warhead is small to keep the speed up, maybe too small to do serious damage to a carrier. And the PLA would still also have to get close enough to use it. The maximum range is about maybe seven miles."

"One of their subs snuck up on the *Kitty Hawk* about ten years ago," Kyra observed.

"True. You know recent military history. Your usefulness just went up," Jonathan said. Cooke raised an eyebrow. The Red Cell analyst had just offered one of his higher compliments.

"What about planes?" Cooke asked.

Jonathan stood and moved to the National Geographic map of the Chinese coast he had pinned to the wall. "The PLA has two air bases directly across the Strait and nine more in range. That's a few hundred planes, but they've only got maybe a hundred fifty modern types, Su-27s and -30s."

"I'd bet money the PLA wouldn't mind sacrificing a few hundred old planes if it meant winning the Battle of the Taiwan Strait," Kyra observed.

"Given the money that the PLA has spent on exotic technologies, I would hope that the Assassin's Mace is something more interesting than just sending out cheap cannon fodder. But we can't disprove anything yet," Jonathan replied. He turned to Cooke. "If you want something more defensible than my impeccable logic, we'll need to do some actual research."

"Take your time," Cooke said.

"Meaning?" Jonathan asked.

"Meaning you get twenty-four hours," Cooke said. "Less if the Taiwanese refuse to give up Tian's men and the PLA gets rowdy again."

"Any word on how that Taiwanese SWAT team is doing?" Kyra asked.

"Two dead," Cooke said. "They assumed room temperature this morning. The third officer is still listed as critical." Another page came out of the manila folder, this one from the Office of Medical Services. "Whatever was in that canister torched his lungs. He's suffering from"—she had to read the language directly from the page—"'severe inhalation injury with persistent postburn refractory hypoxemia.' That means he's got second- and third-degree chemical burns of the trachea and lungs. Oxygen can't diffuse across the lung membranes into his bloodstream. The 'refractory' part means nothing that they're trying is helping him. He'll be intubated and paralyzed with drugs to keep him from fighting the doctors, but it's just a question of when he's going to die, not if."

"What about that dead American?" Kyra asked.

"FBI is still trying to run down which Lockheed division he worked for. The company isn't moving very fast. They're not excited about the idea that one of their employees was committing espionage." She checked her watch. "Tian's going to give his speech in an hour. Start pulling your research together and then come back and join me."

THE GREAT HALL OF THE PEOPLE
BEIJING

Cooke's television couldn't do justice to the Great Hall of the People. The camera, owned and operated by China Central Television, pulled back to a wide-angle shot and panned left to right, showing the breadth of the massive room that held thousands of seats. The People's National Congress had three thousand delegates, and the Great Hall held them all with room to spare. The cavernous amphitheater was an engineering feat. It had been constructed in a mere ten months all by "volunteers," though Cooke wondered whether the Chinese hadn't played fast and loose with that term. Either way, Cooke had no doubt that the construction workers had not been paid, but their work was exquisite. The massive chamber was arranged like an orchestra hall, with two elevated semicircular tiers stretching the hall's full width for seating above the ground levels. There were no support columns under either balcony to block the view of the vast stage. An expansive red banner framed the Politburo and other senior party members seated on the wide dais, with ten towering Chinese flags lining the wall behind them. It was an image meant to convey the full grandeur of the state and it managed to do that quite well, even for those like Cooke who knew enough about the state to keep their awe in check.

The acoustics of the hall were remarkable given its size, but the room was quiet. Cooke watched as Tian stood from his seat and approached the podium in front. He looked the room over, his face fixed in a look of tranquility.

"It makes the Senate Chamber on Capitol Hill look like a high school auditorium. It's like having a stadium devoted to politics," Kyra said.

"Whoever invented the saying that politics is a blood sport was Chinese," Cooke replied.

The president of the People's Republic of China looked down at his text and began to speak in measured tones. Elsewhere in the hall, translators wearing headphones and sitting in closed booths looked down at their own portfolios and began to translate in sync with Tian as his Mandarin cadence came through their headphones. Central China Television had dedicated its CCTV 4 English-only international channel to the speech nominally for the benefit of Westerners living in the country.

Tian offered the pleasantries befitting a head of state addressing his country, speaking with a practiced manner, calm, not so different from the official manner he had used with Dunne in the office at Zhongnanhai. Most men would have been nervous speaking even to just the few thousand in the Great Hall, and Tian knew the real audience was far larger . . . though he was, in truth, talking to an audience of one. There were televisions in the White House.

Tian finally broached the true subject with a grave look. "It is with the greatest sorrow and reluctance that I have convened this special session of the National Congress of the Communist Party of China. Four days ago, the government of Taiwan arrested eight citizens of the People's Republic of China on charges of espionage. I have been assured that these arrests were carried out with the full knowledge and approval of President Liang himself. We have requested assurances of the health and safety of those arrested, but we have been refused even that courtesy."

CIA DIRECTOR'S OFFICE

"This is not how I wanted to start my morning," Cooke said. "It would be nice if the president could convince Liang to declare the whole lot of them persona non grata and send them all back to Beijing."

"Not likely," Jonathan said. "The 'One China' policy keeps us from saying that Tian's boys were even trespassing, much less committing espionage."

"Keeps us on a short leash," Kyra observed. "I bet Tian likes it that way."

"That's what happens when you base your foreign policy on a lie," Jonathan said. "And the longer we stick to it, the more painful it's going to be when we finally have to back out."

"It's better to keep the peace so China and Taiwan can work it out through diplomacy," Cooke said.

"You're assuming that they *can* work it out through diplomacy," Jonathan told her.

BEIJING

Mitchell took a deep breath and regretted it. The Beijing smog was worse than the floating filth in his native Los Angeles air, and that was an impressive feat. The dusky sky of his first night in Beijing three years ago had appeared threatening until one of the embassy officers told him that the dark clouds on the horizon had nothing to do with rain.

Mitchell cleared his mind and cursed his lack of mental discipline. Detecting surveillance while in a car required total focus, though tonight he needed less than usual. He'd chosen to make his run during Tian's speech officially because he hoped at least some of the MSS would be watching it instead of working the street. Unofficially he just couldn't stand to listen to the Chinese head of state. But the surveillance team two cars back had done everything but tap his bumper, relieving him of the need to think too hard about where any unwanted guests might be. But it was night and they had to stay close or lose Mitchell to the tide of traffic. Vehicular surveillance in a crowded city—and few had as many residents as Beijing—was the most difficult kind to perform. Traffic patterns were uncontrollable. Keeping a single car close to the target without being seen was no small task, and moving other cars along parallel side streets was more complicated still.

"Almost there," the driver, another case officer, said.

"Take the corner," Mitchell said.

Mitchell's driver pulled the car into the far right lane. He turned the corner and stopped short, forcing the cars behind to brake hard. Mitchell opened his door and stepped out onto the sidewalk, then turned and said something meaningless to his driver, as though to thank him for the ride. The driver nodded, then pulled out into traffic—he would just drive home—and the chief of station walked in the opposite direction.

Vehicular surveillance was hard enough, but making the sudden shift from vehicle to foot pursuit was agony. The MSS officers could stay on the car, but there was no way the Chinese could have had prepositioned anyone to cover Mitchell's dismount. The only men who could follow him would have to come from the cars, so their numbers would be limited. Mitchell had identified only two cars, the first of which ignored the light, turned the corner at the first available moment, and accelerated as much as traffic would allow.

That left the second. If there were other cars on the side streets, they could add to the count—maybe even providing enough manpower to establish a small surveillance bubble around him, given a minute or two. He refused to give it to them. The ground was going to open up and swallow Carl Mitchell whole before they would get the chance.

THE GREAT HALL OF THE PEOPLE
BEIJING

"Our requests for the prisoners' release have gone unanswered. Taiwan's government has refused even to allow our representatives to visit and assess whether our accused citizens are being well treated and have adequate legal representation. The charges are without merit, the arrests were without cause, the citizens detained are without guilt. Liang must personally account for the well-being and safe return of every one of our citizens." Tian had been talking for two minutes and no one had made a sound. He wasn't looking at the teleprompter or the papers on the podium. The president of the People's Republic of China was orating from memory now.

"The members of the Politburo Standing Committee have discussed these recent events at length. Their resolution in the face of unwarranted and illegal political persecution of our citizens is unanimous and firm. There is no division of opinion among us or among the citizens of this great nation on this matter. It is a dangerous step that undermines cross-Strait relations for Liang to refuse us access to our people."

Tian struck the podium with his open palm. "The arrest of innocent citizens of our nation was a fraud, a first step toward separation, a first step toward secession, a first step toward independence!"

CIA DIRECTOR'S OFFICE

"He just went off script," Cooke said.

"Yes, he did," Jonathan agreed. He scrubbed through the text Dunne had provided and finally tossed the transcript back onto the desk. "It's not in the speech. He's making this up."

"Or Tian left it out of our copy on purpose," Kyra said.

Cooke let out a racial slur that would have cost her a Senate confirmation.

BEIJING

Catch me if you can. Mitchell stood at the corner and looked up the street at the oncoming traffic. He had a free excuse to watch the second car that he'd culled from the river of automobiles and he used it. Two men crawled out as quickly as they could and started toward him. They were more than half a block away.

Only two. I can deal with two. Especially at night. The night changed everything. The playing field was now skewed in Mitchell's favor. The street was a riptide of bodies pushing against the two men—Beijing's twelve million citizens working against their own government for a few minutes. It would buy Mitchell time, at least a bare few seconds at the right moment when the Chinese security services would have no eyes on him. That would be enough, but if the subways were on schedule tonight, he would earn far more time than that.

The light changed and Mitchell merged with the mob of citizens who began to march across the broad Jiaodaokou Dongdajie avenue. He walked no faster than the crowd. The two MSS officers didn't reach the corner before the light changed again and Mitchell was on the other side of the street with a wall of moving cars between. The two men tried to step into the street, but a near miss with a car that didn't bother to slow down changed their minds.

Shaking surveillance was not difficult but rarely done, because it would infuriate the watchers and earn retribution later. The skillful part was to make the watchers think that either bad luck or their own incompetence was to blame. The two men on the other side of the street couldn't prove that Mitchell even knew they were there. All the chief of station had done was get out of a car and cross the street. Like a master musician, it was all in the timing.

The Beixinqiao subway station entrance was behind him. Mitchell didn't stop to pay the fare. His ticket was in his pocket, courtesy of another of his officers who had "decided" to take a midday walk around the city. The two MSS officers wouldn't bother with tickets, but Mitchell's prepaid voucher kept the race on even terms. He was down the stairs and approaching the platform when the two finally crossed the street at a dead run. The trains were on time—something in which Communist governments always took pride—and Mitchell was aboard by the time his pursuers reached the top of the stairwell. They pushed their way down the stairs, knocking aside any number of commuters in their rush, and they arrived at the platform just in time to watch the train pull away. They would likely call their superiors to request coverage of all the stations down the line where Mitchell might exit, but the possible number of stops was large, and getting men into position at the closer ones before the train hit them in sequence would be impossible.

In any city of twelve million residents with traffic to match, the subway was always the fastest way to move away from any given point. Mitchell's immediate need was simply to put distance between himself and the Beixinqiao station and a subway train moved faster than any car could follow or any officer on foot could run.

THE GREAT HALL OF THE PEOPLE
BEIJING

The crowd roared for the first time. Tian turned his head slowly, taking in the wave from one side of the room to the other. It was a subtle thing, but Cooke saw it from seven thousand miles away. Tian was feeding off the energy of the crowd. The president of the People's

Republic of China exuded the air of a god on earth soaking in the adoration of worshipers. To the foreign observers in the room, it made twisted sense. Communist doctrine made atheism the official religion, replacing the worship of a supreme being with complete obedience to the state. The state was God and Tian Kai was the state.

Tian held up his hand and the crowd fell silent. "Our position on the issue of reunification has never wavered. We have made our policy clear through our words, through our laws, and through our actions. Any moves toward secession threatens China's state sovereignty and territorial integrity. We have offered the leadership of Taiwan countless opportunities to negotiate the peaceful way forward. We have offered the open hand of forgiveness and fellowship. We have shown the fist of our determination only when no other choices were left. And now the nationalist leader of Taiwan has made his intentions clear. We will make ours equally clear. We will not allow the misguided and selfish politicians of this province to separate from the mainland, or to separate its people from their destiny as citizens of the People's Republic of China!"

The volume control on the television kept the audience's eruption to a tolerable level. Inside the Great Hall it must have been deafening. The camera cut to the crowd, which, to a man, surged to its feet.

CIA DIRECTOR'S OFFICE

"It's like Hitler at Nuremberg," Cooke said. She hadn't been born when the Führer had given that speech, but she was a History Channel addict. *They'll turn this into a documentary in a few years*, she thought. Sometimes it was hard to recognize when history was being made. Other times it was as plain as a slow-motion trainwreck, and just as easy to stop.

BEIJING

Mitchell detrained at the Dongsi station two stops later and kept his head down. In thirty seconds he was aboveground again. He walked east. The Capital Theater was only a short distance in that direction and a bit south on the Wangfujing road. The Beijing People's Art

Theater Company routinely played to a full house, offering a balance between foreign works and Chinese dramas, and they drew a large number of foreign patrons on any given night, which offered Mitchell a sizable non-Asian element in which to merge.

He already had his ticket for that evening's performance, a well-reviewed adaptation of *The Monkey King*. He entered the theater, early as planned, and walked to the men's restroom on the main floor. The smell was appalling by Western standards. The Chinese tossed their used paper into a special bin instead of flushing it into a sewer system that was not always robust enough to handle large loads. Mitchell breathed through his mouth while washing his hands four times until the French patron occupying the second stall from the end finished his business and left as quickly as dignity would allow. Public restrooms in most any country were not a place to linger, which made them a boon to espionage. The stall door closed and locked, Mitchell pulled out a centimeter-square piece of white duct tape from his pocket. It was innocuous, a piece of pocket litter easily discarded or explained away. He affixed it to the rear base of the toilet, which was more of a trough with a hood at one end over which the individual squatted. The tape matched the porcelain color. It would be almost impossible for any patron to see even if looking down for it. The tiny patch would be more easily found by touch than by sight, and there was only one patron who would be feeling around behind the stall anytime soon, given the communal restroom's odor.

All that trouble just to set up a signal for Pioneer to perform a sign of life.

Mitchell vacated the stall, washed his hands again for real, and left the room. He was a patron of the arts for the rest of the night. Three years in Beijing and he'd never seen *The Monkey King*. Theater hadn't been an interest of his before his current tour, but he'd learned to appreciate it at the urging of his wife. She was waiting for him in the twelfth row and would be keeping a better poker face than he had ever mastered. Laura Mitchell had been a drama major in college and was hoping her husband's final tour would be in London as a liaison so she could spend time in the West End near Leicester Square attending experimental productions.

She deserves it, Mitchell thought. Laura had been a faithful soldier for the last twenty years, helping her husband build his cover in third-world rat holes, and praying quietly during the nights when he came home late. She had never trained at the Farm or performed an operational act, but Laura had spent her life in the clandestine service every bit as much as he had. He owed that woman, the Agency owed her more, and he intended to spend every day of retirement finding ways to overpay on the debt.

THE GREAT HALL OF THE PEOPLE
BEIJING

Tian let the cries go on for more than two minutes before raising his hand. "There is one China! China's sovereignty belongs to the entire Chinese people! Retreat from this act of rebellion. Come together with us to unite all descendants of the Chinese nation who love the motherland!" The Chinese leader was holding nothing back now. "We insist on reunification by peaceful means, but do not challenge our will to block all 'Taiwan independence' movements. Our determination to preserve our country's sovereignty and territorial integrity is absolute! Taiwan's future rejoined with the mainland as one China must not be delayed. I say to President Liang, accept the commencement of final negotiations to reunify our nation!"

CIA DIRECTOR'S OFFICE

Cooke ran her hands through her hair. "He used the word 'rebellion.'"

"And 'secession' and 'independence,'" Jonathan said.

"I guess a bad translation is too much to hope for," Kyra offered.

"No, they got it right," Cooke said.

"How do you know?" Kyra asked. She had watched the CIA director during the speech and was sure that the older woman didn't speak Mandarin.

"Because that crowd reacted like Romans watching a lion eat Christians." Cooke fell back in her chair, suddenly tired. "One aircraft carrier might not be enough."

BEIJING

By her count, Laura Mitchell had been waiting for her husband for fifteen minutes when the chief of station finally settled into his seat. Her
husband looked over and took a moment to appreciate his wife before
he reached for her hand. Laura wasn't a model but she was still very
pretty, a fact that was lost on their Chinese hosts.

He didn't get to see her dressed up like this nearly enough. She
was a teaching specialist for autistic children at the English-speaking
school near the embassy where so many diplomats' children went, including their own son. It was a job that didn't lend itself to dresses and
heels, though she looked good to him in the polo shirts and khaki pants
she usually wore. When she did wear her finest, there was no other
woman as far as he was concerned, but it also left him full of regret
that he'd dragged her away from the States for so many years. He didn't
deserve her patience.

"Done for the night?" she asked quietly. The nearest person was
three seats away and there was a low buzz of conversation throughout
the theater that would have made eavesdropping difficult, but she still
knew to be careful with her words.

"I think so."

"Any of your friends try to come?"

"A few," Mitchell told her. "I had to disappoint them."

"They'll get over it," Laura assured him. More than once, she'd
come to their Moscow home and found that the Russians' security services had vandalized it as payback for some humiliation her husband
had inflicted on them. The Chinese seemed more civilized, for which
she was grateful. It saved on the cleaning bills.

"I hope so," Mitchell replied. "Given how they've been treating me
the last few days, I'd hate to see how they behave when they've got
their dander up."

"Maybe they'd go easy on you if you were walking around with one
of those pretty girls in your office," Laura said. He couldn't quite tell if
she was making a joke.

"You know I don't like to do that. Better to avoid temptation," he
said, serious. Case officers who spent their careers overseas had an appalling divorce rate. Mitchell was determined not to push the percent-
age up.

"You've got the perfect job for someone who wants to have an affair.

Late nights. Long hours," she observed. "Uncleared spouse not allowed to ask what you've been doing."

"I wouldn't do that to you," Mitchell declared. He squeezed her hand again. "You know that, right?"

"I'm still here," she answered.

"Sometimes I wonder why," he said. He thought Laura didn't sound quite convinced.

"Pure compassion," Laura said. "No other woman could live with you."

"I appreciate the pity you take on me."

"It's not for you. It's for the rest of my gender," she told her husband. "I didn't say some other woman wouldn't give you a go. I'm saving her from you."

Mitchell laughed, let go of his wife's hand, and put his arm around her. "You should work for us."

"I already do, love," Laura said. She kissed him on the cheek. "They just don't give me a paycheck."

CHAPTER 6

FRIDAY
DAY SIX

"You called?" Jonathan stood in the doorway. Morning sunlight was pouring in through the blinds, Cooke was sitting on the leather couch opposite the door, and it was obvious to Jon that the woman hadn't slept much the night before. She had to force her eyes to focus on him, he saw, and he knew that she could turn brusque when she was wearing down. He suspected she was running on coffee or something stronger, but it wasn't his place to say anything.

The CIA director looked at the analyst and realized that, in her tired state, she'd forgotten to tell her secretaries out front that Jon would be coming. How he'd gotten past them was something she'd have to drag out of him later when she had the patience. She also realized that he hadn't knocked.

She ignored that fact and waved him in. "How's Kyra?" she asked.

"Hard couple of days, I think. She'll adjust."

Cooke nodded. "She survived Caracas, she'll survive you."

"One can hope," he said wryly. "Though I'm the least of her problems. And yours, I suspect."

You underestimate yourself, Cooke thought, but it wasn't time for that discussion. She held up the Red Cell report that Jonathan had delivered to her a few days previous. "I've been reading this. *Inside Strait—How the PLA Could Invade Taiwan,*" she read off the front page. "That's terrible. How did you get this published with a title like that?"

"I presume you're not reading for the literary merit," Jonathan answered, sidestepping the question.

"No," Cooke conceded. Jon was still on his feet, she realized. "Sit down please." He obeyed. Cooke, relieved, held out the Red Cell paper over the low table in front of the couch and let it drop. "Do you think the Chinese are going to do it?"

Jonathan shrugged. "I'm sure APLAA would tell you that the smart money isn't on invasion."

"I've heard their side. They caveated everything so much I couldn't tell what they really thought. That's why I'm asking you."

"Invasion, probably not," Jonathan said. "But if the PLA took out the Tashan Power Plant, then yeah, I think they're going to move."

KINMEN, TAIWAN
2 KILOMETERS FROM THE CHINESE MAINLAND COAST

The People's Liberation Army invasion of Jinmen Dao, known to the West as the archipelago of Kinmen, began at 0200 hours local time with the faint sounds of boots in wet sand.

The PLA put commandos ashore near Kuningtou for the second time, as their fathers had before on October 25, 1949. That battle had been fought over fifty-six hours along Kinmen's northern coast. The PLA had landed several battalions on the beaches and suffered immediate counterattacks by the Nationalist "Kinmen Bears" riding in American M5 A1 tanks for which the Communists had no counter. Fifteen thousand men had died in less than three days. The victory left Kinmen itself a hallowed ground in the minds of the Taiwanese.

That had been almost seventy years ago. Now, the Taiwanese Army troops stationed on Kinmen had enough firepower to attack the Chinese mainland ports of Xiamen and Fuzhou—artillery range is a measure that works both ways—so the PLA could not ignore them. When the invasion of Taiwan finally began, it was thought, Kinmen's Defense Command would be overwhelmed by superior numbers in short order. They would fight to make Kinmen a bloody win for the PLA and maybe create enough gore to make Beijing reconsider the larger endeavor. The defense would start on the beaches, then fall back into the townships, most of which had stone buildings capable of withstanding heavy fire. The Taiwanese troops would then fall back to the tunnel and bunker complexes at Tai-Wu and Lonpun Mountains, Yangchai, Tingpao, and Lan Lake. The PLA would have to spill blood for weeks assaulting narrow concrete tunnel passages, where they would close up the hallways with their dead.

When the invasion of Taiwan itself was repulsed—the Americans would surely come—reinforcements would arrive or a peace treaty would be signed, the PLA would pull back, and the defenders who had survived the siege of Kinmen would emerge from the ground and take up their watch again. It was a strategy that relied on a number of assumptions, not the least of which was that the will of Taiwan's political leaders would be as strong as that of the soldiers deployed to Kinmen itself. Several of those assumptions would prove wrong this night.

At the same time as their brethren were landing their hovercraft at Kuningtou, a second company of PLA Special Operations Forces rode their own air-cushioned landing craft through the surf of Liaoluo Bay onto solid ground near Shangyi township and unloaded their gear by moonlight. Their mission was to cut off the three major roads that ran through the island's narrow central neck, effectively splitting the island into halves that could not reinforce each other. A third company came ashore on the northwestern coast near the Mashan Observation Station. They all carried light explosives and small arms, nothing larger than a 7.62 mm machine gun. The fifth column forces the Chinese had placed on Kinmen years before had the supplies needed to cripple any targets larger than individual men, and PLA infantry would be standing on this beach by noon with far heavier arms. The soldiers shouldered their weapons, slung their light packs, and dispersed across the islands to their waypoints.

CIA OPERATIONS CENTER

"Sir?" The APLAA analyst didn't take her eyes off her monitor. Drescher read the woman's face, bit off the first snarky remark that passed through his head, and made his way to the woman's desk.

"What?" he asked.

The live feed on APLAA's monitor was thermal, shades of reds, yellows, and grays over a black field, and Drescher needed a few seconds to realize he was looking at a beach at night. He'd never been an imagery analyst, but he could figure that much. "This is Kinmen, east coast," APLAA told him, and then she pointed at a pair of objects sitting on the sand just past the water's edge. "I'm not an imagery analyst, but I'm pretty sure those are Jingsah Two–class hovercraft. You can tell by the double fans on the aft ends. Engines are still warm."

"Taiwanese?" Drescher asked.

"I don't think so. The only people who own Jingsahs in the neighborhood are PLA. Probably the First Group Army, First Amphibious Mechanized Division staging out of Hangzhou. I zoomed out and went looking around the rest of the coastline. I found this." She worked her mouse around on the desk and pulled up several still images. Drescher checked the time codes: the imagery was less than a half hour old. It was clear that the hovercrafts had come onto the beach at a frightening rate of speed and stopped hard enough that anyone inside must have been strapped in to keep from getting thrown around. The final photo showed the hovercrafts had dropped doors by the bows and the bright silhouettes of men were running for the trees. Drescher couldn't see the weapons, but he was sure they were carrying carbines or rifles, given how they held their hands. What kind and caliber they might be, Drescher couldn't tell, but he didn't need that particular bit of information to make his next decision.

CIA DIRECTOR'S OFFICE

Cooke set the phone back on the handset. "That was the Ops Center," she told Jon. "It looks like the Chinese are moving on Kinmen. I have to go." She stood, hesitated, then turned back. "Want to come?"

"Wouldn't miss this," he said, rising.

KINMEN, TAIWAN

The first civilian targets were infrastructure. Power, telephone, and Internet lines were cut and radio transmitters were felled by satchel charges. With the Tashan Power Plant already down, every building on the island that lacked its own generator was dark by 0400, though most of the sleeping populace didn't know it. The few civilians who were awake and realized that the island was dark had no way to tell anyone who mattered.

The first military targets were people. The Taiwanese soldiers garrisoned on Kinmen had kept a high state of readiness for years, but all men must sleep. Sentries were killed with silenced rifles at long distance, shortly after which the commanding officer of the Kinmen Defense Command and his wife were shot in their bed. Other Taiwanese senior officers followed.

The Kinmen Defense Command's three divisions on the larger island were decapitated in ten minutes. The assassinations left eleven dead, including three civilians.

CIA OPERATIONS CENTER

"Assume those were PLA Special Forces," Cooke said. "What's on their target list?" The Ops Center had fallen quiet when the CIA director had walked in.

"The usual, I think," Drescher said. "Power lines, communications, maybe small bridges. Assassinations of key personnel if Taiwanese security isn't up to snuff."

"What's the population of Kinmen?" Jonathan asked.

"Eighty thousand, give or take a few thousand," the APLAA analyst replied. She quietly began to type on her keyboard, double-checking to make sure she hadn't just led Cooke astray.

"Then Special Forces can't take that island," Jonathan noted. "If they want to occupy Kinmen, they'll have to bring in regular forces, and that means they need a beachhead or an airport, maybe both if they're feeling ambitious."

"Do you have anyone watching the airport?" Cooke asked Drescher.

Drescher just looked around the room. A half-dozen people began pounding keyboards and the room started buzzing with low conversation. "Yep," he said.

KINMEN, TAIWAN

The Shangyi Airport was the next target. The massive fireball that had been the Air Defense Command Center surged five hundred feet toward the stars and was visible on the mainland. The primary air defense system guarding the airport followed. The Hawk and Patriot 2 missile batteries purchased from the United States at considerable expense were never used.

The SOF soldiers, joined with their fifth column supporters bearing heavy machine guns, overran the landing strip. They established overlapping fields of fire and killed anyone, soldier or civilian, who entered them. They moved through the buildings and terminals, eliminating security forces and seizing grounded fighter aircraft and weapons stores as they went. It was here that the PLA took its first casualties. A Taiwanese sergeant advanced toward the enemy, took cover behind a concrete Jersey wall at a small construction site, and used his sidearm to kill two PLA commandos running toward the main terminal. The cement barrier gave him excellent protection against small arms fire, and he managed to hold back the enemy for almost five minutes until they flanked him. When the commandos breached the front door, they met their first organized resistance of the morning—Taiwanese soldiers finally armed with weapons heavier than pistols. They held the buildings for almost an hour.

With Kinmen's air defenses suppressed, the first of thirty IL-76 PLA transports filled with reinforcements lifted off in sequence from a runway at Xiamen. The total flight time was less than ten minutes. The transport landed, the pilots lowered the rear access ramp, and almost two hundred PLA soldiers erupted from the back. The plane was stationary for less than one minute before closing the ramp and taxiing off to clear the approach for the next plane and begin its own run back to the mainland. Every IL-76 would make ten runs by dusk. Together they moved a total of four infantry divisions and their associated equipment by nightfall.

The Liaoluo Pier and its two hundred soldiers followed. The PLA used the same tactics there as at the airport. The same results were achieved, though the casualties on both sides were marginally higher. Liaoluo had no landing strip, so PLA Navy amphibious transports and helicopters were used to bring the reinforcements ashore. Small numbers of Taiwanese troops managed to get to the beach with their own heavy machine guns, grenade launchers, and even a pair of mortars. The first amphibious assault craft that landed on the beach suffered a direct hit from a mortar crew that got lucky, jamming the landing ramp closed and trapping its cargo inside. Dozens of landing craft followed and the Taiwanese troops held their defensive positions for almost an hour until they saw the Yuting II landing ship, the first of seven, approaching the shore. Each carried two hundred fifty men and ten amphibious tanks, marking the arrival of the PLA's armored cavalry. The Taiwanese struck back with Javelin antitank weapons and turned the first three tanks into flaming pyres fed by diesel gasoline and the bodies of the tanker crews, but they had no chance to win without air support—*where was the air support?* The only combat planes overhead were Su-30 fighters escorting the monstrous IL-76s. The island's defenders cheered when a vapor trail raced up to one of the Chinese transports and tore it from the sky in a raucous flash. The IL-76 went down, the entire airframe tumbling through the surf before settling in water barely deep enough to drown the crew and troops trapped inside.

PLA helicopters began low runs under the transports, strafing covered ground to kill or flush out anything alive under the greenery.

CIA OPERATIONS CENTER

The Ops Center was normally a very quiet place, or so Drescher had told Cooke. It wasn't upholding the reputation and she was starting to wonder whether Drescher hadn't undersold his unit to her. She assumed that there must have been some semblance of order or control in the room, but if so she couldn't see it, and yet the senior duty officer seemed to have perfect knowledge of how information was flowing around the room. The man was in his element, riding herd on the mob before him, and having far too much fun, given the circumstances.

The rest of the staff wasn't enjoying it so much. The APLAA analyst—a tall, very thin girl with a pixie haircut and angry face—was fighting down an urge to hyperventilate as she read a SIGINT report, whether from fear or pure joy that the long-awaited war with Taiwan had arrived, Cooke couldn't tell. She gave the young woman a reassuring squeeze on her shoulder and a confident nod, which calmed the analyst down and seemed to give her a second wind. Cooke looked over the other analysts, who were all on telephones parceling out the few details they could scrounge up, all of which were surely erroneous. The first reports of any crisis were always wrong.

"You're smiling," Cooke noted quietly to Drescher.

"I love my job." He pushed all the papers on his desk to the side, stacked them, and put them on the file cabinet behind. He was going to need a clean space to work. The director of national intelligence and the president would be calling Cooke, demanding answers, and she could not tell them to be patient. Politicians considered any information, even if they knew it was wrong, better than none. They would have to answer to the press and they could not, they would not, allow themselves to look ignorant. The press had to fill its airtime with something, and if the networks lacked hard facts, they would bring in paid experts to theorize and repeat the same uninformed conjectures until they finally did have real facts. Taipei had no shortage of political think-tank pundits and lobbyists on the payroll willing to spout off, and leaders on the Hill would be screaming alternately for blood and restraint, depending on their politics. But even the networks would tire of the rhetoric and would start yelling at the White House press secretary for something real. The White House would then scream at Cooke to give the president something, anything, that he could repeat to the press. She would tell them that they could not vouch for the reliability of the data, the president would demand the data anyway, and the press secretary would begin to feed false information to the reporters in a bid to buy time. The press secretary would later go off the record and blame the errors on CIA or some other intelligence organ. But to stand in front of the press and admit they knew nothing would make them look incompetent, and that was unacceptable.

"Got it!" one of the analysts yelled. The front monitor wall went black and then live with a satellite thermal video feed.

"What are we looking at?" Drescher yelled back.

"Shangyi Airport," the analyst said.

Cooke grimaced as she stared at the front wall, stunned into silence, then looked back at Jonathan. His face showed no emotion at all.

The Kinmen Air Defense Command Center was a pyre, and the heat outlines of men dead and wounded speckled the tarmac. The closer ones to the burning building were harder to make out as the hot air rising from the fire superheated the concrete and asphalt on which the bodies lay. The corpses that close were roasting like steak in a cast iron skillet. Other men ran over and around the prone bodies further from the fire. Which soldiers were Taiwanese and which were Chinese, Cooke couldn't tell, and she decided it was foolish to think she should know.

KINMEN, TAIWAN

The rest of Kinmen's defenders fell back to the bunkers, taking with them as many civilians as were able to reach the garrisons before the doors were closed and sealed.

The remaining command officers inside Tai-Wu Mountain sealed the complex's heavy outer doors and spent the remainder of the day listening to a dwindling array of reports from their brothers outside. They pleaded for reinforcements and screamed for air support until PLA Navy vessels took up final blockade positions and began jamming the signal.

The Taiwanese command authorities calmly informed the Kinmen

Defense Command before losing contact that its soldiers would be rescued eventually. It was a lie, though the senior Taiwanese military officers didn't know it yet. There would be no reinforcements and no air support. The corrupt president in Taipei who had so eagerly stoked Beijing's animosity for his own ends was terrified that he would need to save his military forces in case China's coup de main of Kinmen was just the first of many.

THE TAIWAN STRAIT
120°00' EAST, 25°00' NORTH,
800 KILOMETERS SOUTHWEST OF OKINAWA

Lieutenant Samuel Roselli checked his course and azimuth for the third time in five minutes and scanned the airspace ahead. It was a clear morning, 0620, visibility a hundred miles in all directions. The lack of cloud cover at least would let Roselli see the MIG patrols coming, but it left his plane nowhere in the sky to hide, and the old EP-3E Aries II would not be outrunning any Chinese fighters. The plane was an old crow, a four-engine turboprop built for surveillance, not combat. It had no offensive weapons, couldn't fly higher than 27,000 feet or come anywhere close to Mach 1 even in a steep dive. For all practical purposes, the EP-3 couldn't fight and it couldn't run. If the MIGs got truly unfriendly, the best he could do was throw the Aries into a dive toward the deck, hold an altitude so low the plane would get a wash from ocean spray, and pray that the waves would confuse an attacker's radar.

Roselli didn't begrudge the Chinese their frustration at watching US spy planes run up and down their coast on a regular basis. He expected the politicians back in Washington would scream if PLA spy planes were making runs near Naval Base San Diego or any of the Navy's other facilities scattered along the West Coast. One day, Roselli figured, they would be. The US wouldn't be the world's lone superpower forever.

"They're going crazy back there. Radio ground traffic all up and down the coast, like an order of magnitude more than they've ever seen. It sounds like every PLA armor unit for a thousand miles is on the move. I miss anything up here?" Lieutenant Julie Ford crawled back into the right seat, which brightened Roselli's mood considerably. He'd flown with copilots far less competent and pretty. The PLAAF had buzzed them several times and she'd held herself together nicely. It was harder for Roselli to imagine a faster way to earn another pilot's trust.

"AWACS says the PLAAF is doing up here what PLA armor is doing down there. Combat patrols everywhere," Roselli said. An Air Force Boeing E-3C Sentry was airborne two hundred miles to the northeast, flying a little higher than twenty-nine thousand feet. The AWACS rotodome was far more powerful than the EP-3's own radar and could see every plane the Chinese had in the air for several thousand miles in all directions. Roselli's EP-3 had links to the AWACS data feed and he didn't like the picture. "I've never seen them keep this many birds in the air."

"Nobody's come by to check us out," Ford said.

"Give 'em time."

"Time" was two minutes, forty seconds. "Incoming," Roselli said. "Three contacts inbound bearing zero-one-five, range one-two-four kilometers, speed five-two-five knots. Intercept in four minutes."

"They're lighting us up," Ford said, her voice calm despite what the EP-3's threat receiver was telling her.

We're still in international airspace, Roselli thought. *Just trying to scare us.* They were flying inside the letter of the law and the PLAAF knew it.

Roselli heard the obscene roar of the fighters through the cockpit glass, the rising and falling pitch of the jetwash scream left by the Doppler effect louder than he could remember ever hearing during flight. They passed the EP-3 in succession less than a second apart and missed the Navy turboprop by less than fifty feet on either side. The EP-3 was heavy for its size, weighing 140,000 pounds on takeoff, but the jet-propelled wake still bounced the prop-driven Navy plane on turbulent air currents, throwing both pilots against their restraints. The Navy technicians in the back grabbed for their chairs and consoles. Two fell, one against a bulkhead, which cost him a cracked rib, the other sprawling on the floor and wondering whether it wasn't safer to stay there.

"They're coming around," Ford said. "Immelmann turns."

The Chinese fighters came about, the two on the flanks peeling around in opposite directions to come in behind. The lead plane's pilot pulled straight up into a circular turn that left him upside down and a thousand feet higher when he matched course with the EP-3. He rolled the Su-27 onto its belly, lowered the nose to drop the altitude, and increased speed to make up the six miles he had lost in the ten seconds it had taken him to come about. His wingmen took up station on either side of the EP-3, doing their best to match speed. The fighters weren't designed for optimal stability at such low speeds in the thinner air and the Chinese pilots had to finesse their aircraft to hold their positions. The lead pilot slowed his plane to a relative stop less than five hundred feet behind the US Navy plane.

"Lead bogey is on our six," Roselli said. He didn't have to tell Ford about the other two at the three and nine o'clock positions. She was looking out the window.

"They don't learn, do they?" Ford said. "This isn't 2001, you know? Touch wings and we have a prayer. They don't."

"Maybe their ejection seats got better," Roselli said. "Or maybe they want us to spend a couple weeks on Hainan Island."

Roselli watched the nine o'clock fighter holding station off the portside wing. He was too close for comfort. That's the point, he thought. *Cat-and-mouse, and we're a fat old rat.*

Ford watched her partner but said nothing, her own poker face holding steady. No sense in being scared until there was something to be scared about.

The lead pilot provided the reason a minute later. The American pilots hadn't changed course or altitude or given him a sign of any kind that they even took notice of his presence. The Americans' conceit angered him. These surveillance flights were arrogance on display, open espionage done in full view of his country. To disregard the pilots sent to confront them showed disdain heaped upon disrespect. The PLAAF flight leader wished he had orders more liberal than those he had received, but they were liberal enough. He turned his radar to fire control mode.

The EP-3's threat receiver almost screamed at the pilots. "Bogey at six o'clock just lit us up!" Ford yelled. "He's got a lock!"

Roselli pushed the stick forward hard and the EP-3 dropped into a dive steep enough to lift the pilots out of their seats until the harnesses pushed back. He pulled hard left, sending the EP-3 into a corkscrew turn as it raced for the deck. Ford activated the electronic countermeasures, and the Chinese pilots suddenly faced radar clutter and air filled with chaff. The dive broke the flight leader's missile lock, but he had never intended to work hard to maintain it. He ordered his wingmen to hold their altitude while he stayed behind the plane as it fell through four miles of air, leveling out less than a thousand feet above the waves. He followed the US Navy plane until it took up course zero-one-five, its four bladed engines pushing it as fast as it could go. Convinced they were going home, the flight leader pulled back on his own stick to do the same.

Roselli watched the Su-27s fall away on the scope. He looked down at his hands and didn't see the tremors his mind told him were there, but he let the computer take over the duty of returning them to Kadena. "He's falling back," he said, relieved. *Did my voice just shake?*

Ford relaxed, let go of her stick, and looked back to the cabin. Prayers and profanities had been uttered aft, some more vocal than others. She stuck her thumb over her shoulder to point toward the SIGINT technicians, who were doing their own best to calm themselves. "I hope they got something that was worth it."

CIA RED CELL

"They almost shot down an EP-3?" Kyra put the cable behind the manila folder of satellite imagery and started to file through it, splitting her attention between the pictures and Jonathan's voice. The first image was an overhead shot of PLA tanks moving in formation down some Chinese highway. She had climbed on M1 Abrams tanks, beige sixty-ton metal monsters whose thirty-foot length was covered with depleted uranium armor, and it wasn't hard for her imagination to fill in the gaps about the formation of dozens rolling across the asphalt.

"And overran Kinmen while you were asleep in bed," Jonathan confirmed. "They've been busy little buggers."

"Sorry I missed it," Kyra said, and she meant it. "They were definitely outside Chinese airspace?" she asked.

"Depends on your definition of Chinese airspace," Jonathan said. "The Chinese think they own the Strait, so by their standard, no. By everyone else's standard, yes. AWACS out of Kadena AFB on Okinawa tracked the entire flight path. EP-3s don't carry weapons. The PLA knows that. They got to take one apart a few years back."

"You'd think the Chinese would be averse to midair collisions after that one," Kyra mused. "Makes you wonder whether they learned anything from the last time they buzzed an EP-3."

"They learned that for the cheap price of one dead PLA pilot and a crashed MIG, they might get their hands on a US Navy plane full of classified gear," Jonathan told her.

"What did Navy Intel get out of the flight?"

"That's another report," Jonathan said, holding up another paper. "SIGINT confirming that PLA Joint Operational Headquarters in Fujian has assumed command of the buildup. The order of battle matches what APLAA says we should see in an invasion force, except for the missile batteries not standing up. They argue that the Chinese would want to soften up the Taiwanese defenses with a long-range bombardment before sending the troops in. But DIA and the Pentagon say the troop numbers are too small for that just yet. And Tian hasn't made any moves to put the Chinese economy on a war footing, and the *People's Daily* ran an editorial this morning saying this is an exercise."

"Which we can't trust," Kyra said.

"Of course not." Jonathan smiled. *Now you're thinking like an analyst.*

"So it looks like an invasion force, but nobody wants to call it because the numbers aren't big enough and nobody wants to risk being wrong and offending the Chinese," Kyra said.

"Correct," Jonathan replied. He watched her study the overhead imagery. Given how bloodshot her eyes were this morning, he was mildly surprised that she could see anything.

"Do they think Tian is moving tanks because the PLA needs to burn up some surplus diesel?" The Vicodin was doing good things for her headache but nothing for her patience.

"Hardly," Jonathan said, unmoved. "But you may be right for the wrong reason. With Kinmen occupied, this could be the buildup of an invasion force for Penghu. If they're going to move on Taiwan in stages, it's the next logical step."

"You could have just said 'I agree,'" Kyra said, satisfied and annoyed at once.

"That wouldn't have been nearly as much fun," he replied. "In any case, we should focus on the Assassin's Mace. APLAA tried to preempt us by offering their collective wisdom on the matter." He tilted the monitor toward her.

"That was fast," she said.

"The China analysts have been waiting a long time for this," Jonathan said. "The running joke is that they have stacks of prewritten President's Daily Brief articles on a Chinese invasion of Taiwan sitting on their desks, though I suspect they had to think about this one a bit."

For the President

Tian Threat Likely Refers to PLA Submarine Force

Chinese President Tian Kai's claim that the PLA Navy (PLAN) could threaten US naval vessels likely depends on four Russian Kilo-class submarines purchased starting in 1995. Despite progress in the PLA's shipbuilding efforts, the Kilos remain the most advanced attack submarines in the Chinese fleet.

- The PLAN fleet also includes seventeen Ming-class, thirty-two Romeo-class, and five Han-class submarines. All three classes are older than the Kilos and suffer from outdated designs and technology that leave them at a disadvantage against newer US submarines.

The PLAN also has four Russian-made Sovremenny-class destroyers in its surface fleet, but getting them within striking range of US aircraft carriers would be difficult. Despite acquiring the Sovremennys, the PLAN surface fleet remains more of a coastal defense force than a long-range force.

- The PLAN surface fleet carries several classes of antiship missiles in its inventory, including a reverse-engineered version of the French Exocet. However, the PLAN has struggled to train its personnel in effective over-the-horizon missile targeting tactics.

This article was prepared by CIA.

The facing page was a montage of photographs of Russian-made ships and missiles. A small map of the Chinese coast covered the lower right corner and displayed icons marking PLA naval base locations.

"I take it you think they're wrong?" Kyra asked. It always seemed to be his default answer.

"Russian-made ships and subs in the hands of the PLA Navy are a threat," Jonathan admitted. "But we know that the Chinese didn't restrict their little carrier-killer research project to buying up Russian equipment."

He walked around a group of short filing cabinets to the whiteboard, then took up a red marker and eraser. He stopped short, staring at the scrawls of his previous thought experiment on the slick surface. Jonathan frowned, then finally began to erase.

"Giving up on detecting confirmation bias?" Kyra asked.

"Hardly," he said. "But the more interesting problem gets the space." He wiped the board clean, then retrieved a large bound volume from a nearby desk and dropped it on Kyra's with a loud thump. "I've been going over the Agency's last National Intelligence Estimate on the PLA—everything the intelligence community thinks it knows about Chinese military capabilities in one report. It's two years old and this is the short version. The long version has an extra hundred pages with the really good intel; it backs up what APLAA said. China doesn't have the combat power to force unification. No exceptions for an Assassin's Mace. The other intel backs that up. Variations on a theme, but everything says the same thing."

"APLAA wrote it?"

"Yes."

"Well, that explains it," she said.

"Yes and no. They accounted for the PLA's known capabilities, no question, and I didn't doubt they would. What we need to determine is whether there are gaps in the intelligence that point to unknown capabilities."

"Where do we start?" Kyra asked, frustrated. "We've got reports on the PLA going back to Mao."

"Nineteen ninety-one, I think, unless we can find something more recent and conclusive," Jonathan said after a moment's thought. "The Gulf War inspired the PLA's push to modernize their arsenal."

"That was twenty-five years ago," Kyra noted.

"Weapons platforms aren't developed on a short schedule."

"And what if we don't find any that APLAA hasn't considered?" Kyra asked.

"Then we tell Cooke that APLAA is right. And I hate for APLAA to be right about anything," Jonathan said.

Kyra held out a paper two hours later. "The original PDB on the 'Assassin's Mace from ninety-seven."

Jonathan took the paper and scanned it quickly, then began reading aloud. " 'Jiang Zemin Speech Augurs Increase in Military Spending. PRC President Jiang Zemin's call for an 'assassin's mace' weapon could spark a significant increase in PLA research and development spending.'" He dropped the article on the table. "I'm sure it was exciting at the time, but it's hardly news to us now. Certainly nothing there that narrows down the technology. What else?"

"Since that PDB was published, nineteen hits that didn't appear totally useless," Kyra said. She laid a printed page on the desk and grabbed a yellow highlighter. She marked off a text block in the list. "These five are NSA reports, all PLA discussions about whether an ongoing project should qualify for the Mace label. Somebody up at Fort Meade probably tapped some PLA colonel's phone. Some projects qualified, some didn't, but none of them say what the criteria are."

"We can assume 'anything that can cripple a carrier' and start from there," Jonathan said.

"Works for me," Kyra continued. "These"—which took up more than half the page with reference numbers and titles—"are excerpts translated from Chinese military publications. Those start in 1999. They all talk about possible changes to PLA military doctrine to accommodate Assassin's Mace weapons but they don't give specifics. This last one talks about proposed changes in PLA Air Force doctrine and strategy to accommodate new weapons, but again, no specifics on the weapons."

"Which month?"

Kyra checked the report header, which mashed together both the date and time when the report had been issued. "May ninety-nine."

"What does it say about the source on that one?" Jonathan asked.

"It's a HUMINT report, human source who has access to the information because of his position, has an established reporting record, and is reliable. That doesn't tell us anything."

"By design," Jonathan said. "The NCS doesn't give information to DI analysts that could identify sources."

Kyra shook her head and threw the highlighter across the desk. "So how can you tell if two reports are from the same source?"

"Call a reports officer and offer to buy him a beer." Jonathan kept his focus on the paper. "Not much fun to be on the other side of the divide, is it?"

"It's necessary," she answered quietly. She saw his point.

Jonathan studied Kyra for a moment before speaking. The girl had gone on the defensive, but not in a hostile way. *Interesting.* "So why only the one report from the human source?" he asked. "If he was in position to report on the project in the first place, why not task him to follow up?"

No dig at the Dark Side of the house? She'd made herself a target and he'd passed up a chance to take a rhetorical shot at point-blank range. Maybe the man had a soft side after all. Or maybe he'd been testing her and had seen what he'd wanted. She wasn't going to ask. "Maybe they did," Kyra said, suspicious. "Maybe the project never went anywhere. Sometimes the assets report data that's not worth writing up."

Jonathan considered the idea, turning it over in his mind. "You don't change military doctrine to accommodate 'new' weapons if those weapons are just more of what you already have." He leaned forward and stared at the paper. "Look at the timeline. Jiang Zemin orders the project in ninety-seven, NSA grabs a flurry of reports about one project that peters out almost immediately, and then nothing until ninety-nine, when the PLA starts writing again about changing war plans. The idea didn't just go away." He put the hard copy down on the desk and pushed it back toward the young woman. "And it's a given that the various *shashoujian* projects are run at multiple facilities and involve different groups of personnel."

"Meaning what?" Kyra asked.

"You were a case officer. Think about it."

A puzzle. Kyra was good at puzzles. She leaned back in her chair and tilted her head to think. *Multiple facilities, different groups, one asset.* She smiled. "There's a compartment of Assassin's Mace reports that we don't have."

"I agree." For the first time, she noted, Burke smiled back. "Your reasoning?"

She rolled the facts around inside her mind, reordering them. It was funny, she thought, how the mind could hold random thoughts simultaneously but struggled to catalog them so a person could verbalize them, which was a linear process. "There's an asset in a position to report on a change in war planning. That means the asset likely had access to the underlying technology driving the change. But if that technology was part of a black program, then we would have to separate that intelligence from the rest of the report because a leak could identify the asset. So the NCS would publish the report"—Kyra waved the paper in the air— "minus the good bits about the technology. But this asset is reporting on a change inspired by an Assassin's Mace technology, which is just one part of a bigger program, so the asset likely has access to other Mace information. The more Mace projects he can report on, the faster the Chinese could triangulate on him if the information is leaked. So the NCS would pull out the stops to keep that from happening, which means that somewhere around here is a nice, fat compartment of Mace reports."

Jonathan nodded. "Just because a reporting stream is new doesn't mean the activity being reported is new," he said. "And just because a reporting stream dies doesn't mean the activity died. Sometimes it just vanishes into a classified compartment."

Kyra narrowed her eyes and studied the man. He'd agreed with her several times over the last few hours and it seemed . . . wrong. She'd only known him for a few days but she could read a man. Any case officer worth her salt could. And Burke was a thinker—

Then she saw it. "You're just saying that to butter me up because you want me to go get that compartment," Kyra said. It wasn't a question.

"You're perceptive," Jonathan said, smiling. "Much more enjoyable than having to explain everything."

Another dig. She enjoyed this one.

It took Kyra an hour to find the phone numbers. The National Clandestine Service refused to publish a phone directory, citing the possible security risk of a foreign power stealing it. After pleas to Deity, enough curses to negate her prayers, and repeated calls to the Agency's telephone switchboard, Kyra finally reached an officer who didn't plead ignorance on China. The words *assassin's, mace,* and *compartment* in the same sentence worked like a wizard's incantation. The officer begged off and hung up, and the return call came a half hour later from a senior NCS manager several pay grades higher who agreed to talk in person readily enough to leave Kyra suspicious.

George Kain's initial manner bordered on sycophantic. Kyra had been trained to evaluate character on short notice, Kain's voice on the phone had disturbed her, and she had been appalled to find her evaluation more than accurate. Kain took precisely one question from Jonathan regarding information on any Assassin's Mace project and switched from fawning to filibuster. He prattled without pause, talking over all attempts to interrupt, offering nothing useful, and staring out the window at the New Headquarters Building. Kyra was sure he hadn't made eye contact with her once in the last hour.

She looked around the Red Cell vault for a wall clock and didn't find one. *How long?* she mouthed silently to Jonathan. He didn't move his head and said nothing, instead curling his hand on his leg into a fist, then sticking out two fingers. Kain didn't see it. The man was in his own world.

Two? She mirrored his sign with her own fingers. *Hours?*

Jonathan nodded, barely.

Way past time to end this. For the first time, Kyra was ashamed to have been a case officer.

She made her own covert gesture at the mini fridge. Jonathan saw the motion, smiled slightly, then nodded again.

Kyra walked to the mini fridge, retrieved a bottled water, then walked back to her seat. She offered the plastic bottle to Kain. "You must be thirsty."

For the first time in hours, Kain paused. "Thanks." He uncapped the bottle, took a swig, and then saw the tactical error too late.

"You've tried very hard not to answer the question," Jonathan said as soon as Kain's mouth filled with Dasani water. "Stop wasting our time. We're not idiots."

Kain swallowed. "If we have anything worth reporting, you'll have to wait until we publish it in finished intel channels."

"The reports we're looking for could be more than ten years old. They'd already be in finished intel channels if you were ever going to release them," Kyra observed.

"Not my problem," Kain said. "If there is any reporting being held back in a compartment, I'm not going to second-guess the decision not to release it."

"This tasking came from Director Cooke—," Jonathan said.

"I don't care if it came from the president," Kain interrupted. He drew another swig from the bottle. "If there's something we think the president needs to know, we'll tell him. We don't need the DI to do it for us, not that your little fantasies even qualify as analysis. And we certainly don't need a pair of failed wannabe operators turned analysts to do it for us." Kain smirked at Jonathan, then frowned at Kyra, stood, finished the bottle, and took his time dropping it in the nearest garbage can. "Thanks for the water," he said. He then strode out of the vault.

"You should have let me choke him," Kyra said.

"You thought I would have stopped you?"

"He should run for the Senate," Kyra said. "He wouldn't be the first case officer to become a politician."

"The two professions do share a disturbing number of skills," Jonathan agreed. "Good move with the water."

"I should've done it an hour earlier," Kyra said. "Now what?"

"I suspected that was coming," he admitted. "Some cooperation would have been nice, but I didn't expect it. Still, we had to make a good faith effort to request access before we ask Cooke to start twisting arms."

"I hope there really is a compartment," Kyra said. "I'd hate to pick a fight just to find out they don't have anything worth fighting over."

"They do. Despite what you might think, an NCS manager doesn't take two hours out of his day to belittle analysts just for fun," Jonathan said. "I'll be back." He marched out of the vault and disappeared into the stairwell across the hall.

Kyra stared at the back of his head until the stairwell door closed and then let out a long breath. It was apparent where he was going. She wondered just how close Jonathan and Cooke really were. *Real close,* she hoped. The bureaucratic games were starting to get under her skin.

CIA DIRECTOR'S OFFICE

Barron's composure had limits, and Cooke's account of Kain's sandbagging had pushed him close to them. Some things he expected to be handled *below* his pay grade. Hearing about them from one of the very few people he answered to always lit his very short fuse. But he expected that had been Burke's intention. Sometimes it really did take a trip to the director's office to make the case officers and analysts stop acting like children protective of their toys.

"They were asking about Pioneer's compartment?" Barron asked. The question was almost redundant. There was no other sets of files that fit the bill Cooke had just described.

"They were," Cooke confirmed. "George Kain stonewalled them. Sat in their space for two hours and treated them like they were complete idiots."

"I'll go talk to him about it. I understand his reasons, but his tactics were faulty, to say the least."

"How many people have access to Pioneer's reporting?" Cooke asked.

"If you count the two of us, still fewer than a dozen," Barron replied.

"Has he fed you anything on the Assassin's Mace lately?"

"No." Barron frowned and took a deep breath. "He's the guy who told us about it in the first place back after the ninety-six Taiwan Strait crisis. By ninety-seven it was clear the project wasn't going anywhere, so we put him on other targets. Every once in a while he still sends us something on the project, but it's just not a high priority. We've been more worried about the Russian equipment the PLA's been buying."

Cooke leaned back. "If there's not much on it, then there shouldn't be an issue letting the Red Cell have access to it."

Barron knew an order when he heard one, but he didn't have to like it. "I'd rather not." He knew it was a weak protest.

"Clark, there are two men that I answer to," Cooke said, talking slowly and clearly, as though to a child. "And at some point, I'm going to get a call from the president or, more likely, the director of national intelligence. That man will start asking me some very pointed questions about what's going on here. And right now, I don't have any good answers, just good theories. If the Red Cell can prove those theories, I'll be a very happy woman, but that's going to be very hard for them to do if your half of the house is refusing to lower the drawbridge and let them inside that big stone wall you case officers have erected between yourselves and the analysts." Cooke stopped to let the tongue-lashing sink in. "If the Red Cell includes any of Pioneer's intel in their report, I'll restrict it to POTUS only," she offered. "No one outside the Oval Office even hears about it, much less reads it."

Barron's face showed that he didn't like it, and *yes, ma'am,* he certainly was going to worry about it, but an order was an order. "How many people are we talking here?"

"Two people. Burke, of course. The other one is your girl, Stryker," Cooke said.

"I can live with that. Just make sure they don't give me a reason to regret it, or next time I'll let Kain have his way with them," Barron warned.

"Fair enough," Cooke said.

CIA RED CELL

"I need glasses," Kyra said. She dropped a stack of reports on Jonathan's desk, closed her eyes, and rested her head on her arms. The morning painkiller had finally worn off.

"You need to learn that caffeine is not a substitute for sleep." Jonathan knew a hangover when he saw one, had never suffered one but had seen plenty in graduate school. She was lithe, he'd noted, not too much body mass to absorb alcohol. The current weather precluded many opportunities for parties, so the woman was either drinking alone or haunting one of Leesburg's several excellent pubs and bars along King Street. A few shots of something harder than beer would cross her line between drinking to relax and drinking to excess. An officer's personal drinking habits could become a matter for the Counterintelligence Center, the unit that hunted moles inside the Agency. Stryker was too new for that, he supposed, but she'd almost gotten killed, might have been self-medicating the stress with something harder than beer, and officers had been fired for alcoholism before. "Is that it?" he asked.

"Finally," Kyra said. She had been logging Pioneer's reports since Kain's flunky arrived with the paperwork to get the Red Cell analysts read into the Assassin's Mace compartment. The forms they signed were the United States Government's version of a blood oath and promised vile retribution if they leaked the information to anyone, even other DI analysts.

Jonathan wheeled his chair over to Kyra's desk and stared at the Excel spreadsheet on her screen. "What's the final count?"

"Two hundred twenty-seven Assassin's Mace reports total," Kyra said. "One hundred thirty-six on aerospace projects. Fifty-seven on antiship missile projects. Twenty on naval projects, nine on lasers, and the rest on weapons that we've labeled as miscellaneous."

"That breakdown matches our thinking," Jonathan said. "Heavy numbers on aerospace and missiles."

Kyra sat back and stared at the screen. It was an impressive list. "What about that stealth fighter the PLA was building back in the aughts? The J-20?"

"That one's trying to be an air superiority plane, not a bomber," Jonathan said. "The Chinese have always had serious issues building decent fighter engines. Still, it's possible that they cross-bred the technology into another project. Any commonalities in the aerospace reports?"

"Most of them named the China Aviation Industry Corporation as the primary conduit for the projects. Only one other company was mentioned, Xian Aircraft Design and Research Institute. According to the cable, the PLA was funding a big effort with Xian under CAIC direction. One of the CAIC senior managers asked for a progress report. Pioneer intercepted the Xian reply and copied a DVD that was part of the package."

"What was the date on that cable?" Jonathan asked.

"June 1999," Kyra said after a brief hunt for the paper.

"What was on the disk?"

"Whoever looked at the file said it was a computer-aided design program," Kyra said.

Jonathan leaned back in his chair. "A CAD program wouldn't tell us much. It's the data files on whatever Xian was building that you'd want."

"There's no record that we got those. But look at this." Kyra leaned over and made the spreadsheet obey. "If we reorder the list of Pioneer's reporting by date instead of technology, almost all of the aerospace reports are dated after ninety-nine. Maybe CAIC made a technology breakthrough, developed some new tech."

"Or stole some," Jonathan said. "They're big on that." He pushed back from the desk with his foot and let his chair roll across the floor back until it stopped near the marker board where he had drafted his list. He stood and walked to the window and stared out at the A-12 monument overlooking the west parking lot. "You don't actually need a fighter to attack a carrier. A bomber could do the job just fine if it could penetrate the air defense umbrella. Very difficult, but not impossible."

Kyra thought for a moment. "Speed?"

"Speed. Altitude. Stealth. Any of those three would solve the problem. When the Cold War broke out and we needed to keep watch on the Russians, we built the U-2. And by 'we,' I do mean CIA. The U-2 was ours—highest-altitude plane ever built at the time. When the Russians figured out how to shoot those down, we went for speed and built the A-12. The Russians never did figure out how to shoot that down, but it was only a matter of time. So the Air Force worked out stealth and built the F-117 Nighthawk. Back in the Gulf War, Saddam had more antiair defenses surrounding Baghdad than the Russians had surrounding Moscow, literally. Three thousand double-A guns and sixtyish SAM batteries. The Iraqis never even managed to scratch the paint on a Nighthawk, much less shoot one down."

"The Serbs managed it," Kyra said. "They shot one down near Sarajevo."

"Dumb luck with an assist from our stupidity," Jonathan said. "Orders forced the pilots to fly the same approach routes from Aviano every night, so the Serbs had a pretty good idea where to point their radar."

"Any of those three would stick in the Pentagon's craw," Kyra admitted.

"It's great fun being the only person with a particular technology. It stops being fun the moment someone else gets it," Jonathan agreed. "The question is how do we prove any of this."

"That one's easy." Kyra put her head down and smiled slightly. "We go out there and debrief Pioneer."

Jonathan rocked back in his chair, surprised at the suggestion. "You're serious?"

"Better to interview the asset in person than just read somebody else's reports about it. Let's cut out the middleman." *And get out of this office.*

The senior analyst cocked an eyebrow. "There's no way with PLA tanks rolling that NCS is going to let a pair of analysts go to China to talk to one of their prize assets."

Coward. Cynic? The two were not mutually exclusive, though Kyra suspected that only the latter was true. There was no question about that one. "It'll never happen if we don't ask."

"Feel free," Jonathan replied without hesitation. "While you're tilting at windmills, see if you can get NCS to cough up copies of those disks that Pioneer handed over."

USS *ABRAHAM LINCOLN* (CVN 72)
240 KILOMETERS WEST OF SASEBO, JAPAN

Captain (USN) Moshe Nagin rolled the F-35 Lightning II Joint Strike Fighter ten degrees to give him a wider view of USS *Abraham Lincoln*. Truth be told, and he never admitted it to his fellow naval aviators, he hated trapping on aircraft carriers. Landing a jet fighter on a moving *Nimitz*-class carrier at night in a squall was a task so hard it made grown men want to wet their pants, and it never got easy with practice. Runways are supposed to sit still and be a mile long. Landing on a ship's deck that was only five hundred feet long and moving at thirty knots was unnatural, and his life depended on some too-young-to-drink boatswain's mate below decks setting the proper tension on the deck cables. Too little tension on the wires and the plane would roll off into the water. Too much and only divine intervention would keep the cable from ripping the tailhook out of the plane. The other possibilities all involved varying amounts of burning jet fuel, live ordnance, and pilot spread over the deck.

Nagin looked past the *Lincoln* and picked out an HH-60H Seahawk flying its own pattern low and slow. Some of his younger pilots mocked the helo pilots, as though flying jets was the only job on a carrier that mattered, but time would solve that. Bold pilots sometimes got to be old pilots only through the gracious courtesy of helo search and rescue teams. He had found religion the first time a Seahawk had pulled him out of the water. One of the engines on his first Hornet malfunctioned a half second into a catapult launch, rupturing the cowling and sending shrapnel into the other. The catapult had obediently thrown his Hornet off the carrier anyway. Nagin ejected just before the plane hit the Persian Gulf. The Seahawk crew that lifted him from the water hadn't even cracked a joke about his flying skills, and that earned them a share of the love he otherwise saved for his wife.

"Break to line up," the landing signal officer ordered through his helmet. Nagin sucked in a breath of sterile, recycled air through his mask and pulled the plane into a turn, rolling hard left.

"Call the ball," the LSO said.

Nagin sought out the "meatball" light on the port side. The yellow dot emitted by the Fresnel lens was agreeably where it was supposed to be, sitting between horizontal green lights above and below. He was riding the glide slope straight as a ruler.

"Fencer eight-zero-one, juliet sierra foxtrot ball, eight-point-eight," Nagin called out.

"Roger ball," the LSO acknowledged.

Nagin held the turn until he'd come around 180 degrees from his previous course, then rolled the plane level. *Lincoln* was ahead and the absurdly short runway was a thousand feet below and moving to the right. Nagin corrected for the drift and nudged the nose up a bit to kill some speed. The LSO stayed silent—Nagin's best indication that he wasn't completely screwing up.

The exact moment the landing gear hit the deck was always a surprise. The plane touched down moving at a hair under 150 miles per hour. White smoke poured off the tires as the rubber went molten from the friction, and for a moment the plane was sliding on liquid made from its own wheels. Nagin jammed the throttle full forward and heard the F-35's single engine scream as it spooled up to full power.

Inertia threw Nagin against his harness, and he knew that the tailhook had caught a wire—the number three—which held with the right amount of tension. His speed dropped, the tires stopped melting, and they caught traction on the nonskid deck. Nagin yanked the throttle back, the engine went quiet, and his speed went to zero.

It wasn't the moment to relax. The carrier deck was a busy and cramped space, and it wouldn't do to drive the new stealth fighter into the water. His shoulders ached where the harness had pressed into the muscle. He wondered if he'd bruised them again.

MAIN HANGAR DECK
USS *ABRAHAM LINCOLN*

Lincoln's hangar deck reeked of jet fuel. Everyone aboard ended up in the hangar sooner or later, where the smell of refined hydrocarbons attached itself to their clothing, and they carried the odor out to their shipmates like missionaries spreading the gospel. Rear Admiral Alton Pollard had lived a quarter century on carriers, which was long enough for his mind to learn to ignore the smell the same way it ignored the feeling of clothing on his skin. He had to think about the odor to notice it, and it was smarter not to think about it.

The hangar deck was almost 700 feet long and 110 wide but still felt cramped when more than a few fighters were parked inside. The new F-35s were off the hardtop above and more than a few off-duty sailors were down to see the planes. The Lightning II was clearly American, looked like a fighter, but it was not fearsome. *What's scarier?* the Pentagon desk pilots had reasoned. *The plane they see up close in combat or the one they never see coming at all?* But in the back of Pollard's mind something nagged at him, telling him that a psychological weapon had been lost. Maybe he was just finally old enough that he couldn't embrace change with any enthusiasm. He shook his head, cleared his mind, and approached the senior pilot, who was holding class on the new plane with enlisted sailors young enough to be his children.

"Admiral." Nagin's posture straightened and he gestured to the F-35. "The replacement for the Hornet," he said. "What do you think?" The senior pilot aboard was still dressed in his flight suit and cradling his helmet in his arm like a football. As commander, air group (CAG), Nagin had exactly one superior aboard. Pollard was the only man who outranked him. The admiral thought a CAG had the best job in the Navy, had been one himself, and missed the job most days. Nagin had the privileges of elevated rank and still got to fly a fighter every day. Being the commanding officer of a battle group had its own rewards, but they never quite equaled the logging of flight hours in the cockpit.

"You tell me," Pollard said. "You've flown one. I haven't." He put his hand on the plane's wing, the first time he'd actually touched a Lightning II. He could have taken one of the new fighters out for a joyride, but Pollard's body didn't quite bounce back from hard carrier landings the way it used to. His back loved flying less every year, and he refused to think what an ejection seat would do to his spine now. He'd had to do that once. Although forever grateful to the Martin-Baker company for building an escape vehicle that worked every time, he was quite sure the compression of his vertebrae had left him an inch shorter. It was a small price to pay to come home to his wife.

Nagin frowned a bit. "Twice the range on internal fuel as the 18Cs, but she has a single engine, which worries me. I don't like single points of failure and that's a big one. And there's no HUD. All the flight data is projected onto the inside of the helmet." He hefted his flight helmet and showed it to the admiral. Pollard took it and examined the inside.

"That doesn't make you sick?" Pollard asked.

"It feels a little unnatural at first, but works fine when you get used to it."

Pollard handed the helmet back to its owner. "What about the ordnance load?"

"No question, she's a bomb truck," Nagin said. "She can lug around five thousand pounds of JDAM hurt inside and six hardpoints on the wings when stealth doesn't matter. That only leaves room for two AMRAAMs mounted inside when you have to go air-to-air, and those have to mount on the bay doors." Those bay doors were open, Nagin gestured inside. "You get two Sidewinders on the wings if you really need 'em and don't care about the stealth."

"Maneuverability?"

"She handles well enough to dogfight, but she's no F-22 like the Air Force boys are flying these days. So she doesn't carry much for it."

"You don't like the pistol?" Pollard asked, working his way back toward the engine. He found the gun mounted in an external pod on the undercarriage almost directly between the wings.

The CAG shook his head. "The gun's fine. It's a version of the GAU-12-slash-U—twenty-five millimeter four-barrel Gatling, pretty much the same thing the Harrier carries. But hanging it off the center pylon degrades the stealth a bit when it's mounted. And I'm not too keen on the ammo load. It handles forty-one hundred rounds per minute but only carries two hundred twenty rounds in the pod. So you've got about three seconds worth of fire before you're left hoping that you've still got some missiles."

"Or some Hornets in the neighborhood," Pollard said. "But nobody dogfights anymore, not like the old days, not at close range."

"That's the problem," Nagin countered. "If the bogeys ever manage to get in close, we could have trouble."

"Then don't let 'em get in close." Pollard watched his sailors stare at the new JSF like it was the burning bush, then finally took his gaze away from the plane and looked at the senior pilot. He motioned him away from the crowd of enlisted men. Nagin fell in behind the senior officer as the admiral sought privacy, looking for space in the hangar deck that was overrun only by equipment and not by sailors.

"Orders came in from CINCPACOM just after you left. The PLA overran Kinmen and caught everyone flat-footed. That island is so close to the coast that the Chinese were able to blitz out of their bases in range without having to move extra assets around. They could take the Matsus the same way and nobody will be able to call it more than five minutes in advance. PACOM is sending out EP-3s to ramp up

ELINT coverage in case the Chinese start getting ready to make a move on Penghu or Taiwan proper. And we're changing course. *Washington* is coming down too. We'll both keep the island between us and the mainland. *Washington* takes the north, we get the south," Pollard told him. "Have you seen the morning intel?"

"Not today," the pilot said, shaking his head. "The flight schedule had me in the air too early. I was going to catch up after I finish up down here. Anything on that PLA carrier threat?"

Pollard shook his head. "CIA and Navy Intel assessments came in. They all say it probably refers to PLA subs carrying Sunburns or Exocets, maybe Shkvals."

"Academy plebes at Annapolis could've made that call," Nagin said.

"True," Pollard said. "But it's the safe bet, and if it comes down to straight ASW, we can handle the PLA Navy."

"I hate people who always make the safe bet," Nagin said.

"You never win big and you can always still lose," Pollard agreed. "But we're getting some help to keep the PLA Navy off our backs." He reached into his pocket and passed a hard copy of CINCPACOM's orders to Nagin, who turned it over in his hand and began to study the small type. "*Honolulu, Tucson, Virginia,* and *Gettysburg.*" The first three were attack submarines: the two named for cities were *Los Angeles*–class, the third was the lead boat of the more modern *Virginia* class. *Gettysburg* was a *Ticonderoga*-class cruiser. "The subs will join us by day after tomorrow. *Gettysburg* is coming up from the south. She's already in the Balintang Channel, so she'll beat us there by a day or so. *Washington* is getting the *Salt Lake City, Columbia, New Mexico,* and *Leyte Gulf.* Not a bad start."

"Maybe *Gettysburg* will clear out the water for us and save us the trouble," Nagin said, hopeful. "We'll be in the PLA's ocean by Saturday." Chinese submarines had shadowed US carriers in past years, at least one as far north as Okinawa. The US Navy usually found the PLA units and chased them off, but everyone on both sides understood that practice made perfect and the Chinese were only getting better. "Even with the help, the numbers will still be six to one in the PLA's favor."

"It'll be a target-rich environment if we have to go 'weapons free,'" Pollard said. "Intel says that at least half of the Chinese sub fleet are old Russian Romeos. Those are easy. It's the Kilos and the Hans that worry me. Imagery puts the Hans to the north, closer to *Washington's* AOR, so we'll probably be facing Kilos if the PLA decides to take a shot at us. Diesel-electrics, nice and quiet, but they're getting old," Pollard said. "If we've got the island between us and them, they'll have to approach us from the south. *Washington* will close off the north unless they want to take the really long route around. That'll limit their approach vectors."

"Not looking to take us into the Strait?" Nagin asked. The attempt at humor wasn't even halfhearted.

"Not if I can help it," Pollard replied. "Too close to too many PLA bases for my taste. I'd prefer not to be the one who has the limited approach options."

"*Nimitz* did it back in ninety-six," Nagin observed.

"The Chinese weren't ready to take a shot at a US carrier in ninety-six. Maybe they are now," Pollard told his subordinate. "And I'd rather make the PLA come to us. We've sold the Taiwanese enough weapons over the years. No sense in us being the first line of defense for them."

Nagin lifted his helmet and held it in both hands, looking at it. He'd been to Pollard's office upstairs and seen the admiral's own flight helmet behind the desk. The moniker *Tycho* was stenciled across the front, scratched and faded. Nagin had shared plenty of beers in plenty of bars with Pollard and heard the old man's war stories from Iraq and Bosnia. The admiral had earned his rank the right way. The man had been ordered into a fight, flown his own fighter straight onto the enemy's home field, fired his guns in anger, and taken fire in return. Nagin respected the man and not just his rank. The admiral didn't fly combat missions anymore, but the old man had been into the devil's own home more than once and could tell his men the color of the paint on the walls inside. Admirals were considered too valuable for that, so Pollard had to settle for sitting on the carrier watching his pilots launch into unfriendly skies. It was the order of military life, and Nagin's turn to leave the cockpit and watch others fly was coming soon enough.

Nagin squared his shoulders and faced the admiral. "If Tian wants to take it that far, we've had a long time to get ready for it."

Pollard smiled. "So have they."

CHAPTER 7

SATURDAY
DAY SEVEN

Pioneer owed his freedom to the habit of catching his mistakes before he made them. He controlled his thoughts with discipline that a monk would have coveted and he always thought twice before moving once. Though he knew it wasn't true, he assumed the enemy would never make an unforced error and that only by doing the same could he survive. He had conditioned himself to settle for winning by stalemate, so it had never occurred to him that misfortune would stalk his enemy the way it had always stalked him.

He'd come to Jingshan Park to clear his mind. It was a more sultry day than usual for Beijing's winters when he arrived, and others had flocked to the park to enjoy the warmth. He found a group of older men standing near the Pavilion of Everlasting Spring—not living up to its name this season—practicing the art of water calligraphy on the cement sidewalk stones near the gardens. Each man held a brush with a white handle long enough for the horsehair tip to touch the ground. They would dip the instrument in water, roll the end on the ground until it came to a fine point, and write pictograms on the stone walkway. It was a practice thought to stimulate the mind, and Pioneer found it calming to watch. He was no artist, but when one of the elderly men had offered him a turn, he took the brush without protest and joined in the craft. His unnamed patron left him the brush, the chill in the air finally reaching his old bones and forcing him to go home for some relief.

Pioneer's characters weren't elegant. There was such a thing as sloppy Chinese handwriting, but artistry wasn't the point. He stayed for hours, finding it easy to lose himself in the hobby, and he paid little attention to the crowd of tourists and locals that he and the other men drew. He wasn't a natural showman. Espionage had taught him to shun public attention, but he felt very peaceful at the moment and he wasn't engaged in an operational act, so there was nothing illegal for anyone to see. Some of their spectators watched them for only a few minutes before moving on; others stayed for an hour or more despite the chill. There was more than enough artwork for them to see. The characters would have disappeared quickly during any other season. A warmer sun would have evaporated the water almost as fast as they were written, but that was not the case today. The temperature fell as the evening approached, and the ground grew colder than the air. The wet pictographs remained, forcing Pioneer and the others to move down the sidewalk to keep a clean canvas in front of them, the crowd moving with them. Finally, the cold became too much for him and Pioneer handed the brush to another old man and walked north to Lotus Lane, a strip along the south shore of Qianhai Lake lined with restaurants and bars. He began searching for something warm to drink. There were a number of coffeehouses, and Pioneer had developed a taste for the Western brew.

In retrospect, the man on the bicycle should have struck Pioneer as being out of place. Normally he was observant enough to notice such things, but his focus on the water calligraphy had been total and he hadn't seen the man ride past him in Jingshan Park three times. As Pioneer entered the pedestrian-only zone of Lotus Lane, the man followed behind him and attempted to dismount his bicycle before it came to a complete stop. The front wheel hit an icy patch on the road and the bicycle shot out from under him as the cyclist put his foot down to catch himself. His shoe landed on the same black ice and went sideways, and its owner collapsed in an ungraceful heap, taking a pair of nearby pedestrians with him. His leg broke under his weight in two places and he cried out in shock at the sharp pain. One of the pedestrians, a woman, shouted in surprise as the bicycle struck her behind the knees, pitching her forward onto her face. Her reactions were slowed by the several drinks she'd had midafternoon, and her face smashed into the concrete, breaking her nose with a cracking noise that Pioneer could hear. The second victim, a man, stumbled as the woman struck him on the way down, throwing him forward onto the decorative cement rail to his right. He caught himself before he went over but couldn't get his own footing on the ice and fell to the ground bruised but still luckier than the other two.

Pioneer turned toward the ruckus, not fast enough to see the accident, but quickly enough to see the full aftermath. The woman was lying on her stomach in shock, blood streaming from her broken nose. He saw the man lying near the rail, a look of pain on his face but trying to get to his feet. The cyclist was clutching his leg, which was bent at an unnatural angle that made Pioneer sick. Without thinking, he moved toward the man to help him. The man rolled onto his side, and Pioneer saw a two-way radio fall from his coat. It was a Motorola, black, somewhat larger than the kind that a tourist might have for personal use, and was attached by wire to a clear acoustic tube speaker that it had ripped from the cyclist's ear on its way to the ground. The man tried to grab for the radio and earpiece but they were out of reach, and then he made the mistake that fully destroyed his cover.

Pioneer leaned toward the downed man. The cyclist saw him approaching and froze. He was a junior officer who lacked experience, and his panic was strong enough to override the few months of training he did have. His instincts told him to avoid contact with the target— usually the right response, but not now at a moment when the target was entirely focused on him. The officer jerked away, exactly the wrong move for a crippled man in need of immediate help. The cyclist realized his mistake and made a second by looking directly at Pioneer to see if the target had penetrated his cover, as if the earpiece hadn't been enough. The clear plastic coil would have screamed *security service* in any country.

Pioneer looked directly at the crippled man's face and saw . . . *recognition*. He was quite sure they had never met. Pioneer's memory for faces was good. It was the necessary by-product of years of counter-surveillance practice, but the injured man's look settled the question in Pioneer's mind as to who he was. Pioneer reflexively held his own features rigid to show nothing in return. His mind sorted the possible responses and only one fell out that would preserve any hope of his continued survival at all.

He retrieved the radio and earpiece and held them out to the man.

The cyclist's face showed as much surprise as pain as he took them from his prey. It was not an act he would have expected. Maybe this target hadn't figured out that he belonged to the MSS? Was that possible?

Pioneer wasn't nearly stupid enough for that, though he didn't know that the woman with the broken nose and the man by the railing were MSS as well, as were six other people in the immediate vicinity. Pioneer helped the cyclist to stand on his one good leg and moved him inside to a bar ten feet away, where he could at least be warm while he waited for medical assistance. He retrieved a rag with ice from the bartender and returned outside to the woman, who had been helped to a sitting position by her MSS partners. Her coat was ruined by the bloodstains and Pioneer feared she would faint if she took a look down at herself. He gently tilted her head back and applied the ice, then helped her stand and moved her into the bar to sit next to her partner.

The medics arrived, splinted the cyclist's leg, and wheeled him out of the bar on a gurney while helping the woman to the ambulance. Pioneer watched them go and then went on his way to the coffeehouse. He was moving entirely on automatic pilot, keeping up the good show even while his brain screamed that it was futile.

They know.

How did they know? When and where exactly had he made the mistake that had tipped them off? He couldn't come up with an answer but he couldn't stop thinking about it. Finally, he forced his mind away from the obsession as best he could. It was a riddle without a solution. Other spies had been exposed by the most trivial of errors, and his error surely had been trivial because he could not, for the life of him, identify what it had been. He likely would never learn how they had been tipped off to him unless they wanted to tell him at his trial, and that was unlikely. It would be a closed-door hearing with him absent in a cell.

His time as a spy was over, but he still had one operational act left to perform. After that, the sole remaining question of how long he might live would be completely out of his control. Would the CIA fight for him? Even if the Americans had the will to exfiltrate him, time was still not his friend and never had been. Before, it had at least left him alone. Now it would torture him. Assuming that they would decide to save him, the CIA would need time to position enough assets to act, while the MSS could arrest him almost at its leisure. Why hadn't they done so? Maybe they had only recently become aware that he was a traitor? They didn't know the extent of his crimes and were still exploring the magnitude of his treason? He had no answers to questions that he wouldn't be able to stop asking. They would be like a merciless children's song playing over and over in his head until he was ready to scream.

Answers wouldn't change the fact that Pioneer was now a dead man walking free with one hope only. Every case officer he'd ever worked with had promised to get him out of China if he were compromised. It was time for one of them to keep the promise.

CHAPTER 8

SUNDAY
DAY EIGHT

Mitchell was driving, which was no small feat for an American in Beijing. The written driving test had a hundred questions and the English version was nearly incomprehensible. Most of Dunne's people who had licenses had taken the test repeatedly, often sharing and memorizing the right and wrong answers among themselves to improve their scores. Mitchell took the test in Mandarin, a notable feat itself, and passed with a perfect score, which was unheard-of for an American. Yet he still preferred to use the railways as a matter of course. Traffic in Beijing flowed through the streets like floodwaters through a Venetian canal, and the rules of maneuver were mostly unwritten. Motorists acted on instinct and moved like schools of fish, where a single car's turn could lead a wave behind it. It had taken Mitchell months to develop a feel for the flow and pace of traffic here, but it was worth the effort. It made life miserable for the Chinese security officers who had to conduct surveillance.

He made the turn onto the Wangfujing Dajie road and pressed the accelerator. His eyes moved back and forth between the road and the rearview mirror every few seconds. The MSS was back there. Vehicular countersurveillance was a difficult skill to master, largely because it meant the driver had to spend more time looking to the rear than ahead at the road. But the Russians, giving Mitchell no end of practice, had quickly fixed the habit in him.

At least five cars had made the last three turns with him. He wasn't sure which were driven by security officers, but he was certain at least two and possibly three of them were following him. He had no issues with that. His only stop tonight would be for gas.

Pioneer stood in front of the Capital Theater, watching the traffic as though waiting to flag down a taxi. It was his preferred site for such operations. Pioneer enjoyed the performing arts and could speak intelligently about a broad range of plays, particularly Western musicals. The music of *Les Misérables* haunted him. Jean Valjean's story of a man living a life of secrets felt like his own, and Pioneer had learned some of his limited English by following the libretto's text as he listened to the album in his apartment.

It was cold enough that Pioneer's breath was visible in the air; yesterday's warmth was gone. He wore a black overcoat and red scarf—not the blue one that he usually wore—positioned not to obscure his face. This operational act didn't require him to do anything except be recognizable from a short distance. Pioneer carried no classified material tonight. There was nothing on his person that could incriminate him if he were searched, and yet he was more tense tonight than he had been any other night he could remember. Perhaps the evening he had first walked in and volunteered to work for the CIA could compare, but his stress that night almost twenty-five years before had merely been compounded by nervousness. Ignorance worked in his favor then. Now his anxiety was multiplied by experience. He wondered if the MSS had tracked how often he changed the colors of his scarves, the answer to which was *never* until tonight. He hoped that they wouldn't realize that the change had to do with something more than mere fashion.

Mitchell approached the theater. He moved the car one lane to the left out of the rightmost lane. It was a purely diversionary maneuver that forced the MSS officers in the cars behind to watch his car instead of the sidewalk to his right as he passed the Capital Theater. The patrons, both Chinese and foreigners, were still mingling in front in a sizable crowd. Mitchell wished that he could park the car and buy a ticket to whatever was playing. *The Monkey King,* which had been as good as the reviewers claimed, had left the station chief thinking about another night out at the theater with his wife.

The time window for the sign of life was five minutes. There would be no contact between them, which would make it impossible for some counterintelligence analyst to prove that the close proximity wasn't a coincidence. That was the theory. Proximity might be enough to set the MSS off, depending on their level of paranoia, if they were watching Pioneer . . . and the Chinese were a paranoid bunch.

Mitchell didn't slow the car or turn his head to look for the asset. It was all done with the eyes. He looked right. Pioneer was there as scheduled.

Sign of life. He's still free, Mitchell thought. But Pioneer was wearing the red scarf, not the blue, and the CIA officer was sure he felt his chest seize up.

They're watching him.

He made the left turn onto the Jianguomennei Dajie, the artery road that passed between the Forbidden City and Tiananmen Square, both landmarks west of his position. He straightened out the car and drove east toward the embassy district. He said nothing until he arrived at his office, closed and locked the door, and dialed the number for Barron's office. Only here could Mitchell open up. The room was swept for microphones and other such gear on a schedule. "Hey, boss."

"How'd it go?" Barron asked.

"He's alive and running loose, but they're on him," Mitchell said.

"Then why not pick him up? Any chance that the locals don't really know?"

"Maybe, but I wouldn't bank on it. Pioneer called it, not me," Mitchell said. "And it could explain why the package wasn't at the drop site."

"That means there's a high probability that you've been burned too," Barron said. "Betcha the MSS had a microcamera inside that bathroom or outside pointing at the door."

"Probably a safe bet," Mitchell admitted. "Sorry you're going to have to find a new station chief. Makes me wonder why they didn't pick me up."

"They're still trying to pull apart the entire network, most likely," Barron said. "We don't know how long he's been under surveillance. They could have been watching him for a year now, for all we know."

"We can't leave him hanging, boss," Mitchell pleaded, his voice rising. "Twenty-five years has gotta count for something. We've gotta get him out." His own emotion surprised him. He wasn't a young man and thought he had mastered the art of keeping his feelings out of the way of his professional judgment a long time ago. It was a dangerous weakness and it disturbed him to see it in himself.

"It counts for a lot. We won't hang him out to dry," Barron said.

"I want to run the exfil to get him out."

"No promises," Barron said. "We don't play the game stupid. When in doubt, get out. Live to fight another day."

Mitchell frowned. The mantra had sounded smart the first time he'd heard it. Now it felt like a coward's motto. "Words to stay out of jail by," he said, not feeling the truth of them.

On the other side of the world, Barron nodded. Mitchell wasn't a stupid man. He was always professional. "We'll make sure Pioneer stays that way. I don't care what anyone says, yes or no, we owe him. I'll talk to Cooke."

REPUBLIC OF CHINA SHIP (ROCS) *MA KONG* (DDG–1805)
TSO YING NAVAL BASE
KAOHSIUNG CITY, TAIWAN

Captain Wu Tai-cheng stared down at the bow of the *Ma Kong*, sucked in a lungful of the cold open air, and enjoyed the swell of pride that rose in his chest. The ship was lit up by the dockside lights, and the hard metal structures of the vessel's radar masts made for a frightening image illuminated against the black sky as he turned his head to look up. His pride was entirely justified. This was a vessel to be feared. He knew it and the Chinese knew it. There were only four *Kidd*-class destroyers in the entire world, Taiwan owned them all, and he commanded one of them. The Americans had built them for the shah of Iran, but that corrupt old tyrant had lost his throne to the mullahs before taking delivery. So their builders had put them to use, calling them the *Ayatollah*-class as a joke. Wu's ship had once been called the USS *Chandler* before the Taiwanese government bought it and its sister ships years before.

Ma Kong was not as capable as the *Arleigh Burke*–class destroyers that the Americans wouldn't sell out of fear that the Chinese would be upset, but it was a deadly vessel in its own right. Its engines were quiet enough that it could hunt submarines, it carried the Harpoon missiles that could crack an enemy surface ship in half, and any plane within range of *Ma Kong*'s RIM-66 missiles and Phalanx guns lived only by Captain Wu's good graces. Together, the four ships gave his country a considerable defense against the PLA's air and naval forces. It irked Wu that the Americans still refused to sell his country its very best weapons, but *Ma Kong* still made the Chinese think twice, he was certain.

As Wu stared out past the dockyard perimeter toward the city lights, an entirely different emotion rose up inside him. *Fools,* he thought. The PLA had taken Kinmen in a day and the stupid fools who ran his country were cowering in their comfortable offices, dithering about what to do. "President" Liang—the man didn't deserve the title in Wu's opinion—was a fool. His arrogance had cost his people dearly, and now his fear of the Chinese was just raising the price they would have to pay to free their countrymen.

The dock to the ship's port side was busy as the workers loaded ammunition, fuel, and other supplies aboard, but the process was going far too slowly. It had taken too long for even those orders to come down from Navy General Headquarters. *Ma Kong* should be in the Strait already, he thought, churning through the water at thirty knots toward that sacred island with her sisters and planes overhead to lay waste to any Chinese soldiers they could catch out in the open. He had ordered his chief engineer to fire up the ship's four General Electric turbines in anticipation of that very order, which had yet to come. The other captains in port were acting more cautiously, but Wu was not such a man. The order would come, he was sure. It *had* to come. To let the Chinese have Kinmen without a fight would be inexcusable.

And if the order didn't come before, the Americans would come to Taiwan with one or more of their carrier strike groups and then the order would come. With American ships and planes strengthening the rubber spines of the government bureaucrats, *Ma Kong* would finally put to sea and lend her strength to the US Navy's strike groups, fighting alongside her former family of ships, and then the PLA would see the terrible mistake they had made.

He turned his back and walked aft toward the ship's stern, stepping in and around the crates that were stacked up on the deck. He passed through the maze, enlisted men and junior officers parting before him to let him pass without a word, and finally arrived at the helipad, where deckhands were securing one of the ship's two helicopters for transport, this one a Sikorsky S-70B Seahawk. Two of the *Ma Kong*'s RIM missile launchers were just beyond with a pair of engineers checking and double-checking them. Wu had told his crew in plain terms that very morning that their lives depended on those weapons in more ways than one. Wu set his course for them.

The deck was noisy tonight and so he didn't hear the whistling sound until the last second. And then the night was lit up as the ship bucked underneath, tossing him across the deck along with boxes, crates, ropes, and bits of the men that were once part of his crew.

Wu crashed down flat on his back, almost at the stern, lucky his spine hadn't broken, and it took him several seconds to realize that he could hear nothing. His eardrums were ruptured and his ears and nose were bleeding in a gusher. He pushed himself onto his side, mildly surprised that his arms were still working, and he tried to stagger to his feet. It took him three tries and he succeeded only when his blind groping led him to the stern railing. Then he managed to open his eyes.

The explosion had erupted amidship, just forward of the helipad, starboard side, tearing a hole in *Ma Kong* so large that he thought it might have ripped the ship almost in half. A fire blazed out of the hole, smoke rolling skyward into the deck lights, but he knew that wouldn't last long. Part of the hole was below the waterline. *Ma Kong* was flooding. He prayed that the crew below was closing the watertight doors and starting the pumps, if they still worked. He couldn't hear his own men screaming as they moved around the deck. He tried to yell an order but no one responded. Wu couldn't hear his own voice and he wondered if the rest of his men were as deaf as he was.

He staggered forward and fell to his knees. His sense of balance was destroyed along with his eardrums, and he wondered whether *Ma Kong* wasn't listing. If she had taken on that much water that fast, then she was surely dying, on her way to the bottom of the harbor, and some of his men caught below would drown. He pushed himself back to his feet and tried to move forward again to help the wounded, to organize the damage control parties or give the order to abandon ship. Then he began to fall forward again. An ensign caught him as he dropped to one knee.

The second explosion lifted them into the air and sent them both over the rail into the water. Wu managed to grab a quick breath of air before he plunged into the cold, black harbor. He found his mind strangely focused not on his own survival but on that of his ship. Had munitions on the deck cooked off? Did a fuel drum under pressure explode from the fire's heat? Wu didn't know. After a few seconds, something inside his mind told him to push for the surface, but he realized that he didn't know where the surface was. His sense of balance told him nothing. He opened his eyes and managed to turn his head until he saw the dim light of the fire above the water. He tried to push up for that. His clothes were heavy with water and his broken bones made him want to pass out when he moved, but he finally managed to push his head above the surface.

Ma Kong's entire aft section was burning. The Sikorsky helicopter was a flaming wreck and everything else on the deck was engulfed. Wu saw that the men on the bow were throwing lines to the wounded in the water.

Wu's head slipped under the water for a moment and he kicked his one good leg to surface. He managed to wave an arm and he saw one of the crew point in his direction. Then he went under a third time and found he didn't have the strength to rise above the water again.

I'm going to drown.

A hand plunged into the water and grabbed his arm. Captain Wu Tai-cheng of the now-dead ROCS *Ma Kong* broke the surface of Tso Ying harbor and sucked in the cold salt air. His first thought was to question whether President Liang had another reason to be afraid of the Chinese that he hadn't shared.

CHAPTER 9

MONDAY
DAY NINE

Truman called the Oval Office the "crown jewel of the American prison system," but unlike most federal inmates, every president of the United States is allowed to decorate his cell to his personal tastes at the considerable expense of the taxpayers. Harry Stuart had been more frugal than most in that regard. The office now satisfied the colonial tastes that stemmed from his heritage as the eighth president from Virginia, but a few pieces were constants that carried over through administrations. The *Resolute* desk sat in its usual place at the room's south end, flanked by Old Glory and a Seal of the President flag with gold curtains behind framing the window to the South Lawn. Stuart had raided the Smithsonian for Lincoln and Washington portraits and a Churchill bust. Any piece of artwork in the office would have fetched hundreds of thousands, perhaps millions, on the open market. The furniture could have paid for the BMW Cooke almost never got to drive. The room was a fine museum of American history in its own right. The CIA director would have liked more time to study the pieces, but the commander in chief had given her less than five minutes before ordering his staff to place a call to the president of the People's Republic of China.

"This attack is not in the best interests of your people, Mr. President." Stuart was not given to fits of temper, but he was a man who did not enjoy surprises. No president did. Those who sat in the Oval Office all prayed for an orderly world, even the ones who were not religious despite their public image, and they rarely got it. Surprise was one of the few constants of the job and the PLA attack on Kinmen had set the new standard for it. That particular patch of soil in the South China Sea was so small that it wasn't labeled on most maps, but it now had the undivided attention of the United States' commander in chief.

"Mr. President, is it not the policy of the United States that Taiwan and all her territories are part of China?" Tian's voice was smooth over the speakerphone. Cooke knew that Tian Kai had been a government functionary his entire adult life, but the man was debating like a trained lawyer. He certainly was smart enough never to ask a question for which he didn't already know the answer.

"It is our policy that we oppose any unilateral change in the relations between China and Taiwan." Stuart was on the defensive. "Your attack on Kinmen is just such a change. Your attack on the *Ma Kong* is just such a change—"

"And what evidence do you have that we sank the *Ma Kong*?" Tian interrupted.

Stuart stopped short, surprised that Tian would ask such a question under the circumstances. He looked over to Cooke, who shook her head. It was a request—she couldn't give orders to this man—not to reveal classified information to his Chinese counterpart. "Are you trying to tell me that you didn't sink it?" Stuart asked.

Good, Cooke thought. *Deflect a question with a question.*

"I question the separatists' ability to maintain the military equipment that you have been selling them," Tian said. A nonanswer.

"Yes, Mr. President, we built those *Kidd*-class destroyers, so I can promise you that they don't just spontaneously explode anchored at the dock, good maintenance or not." Ingalls Shipbuilding of Pascagoula, Mississippi, did fine work, he was sure.

Tian didn't respond and Stuart let that silence hang pregnant in the air for a few moments before continuing. "Your government made certain decisions without any prior consultation, no bilateral or multilateral negotiations of any kind, or any effort to resolve your dispute through the UN Security Council. We object to that." It was a hard thrust back at the Chinese president to regain the initiative.

"Mr. President, the UN has no role here," Tian answered in a blunt parry. "We are suppressing a potential rebellion, as your President Lincoln did when your southern states tried to secede. I ask you to respect our sovereign right to maintain the 'domestic tranquility,' as you call it, of our union." Tian's English was perfect, if accented, his grammar and diction exact, and Cooke found it unnerving to hear the shades of a British accent coming from the mouth of a Beijing-born oligarch.

"Mr. President, it seems to me that it's the PLA who's disturbing your domestic tranquility at the moment, not the Taiwanese," Stuart said, his frustration starting to show.

"Not so," Tian answered. "Liang is trying to save his political career by fomenting insurrection in the province. We cannot allow him to succeed. China's long-standing position is that Taiwan will not be allowed to declare independence."

"The United States respectfully disagrees with your assessment of President Liang's intentions." It was a weak rebuttal and Stuart knew it.

"You are entitled to your own interpretation of events," Tian said. "However, as this is an internal security matter, it is our interpretation that matters here, sir. Liang would not have set himself on this present course if he did not believe the United States would intervene. And so the People's Republic of China formally asks the United States not to interfere in our domestic affairs. There are no American interests at stake and our military action has been quite restrained."

Restrained? Cooke thought. *Hardly.*

"Mr. President, *restrained* is not the word I would choose," Stuart said, echoing the CIA director's thought. He leaned in toward the telephone mic. "Your attacks were unprovoked. The senior military officer on Kinmen and his wife were shot in their home. Yes, we know about that, and don't bother asking me how because I won't tell you. The power grid is wrecked. The airport is a smoking ruin. The *Ma Kong* was cut in half, sitting at the bottom of her dock, and a number of her crew went down with her. None of that, by definition, is restrained. But in case there was any question, peace and stability along the Pacific Rim have always been and continue to be American interests, even if they are no longer yours."

All done being diplomatic, Cooke thought. She decided that she preferred Stuart that way.

"Of course they remain ours," Tian said, refusing to take Stuart's bait. "We have chosen to demonstrate our resolve and our capabilities on a limited scale. Kinmen is hardly worth our notice or yours. It is our sincere hope that by our seizing this minor spit of land, President Liang will have to face the reality of his situation and choose to back down. But our strategy of restraint can only work if the United States does not offer Liang false hope by intervening. Any show of support from you, Mr. President, could only prolong the conflict and cause unnecessary suffering."

It was a neat trap. *Do nothing and China wins. Act aggressively and get painted as a scapegoat,* Cooke thought. She guessed that Stuart wanted more time to think, and he wasn't going to get it sparring with a Chinese president who'd had days to practice this conversation. Doubtless, there was nothing Stuart could say for which Tian didn't already have an answer . . . nothing diplomatic, anyway.

Stuart proved her right. "President Tian, thank you for taking my call," he said abruptly. "I do hope that this can be resolved swiftly and without unnecessary loss of life, or any interruption in trade between our two countries."

"Of course. We are committed to stability and the preservation of our trade relationship with the United States. Your economic well-being is in our interest, as you know, as ours is in yours. We have invested in so many of your government securities and we do not wish to see them devalued," Tian replied. "Your servant, sir."

And the line went dead.

Stuart fell back into his chair and clutched the armrests with a frustrated grip. "We just got caught with our pants down and our laundry still hanging on the line."

"You didn't exactly strip the paint off the walls," the secretary of defense observed. General Lance Showalter (USMC, retired) stood a head taller than Cooke, half again as wide at the shoulders. The observation was kinder than the one running through Cooke's mind, but generals had to be diplomats as much as State department officers.

"Tian was right," Stuart said. "We don't have any evidence that the PLA took out the *Ma Kong*. We know they did it, but we can't prove it, and without that my hands are tied." He looked at his CIA director. "Any information on that?"

"Unfortunately, no," Cooke replied. "Nothing on radar and this definitely wasn't a Chinese sapper team. Security at the Tso Ying Naval Base is too good to let that happen. Navy Intelligence thinks that a Chinese submarine must've slipped through the Taiwanese sonar nets and put a torpedo into her."

"That would be one quiet submarine," Showalter said.

"Agreed," Cooke said. "Not to mention it begs the question why they would only take out the *Ma Kong*. There were a half-dozen other vessels in port, including the *Kee Lung*, which is another *Kidd*-class destroyer. The *Kidd*s are a cornerstone in Taiwan's air defense network, so if this attack was the precursor to an invasion, the Chinese would take both ships out if they could. If the PLA Navy could get a submarine that close, they could've turned this into Taiwan's Pearl Harbor. So why take out one ship and not the others?"

"So is this the prelude to invasion or not?" Stuart asked.

"We don't know," Cooke admitted. It hurt to say it.

"Figure it out," Stuart ordered. "Until we do and can prove it, I don't have room to move. Kinmen really is a piddling little spit of land." He slapped the couch arm with his open hand and stared out the windows in thought. "A lot of the public wouldn't be happy about going to war with China over Taiwan itself, much less over an island you can't see on most of the world's maps." The president exhaled and turned back toward his guests.

"We're not done yet, Harry," Showalter consoled him. The SecDef was one of the few who could show such familiarity with Stuart in this office.

"No, but I think we're going to be playing for a draw on this one. At least the Taiwanese legislature is screaming impeachment. Liang's probably hiding under his desk," Stuart said. "We can't afford any more mistakes. The talk shows are already going to have a field day with this and I'm sure the *Post* headline tomorrow morning is going to be all kinds of calm and restrained. And I'm about to order my secretary to tell anyone calling from the Hill that I'm in an undisclosed location. I might have to send you out to do the rounds," he told Showalter.

"I'd rather be shot."

"I'd rather shoot you than go on television myself to talk about this."

"And you call yourself a politician," Showalter scoffed.

"I am a *tired* politician. Seven years in this office feels like seventy outside. There's a reason all presidents go gray in here," Stuart said, and followed the admission with a sigh. "What's the next move?"

Showalter reached over the side of the couch to retrieve a map case and unrolled it onto the coffee table. As a soldier, he'd carried the case through two wars. As a civilian, he only pulled it out when he was ready to recommend that death and destruction become the official policies of the United States Government. Underneath the flimsy plastic cover was a large satellite photograph of the Taiwan Strait with map markings overlaid. Showalter pulled out a grease pencil and circled a small island. "Here's Kinmen. Six townships, population of seventy-five thousand. It's so close to the coast that for the PLA, putting troops on it was more like a river crossing than an amphibious attack. The Potomac is wider in places. The Taiwanese excavated some serious bunker and tunnel complexes in response to all the shelling during the Cold War, so the PLA would take high casualties clearing them out. Now that most of the shooting is over, they don't have to. They just have to keep the troops penned inside, and there won't be reinforcements coming from Taipei. Liang has to hold them back to defend against a larger possible incursion into the Strait."

"Can we liberate the island?" Stuart asked.

Showalter shook his head. "Horatio Nelson said 'a ship's a fool to fight a fort' and he was right. We'd have a tough time protecting battle groups in China's littoral waters, and sustaining air superiority that close to the mainland would be tougher. PLA supply lines would only be a few miles long, while ours would stretch more than a few thousand. Any planes we sent over Kinmen would be within range of SAMs on the mainland, so we'd have to use the B-2s to attack sites on Chinese soil. You order that and we'll have more to worry about than just liberating Kinmen."

"So Kinmen is a done deal," Stuart said.

"The PRC owns it now," Showalter said, nodding his head. "Taiwan will only get it back if Tian is feeling generous."

"Yeah, well, this isn't going to go further," Stuart said. "We're going to make sure of that."

"'This will not stand?'" Showalter offered.

"I may not be able to run the PLA off of Kinmen, but it's the last island I'm going to let them take without a fight," Stuart told him. He turned back to Cooke. "So what's Tian's next move? And don't tell me you don't know."

She reached into a lockbag and pulled out a three-page paper stapled at the corner. "One of our Red Cell analysts drafted this a few years ago. It's a model plan for how the PLA could take Taiwan with limited resources. Most analysts believe that China would want the invasion to go quickly to limit our ability to respond or for anyone to intervene diplomatically. This," she said, passing the Red Cell paper to the president and a second copy to Showalter, "posits a strategy where they hit fast, stop fast, and supposedly give Liang time to think things over. But what they're really doing is giving the PLA time to regroup and prepare for the next stage while confusing the diplomats as to China's real intention."

Stuart ground his teeth together. "That sounds familiar."

"Yes, it does," Cooke agreed. "And if Taiwan surrenders at any point, so much the better. Stage One calls for an assault on Kinmen. Stage Two is a push on the Penghu." The CIA director took Showalter's grease pencil and tapped another landmass in the Strait, this one more than halfway to Taiwan. "The Pescadores are a natural staging point for a full-on invasion of the main island. Sixty-four islands, but the largest one, Penghu, has air- and seaport facilities that would let the PLA resupply its biggest transports, and it's less than fifty miles off Taiwan."

"Why not increase the pressure by taking the Matsus or some of the other smaller islands closer to the mainland?" Stuart asked. "Easier to grab, fewer casualties."

"They're not in the direct path of an invasion like Kinmen. And if the PLA seizes control of Taiwan, Tian will get them all anyway," Showalter answered.

"And your people don't think Liang will back down?" Stuart asked Cooke.

"Nobody is optimistic," Cooke said. "He's too corrupt to care about the soldiers on Kinmen, and he's no strategic genius. If his party loses the election, he loses all protection from prosecution on corruption charges. He needs friends in power, so he was desperate enough to light this tinderbox in the first place. He wanted the Taiwan public focused on an external threat. They're focused now, but if Liang shows weakness and backs down, he loses everything. And Tian's right. Liang is almost certainly banking on you to stop the PLA and get Kinmen back for him."

"So where does this hit on the *Ma Kong* fit into this?" Stuart asked, waving the paper in the air.

"The Red Cell has a theory, but I'm not prepared to explain it in detail—" Cooke started.

"Then give me the short version," Stuart ordered.

"Yes, sir," Cooke said. She hated to share unproven theories, but an order was an order. "It was a weapons test."

Stuart stared at the CIA director, surprised. "What kind of weapon?"

"We don't know exactly, but something designed to kill an aircraft carrier." She spent less than a minute on the history of the Assassin's Mace project. "Basically, if this 'assassin's mace,' whatever it is, can take out a *Kidd*-class destroyer, then it might be able to take out a carrier."

Stuart rolled his eyes, dropped the paper on the table, and slumped back into his chair. "So the Chinese think they have a way to kill carriers. No wonder Tian was shoving it all in my face."

"We don—," Cooke started.

"'We don't know,' yes, yes," Stuart cut her off. He sucked in a deep breath in frustration. "Lance, could Taiwan defend the Pescadores without our help?" Stuart asked.

"No," Showalter said. The man's response was quick and final. Cooke raised an eyebrow. "But if you want, we can draw a line in the sand there. There's fifty miles of South China Sea between Penghu and the mainland coast. With Taiwan's support, we can make it feel like fifty thousand. *Lincoln* and *Washington* are both en route. *Lincoln* is sailing south, three days out of Yokosuka. *Washington* is one day east of Guam. We can back them up with the air wing at Kadena, and if you want to start hitting some ground targets, we can start flying the B-2s out of Kansas." He considered knowing the position of all twelve US carriers a basic function of his job.

"But we could lose a carrier to this . . . thing, whatever this thing might be," Stuart said. He sounded more tired than before.

"Harry, you could lose a carrier even if they don't have this thing," the SecDef said.

"Sir, if I may?" Cooke interrupted him.

"Yes?"

"In my job, I'm not supposed to recommend policy. I'm just supposed to give you the intelligence and the analysis. But I can tell you what the likely implications of any course of action might be. Sir, if you turn those carriers around, it will send a very loud message to every one of our allies on the Pacific Rim and a louder one to our enemies everywhere else. And I don't believe I have to spell out to you what that message is. But it will be final and irreversible, and the United States will never recover the influence we will lose. You'll change the world and not in a way you will like, sir." Cooke sat back and realized that her heart was pounding harder than she could ever remember.

"That was bold," Stuart said quietly.

"Yes, sir. I'll understand if you want me to—"

Stuart cut her off once again, this time with a wave of his hand. "I like bold. And it helps that I agree with you." He left the implied consequences of disagreeing with her unsaid. "Any ideas about what story I should feed the press about the carriers going in?"

"You could make a statement that the carriers are there to protect the right to free maritime passage through international waters during hostilities," Showalter offered.

"You wouldn't even be lying," Cooke said in agreement. She pointed at the map and traced a line. "Taiwan sits in the Luzon Strait connecting the Pacific with the South China Sea north of the Philippines. That is the major shipping lane linking Japan and the Koreas to Indonesia and the Indian Ocean. If Tian takes over and creates a Kinmen–Pescadores–Taiwan line under one flag, he could close off access to commercial shipping at will through both the Taiwan and Luzon Straits."

"I like it." The president of the United States smiled and nodded. "Lance, pull the plans off the shelf for defending the Pescadores. And send that Red Cell report to the carrier groups. If that's the PLA's playbook, I want them to know it back and front."

CIA DIRECTOR'S OFFICE

Barron had a whole pot of coffee waiting in Cooke's office this time when she came through the door. The CIA director downed two mugs of it to give herself some time to think and she drew a third before sitting down.

She opened the file and pulled out a research paper. "The Red Cell came up with this a few years ago. I just shared it with the president."

Barron took the paper and scanned the abstract. "That's not bad," he said. "If they're right, Penghu and the rest of the Pescadores are next on the menu." He dropped the paper on the table.

"The president liked it," Cooke said. "We need to get an idea of when the PLA could make a run on the Pescadores. What's the holdup with Pioneer?"

Barron sucked in a deep breath and Cooke felt her intuition scream. She said nothing. The NCS director needed the chance to break the news in his own way. "Chief of station says that Pioneer's been burned," he said, sotto voce. It was the worst thing he could have said at that moment and he knew it.

Cooke closed her eyes, covered her face with her hands, and gritted her teeth so hard she was afraid she was going to break her jaw. "What happened?" she asked slowly, her voice controlled.

"We don't know," Barron admitted.

"Do we know how long he's been under surveillance?" Cooke asked.

"No." Barron had done nothing, but felt incompetent all the same.

"I assume Mitchell has an exfiltration plan?" asked Cooke.

Barron confirmed the assumption with a nod. "We've had one in place for twenty years."

"Always risky," Cooke said. Exfiltrations were rare. Most foreign assets retired in place or left their homeland on their own. "How long before Mitchell can get him out?"

"Hard to say, given the increased security over there," Barron admitted. "I'd send a separate team to do the job if I could, but with Beijing in lockdown, it'll be tough to get more than a few people in on short notice without raising red flags. So it might just be grab-and-go."

"That's a devil of a thing to do to a man," Cooke said. It wasn't a criticism. "Ask him to walk out of his whole life on a moment's notice."

"Better than getting shot by the MSS on a moment's notice," Barron said.

Cooke sat back in her chair. "Anything else?"

"Yes," Barron said. "The Red Cell just put in a request to send a pair of analysts to China to debrief Pioneer."

Cooke nodded. "Burke and Stryker think they've got something developing on their Assassin's Mace theory."

"Normally, I wouldn't let a DI analyst within a hundred miles of an asset that sensitive, but if they're on to something with this Assassin's Mace idea, I might be inclined to give them some latitude. But even if we send them, there's no guarantee we can get them and Pioneer in the same room. Sending a pair of analysts might just be feeding the surveillance monster. I'm fine with sending Stryker, but Burke sounds too high-risk to me."

"He's done time in the field, so he's got some ops training," Cooke replied. "Firearms, Crash-and-Bang, the usual stuff we run analysts through before we sent them to the sandbox"—Iraq. "I'll get his file to you."

"Crash-and-bang isn't the same as training to operate in a hostile countersurveillance environment."

Cooke nodded. "True, but risk is the business," she said, finishing the argument. "Greenlight the Red Cell TDY to Beijing."

"They don't say two words to Pioneer without one of my people in the room," Barron said.

"Agreed," she assured him. "But I want Mitchell to give them full cooperation. None of those station chief king-of-the-hill games."

"Mitchell will love that," Barron said.

"He'd better learn," Cooke said. "If the Chinese are going after the Pescadores, I want Stuart to have plenty of warning this time. If the diplomats fail, the PLA won't just be rolling tanks for the next part. They'll be flying planes, and those move just a bit faster."

CIA INFORMATION OPERATIONS CENTER
WEST OF MCLEAN, VIRGINIA

The Information Operations Center was one of five CIA divisions set up to attack problems not bounded neatly by national borders. Drug trafficking, terrorism, nuclear proliferation, and counterintelligence each had earned their own units, but IOC had outgrown most of them in little more than a decade. The criminals engaged in the other offenses were not blind to technology's march, and the Internet had come to underpin their activities as much as money. IOC pursued them all, fueled by a budget that would have placed it easily in the Fortune 1000.

Kyra was surprised to see that Jonathan knew his way through the Analysis Group spaces. It was a cubicle farm like the one she had expected to see in the Red Cell, but the sheer number of workspaces was enormous. There were dozens, easily more than a hundred, all flanking a single aisle that ran more than a hundred yards from end to end. The vault took up the entire side of the building on this floor alone.

Farm *is too small,* she decided. *A cubicle plantation?*

"Twenty years ago, there was exactly one analyst working computer security issues," Jonathan muttered quietly to her.

"I guess somebody figured out that the Internet was changing the world."

"A rare case of the Agency staying on top of technology instead of playing catch-up," he agreed. Jonathan steered her by the arm to a private office at the end of a wall opposite the analyst pens and pushed the door open without bothering to knock.

"Jonathan!" Kyra heard the voice, basso, but her position kept her from seeing the man in the office. "Get in here and close the door before someone sees me consorting with the Red Cell."

"I apologize for what you're about to endure," Jonathan said quietly. He held out his arm in gentlemanly fashion to let Kyra pass.

Kyra stepped into an office large enough only for the desk, a file cabinet, and a shabby visitors' couch that looked far older than the room itself. The desk was overrun by no less than four computer monitors and Kyra counted at least five hardware towers on the floor, making the rat's nest of wiring underfoot entirely predictable. What space was left on the desktop was overtaken by papers and DVD jewel cases with assorted classification markings scribbled on them in permanent blue ink. The room's occupant was reasonably handsome, young, with two days' growth of blond beard on his face, but his threadbare military sweater was hardly the height of fashion. He smiled innocently, and Kyra got the impression that the man was utterly ignorant that his clothes were totally without style.

"Kyra, meet Garr Weaver," Jonathan said.

"One of the few here who will still speak to Jon. How did Mr. Burke here convince you to hook up with his outfit?" Weaver spoke with a light southern accent that seemed mixed with occasional New England inflections on the vowels. Weaver was either raised in the South and educated in the North, or the reverse. Kyra settled on the former, given that his southern accent was more prominent than the Boston cadence.

"He didn't—," Kyra started.

"A volunteer!" Weaver exclaimed, taking Kyra's answer and logically extending it to the wrong extreme. Weaver stood and offered his hand, which she shook before sitting on the couch. Up close she saw it was covered with the hair of a hundred visitors. She was appalled that she would have to attack her shirt and pants with a lint brush when she got home but tried not to show it.

"A directed assignment," Kyra said.

Weaver's eyebrows went up in mock surprise. "The seventh floor has instituted the draft again?"

"Don't mind the interrogation," Jonathan advised. "Garr is one of the Red Cell's emeritus members."

"I did a rotation there a few years ago when I got swept up by one of Cooke's press gangs. Jonathan and some heavy drinking made it tolerable," Weaver said. Kyra figured that the last part was a lie. "So what can I do you for?"

"A favor, I hope." Jonathan held out the CD. "This is a custom software program developed by a Chinese aerospace company, but we have no follow-up on it. I need you to take a look at it."

"Excellent. I love tearing foreign software apart." Weaver extracted the disk by the edges and placed it carefully in the tray sticking out of a

Macintosh tower under his desk. He pressed a button on a grubby key-board and the tray slid shut. "Anything you can tell me about the asset who handed this over?"

"No," Jonathan said.

"Ah. One of those," Weaver said. "Does the company have a name?"

"Xian Aircraft Design and Research Institute," Kyra said. "It might have also been filed under China Aviation Industry Corporation."

"Ah, the Chinese. The source of all cyberevil in the world, or so the Pentagon thinks," Weaver said. The disk finished loading and a single icon appeared on one of the monitors. Weaver called up a window displaying the file's statistics. "Not a very big file, a Linux binary, almost a hundred megabytes."

"The Chinese use Linux?" Jonathan asked.

"A variant called Red Flag Linux," Kyra said.

"You know Linux?" Weaver asked, surprised.

"Computers are a hobby," she admitted.

"A woman with some geek cred. Jonathan, you've been holding out on me," Weaver said. Then he turned serious. "About, oh, fifteen years ago, the Chinese government got worried that Microsoft might have put backdoors into Windows that would give us or NSA covert access to their systems. The source code to Linux is free, so the Chinese decided that it would be safer to own their own operating system for critical functions. So they created their own variant called Red Flag Linux. The logo is a marching penguin carrying a Chinese flag. I'm not kidding."

He double-clicked the icon. A Linux virtualization program launched, followed by the application. The program filled Weaver's monitor with a blank window divided into quadrants, all black, and a small toolbar of icons across the top under a menu of Mandarin characters. "It looks like a pretty standard CAD program, I think," Weaver observed. "Did you get any of their data files that we can load up?"

"No," Jonathan admitted. "Or if we did, the NCS wouldn't hand them over."

"Always a possibility with that lot," Weaver conceded. "I can build some test objects later to scope out the program functions. What I can tell you right now is that these"—Weaver pointed to a set of characters in the upper left quadrant—"are probably simple measurements fields: height, width, scale, and so on." He clicked his mouse several times and rendered a cube with each quadrant displaying the object from a different vantage point in two dimensions. The upper left window showed the cube in three. "Yeah," Weaver said. "Definitely units of measurement, all metric, probably—centimeters, meters, whatever. I'm not sure what this one is," he said, pointing at a label of unreadable characters. "This measurement field doesn't change when I change the object size. I'll call APLAA and see if they'll send me a translator to read the label. But if all else fails, I'll just reverse-engineer the algorithm behind that field."

"'Just,'" Jonathan mused. "How long?"

"If APLAA will help, a few hours, maybe. But that's unlikely," Weaver said with certainty. "We are a bit of a drive from headquarters out here. They won't be anxious to come this far out in the snow, even if the Agency does reimburse the mileage."

"They'll beg off," Jonathan agreed. "So without their help?"

"I'll have to tear the app apart. A week if I put in some long hours," Weaver replied.

"Any way you can speed that up?" Kyra asked.

Weaver turned slightly in his chair and considered the woman. Kyra wasn't sure she liked the look on his face. "I've been known to work a minor miracle with the proper incentive."

"And what incentive are you looking for?" Kyra asked.

"You and me. Lunch in the Agency dining room," Weaver said. He was perfectly serious.

"You're bold," Kyra answered. She kept her face neutral.

"Life gives nothing to the meek," Weaver told her.

Jonathan raised an eyebrow and looked at the young woman. Kyra didn't flinch, whether from case officer training or just personal experience with software engineers, Jonathan couldn't tell. "What text editor do you use? Vi or Emacs?" she asked.

"Emacs," Weaver said.

"Sorry, I'm a Vi girl. I don't go out with Emacs guys." Jonathan suspected that Kyra would have picked whichever option Weaver hadn't.

"I'll convert."

"I can't respect a coder who's willing to abandon his preferred text editor for a woman he just met. That's just bad form. Shows desperation." Kyra paused for just the right effect. "I'm embarrassed for you now."

"Hey, I'm not a Linux fanboy with bad hygiene," Weaver said. "I know how to show a girl a good time."

Kyra cocked her head and smiled, and Jonathan sensed Farm train-ing was coming into play. Weaver was out of his league. Dating any woman was an exercise in codebreaking for men under normal circum-stances. Chasing women trained in covert operations and espionage recruitment elevated the game to a new level, southern charm notwith-standing. "I'll make you a deal," she finally said. "You reverse-engineer that app and figure out what that number means for us in three days. Reconstruct it in C plus plus. If your interpretation of the algorithm is sufficiently elegant, I'll let you take me to the ADR."

"Objective-C would be prettier."

"And cheating if you use the Cocoa framework. You do that and you only get to take me to Starbucks. I like a man who can write his own root class from scratch," Kyra chided. Jonathan was completely lost in the jungle of jargon that the two were tossing around.

"Three days, eh?" Weaver scratched his stubble. "You're on. Jon, you'll have to excuse me. I have a deadline to meet."

"You realize that I didn't understand a word of that?" Jonathan asked the pair.

"Suffice it to say that your partner there will be enjoying a rack of lamb with me in the ADR a week from today."

"You're assuming that your code will be elegant enough to meet my standards," Kyra said. Jonathan couldn't tell whether she was teasing. "That's a subjective measure and totally out of your control."

"Let's just say that I have a high opinion of my coding skills," Weaver told her, smiling. "And I appreciate the challenge, no matter how this turns out."

"I doubt your team chief will appreciate us monopolizing your time," Jonathan said.

"Did you tell anyone here that you were coming?" Weaver asked.

"No," Jonathan said.

"The word will get out. It always does. If anyone asks, I'm working with you in the interest of damage control."

"Whatever makes you happy," Jonathan said. "Good to see you, Garr."

"Always my pleasure. I'll call when I have something."

"Good luck," Kyra said with a wry smile.

"Luck is for people who lack skill," Garr replied. He turned back to the monitor, and Kyra watched the cybersecurity analyst vanish in a moment into his own little world.

CIA OPERATIONS CENTER

"In a hurry?" Drescher asked. Kyra's manner was impatient.

"I'm on my way to the airport," she said. "Pictures of a hundred dead bodies?"

"Much better," Drescher said. He pressed a button and the Ops Center monitors blanked out the news channels and replaced them with single feed. "A few hundred Chinese tanks rolling for the coast. Pretty shot too. Low-orbit, great lighting, the overhead angle is almost straight down. Satellite imagery doesn't get prettier than this."

"Where are we looking?" Kyra asked.

"Nanjing, Guiyang Army Base," Drescher replied. He held out a map of the Chinese coast with symbols marked on the page. "Eleven infantry divisions, eight special forces regiments, two armored divisions, one artillery division, and a pair of reserve units," Drescher read off a paper prepared by his APLAA analyst. "Total manpower around three hundred thousand. No heat blooms in any navy ships along the coast, so all those tanks are just for show until they get their air bridge set up. That's where the real action is."

He handed over a set of photographs. "I don't think they're lining these up just to send us a message. Too many working bodies around the planes." Some of the dark specks marking the ground crews in the pictures were standing by spaghetti hoses of jet fuel lines snaking up to the planes. "There's activity at Shantou, Fuzhou, Zhongshan, Taihe, and Zeguo. But that's not what's interesting." Drescher pushed another set of photos into her hands, then turned and put his finger down on a map of China taped to the wall behind his desk. "All of that other activity is along the southeastern coast, but those were taken over Chengdu."

Kyra saw where his finger had landed on the map and her eyebrows went up. "You're on your way to India that far west."

"That's why it's interesting. Thought your partner might like to know."

"Has Taiwan responded?" Kyra asked.

"Nothing significant. Increased air patrols, but they're all staying inside Taiwanese airspace." Drescher rested a hand on the photo stack. "No heat blooms in Taiwanese Navy ships in port. Tian has got Liang shell-shocked. The PLA storms Kinmen, Taiwan tries to start moving, and the PLA knocks out one of their best ships while it's still in port.

Liang's probably too scared to make a move. He hasn't got a skirt to hide behind until *Lincoln* and *Washington* show up."

"Thanks," Kyra said.

"Talk to you on the other side," Drescher said with a slight bow.

UNITED FLIGHT 897

"At least we got business class. Economy would have killed me," Kyra said. Agency regulations allowed travelers to upgrade on flights over eight hours, which Kyra had hoped would give her a fighting chance to sleep.

"It won't help," Jonathan said. The woman sounded very satisfied with herself at getting approval for the trip, and had been from the moment she saw his surprise when they received the notice. He was still wondering why Cooke had approved the trip and quietly hoped that the chief of station at the other end wouldn't just out them to the Chinese on arrival. He imagined that Carl Mitchell would be less than enthusiastic about taking responsibility for a pair of analysts, given current events. "China is thirteen hours ahead of us. Your body clock will be jet-lagged no matter how much sleep you get. You'd do better to stay awake for a while."

"Pessimist," she accused him.

"Realist. There is a difference," Jonathan said. His eyes didn't shift from the copy of the *Economist* on his tray table. "Optimists make poor analysts," he said. "They aren't critical enough."

"That's just morose."

"Reading the PDB every day will do that to you," Jonathan said.

"The president does that, and he still smiles."

"A politician's job depends on smiling. Mine doesn't. It does depend on my being awake, even after fourteen hours on a plane. Yours too. So lay off the wine," he advised her. "You don't want to fight jet lag and a hangover at the same time." The plane had only been in the air for half an hour and Kyra was already working on her second glass. Dinner was still a few hours off, so she was drinking on an empty stomach, and he knew that case officers favored bars and pubs as places to meet assets for reasons that had nothing to do with security. CIA's clandestine service was still a boys' club that ran on a machismo that made an inability, or unwillingness, to imbibe alcohol a fatal weakness among one's peers. Mormons and Muslims got a pass, but the rest were expected to follow the unwritten rule, and Burke had no doubts that Stryker could match the men drink for drink.

"Why? The coffee is free," she deadpanned.

"So is the turbulence."

"Speaking from experience?" she asked.

"I don't drink," Jonathan said, his voice suddenly cold.

Alcoholics in the family tree? They weren't nearly close enough for her to ask that question, and Kyra knew when to turn a conversation. "Sounds like you've traveled your share for work," Kyra said. She didn't refer to the Agency by name. Even on a Boeing 777, business class was cramped quarters, and they had no idea who was a foreign national and who wasn't. The case officer had already picked out several of their fellow travelers as Chinese nationals and heard at least four other languages being spoken that she couldn't identify at the moment. One sounded vaguely Japanese, though Kyra couldn't really distinguish some of the Asian tongues from each other. Some of the other languages closer to his side of the aisle sounded like they came from Eastern Europe. She didn't know what anyone around her was talking about, but the conversations were animated enough that she assumed they were discussing the Kinmen invasion. Every passenger on the plane was flying into a country that was at war, and she couldn't imagine what else they might talk about under the circumstances, even if Jonathan seemed determined to avoid the subject.

"I've flown domestic plenty. London a few times, Rome once. I hiked the Okinawa battlefields. And I did a tour in the sandbox."

The sandbox, she thought. *Iraq.* "You see any action?"

Jonathan shrugged. "I was at Camp Doha before the war. Saddam sent some Scuds over during the buildup, but nothing close. Then I was in the Green Zone for a year. Zawahiri's boys sent some mortar rounds our way. There were some car bombs. Nothing too close." He shifted in the seat and stretched out his legs to work out the kinks. "So you going to tell me what happened down in Venezuela?"

Her head twisted in surprise and he saw pain flash across her eyes. "Cooke told you about that?"

"Only after I made a few deductions about why she brought you to the Red Cell."

Kyra frowned and looked around the darkened cabin. Most of the passengers were settling in to sleep or starting to watch movies. She reached down and rolled up the long shirt sleeve on her left arm. She still had a padded gauze bandage taped across her upper arm. She pulled it back and turned so the senior analyst could see the back of her arm but her body blocked the view of wandering eyes across the aisle.

Jonathan looked down at the wound. The girl had a lateral laceration running across her triceps. No question, she had lost some meat and the scar was going to be ugly. He tilted his head and studied the wound. "Seven-point-six-two-millimeter round?"

"Lucky guess," she said. Kyra replaced the bandage and pulled her sleeve down.

"It's a common caliber used by South American militaries," he said. "They were close."

"Yeah, they were," Kyra said. "You ever make it to Beijing?" she asked. *Please let it go.*

He paused, as though considering whether to grant her unspoken request. "No, unfortunately," he said finally. "It would be very useful if one of us had spent time on the ground there. I'm told it can be a difficult city to navigate."

"Not a problem," Kyra said.

"Optimist."

"If we can't find our way around a foreign city without a map, then we're working for the wrong agency," she said. It surprised her to finally see Jonathan smile.

CIA INFORMATION OPERATIONS CENTER

Weaver put the soda can a safe distance from the keyboard—he'd lost more than one electronic device to carbonated drinks—and turned his attention back to the monitor. It was dead quiet inside the vault except for the hum of the server fans mounted in the rack under his desk. He had the vault to himself and he preferred it that way. It was difficult enough to translate hexadecimal code into assembly language without the distractions of other analysts talking in the hallway.

Reverse-engineering a compiled computer program was the most difficult craft a programmer could master. Writing programs in the first place, even complex ones, was child's play by comparison. The programmer could use any one of dozens of languages to create one. Any of those languages made life easy for the coders by letting them use English words—called *source code*—instead of forcing them to use pure numbers, which was all that computers really understood. Those English commands were converted into those numbers by a compiler, a one-way translator between the two.

Reverse engineering was the craft of turning those raw numbers back into English commands with no source code to act as a guide. It was like trying to translate demotic Egyptian without benefit of a Rosetta Stone. Humans thought in the base-ten counting system, where the numbers ran 0-1-2-3-4-5-6-7-8-9 before adding a second digit to make 10. Computers thought in eight-bit binary—base two—where the sequence was 00000000-00000001-00000011, on to infinity. But it was easy to misread the streams of 0s and 1s while suffering a boredom that no Coke or coffee could cure. So Weaver used a decompiler to convert the binary numbers into hexadecimal—base sixteen. Weaver could at least think in hexadecimal, which counted 0-1-2-3-4-5-6-7-8-9-a-b-c-d-e-f. But from there, he had to look at the numbers and try to turn them back into source code that performed the same functions.

The private sector paid good money to the few who could reverse-engineer programs. It was a useful skill to any company looking to steal a competitor's software trade secrets, and Weaver had just the right amount of insanity for the craft. His skills should have brought more than double his government salary, and Microsoft and Google had both made generous offers, but Weaver's patriotic streak kept him tethered to government service. He supposed that he could have made a healthy living performing corporate espionage, but he could perform the same acts here without worrying about the law. If Weaver hadn't kept himself pumped full of caffeine—the true blood of programmers everywhere—he would have slept the sleep of the righteous.

The program that the Red Cell had brought him was straightforward. The Chinese coders who'd written it had been competent but uninspired. Programming was a craft where efficiency created a natural elegance, but the best algorithms ceased to be lines of code and became something beautiful, all pure in their efficiency and working together in a modular harmony. The lines of code that Weaver spent the night reconstructing weren't even close to that, which was both a blessing and a curse. It made them almost predictable to reverse into assembly code. It also made them boring, which was not helpful, given that it was well past midnight.

The algorithm Weaver extracted from the Chinese CAD program was longer than expected and more complicated than its size implied. MIT had required him to take an introductory course in differential equations, and he'd only gotten a middling grade, so it took him an hour to realize that the algorithm was one of those. He had borrowed a colleague's textbooks—Weaver had sold his own back to the college hours after the final exam—but they hadn't helped him one whit. It occurred to him that, given that the algorithm was integrated into a CAD program, texts on general mathematical theory weren't going to help him much. Geometry or mechanical engineering texts, or maybe physics, would be more relevant.

The other equations measured the simplest of physical properties—length, width, depth, area. This one stayed constant when the dimensional variables were kept proportional: changing an object's overall size did not change the equation's output, but changing its shape did. He was overlooking . . . what? Mass? Weaver ruled it out. That would have changed along with the area measurement. Tensile strength? Not possible without inputting the specific material the shape would be cut from, and Weaver couldn't see a way to enter that value into the program. He considered that it could be a parts number generator, assigning unique identifiers to each new part being designed so it could be located in some database. But the equation was too complex for that. Was it some other engineering function that he wasn't familiar with?

He finally asked an APLAA analyst to help him identify the related pictograph on the CAD program's interface. The APLAA analyst had wasted an hour searching out the Mandarin pictograph radicals of that label before realizing they weren't likely to be in a standard usage dictionary. She found them in a technical dictionary in short order—*hengjiemian*. The literal translation was . . . "cross-view"? That made no sense to Weaver. Yes, mechanical engineers used CAD programs to create cross-section technical drawings, but where was the connection to a mathematical formula that changed its product when the object's shape changed but not its size?

Still, even if he had the source code in hand, it was probable that he still wouldn't understand what the mathematical calculation was supposed to tell him. It was one thing to know that a piece of source code calculated $e=mc^2$. It was another to know that that particular formula explained why nothing could travel faster than the speed of light. This Chinese algorithm promised to be far more complex than Einstein's simple formula. But Weaver wasn't going to fail. Identifying the equation's purpose was now a point of professional pride. Lunch with Stryker was just going to be the capper. She was one of the few DI officers that he'd met of late who weren't either taken or socially useless introverts. Besides, the woman knew how to write code. That and the fact that she was easy on the eyes made her worth the effort.

Weaver rolled back from the desk and dropped the soda can in the garbage. It was late enough that the pitiful amount of caffeine in a cola wouldn't keep him awake. Time for the coffee mug.

CHAPTER 10

TUESDAY
DAY TEN

The airport was in the Chaoyang district, northeast of the city in a suburb no longer considered remote. The '08 Olympics had fixed that. If the government had spared any expense to ready the city for visitors that year, it had not been here. Beijing's largest airport left no question that the host country had become a deserving member of the first world. Terminal 2 was all painted girders and steel rising to a low hangar ceiling, well lit and devoid of any obvious Chinese influence. The size was impressive and the architecture was not, which was a disappointment to Kyra. Growing up in Charlottesville had given her an appreciation for the architectural influences of Mr. Jefferson. She wanted a country with such a unique heritage to make a unique first impression. The building was a justifiable source of pride for a nation whose citizens had starved to death by the millions under Mao, but Kyra hoped they weren't losing their own culture in bits and pieces in a bid to prove their national standing.

The views of Beijing seen from the taxi window as they traveled the Shoudou Jichang Airport Expressway southwest into the city did not change that impression. It was as modern a city as any she had visited, better than most, with construction that was threatening to crush out the buildings that still matched the Beijing that Kyra had pictured in her mind. Rental cars were not available to foreigners, so they had settled for a simple taxi. It was the most random option available, and random behavior was a counterintelligence officer's worst enemy and therefore Jonathan and Kyra's second-best defense. The first was to say nothing during the drive and do nothing openly illegal for the rest of their stay.

The expressway terminated in an exit onto the Dong Sanhuan Beilu Freeway near the northern embassy district, one of the four major roadways that circled the city center. From there, the driver took them on a tour of the small side streets that left Kyra grasping for a sense of direction. Despite her boast on the plane, she had spent a good chunk of the flight staring at maps and guidebooks that

she'd pilfered from the CIA Library's map office. The case officer—
she still couldn't think of herself as an analyst—had been trying to
memorize the major street names. She couldn't feel comfortable
entering a hostile territory without arming herself with a detailed
knowledge of the terrain, but she had finally given up on that dream.
The endless *dajies* and *zhonglus* labeling the streets had all run together within minutes, and so she had settled for a general overview
of Beijing's asphalt geography. The city center was an elongated box
with Tiananmen Square and the Forbidden City at its center and
Nanhai, Zhonghai, and Beihai Lakes to its immediate west. Most
of the major streets ran north-south and east-west. It was only the
smaller side streets that were laid out in haphazard fashion. Seen
from above, it made more sense to Kyra than Washington DC's design; she had cursed Pierre L'Enfant's name more than once and not
because he was French.

Despite being American-owned, she knew that the Holiday Inn
Crowne Plaza was not a safe harbor. The staff was almost entirely
Chinese and the security briefings detailing the MSS counterintelligence presence in Chinese hotels had been near-terrifying. They
were on enemy soil and the locals had all the advantages. There was
no guarantee that their rooms had been assigned at random. They
were assigned adjoining rooms, which seemed overly convenient.
Searching for surveillance equipment would be an obvious giveaway.
She had no doubt at all that her bag would be searched the first time
she stepped out.

Jonathan went straight for the television. The channel was irrelevant; he increased the volume until it was far louder than necessary.
"Under the circumstances, I would have preferred housing at the embassy."

"No room at the inn, I guess," Kyra answered. "State Department
will have a brigade of Foreign Service officers in country trying to talk
Tian down."

"I doubt the PLA is going to allow diplomats to stop them now,"
Jonathan said. "Our friends do know we're coming?" Cables from headquarters to field stations were not always read on schedule, regardless
of how they were marked.

"They should," Kyra hedged.

"Call the concierge and get another taxi to take us over in an hour."

"See you then," she told him, moving to the shared door that led to her room. "And clean up. You need the shower."

"Don't lie down," he warned. "I don't want to have to wake you up."

US EMBASSY
BEIJING, CHINA

"This is not a good time," Mitchell said. Stryker was a case officer, or had been, which nominally put her on Mitchell's side of the CIA divide. But she wasn't one of his officers and she was keeping company with a DI analyst. Those two facts alone made her suspect.

"When would be a good time?" Kyra asked, impatient.

"After the war."

"We can't wait that long," Jonathan informed him. He'd dealt with enough NCS officers to know that Mitchell might be serious.

"Beijing is not a safe operational environment at the moment."

"Is it ever?" Kyra asked.

"No," Mitchell conceded. "But the locals are on a bender. They're harassing everyone who leaves the embassy short of the ambassador. My case officers are getting manhandled in the street. It takes a major operation just to pass a message to any of our local assets, much less get a meeting with them. And now I get this"—the COS waved a headquarters cable in the air —"ordering me to get you in the same room with Pioneer, who you're not supposed to even know about. Kathy Cooke says you get to talk to him, fine, I know how to take orders. But I'd love to know how you found out about him."

"That's hardly relevant at the moment," Jonathan said.

"What is relevant is that I don't know if I can put you in the same room with him."

"Surveillance is that tight?" Kyra asked.

Mitchell dropped the headquarters cable on his desk and slumped back into his chair. "He's been burned," he admitted.

Kyra stared at the chief of station. The security measures in place to protect Pioneer had been in the file and they were impressive. Losing an asset through bad luck and random chance was bad enough, but it happened. Someone's career would die if the breach had come from operational error. "How?"

"We don't know," Mitchell admitted. "We pulled off a sign of life but that's the only direct contact we've managed for two weeks. We've lost a dead drop. I don't know if the MSS intercepted it or some third party just randomly picked it up. That could happen, but that's an awful lot of bad luck given everything else that's going on."

Jonathan frowned. "This started at the same time as the surveillance crackdown?"

"They started around the same time, yes. Whether they're connected, I don't know, and at the moment I don't particularly care. I'll leave that for you analysts to figure out. What I do care about is getting him out of the country without burning my officers. I've got headquarters screaming for intel that I can't provide, we've lost our best asset, and the MSS could wrap him up at any time. If they do, they'll put it on the front page of the *People's Daily* and our other assets will decide we can't protect them and they'll go dry. So, no offense, but I have bigger worries than arranging a meeting that could get Pioneer killed and you arrested. I'd be doing you a favor if I just turned down the request, orders or not."

"But you won't," Kyra said.

"Don't test me," Mitchell said. There was a difference between being bold and being brash, and Stryker was leaning toward the latter. "Getting Pioneer out is my priority, and once we start an exfiltration, I'm sure not going to put it on hold for a few hours so you can have a chat while the MSS is tearing Beijing apart to find him. If we can get him out of the country, you can talk to him then. Until then, I don't want to hear it. And you go over my head and I'll kick you out of the country. You understand me?"

Jonathan opened his mouth to answer, but Kyra cut him off. "Understood."

CHAPTER 11

WEDNESDAY
DAY ELEVEN

"This"—Stuart threw OPLAN 5077 onto his desk—"calls for nuclear weapons." He knew the plan had been revised a few years before and he wondered which general had thrown in that little provision.

Showalter closed his own copy. The operations plan laid out the logistics and mobilization schedule of all US military assets to be used in the defense of Taiwan. It was the product of more than thirty years of work by the Pentagon's best minds. No single president could match that level of collective experience, though several had been arrogant enough to think they could. "Only as a strategic option. Mr. President, you need to have the flexibility—"

"Unacceptable."

"Any OPLAN that doesn't at least have weapons of mass destruction as an option for this would put you in a weak position from the start. Mr. President, if the Chinese are unable to counter our carriers, they could choose to use a nuclear weapon—"

"Tian is not going to nuke our carriers and I'm not going to even consider nuking the mainland. I wouldn't order a nuclear strike even if the PLA was marching on Taipei, and I sure wouldn't order a *first* strike. Seventy years on and we're still catching grief over Hiroshima. So I am *not* going to nuke Beijing over that little Kinmen sandbar in the Strait."

"If I may, sir," the director of national intelligence cut in. Michael Rhead had been a deputy defense secretary when the plan was revised. "The OPLAN would be deficient if it didn't offer a full range of options, however unlikely some of them might be. Besides, the OPLAN has been a priority target of the Chinese intelligence services for years. If they've secured a copy, they'll think the option is still active—"

Stuart didn't miss the implication. "Do you have any intel to back that up?" Stuart demanded. "That they have an asset inside my administration?"

Cooke said nothing. It was Rhead's question to answer, but the odds that the Chinese had an asset inside the administration were so high that she considered the question to be almost nonsensical. "No, sir," Rhead answered. "But I'd be stunned if they didn't. If you look at the history, there hasn't been a time since 1947 that the intelligence community hasn't been penetrated by somebody. In any case, the director of the National Counterintelligence Executive would be in a better position to answer that question with hard proof."

"NCIX reports to you," Stuart observed.

"Yes, sir," Rhead said, "and they are working a number of Chinese espionage cases with the FBI—"

"None of which are inside the Pentagon," Stuart said.

"That was a hypothetical—"

"I'm not going to be paralyzed by hypotheticals," Stuart said. He put a hand on the OPLAN binder and pushed it back. He was tempted to scrounge a cigarette. He'd kicked that habit years ago rather than face cancer, but like all true addictions, the nicotine craving never truly went away. It helped his resolve that the White House was a US federal building, wherein smoking was illegal, the Oval Office included. "Kathy, do you have any assets in Beijing who can tell us whether the Chinese have a copy?"

"One," Cooke conceded. Technically it was still true. Pioneer was physically in Beijing, even if he could no longer pass information in a timely fashion.

"Who?" Stuart asked.

"A senior systems administrator inside the Ministry of State Security," she told him. "His code name is Pioneer."

"Have you tasked him specifically on that point?"

"Harry, this isn't a courtroom." Showalter usually avoided such informality, but he saw the prosecutor in the president coming out.

"It is if I want it to be," Stuart said. "Answer the question, Kathy."

"His standing requirements are to report any MSS acquisition of sensitive military information," Cooke said. "Getting a copy of the OPLAN would certainly qualify."

"And he hasn't flagged this"—Stuart lifted the OPLAN—"as showing up stolen." It wasn't a question. His line of reasoning had been carried to its logical conclusion, or at least as far as the lawyer in Stuart wanted it to go.

Cooke would have preferred that he had asked the logical next question, but she knew he would not, leaving her to give him the answer to it anyway. "That is true, sir. However, I regret to inform you that operational conditions on the ground in Beijing have left us unable to maintain secure communication with Pioneer. In fact, we have reason to believe that the MSS has identified him as a CIA asset and has him under direct surveillance. Given that, the director of the National Clandestine Service has determined that it's necessary to terminate Pioneer as a CIA asset and exfiltrate him as soon as possible."

Rhead jerked in his chair toward Cooke. "Who screwed up?"

"Sir?"

"How did the Chinese figure out that he was ours?" Rhead said, his voice rising.

"We don't know," Cooke said.

"When was he compromised?" Showalter asked.

"Again, we don't know," Cooke said. She despised not having the answers. "But recently, we believe." *We hope.*

"How long has he been in service?" Stuart asked.

"Since 1991," Cooke told him. She could have told them the exact date when Pioneer walked into the US embassy in Tokyo and offered himself up, but that was a level of detail the president didn't need.

"And we lost him on your watch," Rhead said.

"It's your watch too, Mike," Showalter said.

"We're not going to lose him," Cooke answered. "Yes, he'll no longer be in service as an asset, but we're going to get him out. He'll still be of use to us here. He knows more than he's—"

"You lost our best asset in Beijing and you just don't want to—," Rhead started.

"There's no time for that," Stuart said, cutting everyone off. "It's possible to do everything right and still lose the game. So put the knives away and save them for the PLA."

"Kathy, your people are sure about this?" Showalter asked.

"That's he's been compromised? He's sure and that's what matters."

"Hardly," Rhead said. "He's just an asset."

"He's as close to a professional intelligence officer as you can get in this business without having gone through the Farm," Cooke answered.

"You want to burn him, Mike?" Stuart asked.

"There are times when burning an asset is worth the gain," Rhead answered. "Stopping a war with the Chinese would be one of them if this man can feed us the details on the PLA's current operations."

"If he's really been compromised, he couldn't give us that," Cooke noted. "Best case, the Chinese would just roll him up. Worst case, they'd feed him misinformation and then we'd confirm he's one of ours by acting on it." She didn't have to mention that the best case would still be an epic disaster.

"We've got two carrier battle groups sitting less than two hundred miles from the Chinese coast," Rhead said. "We should get someone in the room with him, calm him down, send him back in to see what he can deliver for us. If we weren't sending carriers in to protect twenty million people, I'd say pull him out. But we're facing a war with our ability to maintain alliances in the Pacific for the next few decades on the line. Bad enough to lose our best asset in Beijing, but we stand to lose a lot more if we botch an exfiltration, which could be real easy to do if he's under surveillance. We should cut our losses."

"We owe this man—," Cooke said.

"We owe him nothing," Rhead cut her off. "Traitors don't work for charity. They have their own agendas and we paid this one. He got what he wanted."

"That's cold, Mike," Stuart observed.

"That's pragmatic, Harry," Rhead said, speaking informally to the president for the first time in Cooke's presence. "Kathy's people make deals with devils and I wouldn't put this country's long-term interests at risk for someone like that."

"He's a dead man if we abandon him," Cooke replied. "Done deal. He gets a bullet in the back of the head."

"If we try to save him, we're risking our long-term relationship with the Chinese," Rhead said.

"We're risking that right now anyway," Stuart said. The president leaned forward, put his hands together, and pressed them against his chin.

Stuart said nothing. Cooke held his gaze, refusing to look over at Rhead, whose stare she could feel on her skin. "The only way out is through, eh?"

"Mr. President—," Rhead started.

Stuart cut him off with his hand. "Kathy, proceed at your discretion, but if your people get caught, getting them out won't be your job. It'll be Aidan Dunne's. No ops to save them from jail. Mike has a point. Anyone who gets arrested will be spending a few years in jail. Understood?"

Cooke nodded slowly. "Yes, sir."

CIA DIRECTOR'S OFFICE

As a rule—and it was a rule that was given no exceptions—the Farm did not graduate case officers if there was any doubt about their skills. There was a wall in the Old Headquarters Building main entrance with one hundred two chiseled gray stars, each marking a dead CIA officer. Beneath them sat a black book under glass, bound in Moroccan goat-skin leather, the pages handmade of parchment paper, with the names of the deceased each handwritten in calligraphic style next to a gold star. The Book of Honor had only fifty-four names. Forty-eight dead officers remained anonymous, some more than fifty years after having made their final sacrifice for their agency and their country. They died not because their training hadn't been equal to the game. It was simply a fact that the game had rigid rules and, at times, no rules at all. Some-times luck just ran bad and sometimes no training was enough.

So the exercises at the Farm were constantly revised, trainees were graded by unforgiving instructors, and there was no curve given. Train-ees were either "satisfactory" or "unsatisfactory." Those who couldn't achieve the former rating received desk jobs. Those who did went to the field and ran operations. It was that simple.

Cooke stared at Kyra Stryker's file on the flat panel monitor. She had achieved the "satisfactory" rating in every Farm exercise with no excep-tions. The instructors' comments were devoid of negative criticism, and even the known curmudgeons on the Farm staff had found occasion to pay her random compliments. Stryker's memory was near-photographic and her surveillance detection ability was unusually sharp. The report on her escape-and-evasion exercises was fascinating despite the dry prose. Few students managed to stay free in the woods of the Virginia Tidewater for the several days they were hunted by their instructors, but Stryker had managed it. The spotters spent days searching the brush in lines while the dogs sniffed the swamp marshes. The woman had disappeared into the woods and that was the last anyone saw of her until the morning the exercise ended and she'd walked back out. She endured the kidnapping, the screams and taunts, and the humid sweatbox room during the simulated interrogation course well enough. Her qualification scores with the Glock 17 and the HK417 were excel-lent, and she'd done as well with the 40 mm grenade launcher as any woman her size could have.

They had tried every way to break her under stress and failed. One instructor's typed comment summarized Stryker more neatly than any other phrase Cooke could imagine:

"She's solid."

Stryker's career should have been textbook—several field tours, moving from less important and dangerous posts to hard-target countries, an occasional headquarters rotation, eventually a series of station chief posts, one or more in Europe or Asia, maybe working Beijing as a real assignment before being brought home for good. With luck and her tickets punched, she would have been tapped to join the NCS leadership team or maybe take a senior DNI post. Reaching the Senior Intelligence Service should have been an inevitability.

Cooke considered it an injustice, if so polite a term could be applied, that Stryker's career had imploded six months after her graduation from the Farm.

"Mitchell's exfil plan?" Barron was standing in the doorway to Cooke's office.

"Stryker's service record," Cooke corrected him.

"You thinking about giving her to Mitchell?"

"I'm considering it," Cooke said.

"That would be one fewer officer we'd have to get into the country," Barron admitted. "And Rhead would have a stroke. Win-win."

"Fine by me," Cooke agreed. "Stuart left the call to us, but he promised there wouldn't be any ops to save our people if anyone gets pinched."

"We don't have any Chinese agents in custody to bargain with anyway. I suppose we could always exhume Larry Wu-tai Chin. Or rearrest Wen Ho Lee," Barron said, a smile breaking across his weathered face.

"No leverage there," Cooke said, half-serious. "The Bureau couldn't convict him the first time."

"True," Barron said. He pulled the guest chair away from the desk and let his body fall into it. The man appeared tired and Cooke couldn't fault him for it.

She turned the monitor off, drained the last bit of cooling black sludge from her mug, then stared at it. "What makes a person turn on their country?"

"Is that a rhetorical question?"

"If we're going to expose Stryker and Mitchell to that kind of risk, I'd like to think we were doing it for someone who was worth it," Cooke said.

"It's bad tradecraft to spend too much time asking traitors why they're doing what they do," Barron said. "You ask them that and the ones that are angels might reconsider. The ones who are devils will just lie, which is usually preferable to hearing the truth. Quite frankly, I don't want to know the private secrets of dirty people, strange as that sounds. Better to take them as they come. Judge them by their reliability and credibility, not their integrity."

"That doesn't make it easier to risk good people for bad."

"Our people are breaking Chinese law every time they set foot on the street," Barron pointed out. "It's just a matter of degree what they'll have to do to get Pioneer out. But I do know how you feel."

"Do you?" Cooke asked. It was a genuine question, not a try at sarcasm.

"Yeah." Barron sucked on his teeth. "Three of the stars on the Memorial Wall were mine. The first one died in Baghdad. Charlie Lyman. He was on his way to meet with an informer when a roadside bomb took out his Humvee. We had to pick him and his Iraqi translator up with shovels. The second was Tim Pratt. An Afghani drug courier shot him in the head while he was doing counternarcotics work outside Ghazni. It took us two days to find his body. The birds led us to him." He stopped speaking.

"And number three?"

Barron sighed and lowered his head a bit. "Emmanuela Giordano. We called her Emma. She bought it in a car wreck in Moscow. Stupid buggers had her under close surveillance, and the moron driving the lead car actually managed to hit her in the rear quarter. She wasn't even trying to lose them. The idiot just panicked in bad traffic and spun her out on the freeway. The car rolled three times and a truck didn't stop quick enough. Hit her broadside on the driver's side door."

"Anyone else with her?"

"Me. Four broken ribs and a concussion. I have just enough hair to hide the scar."

Cooke smiled. "Glad you made it."

"Me too," Barron said. "Emma was dead on the scene. I spent six months in recovery and got sent to Beijing for my next tour. The next year, Pioneer made contact and I set him up as an asset. So I can tell you that he's as close to one of the angels as we find in this business."

"Good reasons for turning traitor?" Cooke asked.

"One reason, and it's a good one," Barron said.

"I thought you didn't ask the reasons."

"I didn't ask. He volunteered it," Barron said. "If I never did anything else here, getting him set up made everything else worth it. I'd sure like to see him again."

Cooke finally set the mug onto the desk. "Do you think Stryker can handle the mission?"

Barron sat back and stared down for a moment. "Hard to say. She passed the Farm. She's not a seasoned officer and Beijing is a tough place to do the work. But she survived Venezuela. Some of that was dumb luck. A lot wasn't. She trusted her instincts."

"Well, that's the real issue, isn't it?" Cooke asked.

"It counts for a lot," Barron admitted. "So what'r'ya gonna do?"

"Trust my instincts, I suppose."

"Your call." Barron stood up to leave for his office. "Either way, we'll get it done. No excuses."

CHAPTER 12

THURSDAY
DAY TWELVE

Kyra had hoped that a walk on the streets would offer the distraction she had needed so much for weeks, but the reality was disappointing. If not for the signs in Mandarin, the neighborhood surrounding the US embassy could have passed for a great number of cities that she had seen. The architecture was all avant-garde, even daring, and certainly impressive to her untrained eye. The city had become a laboratory for architects, and the modern constructions were devouring the sections that still matched Kyra's notion of what a Chinese city should be. But her first impression of the city she saw from the taxicab had been right. The Chinese were making their home a modern place at a cost that the case officer found depressing.

Mitchell had warned her and Burke about leaving safe ground, ordered them against it really, but Jonathan had buried himself in papers and research and Kyra had had enough of that. Her mind was screaming to do something besides sit at another desk and stare at another monitor. She could have that life anywhere, and Kyra had joined the Agency hoping for something better. Now she was standing in one of the great countries—illegally, she admitted—that all case officers hoped to see in their lifetime. It was the new field where case officers could test their skills against an enemy that was respected, skilled, and persistent. It was the kind of assignment that Kyra had hoped to earn, would probably never have now, and so she was determined that she hadn't traveled so far to see nothing but the inside of the embassy compound. Throwing her out of the country was the worst penalty Mitchell could lay on her and she'd been through that once. So Kyra checked her rear pocket for her passport and Chinese yuan and slipped out through the south gate past the Marine guard onto An Jia Lou Road. The embassies of South Korea and India sat across the street and the embassies of Israel and Malaysia just beyond with their own guards standing watch over the darkened street. Kyra worked her way south until she passed the Israeli embassy and diplomatic housing complex to the south and the loose pedestrian crowd began to change from Westerners and South Asians to Chinese natives.

Following the map in her mind, she turned southeast when she reached the Liangmaqiao Road and began a long walk. The developed neighborhood of the foreign consulates gave way to a series of half-finished construction projects and then finally to the more traditional Chinese districts that she'd hoped to see. Checking her watch, Kyra decided that she had traveled over two miles; her feet were already hurting. Her sneakers were not designed for long walks. She would have some blisters. She ignored the sore spots and kept up her pace and fixed her eyes on the skyline. The Forbidden City lit up the cityscape in the distance. She doubted that she could make the trip on foot tonight.

The first blow caught her square between her shoulder blades and knocked her into the brick wall to her right. Kyra got her hands up to protect her face before she made contact but still hit hard enough to scrape her palms on the rough stone. Stunned, she turned her head and saw a Chinese man, well dressed in a British-cut suit, average build, just a little taller than herself. He looked at her, stoic, no expression on his face, but he was clearly focused on her. He stood still as the crowd flowed around him.

Kyra twisted her neck in a circle to straighten out the kink that the body check had given her, then stared straight at the man as a strange emotion settled over her. The tear along her arm throbbed as her heart started to pound. She thought for a moment that she should have been furious, but she felt detached . . . almost unfeeling.

You want to play? she thought.

Kyra turned away from the man and began to walk again. She turned her head briefly to check for the tail. He was barely an arm's length behind her. She approached the cross street, then stopped and braced herself. It was a good guess. The man walked into her hard enough that she would have sprawled onto the street had she not prepared herself for the hit. This time she didn't bother to look back.

Something cold rose up inside her chest and her thoughts went blank. The light changed and she began to cross with the small mob. The man behind bumped her again as she approached the opposite sidewalk, a subtle move intended to make it look as though she had tripped trying to step up on the curb. She was agile enough to clear the rise, but the feeling inside her grew stronger and she lost all desire to suppress it.

An alleyway cut into the wall on her right fifteen feet ahead. Kyra quickened her pace just a bit, and a brief glance confirmed that she had managed to put a few pedestrians between her and the man be-hind. She approached the alley, then made a quick turn and ran into the dark space.

Alpha saw the woman break to the right and sprint into the alley. He pushed a pair of random lovers out of his path and rushed forward to the dark hole between the buildings. He stared into the dark and re-alized he could see nothing beyond, but there was no light at the end of the alley to suggest another exit. The woman had to be somewhere in front of him, but the streetlamps behind him destroyed his night vision and he wouldn't recover it until he stepped into the darkness. He took the step and moved into the black space.

The metal rebar caught him flat on the nose and shattered his upper lateral cartilage into pieces. Blood gushed out in an instant into his mouth and throat and he gagged. The pain tore through his head and he couldn't think. All he managed was the reflex to move his hands to his face to cover the wound.

The blow sent a vibration through the rebar that rebounded through her arm, and Kyra felt a burst of pain try to erupt from her gutted tri-ceps. The Vicodin let her ignore it. Kyra swung for his kneecap next. Her aim was off in the dark and she missed the patella on the first try. The second try connected squarely, dropping Alpha to the concrete and forcing a cry from him despite the blood in his throat leaking from the gusher in the middle of his face.

Kyra was yelling and crying now, had lost all self-control and knew it, but she couldn't stop herself. The trained part of her mind watched with detachment as she went wild, unable to regain herself. She didn't understand that she was cursing, and that part of her mind that was quietly observing the scene caught bits of English and Spanish screams directed at the pathetic, crippled figure on the ground curled into the fetal position.

She didn't know how long it went on. It felt like minutes, certainly, but the beating could only have lasted for a few seconds. Then the rebar slipped from her fingers and fell to the concrete with several loud clangs as the ends took turns hitting the ground faster and faster until it came to rest. She didn't know why she stopped, but Kyra wasn't a killer. She stared down at the silhouette for a brief moment, then turned and ran.

She paused at the curtain of light dividing the street from the darkened alley. Her heart was pounding hard and she couldn't control her breathing. No pedestrians had stopped. The traffic had been loud enough to drown out the noises from the alleyway.

Kyra turned back toward the embassy district and began to run.

THE WHITE HOUSE

"That's it, Mr. President." Barron closed the book and set it on the table. There were five printed copies of Mitchell's plan to exfiltrate Pioneer in existence and they were all in the Oval Office. Stuart, Rhead, Showalter, Cooke, and Barron had copies, all received in that order. Barron would collect them all once the meeting was over, carry them back to Langley in a lockbag, and shred them personally. He found himself hoping that the DNI would demand to keep a copy so he could tell Rhead off in front of the president. Barron despised Michael Rhead for several excellent reasons, but the most important one was sure to come out in the next five minutes. He'd been waiting for this particular fight.

Stuart didn't close his own leather binder. "It seems too simple."

Barron nodded. "The more complicated they are, the more likely they are to fail. Simplicity leaves room for flexibility when things don't go as planned. Besides, with the MSS putting the lockdown on everyone over there, our resources are limited."

"'Captains talk strategy, generals talk logistics,' eh?" Stuart asked.

"It's the literal truth in this case," Cooke said. She set her own book on the table next to Barron's.

"Who's going to perform the retrieval?" Rhead said. The DNI had been remarkably uncritical of the plan. He seemed almost at peace with Cooke's decision to proceed with the operation.

Barron watched as Cooke took a breath. "They've got blanket coverage on most of the long-term residents that pass through the embassies there, not just our people. It's—"

"Who?" Rhead repeated.

Cooke looked Rhead straight in the face. "Kyra Stryker," she said.

Rhead slammed his binder shut and beat the leather book on the coffee table so hard that Cooke feared for its structural integrity. "Are you out of your mind?" the DNI yelled. The Secret Service officer standing by the door shifted his stance automatically in response to the sudden display of aggression.

"Mike!" Stuart shouted at the man. The DNI looked at the president, unapologetic for his show of temper. "There's only one person who gets to yell at people in this office and you aren't him. Care to explain yourself?" It was not really a question.

"Kyra Stryker is a case officer I ordered Director Cooke to fire a month ago for incompetence and insubordination. And you"—Rhead leveled a finger at Cooke—"disobeyed that order."

"And I'd do it again."

"You're fired!" Rhead snapped. "I want your resig—"

"Put a lid on it, Mike! I decide who gets fired in here," Stuart practically yelled at the man. "Kathy, what's the story on Stryker?"

"Stryker is an excellent case officer, Mr. President," Cooke started. "She graduated from the Farm last spring with the second-highest score on record. Her first assignment was to Caracas—"

"She botched a clandestine meeting with an asset and almost got herself arrested," Rhead cut her off. "And you sent her right back into the field, against my orders, to exfiltrate an asset in a city that's even more hostile! You're as incompetent as Stryker!"

Stuart silenced Rhead with a look. "Kathy, I'm assuming there's another side to this story?"

"There is, sir. The meeting in Caracas did go wrong, that's true, but it was a meeting that Stryker had argued against."

Barron nodded. "There were clear signs that the asset was a double agent working for the Venezuelans. We determined that he couldn't have had access to the intelligence he was providing us even though it was checking out. So we decided to terminate the relationship rather than risk our people." He stopped suddenly, clenched his jaw, and fought the urge to launch out of his seat. Surprised, Cooke saw that he had balled his hands into fists. She'd never seen him so tense. When he finally spoke, he was fighting to keep his demeanor professional. "But the chief of station refused our assessment and ordered the original case officer to maintain the relationship. He refused, so the COS took him off the case and assigned Stryker. He threatened to terminate her assignment if she didn't go. Even so, she went under protest. She made it to the site and figured in two seconds that the meet was an ambush. There were at least a dozen SEBIN commandos hiding around the bridge. Stryker outran them on foot but she took a bullet in the arm for her trouble. She got to a safe house and had to perform first aid on herself with some hemostatic gauze and morphine and almost overdosed. We evaced her to the States and she's spent the last two months on medical leave."

"Your chief of station sounds incompetent," Stuart said.

"He's not our chief of station, strictly speaking, sir," Barron said. "He's not a CIA officer."

"Who are we talking about here?" Stuart asked.

"I think Director Rhead should answer that question," Cooke said. Heads turned in the DNI's direction.

Cooke sat back and Barron suppressed a smile. Rhead looked like he was suppressing the urge to strangle the CIA director only because the Secret Service officer would have beaten him if he had tried. "Sam Rigdon."

"Rigdon . . . ," Stuart said. "Why do I know that name?"

Barron turned to Rhead. "Are you going to tell him, or am I?"

Rhead gritted his teeth. "Because, Mr. President," he said, "he was your ambassador to Kenya during your first term. And he donated money to your reelection campaign."

It took almost ten seconds for the implication to register, and then Stuart ran his hands down his face, pale white. "You gave a chief of station slot to a campaign donor?"

"Six months before you nominated me to take over CIA," Cooke told him. "The acting director at the time had no political leverage to stop the appointment."

"Rigdon was a CIA analyst for five years before he went to the private sector—," Rhead started to argue.

"Analysts read reports and give bad PowerPoint briefings," Stuart said. "They don't run ops! What were you thinking?"

"I was thinking that you had a major contributor with some qualifications who was more interested in playing spy again than in being a diplomat to some rat-hole country that nobody cares about!" Rhead shot back. "We give ambassadorships to donors! Chiefs of stations are just the intel equivalent, they answer to me, and there's no law that says they have to be CIA bodies."

"Unbelievable," Stuart muttered. "Talk about politicizing intelligence."

"Is he still in Caracas?" Showalter asked.

"Yes," Cooke said. Barron had done his duty and it was time to get him out of the direct line of fire. "Director Rhead disagreed with our after-action report and refused to let us remove Rigdon. Instead, he decided that Stryker was at fault and ordered her fired."

"Don't talk about me like I'm not here!" Rhead snapped.

"Shut up!" Stuart ordered. "I've heard enough from you."

"Harry—," Rhead started.

"*Shut up!*" Stuart yelled. Rhead slumped back and closed his mouth. "Get Rigdon out of there right now, Mike. Do it or I'll have State revoke his passport and he can stay in Caracas. Kathy, put somebody in who can do the job. And I don't care if we have to give Rigdon his money back; once he lands in Miami, shut him up. I don't even want to think what the *Post* headline would read. And don't get me started on what could happen on the Hill if this gets out. Mike, are there any more Rigdons out there? Don't talk, just nod." Rhead shook his head. "Good. Kathy, can Stryker get the job done in Beijing?"

"Yes, sir, we believe she can," Cooke said. "Nothing's guaranteed, but we believe that for this assignment, she'll do as well as anyone else that we could put on it."

"When will you pull Pioneer out?" Stuart asked.

"We haven't asked Stryker to take the mission yet," Cooke said. "We need your approval for the operation first."

"You trust her?" Stuart asked.

"Absolutely, sir," Cooke said.

"Then it's your hide. Tell her godspeed."

"I will, sir."

"And Mike?" the president said, turning to his director of national intelligence.

"Yes, Mr. President?" The DNI sounded hesitant.

"You will *not* pull a Valerie Plame on that girl. If I see Stryker's name in the *Post*, so help me, I'll turn the attorney general loose on you. You understand me?"

"Yes, Mr. President." Resignation this time. Cooke watched the DNI's shoulders slump down.

BEIJING

Kyra had not wanted Mitchell to be an impressive man. Quite the opposite, she had wanted him to be very much the one kind of station chief she already knew, arrogant and unruly. It would have saved her from the guilt of staying silent about beating a Chinese intelligence officer near to death, and that emotion was hollowing her out. Mitchell clearly was competent and he seemed like a decent man, which almost certainly meant he would send her, and probably Jonathan, to the airport the minute she confessed. But the right thing and the proper thing weren't the same at the moment.

Mitchell was past his prime, in his midfifties by her guess. His time as a field officer was nearly finished, and clearly it had not been wasted. His office walls weren't covered with trophies like some station chiefs', with ceremonial weapons or gifts from foreign intelligence services. Mitchell's office was far more spare. In fact, he had allowed himself only one significant career decoration, but it told enough of his story to make Kyra feel small. Under the glass covering his cherry desktop was a framed array of some fifty challenge coins collected from military divisions and brigades, foreign and domestic, mingled with a few from foreign intelligence services. It was a modest tribute to a covert career that entitled the man to far more hubris than he had shown her. Mitchell had led the life she wanted for herself. Now denied, she wanted to hate him for it but had no good reason to disrespect the man.

Mitchell interrupted her thoughts as he turned around in his chair and pulled printout from the laser printer that sat behind his desk. "Read this," he ordered. Kyra took the cable.

```
ACTION REQUIRED: EXFILTRATE PIONEER

1. D/CIA DIRECTS COS TO EXFILTRATE PIONEER.

2. GIVEN EXTRAORDINARILY HOSTILE CONDITIONS
ON THE GROUND, COS IS AUTHORIZED TO REDI-
RECT ALL AVAILABLE RESOURCES AS NECESSARY.
D/CIA REGRETS THAT LOCAL SECURITY LOCKDOWN
PRECLUDES SENDING SIGNIFICANT ASSETS IN
SHORT ORDER TO ASSIST. IF REQUIRED, COS IS
DIRECTED TO MAKE USE OF OFFICER STRYKER IN
ANY CAPACITY NECESSARY IF SHE IS WILLING.
STRYKER IS QUALIFIED AND HAS FULL CONFIDENCE
OF D/CIA AND D/NCS. PERSONNEL FILE ATTACHED
FOR COS REVIEW.
```

3. ANY OFFICERS DETAINED DURING THIS OPERA-
TION BY LOCAL SECURITY SHOULD NOT EXPECT IM-
MEDIATE RELEASE.

Stryker has . . . full confidence of D/CIA, and D/NCS. She read the
phrase again, struggling and failing to say something meaningful.

Mitchell gave her another few moments of silence before he finally
spoke. "Are you in?"

"I wasn't expecting this," Kyra said.

"Nobody was," Mitchell said. "If you don't want to take part, no one
will hold it against you. You're not familiar with the ground here and it's
hostile territory. But Cooke wouldn't ask if Pioneer wasn't worth it."

Kyra nodded. She reread the second paragraph, then nodded her
head. "I'm in."

"You sure?" Mitchell asked. "You understand paragraph three there?
Anyone who gets arrested is going to do serious jail time here, maybe a
life sentence. Pioneer is that big."

She tried to weigh the idea of having Mitchell's life against a long
stretch in Chinese prison but found that she couldn't think. Her logic
and her emotions were taking her in different directions. She closed
her eyes and tried to shut out the world but it didn't help. Finally she
cleared her mind and said what felt right. "I understand," she replied.
"What's the plan?"

"We have a plan, but conditions out there are forcing us to revise it.
The MSS and the other locals have been smothering us. It's all been
deterrence surveillance on long-term residents, so my people have a
high probability of getting burned if they try—"

"But I'm disposable," Kyra said, interrupting.

Mitchell fell silent for a moment before answering. "I don't use that
word. You're trained, you're anonymous to the MSS, and you don't have
to worry about your long-term cover here. I went over your file. You
would've wiped the floor with me at the Farm twenty-five years ago.
So you're not disposable. You're valuable. Unless you think you can't
handle it."

Can I? Two hours ago, before beating a man into the ground with
a piece of rebar, she wouldn't have had a doubt. Now she didn't know.
Kyra said nothing.

Mitchell shrugged. "Just speaking truth." He reached back into
the safe and pulled out a black binder. "Here's the exfil plan. Go over

it. We're going to make some changes in the next few hours, but you need to know what's in here if you're going to help us with that. We'll be meeting in the conference room to go over everything at nineteen thirty."

Kyra nodded. "What about Jon?"

"Burke? He doesn't need to know—," Mitchell started.

"Yes, he does," she said, more vehement than she'd intended.

Mitchell frowned. "He's had some training, crash-and-bang, fire-arms, but nothing like he'd need to help with this."

"I didn't ask for his help," Kyra said. "But he's read into everything, the same as me. There's no reason to cut him out."

"He's an—"

"'He's an analyst' isn't good enough. Not this time."

Mitchell cocked his head, surprised. "What's this guy to you?"

"Burke can be a jackass, but he's my partner on this one. You want my help, you tell him what's going on."

Mitchell stared at the woman and let out a long, exasperated breath. "Fine."

TIANANMEN SQUARE
BEIJING, CHINA

The protest was large and loud, but organized in typical Chinese fashion. The protesters carried signs written in a mix of Chinese and English. The grammar for the latter was surprisingly good. Jonathan picked out the CNN camera crew, which was circling the finest-looking female reporter he'd seen in some time. He and Kyra stood at a safe distance and dead center in the reporter's line of sight, though not close enough to draw her attention. The spot kept them behind the cameras and lights illuminating the darkened square. There was no question that the MSS was watching the feed.

A BBC reporter stood to the east taping a segment, her back to the crowd. Kyra loved a British accent, but she couldn't hear the words over the chanting locals. Officers of the People's Armed Police stood around the edges of the square glaring at foreigners but doing nothing to stem the steady flow of natives to the crowd. The protesters were bundled up against the cold and exhaled hundreds of little clouds of freezing breaths as they yelled and chanted. In the center, one man was preaching against the treacherous Taiwanese through a megaphone, and Kyra wondered whether it was also government-issued. She couldn't imagine that the man kept one handy in a closet at home just in case a mass protest erupted—not in this country. Maybe in the US, but not in the People's Republic of China.

Kyra tried to estimate the size of the crowd but couldn't settle on a number with any degree of confidence and gave up the exercise. Tiananmen Square was the largest open space in Beijing but she didn't know the actual dimensions, which could have simplified what should have been a simple mathematical problem. The Forbidden City consumed the view across Dongchang'an Jie Street to the north with its massive wall, enclosing a palace almost a kilometer square. The Tiananmen Gate of Heavenly Peace crossed the palace's perimeter moat to the Taihemen Gate of Supreme Harmony, through which visitors could visit the Imperial Gardens, the Qianqinggong or Palace of Heavenly Purity, and the dozens of other buildings housed inside the complex. The Great Hall of the People stood to the west and Mao's mausoleum to the south.

It was a clear night and cold, which would make it trivial for one of NRO's satellites, or even the commercial birds for that matter, to get some clear overhead shots. Calculating the crowd's size using a high-resolution bird's-eye photograph would yield a number far more accurate than anything she could guess at, even if she had known the dimensions.

"Fifty thousand at least," Jonathan said, reading the young woman's mind.

"You've seen protests this large before?"

"A couple of times in the Middle East, usually whenever the Israelis moved on the West Bank. This is all theater. I doubt the masses even know what their signs say."

Kyra stared at the placards and realized in an instant that more than a few were written not in good English but in perfect English. The grammar was too good to believe the signs had been written by the commoners carrying them, and she wondered which government propaganda department was responsible for cranking out protest signs in foreign languages.

"I've seen a few in Washington, on the Downtown Mall," Kyra said. "A couple of inaugurations and the Fourth of July fireworks."

"You wouldn't remember it, but the one here back in eighty-nine got real bloody." He was lost in thought for the moment and was talking as much to himself as to her. "Deng Xiopeng called out the tanks. The whole city went into lockdown and there were some pretty serious riots in the streets—Molotov cocktails, burning troop transports, the works. The PLA gunned down a few hundred students, maybe as many as a thousand, and they jailed at least that many over the next decade. They never made the final body count public, if they ever bothered to total one up. The party tried to erase the whole event from the history books and they've been real skittish about letting anything like it start up again."

"One of our people should write this one up," she suggested.

"Don't bother," Jonathan said. "Leave the cable writing on this kind of thing to State. Nothing here is worth classifying, and the press is watching, so the Open Source Center will get a report to the analysts. Save your energy for more complicated problems."

He turned and started walking away from the protest. He said nothing for almost a minute. She smelled street food but could not find a vendor within sight.

"They want me to help with the exfil," she said quietly.

"I know. I saw the cable," Jonathan said. That surprised her. She wondered how he'd managed that feat. There was no way that Mitchell would have shared it. "It's a very bad idea."

"You're an expert on covert ops now?" Kyra asked.

"No, but I'm not totally ignorant on the subject. You don't know the city and you don't speak the language. You don't have diplomatic cover and I'm not sure the Chinese would respect it if they caught you." He stopped himself and Kyra stared up at him, surprised. He never looked at her, just stared straight ahead. He finally started again. "The chances of you getting nabbed and spending a few decades in a Beijing prison seem very high to me."

"It's a possibility." She was hedging, but it was as close as she wanted to come to admitting he was right.

He looked down at her, surprised. "Then why do it?"

Kyra gritted her teeth, closed her eyes, and turned away from him as she stopped walking. He said nothing.

"I went for a walk," she said.

"Outside the embassy?"

"Yes."

"That wasn't smart," Jonathan said.

"No, it wasn't. I was followed. Beat up, actually," she admitted.

Jonathan paused before answering. "And you gave as good as you got."

I really wish you'd stop reading me like that. Kyra nodded. "Better than I got, actually. I took a piece of rebar to his nose and his knees. It was like I was watching someone else do it." She finally turned around and looked up at Jonathan.

"Nobody tried to stop you? Did anyone follow you back to the embassy?"

"No, and I don't know. I wasn't exactly working a surveillance detection route," she admitted.

"Then he was the only one following you. If he'd had partners, they'd have nailed you."

Kyra nodded. She felt numb. "I feel like I'm crippled," Kyra said. "Or busted."

"It's called post-traumatic stress disorder. You should talk to one of the counselors at the Employee Assistance Program," he said. "It helps."

"You had PTSD, didn't you?"

"Once, after Iraq. I was one of the analysts that George Tenet sent over to find all those weapons of mass destruction. I was working inside the Green Zone when some insurgents set up one of those hit-and-run mortar attacks. A round hit near my position." He frowned faintly at some memory that he decided not to share. "It doesn't mean that you can't do your job," Jonathan assured her. "It does mean that you should think long and hard before you sign on for Mitchell's op."

"We need to get Pioneer out." She winced as she realized that she had spoken the crypt in public. She looked around. No one was in earshot.

"I'm sure Mitchell appreciates your devotion to duty," he said.

Kyra wanted to swear at the man but she held her tongue. Analysts, it seemed, could use logic to read people as well as case officers could for all their training.

They crossed the street and left the official bounds of the square. The noise of the crowd was slowly fading behind them. "I know that Kathy Cooke asked you. Just because the request came from higher up doesn't make it any smarter," Jonathan told her.

"What is it with you two?" Kyra asked, exasperated.

Jonathan frowned. "What are you talking about?"

"Oh please," Kyra exclaimed. "She could've hid me anywhere in the Agency, but she gave me to you and walked down to do it in person. And CIA directors don't give briefings to line analysts or invite them to hang out and watch Chinese presidents give speeches. She's done both and it wasn't my company she was after. You two know each other and it isn't just professional."

Jonathan turned his head a bit and looked over at her but said nothing. "I can keep a secret. I work for the CIA," Kyra said. It felt good to finally have Jonathan on the defensive.

"Those two don't go together as often as you might think." He sighed and shoved his hands deep in his pockets. "Kathy wasn't playing in that game at the War College when we met. She was deputy director of PACOM's J-2 intel shop and she was running the game. So she wasn't thrilled when this civilian decided to work around some of the rules he thought were less than realistic. We ended up talking naval tactics over dinner. She asked me out, if you can believe it. She retired from the Navy after that tour, came back to DC, and started a wargaming think tank. Offered me a job, which I declined, but we picked up where we'd left off on the personal side. Then Lance Showalter became the SecDef. Kathy worked under him at PACOM, and suddenly she's on the president's short list for CIA director. She got the nod and that was that."

"She shut you down?" Kyra asked.

"'Bad practice to date subordinates,' she said. And some of the good old boys like Rhead have been looking to run her out, which makes me a liability she can't afford."

"She won't be running the Agency forever," Kyra observed.

"George Tenet had the job for seven years, and Kathy Cooke is better than Tenet ever was," he replied. "And people change." He fell silent for a half block and didn't speak again until they reached a corner. "But she's not here on the ground. Mitchell doesn't want to lose a major asset on his watch, and you don't know what he's telling her. And I doubt that you're being objective."

"I have reasons," Kyra protested. It sounded weak to her. It must have sounded worse to the analyst.

"You don't have anything to prove," he said. "Don't do this for your career. Don't do it unless you really believe in it."

Kyra stopped walking. "We owe this man. You've read his reports."

"I have."

"He's taken more chances for us than we can count. Twenty-five years and they could have found him and executed him a dozen times. That kind of pressure can break a person, you know? He's probably so paranoid that he doesn't know what it's like to feel normal anymore. What does that say about us if we use someone like that and throw them away because we're not willing to take a risk?" she asked.

"Smart risks, fine," he replied. "I'm not sure I'd call this a smart risk."

"We play the hand we're given," she told him. "If he's willing to gamble with his life every day for us, we have to be willing to do the same for him at least once. If we don't, we're no better than the Russians or the Chinese or anyone else who throws assets away when they're done with them. And we are better than that. This isn't about logic and odds and doing the smart thing. This is about paying a debt. It's about doing the honorable thing."

Jonathan just looked sideways at her. There was no arguing with emotion and particularly not this patriotic kind. But his own thoughts were jumbled up, he couldn't straighten them out, and it disturbed him. "Just don't let the honorable thing earn you a star on the wall," he finally said.

CIA DIRECTOR'S OFFICE

The green phone rang and Cooke lifted the receiver. "Cooke."

"Barron. I just got the call. Stryker accepted escort duty for Pioneer."

Cooke nodded despite being alone in the office. She looked up at the clock. "When?"

"They hit the street tomorrow at dusk," Barron said. "She'll have a ninety-minute window to get him to the meeting site. Their flight out leaves at twenty-one hundred local time, so they'll have a few hours to hunker down."

"The MSS will be all over the airport by then," Cooke said.

"No help for it," Barron said. "But, yeah, trust me, I'd love to have the Navy send in a sub and use a SEAL team to extract him by sea."

"The Navy wouldn't cut one loose for us. It's a bad time to have a war," Cooke said.

"The Chinese forgot to call us first," Barron admitted. "Awfully inconsiderate."

"I thought so," Cooke agreed, smiling for the first time in days.

"I'll call as soon as we know something."

"I'll be here," Cooke said. She hung the green phone back on its cradle and stared out into the early dawn rising across the George Washington National Forest.

CHAPTER 13

FRIDAY
DAY THIRTEEN

Beijing's air under the streetlamps looked like the fall morning fog that rolled off the James River bend at Scottsville where Kyra grew up. Her bedroom had given her an open view of the river valley, which was usually covered by mist formed by the supersaturated air hiding the trees along the shorelines. She had always cursed the pervasive humidity in Virginia, which never died except during winter, but this urban fog was a deep, dull gray. It disgusted her to see the monochrome color so clearly in the headlights of hundreds of cars, and the smell made her want to retch her dinner onto the sidewalk. She could feel the particulates seeping into her lungs, and the urge to hold her breath was overwhelming. She assumed that her body could learn to ignore the odor, but she imagined that, given time, the air would paint her lungs with a black coat of toxin and guarantee cancer or worse.

Kyra hoped that she would get a few minutes in the safe house to wash the city air off her skin, but her discomfort was a minor issue. Her immediate concern was the fog's effect on surveillance. For her, it would make detecting surveillance a more complex chore than usual. Her forward visibility was less than fifty feet; people faded into hazy shapes beyond that range, but that worked both ways. MSS teams would have to ride her closer than they might otherwise prefer. They would likely give her some distance, but in the gaseous soup the instinct would be to close the distance to keep her in sight. It seemed counterintuitive, but the plan said that her best countermove was to help them do exactly that. It made her nervous but she trusted the plan. The variables were eliminated or controlled in ruthless fashion as far as Mitchell could manage, but the odds still were not in her favor. *Don't think about the odds,* he'd said. *Follow the plan, choose your moments, remember your training.*

Of course, Mitchell didn't know that Kyra had nearly beaten an MSS officer to death in an alleyway the night before. That man was surely in a hospital. If he had identified her and the MSS picked her out tonight as the woman responsible, they would probably be looking for payback. Then again, they were keeping their distance tonight.

Maybe finding one of their officers crippled had made them think twice about their tactic of playing rough. The change introduced a new level of uncertainty.

Maybe I shouldn't have done this, she thought. Jonathan was right. She really hadn't been thinking straight. No help for it now. The MSS had fallen back. That worked in her favor for the moment, and all she could do now was follow the plan.

Her first task was to let the MSS keep her in sight. They were working hard at that, and it was now an advantage that Kyra was taller than the average Chinese woman and had far lighter hair. Her second task was to make them believe she was unskilled and a desperate choice on Mitchell's part. Too tall, too blond, badly dressed for a covert operation—an American woman with a bright red backpack had no chance of mixing with the pedestrian crowd here no matter what she tried.

That she was even trying was a false assumption.

She fumbled to put on a baseball cap, then pulled off her coat and reversed it far too slowly after turning the corner, to make a few other clumsy changes to her appearance. All were awkward. Amateurs could have done as well. Kyra was no amateur.

Her third task was to let them see the red backpack. The bag could not have been more visible had it been the blaze orange color she'd worn those times when her father had dragged her into the woods hunting Virginia white-tailed deer. Here it would create a constant point of reference for anyone following her at a longer distance, even through the fog. No matter what else she did to change her gross profile, the surveillance team could always look for the red backpack. In the polluted air, with visibility low and the crowds heavy, it would draw their focus.

Then she would perform an act of magic.

Every magic trick has three parts. Kyra had already delivered the "pledge" to her hostile audience. She had offered them an ordinary American woman walking for twelve blocks. Kyra memorized the route before stepping out—so many blocks in one direction, then turn, so many blocks in the next direction. A few landmarks had kept her on the track. With those in sight, Kyra maintained the appearance of a disinterested expatriate wandering the Beijing *dajies* and *dongdajies*. She did nothing unusual, and the resulting boredom would set up the gallery to focus on the "turn," when she would give them something interesting to watch. The MSS would have to wait a few minutes for the "prestige," the act of misdirection that would complete the trick.

They wouldn't appreciate the artistry when they finally realized that a trick had taken place. This act would be subtle. It would not be a performance meant to impress.

Pioneer lived in a studio flat on the tenth floor of an aging tower. The building was a cylinder, twice as tall as the Watergate and topped by a roof that extended past the exterior walls. Lit apartment patios lined up in neat columns and drew muted vertical concrete stripes in the haze.

The building was less than a block ahead now and Kyra could sense the surveillance team behind her. She wondered if these particular foot soldiers knew about Pioneer. Given the extent of Pioneer's treason against the state, Mitchell considered it likely that the MSS would have compartmentalized his case. The Ministry of State Security was not small, and anyone low enough in the organization to be stuck following random Americans on the street likely wouldn't know about him, and therefore where he lived. It was a gamble, but an unavoidable one. Depending on the efficiency of their internal communications, she would likely have a few minutes before the Sixth Bureau pieced anything together. If they were like CIA's bureaucracy, she could have days. Another gamble—the enemy's response time was unpredictable.

Kyra entered the building.

The cramped lobby was not well lit and the dark paint and carpet soaked up most of the available light. The elevator was ahead to the left, out of the line of sight of anyone at the front door. Unless the surveillance team wanted to enter the building to maintain pursuit, they would have to fan out to cover all the exits. There were two others, one a fire exit to the east, the other a cargo entrance in the building rear. Spreading the team out would actually help her. Her magic act would work best if played out for a small audience, the smaller the better. A single witness could be more easily confused than several who might each notice different details and piece together the truth more quickly. If only one man saw the trick, he would call out to his team, out of sight at the other exits, and they would have to take his word for what he saw.

Kyra called for the elevator. Then she closed her eyes and listened. Turning back to look around the corner and watch the door would have been obvious, but sound carried through the lobby just fine. The elevator took more than a minute to reach the lobby floor, and the building's main entrance door didn't open during that time. Either she was alone, the best possibility of all, or the surveillance team was splitting apart to surround the building. They might have been calling for additional assets, but even so it would likely take them longer to arrive than she planned to give them.

Kyra stepped into the elevator car and wondered where the hidden cameras were.

The view of the Forbidden City was one of the few amenities worth the rent Pioneer had paid for more than twenty years. Looking south he could see the Qianqinggong, the Palace of Heavenly Purity, rising above the northern wall. Beyond it farther to the south was Tiananmen Square. He couldn't see the square from his bedroom but he knew it was there.

The MSS knew what he was. There was no question about that. They had not dragged him away to be shot only because they wanted to expose the larger network of which he was a part. He had signaled the CIA and only after did it occur to him that it might have been exactly the wrong play. CIA now knew he was exposed, and there would be no more covert meetings. They might not come for him. Pioneer would live out his last days working for the party until the MSS decided that there was nothing else to be gained from watching him, and then they would come for him some night, take him away, and shoot him in a grubby basement. He didn't know how many more days he had, but the length of his life would be set by some MSS officer's patience.

There had been a disturbance in the apartment above his the night before, heavy knocking on the floorboards. Perhaps the MSS had taken over the apartment. They could have installed fiber-optic cameras in the ceiling when he had gone for dinner. His first impulse was to search for them, but he had concluded that it was futile. If the MSS wanted to watch him, they would watch him and he couldn't stop it. They could enter his home anytime he left within moments of his departure. Any person he passed in the hallway could be the MSS officer who would soon put the pistol to his head. Any apartment in the building could be an MSS watch post. The same held true for any apartment in any building he could see from his own home. He'd felt alone for years, but now his home was filled with a sense of murderous hostility.

Despite that, he felt a strange calm. He wondered if the unknown

God was with him, whispering peace to his soul. Somehow he couldn't bring himself to believe it. Could God love a traitor? Perhaps, he supposed. A loving God surely could not love the party, so perhaps God could love one who fought them. Perhaps there was some reward waiting for him after death instead of the oblivion that the party promised. Either was a more tempting path than what he was living now. Suicide had occurred to him, but Pioneer felt that would be a surrender to the enemy. He had fought the party for more than half his life and he could not give that up so easily. No, if he was going to die today, they would have to kill him. He would not do their job for them. If he couldn't hurt them any other way, they would at least pay for the cheap bullet they would use on the back of his head.

Someone knocked on his door. Pioneer turned and didn't rise from the table. The knock came again after a half minute.

They had come. The MSS officer in charge, whoever he was, wasn't a patient man after all.

Pioneer pushed his half-eaten plate of lamb roast across the table, wiped his mouth, and stood. He walked to the entryway, gripped the knob until his knuckles cracked, and opened the door to look his short future in the face so he could spit on it.

"Jian-Min!"

The blond woman leapt at him. Only the smile on her face kept him from backing away in a panic, and he found his arms full of an American girl he did not know. She jabbered at him in Chinese with an accent poor enough that he questioned whether she understood her own words or was just repeating memorized phrases like a good foreign actress.

Pioneer had never seen her before, so there was no question the MSS wouldn't be able to figure out their relationship. Almost certainly that would put them on alert. If she was CIA, here to exfiltrate him from China, they wouldn't have much time.

"I missed you so much. It's been so long!" she said in her poor Mandarin. In fact, her intonation sounded robotic, like she didn't understand what she was saying.

"Yes, it has." It was best to keep his answers short and simple. If this woman didn't speak Chinese, she wouldn't be able to form answers to complex statements. Her replies would be nonsensical if he even asked her a simple question, and that would almost certainly bring the MSS running.

"I'm so happy you are free tonight. I promised you dinner at the Yueming Lou if you would show me the Forbidden City, remember?"

Pioneer stepped back. *Yueming Lou.* He had almost forgotten, but in the instant she said it, the memory came back with force.

Yueming Lou, he thought.

The Yueming Lou was a three-story restaurant in the Xicheng district converted from a church by the owners and popular with the Western tourists. The food was good, not excellent, traditional Hunan, and the prices were reasonable. He enjoyed it more for the third-story terrace views of the northern Beijing lakes and the *hutong,* the ancient narrow alleyways that had once spiderwebbed across Beijing before the party rebuilt the city after the Revolution. Pioneer had dined there many times, at least yearly, under orders that his case officer gave him starting in the third year of his treason. The request surprised him initially. Once he had earned the trust of his case officers, in the fifth year of his labor, they made their reasoning clear. Not every asset earned the promise of exfiltration to the United States. Many didn't really want it. Abandoning home was not an easy matter even for traitors and especially for those motivated by ideology and not money. Among those who did want the promise, relatively few proved themselves worth the risks involved. Pioneer had.

Clark Barron—Pioneer had not known him by that name—was the case officer who made the promise. When Pioneer had asked him about the details of the plan, Barron had refused to answer. It was better if he didn't know the details. What he did need was the signal that the plan was in motion. When the moment came, Barron explained, the case officer would give him a code phrase. "Whatever you're doing," Barron said, "drop it. Walk away. We'll give you some warning if we can so you can pack some things, one bag at most. But when you hear that phrase, you leave with the contact right then. Whatever the contact tells you to do, follow their orders and they'll get you out." What Barron didn't say, but what he had implied, was that hearing the code phrase meant that after he left China, he would not be coming back.

The code phrase was *dinner at the Yueming Lou.* The woman was here to keep Barron's promise.

Pioneer stepped back and for a moment Kyra wondered whether his nerve was going to break.

The man looked at her. His face became a serene mask, but she had seen the brief emotion on it. The look on his face at that moment was a pure expression of his true feelings before it hardened to control his surprise.

For the first time in her life, Kyra had seen pure, unrelieved bitterness. It was hatred so intense she couldn't understand what could cause it.

Then he looked at her again and she knew that she was not the target. *They* were the target of his anger, whoever *they* were, the ones who had driven him to choose this life. They had led him to this moment when he had to abandon his homeland or die. Kyra Stryker had no idea exactly who they were, but in that moment she hated them as much as Pioneer did, and then she understood.

She looked back at him. *They'll have to kill me to stop me from getting you out*, she thought. Kyra hoped that he understood.

Pioneer eyed the young woman. She was still smiling, but it was a facade. There was a hard look in her eyes that sent him a very different message and, in the instant he saw it, he trusted her. She couldn't speak Mandarin, which perplexed him for a second. Why did they send someone without that skill? Something was wrong. But this girl had come for him anyway, and that meant she was a bold one. He hoped it would be enough. His options were limited at the moment.

"I remember. Let me get my coat. It's very cold outside," he said in his native tongue. He saw that she tensed up as he started speaking. She clearly didn't understand a word he'd said, but she relaxed when he turned away, walked to the closet, and retrieved a thick jacket. Then he indulged in a moment to look around home. It had never been a beautiful place, but it had been his shelter. The dishes were undone, food was still on the table. His books were lined up neatly on the shelf by a small television where he spent most of his nights watching party-approved foreign movies. The bed was unmade and his dirty clothing would now sit in the basket until the MSS took it away, searched it, and then burned it. His desk was neat at least. It was a writing desk built by his father for his mother from light brown Chinese elm with a matching chair. It was one of the few gifts that his parents had been able to leave him. He'd committed much of his treason sitting at that desk as he typed out reports on his laptop for the CIA. There was not much here that he could live without, but the desk he would miss. He prayed that rather than destroy it, some MSS officer might appreciate

the craftsmanship and take it for his own. He thought for a moment that it might have been better to burn it, but in truth he wanted it to survive even if he couldn't be there to own it. He'd known for years that he wouldn't be able to take the desk to the United States were he ever exfiltrated. It was far too large and he'd known there wouldn't be enough time to pack it up and ship it out of the country.

The CIA had not confirmed that they would be getting him out, so he had packed nothing. He did have a few photographs of his parents in a small envelope; he slipped them into his pocket. His parents were dead. It was the first moment that he was grateful for the party's one-child policy. He had no siblings, so there was no one else to leave behind. No wife, no children, no lover, not even a pet. He'd only allowed himself a few friends at work, who would wonder tomorrow morning where he was. The party would almost certainly never tell them the truth about his disappearance. Perhaps the MSS would feed them a lie about his being killed in an automobile accident. He hoped they wouldn't stage one and kill someone to provide a plausible foundation for the story.

He put on his coat and took his last look around his home. *Thank you,* he thought. He had suddenly become a sentimental fool, but this once he could not bring himself to care. A man who couldn't be sentimental at such a moment didn't deserve to live.

He looked at the young American woman and smiled. *"I'm ready. Lead on,"* he said. He motioned with his hands so she would understand.

Kyra took him by the hand and led him out the door. He turned, locked it, and they walked down the hallway toward the stairwell.

The stairway shaft leading to the first floor was filthy beyond anything Kyra had ever seen. She refused to touch the handrail and prayed that she wouldn't fall, more out of fear of touching some organism that she'd never be able to clean off than for physical safety. She was unsure that the builders had ever painted the walls, much less repainted them over the years. Years of grime covered the steps, and the smell rising from below was ugly enough to be nauseating.

Kyra held Pioneer's hand as they took the stairs by twos as fast as she thought was safe. They'd covered less than half the distance to the ground floor when she heard a noise from above. Several pairs of feet struck the metal stairs. She took a short moment to judge their direction of travel by the volume and decided they were descending the steps at least by threes. Kyra grabbed Pioneer by the arm and led him down the next flight to the sixth-floor exit. She tested the knob, found it unlocked, and no one was standing on the other side. Kyra pulled her charge through the door and closed it as quietly as she had opened it. She scanned the hallway and looked around the corner for any alcove deep enough for them to hide. There were none. The choice was to remain in place or run around the curved hallway to the opposite stair-well. Kyra judged the distance and decided they could not get out of sight before the men on the stairs would reach their level. She pushed Pioneer against the wall next to the door hinge so the opening door would give him some cover. She stood on the opposite side and set her balance for a strike to the face of anyone who came through.

The feet on the stairs reached their level. The men on the other side did not test the door. They continued down and Kyra counted to thirty before cracking the door. Without it closed and impeding her hearing, she took another moment to judge their distance and direction. The men were nearing the bottom and still moving.

She had focused on sounds in the stairwell too much. The MSS officer came around the corner, his feet silent on the worn carpet, and he caught Kyra across the face with a stiff forearm, pinning her against the wall. Pioneer grabbed for the man's head. The attacker kicked backward into Pioneer's stomach and knocked him to the ground with a hard grunt. It was a moment's distraction that he couldn't afford, and Kyra made him pay for it.

She kicked her own foot back against the MSS agent's knee, and the man's joint bent in the wrong direction almost to the point of breaking. He cried out and staggered back, unable to keep his weight against the woman to pin her to the wall. Kyra threw a hard elbow, caught him square on the nose, and she felt the crunch against her arm. The adrenaline killed the pain from the unhealed wound in her triceps; she felt nothing but the hard hit of the man's face against her elbow. Her attacker fell back further, his hands over his face to hold back the blood that started to flow from his damaged nose. Kyra drove her foot into his stomach, but the officer was too close to the wall and Kyra's kick compressed his solar plexus enough to drive the wind and vomit out of him. He started to double over. Kyra pivoted, stepped forward to close the distance, grabbed his hair, and pushed down as she drove her knee against his face. The bones she had cracked before shattered this time. The strike knocked him backward against the wall. Kyra finished him with a forearm across his throat. The officer fell to the floor, curled into the fetal position, unable to make a noise other than a rasping gurgle as he tried to suck in air and tasted his own blood for his trouble.

Kyra led Pioneer around the bending hall to another stairwell. She had planned to cross over to the building's other side at some point, but Mitchell had left it to her discretion when to make the move. They entered the second shaft, as filthy as the first, and she listened. There were shouts from far above and below, but Kyra started down anyway.

She surprised her charge by leaving the stairwell again on the third floor. Pioneer watched as the woman reached into her pocket and pulled out a disposable cell phone. It had only two numbers preprogrammed. She speed-dialed the first as they ran. Eight doors down on the left, a door opened and Pioneer heard a telephone ringing inside. Kyra pushed him in.

The apartment was decorated in modern Chinese fashion with only a few nods to traditional furniture. The television was on with the volume unduly loud, the blinds were drawn, and the lights dimmed. A Chinese woman stood behind the door and closed it behind them.

"You're Kyra?" she said.

"I am. You speak English?" Kyra said.

"Duke University, class of 2003. The package is on the counter by the stove." Kyra nodded and made for the tiny galley kitchen.

The woman turned to Pioneer. She was Kyra's age as best he could judge. She was young, lithe, taller than the average Chinese woman by several centimeters, with blond hair, which shocked him. He had seen her on occasion in the building lobby, but never often enough to warrant his close attention and always with black hair. Now, with light hair and casual Western clothing, he realized that she was not pure Chinese. He inspected her face closely and saw that her Chinese features were softened by some Western traits. "*You are Long Jian-Min,*" she said. Her Mandarin was flawless.

"*I am.*"

"*I have waited a long time to meet you, but I had hoped that it would be some other way,*" the woman said. "*My name is Rebecca Zhou.*"

"*You are American?*" Pioneer asked.

The woman nodded. *"My grandparents fled to the United States during the Revolution when they were very young."*

Pioneer stared at her. *"How long have you lived here?"*

The young CIA officer smiled at him. *"Six years."*

"Six years? CIA officers have lived in my building for six years?" He was astonished.

"CIA officers have lived in your building for almost as long as you have been working for us. You are a very valuable man. We are the fourth team to hold this post. Our job was to watch you, report back on your condition, and assist in your evacuation if it became necessary," Rebecca said.

"Then you knew that the MSS was watching?" he asked.

Rebecca shook her head. *"Not until you signaled. The MSS has been far more subtle than we ever expected, so we didn't know until you discovered it yourself. But they have overreached, trying to use you to find a larger network of assets that doesn't exist. We changed some of our tradecraft just for you. They didn't realize this, and so they waited too long to arrest you."*

Kyra emerged from the kitchen with an open box. She dropped the red backpack, shed her coat, and began to pull off layers of clothing. Pioneer wondered for a moment just how much clothing she intended to remove.

Rebecca reached into the box and pulled out a bundle of clothing. *"Please put this on, and hurry."*

Pioneer looked at Kyra, who had removed all but the base layer of her clothing. Rebecca took Kyra's outer-layer shirt and pulled it over her head. Both women were wearing casual blue jeans cut slightly large to facilitate quick movement. Standing next to Rebecca, he saw that her appearance was similar to Kyra's from moments ago. Not similar, he realized. Identical, as much as two unrelated women could appear. *"And where is my twin?"* he asked.

"My husband, Roland, is in the bedroom, waiting for your clothing," the young woman answered.

Pioneer removed his coat, shirt, shoes, and pants and handed them over. Rebecca took them and disappeared into the darkness in the rear of the apartment. He donned the clothing the woman had provided for him. The fit was perfect. *How did they know?* he thought. He supposed that over the years, at least one of the people who met with him had had a trained eye for clothing sizes. Or had they been in his apartment as well? He doubted they would ever tell him.

Kyra pulled out another package from the box, this one zipped inside a black nylon case. She gestured for Pioneer to come with her and led him into the light of the kitchen.

The disguise package was descended from the "Silver Bullet" technologies developed by the Agency's Directorate of Science and Technology in the 1970s to help case officers penetrate KGB surveillance in Moscow. Kyra had never seen the original disguises. They were older than she was, but the pieces she applied to his face and body were realistic enough to make her stomach turn. The sight of blood had never fazed her, but holding body parts realistic enough to pass close inspection was another matter. They took thirty seconds to apply. She stepped back, inspected him, nodded, and led him back to the entryway. He looked around for a mirror but could not find one.

Rebecca was waiting with another man who was dressed as Pioneer was when he had entered the apartment.

"Are we ready?" Roland said in English.

"Ready," Kyra said.

Rebecca reached down and hefted the red backpack. It was full of books, newspapers, pencils, and other items common to any Western exchange student. There was nothing to incriminate the carrier. The color was the only feature that made the pack important. *"You have the keys to your car?"* Rebecca said.

Pioneer nodded. It took him a moment to understand that she was asking for them. He handed them over. He was about to tell her where to find the car when it occurred to him that she surely knew.

Roland turned to Pioneer and spoke in his own perfect Mandarin. He also appeared Chinese, but Pioneer inspected his face and saw that he looked more like a Beijing native than his wife. *"I regret I didn't get to know you better. Perhaps we'll get to talk in the United States one day soon."*

"I hope so," Pioneer said. *"You have my gratitude. But you could be arrested. Why would you do that for me?"*

Roland grinned. *"The director says that risk is our business. It's what we do. And you have earned it."*

"Thank you." The words felt insufficient.

"Thank us after you're out of China," Roland said. Pioneer nodded and smiled. Roland turned to Kyra and switched back to English. "We leave first. Give us ten minutes to draw surveillance. You'll get a call, one ring only, if they figure things out before time is up. If that happens, you run. Which stairwell did you come down?"

"The west," Kyra said.

"Anyone pass you?" Roland asked.

Kyra nodded. "We had to switch over on six."

"We'll take the central elevator down. They'll think that's as far as you went when you left the stairwell. Take the east stairwell. Turn left when you get outside, one block, and then cut through the park. That'll send you north. The taxi will be waiting on the far side," Roland said. "The driver is one of ours. We'll buy you as much time as we can."

"Done deal. You're on the clock," Kyra said.

"See you in the States," Roland assured her. "Ready for dinner and a movie, hon?"

"Six years. You have no idea how ready I am," his wife answered. She put the red backpack over her shoulder, then turned back to Pioneer. She leaned in close and put a hand behind his head. She whispered something in Mandarin that Kyra could not understand.

"You were never alone."

Rebecca smiled at the man and took his hand as his facade finally cracked and he began to sob. His body shook and he covered his face, trying to hide the sudden shame he felt at crying before women. His knees felt weak. He feared that he would fall to the floor when Rebecca put a hand to his shoulder and pulled him close, saying nothing, until he could compose himself. Though he had controlled his emotions for decades, it still took a full minute.

She stepped away, took Roland's hand, and the husband-and-wife team walked out into the hallway. Kyra closed the door and marked the time on her watch. It was going to be a very long ten minutes.

The deadline came and the phone never rang. Kyra took Pioneer by the hand and they ran anyway.

MARRIOTT HOTEL, ROOM 745
3C CHONG WEN MEN WAI STREET
CHONG WEN DISTRICT, BEIJING

The hotel suite that Mitchell had arranged was larger and far nicer than Jonathan had expected. The US Government was not usually extravagant when paying for travel accommodations, but the NCS had its own standards. The analyst had heard stories, exaggerated he'd thought, about how well some case officers lived on the road, but this

room lived up to them. The suite featured a very large sitting and dining area, divided from the kitchenette by a wet bar, and a bedroom
separated by a sliding French door with opaque glass panes set in a
grid. Jonathan parted the suite's heavy white curtains an inch, which
was enough to see that the view of the Forbidden City was inspiring.
The food service had been excellent, with classic Italian cuisine on
the menu as well as the local favorites. The television dominating
the near wall was an impressive plasma display so large that Jonathan
knew he would never be able to afford one for his own home. Mitchell
had the volume up high enough to annoy both Jonathan and anyone
who might try listening through hidden microphones. The senior analyst wished that he could afford such places on his own salary when
he was traveling privately. Analysts didn't get approvals for this kind
of accommodation. Jonathan accepted that with a grudge, but he had
no desire to play on the case officers' field, no matter what the perks
were.

In truth, he had no interest in the room's interior design. He shifted
his feet, clasped his hands behind his back, and tried to suppress the
part of his mind shouting that his study of it was an effort at self-
distraction. He was trying very hard not to wonder where Kyra was at
the moment.

Mitchell had chosen the suite at random. Beijing had thousands
of hotels, likely hundreds of thousands of rooms for rent, and even
the MSS could not bug them all. At least that was the theory. There
was still a decent chance that somewhere in the basement the MSS
was listening, but Mitchell didn't seem worried. Jonathan was sure it
was a poker face. No cover story would hold up if they were raided.
If they were arrested and Pioneer identified, whatever they told the
Chinese government would be irrelevant. The MSS would consider
proximity to be guilt, and none of them would set foot on United
States soil again for a very long time. Jonathan had been in war zones,
but he doubted that he had ever been in as much danger as he was this
evening.

Mitchell sat at the cherry dining table finishing the remains of his
risotto while a plate of pastry fritters waited on the side. Jonathan
had tried to beg off the food—his jet-lagged stomach didn't think it
was time to eat—but Mitchell insisted and the analyst took a bowl
of gnocchi. Mitchell had ordered frittate for Kyra and Pioneer, and it
was keeping warm under a tray cover. Jonathan was sure she would

appreciate the wine. His initial thought had been to wait to order until she arrived—he refused to think in terms of *if*—but he supposed that once Pioneer was in the room, Mitchell wouldn't want anyone coming to the door.

Jonathan looked at the digital clock on the writing desk by the window. "We're behind schedule," Mitchell said.

"We have a schedule?" Jonathan asked.

"Always," Mitchell said. "Twenty minutes late, but she's still inside her window. If she doesn't get here in the next ten minutes, we might have to push everyone back to the next flight." He set his utensils on the plate, picked up a fritter, and walked over to the window.

There was a knock at the door. Jonathan resisted the urge to answer it, instead letting Mitchell take the job in case there was some private entry protocol he'd arranged. If there was one, it was subtle. The senior NCS officer simply looked through the peephole and opened the door. The woman at the door was shorter than Kyra, with shoulder-length dark hair. She was dressed in casual clothing and dragging a wheeled suitcase behind. She marched past Mitchell and he closed the door to the hallway.

"John, this is Anna Monaghan," Mitchell said. "She's with S and T"—the Agency's Directorate of Science and Technology. "John's an analyst."

Anna offered her hand. "Cooke told me about you before I got on the plane."

"Then you're a recent import?" Jonathan asked.

"I am," Anna said. "Just got in. Hate the flight from Dulles. Coming down over Russian airspace drives me up the wall."

"The Russkies don't shoot down airliners anymore," Mitchell said. "And you won't be here long enough to get lagged. After you do your beauty work on our friend, you're on the first flight out tomorrow," Mitchell said.

"A shame you won't get the suite when we're done," Jonathan said.

"I wish," Anna said. "Same hotel, but I'm six floors down with the common folk." She scanned the room and looked to Mitchell. "Stryker's still on the street?"

"Stepped out ninety minutes ago. She's still got ten minutes," Mitchell said. "Fifteen before I get really worried."

"I'll set up in the bedroom. I need to steal the desk, and I *am* taking a shower."

"No arguments here," Mitchell said. The woman rolled her case into the bedroom and closed the sliding door.

Kyra and Pioneer entered the Marriott lobby twenty-two minutes behind schedule. The taxi driver had taken a winding route to find any persistent cars behind, and their surveillance detection run on foot had not turned out any hostiles. It still wasn't a given that they were alone, but having made it this far was a promising development. Unless the MSS was running a particularly sophisticated operation, waiting to learn the hotel room number so they could arrest Pioneer together with his handler, their odds of escape had risen considerably. She hoped that their body doubles would not have to spend an unpleasant evening in the local lockup. The MSS would not be able to prove that their proximity and similar dress to a known traitor and his escort was sure evidence of participation in a conspiracy, but Kyra doubted that the MSS required proof beyond a reasonable doubt. She suspected that their threshold for conviction dropped as their annoyance level rose, and once they realized that Pioneer was no longer under their watch, the annoyance level would be stratospheric.

Jonathan had been right. She was craving a shot of anything she could lay hands on, knowing this would be a terrible time for it. If the operation went south and Roland and Rebecca went to prison . . . she knew without a doubt that the imprisonment of two fellow officers as the price paid for her sake would drive her down into the bottle.

Kyra cursed herself for letting her mind wander. It was like Venezuela again. She had picked a poor moment for self-examination. *Still not safe*. She exhaled, scanned the lobby, and found the elevators. She led Pioneer away from the front desk toward the lifts and reached for her front pocket. She extracted the disposable cell phone, a low-end Nokia.

She dialed the second number preprogrammed into the phone, which was the chief of station's number for his own rented disposable phone. Both units were destined for secure disposal, where and how Mitchell hadn't bothered to tell her. This would be the last call her phone would ever make.

She was surprised to hear Jonathan's voice on the phone. "We've been waiting on you for dinner. Your frittata is cold," he said. No doubt Mitchell had coached him on what to say. The first sentence was the pass phrase. The second was a bit of a rebuke. *You're late.*

He's never made a call in Beijing, Kyra realized. *The MSS won't have his voiceprint.* They would almost certainly have one of Mitchell, and having her talk to Jonathan would fit their cover story better if the cell phone was intercepted. They had come through customs together, so surveillance video and voiceprint matches would come together to support the cover story that they were traveling companions.

"Sorry, I was talking to some friends," she replied. "I hope the food didn't cost too much," Kyra said. *Pioneer is with me. Where are you?*

"Not too bad. Given the exchange rate, ten dollars and twenty-two cents, not counting the service fee." *Room 1022.* The Third Department could figure out eventually what Jonathan had really said. First, they would need to separate the conversation from every other call made in Beijing by a Westerner at the same moment, triangulate Kyra's position, and translate the conversation into Chinese. They would have to be bright enough to look up the Marriott's price for frittate and realize that Jonathan was quite mistaken about it, given the day's yuan-to-US dollar exchange rate. Kyra had worked in bureaucracies long enough to know that they wouldn't manage the feat and get an armed team to room 1022 in the next hour.

"Warm it up for me." *Coming up.* She turned off the phone and led Pioneer to the elevator.

Jonathan closed the phone and returned it to Mitchell. "Thanks," Mitchell said. "I don't know if the Chinese have a voiceprint of me they can match up, but no sense taking the chance. Don't want them tracing my voice to find us." He didn't know how many they'd been able to collect of him over the years. None would be preferable, and anything higher than zero was bad news as far as the chief of station was concerned. Mitchell checked the clock. "We're doing okay. Might be able to make up a little time on the road to the airport if traffic isn't bad. We don't want to be sitting around at the airport for a long stretch anyway."

"You're coming too?" Jonathan asked.

Mitchell glared at the analyst for a moment, then suppressed his frustration. "I tried to retrieve a dead drop before we figured out that Pioneer was burned. The MSS was probably watching the drop site, so I'm burned too. Hard to be a chief of station when the enemy knows what you do for a living. I'm Pioneer's escort back to the States and I'm not coming back. My wife's packing up the house right now and she's flying home tomorrow. Anna's going to give me a makeover after she finishes up with Pioneer and Stryker."

"Hard way to end a tour," Jonathan said. It was as close to showing compassion as he could come with a stranger.

"I was almost done here anyway. Would've been home by Independence Day," Mitchell said. He smiled. "Next time I'm back at Langley, you're going to have to explain to me how you talked Cooke into approving a debrief with Pioneer."

"A shame they don't have a bar at headquarters. I don't drink, but I'd buy you a beer for not throwing us out of your office when we showed up and told you what we wanted."

Mitchell chuckled. "To be honest, I was more surprised than angry, at first anyway." He checked the clock again, walked to the door, and pulled it open. He'd timed his own ascent from the lobby to the room to get a ballpark estimate of the travel time. Kyra and Pioneer were approaching the room. Mitchell closed the door behind them and led them out of the front room. "Any problems?" he asked.

"We confirmed surveillance at his apartment," Kyra replied. "No one followed us after we left the building. I think our friends were able to draw everyone away. Good people. I hope they don't get picked up."

"They might," Mitchell conceded. "But Becca's been toting that red backpack for years. If the MSS has been watching the building for any time at all, they'll have seen her wearing it. They might figure out what happened after a while, but they'll never be able to prove it."

Mitchell turned to Pioneer and spoke, this time in accented Mandarin. *"Long Jian-Min, it is my honor to meet you in person. I regret that I cannot give you my name. Perhaps in the United States I will be able to do so. In a few minutes, we will dress you and take you to the airport. This gentleman needs to ask you some questions after we have delivered you safely out of the country, if that would be acceptable?"* Mitchell was intentionally vague with the details, more out of habit than any particular concern that they had missed some listening device. Pioneer nodded politely.

Jonathan moved close to Kyra. "Good to see you without a pair of handcuffs."

"You softie."

"Hardly. The Chinese built a big airport," Jonathan explained. "I need somebody to watch my carry-on while I'm buying dinner in the airport terminal."

"So it's still all about you?" Kyra asked.

"Of course," he said.

"Ah."

"All right, people," Mitchell said. "Enough with the touchy-feely. We're on the road in forty-five." He pointed toward the back room. "Get our man back there. The clock's ticking."

Monaghan's tools of the trade were on display. The Directorate of Science and Technology officer had left a lucrative future as a makeup artist at Fox Studios in Los Angeles to work for the Agency, and Kyra had no doubt that the woman had been very good at her job. The portable electronics she was carrying were fascinating. During the Cold War, producing fake travel documents required a skilled forger with a steady hand who could copy signatures and poor-quality typesetting, but it wasn't done by hand anymore.

"You're going out through the airport?" Monaghan asked.

"Not much choice," Kyra said.

"Then I'll have to set you up with something better than a gross profile change. If they're looking for him"—Monaghan nodded toward Pioneer, who was sitting in the corner—"you can expect close inspection, maybe less than two feet."

"How are you getting out?" Kyra asked.

"Oh, honey," Monaghan said. "I've got my ways. Besides, I'll be fine having a long cup of coffee with some handsome MSS officer if they really want me to stay. They won't have anything on me. I'm leaving the gear with our people here." She picked up a Ziploc bag full of bottles. "You go on into the bathroom and use this. You'll make a real pretty brunette. And I hope you like short hair. Do you wear color contacts?"

"No," Kyra said.

"You do now. A shame to cover up those pretty green eyes, but there's no help for it. I'd bet that the MSS doesn't know your eye color, but I'm not going to take the chance. Those boys have cameras everywhere. And you're going to wear glasses too." Monaghan picked up another Ziploc and pulled it open. "I'll get started on our friend here. I'll finish you up when I'm done with him." Monaghan took Pioneer gently by the arm, led him to a chair, and picked up a bottle of spirit gum. Kyra squeezed his arm, then left him and stepped into the bathroom.

They took separate cars. The airport traffic was light, which Kyra might have considered a sign of divine intervention had she been a religious woman. The open road meant no delays en route to the airport and offered the added benefit of keeping the enemy from hiding in traffic. Identifying hostile surveillance on foot was relatively easy compared to performing vehicular detection on any freeway during peak hours, and Kyra was sure that Beijing's freeways were worse than most. At the moment, she wanted every advantage she could claim.

Jonathan watched Kyra's eyes look to the rearview mirror every few seconds. Courtesy of Monaghan, the woman was, by all appearances, a middle-aged brunette, short hair, glasses, wearing casual clothing and a bit overweight. Her height was unchanged and Monaghan hadn't toyed with her build, though she was slightly broader across the shoulders and larger in the chest. Except for the added weight, it wasn't a bad look for her, and he idly wondered how much of it she might choose to keep once they returned to the States. *If we get that far,* he thought.

Out of the corner of her eye, Kyra caught him studying her. "Sorry you didn't get a makeover?" she asked. Jonathan hadn't performed an operational act since their arrival, so there had been no reason to change his appearance. The MSS had no reason to suspect him of anything.

"Hardly," Jonathan said. "Anyone on us?"

"Don't think so," Kyra said. "A couple of possibles, but they're giving us plenty of space." She had watched the same Hafei Motor sedans hold their distance behind the minivan for more than ten miles. The black cars were trading positions every few miles, but they weren't driving aggressively. They were almost lazy and let any number of cars get between them and the embassy SUV. "No sirens. Always a good sign." She was only half joking.

"You won't be able to come back here," Jonathan said. "You know that."

"I know." Kyra regretted not seeing more of the city, or the countryside for that matter—the Great Wall at least. There was so much history, and it would all be denied her now. *Ironic,* she thought. It made her feel like her rebellious walk on the streets had been justified. She hadn't joined up to play tourist. She had always wanted to prowl the side streets and see the underbellies and dirty corners of the cities where the Agency would send her. She'd had to fight the MSS for it, but for one night, she had gotten a true taste of the real Beijing. She wanted more, always would, but what she'd seen felt good and that was something she hadn't felt for a while. "I'll survive."

"Good for you," he said. Kyra turned to look at him, but Jonathan was staring out the car window at the skyline and she couldn't see his face.

Time to get serious, she thought. "When you get to the waiting area, don't talk to Mitchell or Pioneer," she advised. "They should be sitting apart. Try to keep some distance from both of them. If you have to sit near one of them, sit near Mitchell. Otherwise, let him find you when you deplane in Seoul."

"No problem." Jonathan knew the practice perfectly well but nodded assent.

"Monaghan is good," Kyra said. "She does solid work. But if the MSS does pick either of them up, you just get on the plane, then call the embassy when you land." The telephone number was scribbled on a blank index card in his wallet.

"If that happens, Pioneer is dead," Jonathan said. "And Mitchell goes to prison."

Kyra said nothing for a moment. He was right. If Pioneer was detained, there would be no saving him from a sure bullet to the head after a trial that would be finished in a few weeks at most. "No. But somebody will have to tell the director ASAP."

"Agreed." They lapsed into silence. The GPS unit mounted on the dash guided them into the airport and Kyra pulled the car into a covered garage. Someone from the embassy would come out to retrieve it later.

Kyra killed the engine. "I'll go in first. Follow me in five minutes."

"See you in Seoul."

Kyra moved through boarding security without drawing attention, retrieved her carry-on, and worked through the masses toward her assigned gate. The airport crowd was thin, but the number of uniformed guards moving through the terminal was far higher than the night she and Jonathan had entered the country. Soldiers were standing by the doors leading to the boarding ramps. To her eye, there was no sense of urgency on their part. They stood to the sides, close enough to the boarding lines that some of the Western passengers seemed uncomfortable with the attention. The Asian passengers seemed unmoved by the scrutiny. The sense of calm was a good sign. A blatant show of hostile sorting through departing passengers would be the surest sign that the MSS had figured out something was up. Kyra had managed her magic trick almost two hours ago. Mitchell's liberal estimates gave them at least another hour before the MSS would figure out that Pioneer had disappeared. Jonathan was not so optimistic, but even if his calculation proved better than Mitchell's, the MSS would still be losing the game. There were so many ways to leave Beijing, the MSS couldn't cover them all. Even with the help of the PLA and the other security services, they would have to spread themselves thin in a panicked effort to canvass the major travel hubs. Even then, they would have no assurance that CIA hadn't simply driven him out in a car. The options were legion, China was a very large country, and the security resources were not unlimited. Time and geography were finally working against the MSS.

Kyra found her gate and scanned the waiting group. Mitchell had advised that flights to Seoul at this hour were usually full, and the numbers seemed to confirm that guess. There were few open seats. She did not have her pick, and that alone gave her plausible deniability that she knew any of her covert traveling companions. No security officer could reasonably use the seating arrangements here to infer personal connections. She chose one of the few open seats, settled herself, and stared out the bay windows to the dark tarmac.

Two guards stood by the boarding door, watching the seated passengers. Kyra saw them study her for a moment, but neither made a move in her direction. Her watch, an atomic piece accurate to within hundredths of a second, showed eight minutes to the posted boarding time. Mitchell had tried to time their arrival at the airport to get the group to the gate with little time to spare and therefore to be observed and identified by any officials. It was strange how time could be both an ally and an enemy. Jonathan was five minutes behind her. Mitchell and Pioneer should have been there already, but she couldn't pick them out in the crowd and didn't look around for them. Still, the crowd was calm moving through the terminal. Likely they would have been excited had the soldiers been dragging men away anywhere nearby. Mitchell and Pioneer were still loose, if they were here.

If the airline delayed boarding, it would be the first sign that something was going very wrong.

The boarding was announced in Chinese, English, and another language she did not recognize but assumed was Korean. The crowd stirred and Kyra released the breath she hadn't realized that she'd been holding.

It was a mistake. She heard the shouting before she saw the running guards following two civilian men in suits. The waiting passengers turned en masse as four PLA soldiers in fatigues with weapons drawn slowed to a fast walk, led by the civilians holding portable radios. Other mixed groups of suits and fatigues ran past, moving out to cover the other boarding areas.

The suits—Kyra assumed they were MSS—were speaking loudly in Chinese and the crowd parted before them. They reached the podium and cornered both the guards on duty and the airline staff who were preparing to open the door to the passengers. The guards who had been standing over the crowd shook their heads vigorously to some question. The MSS officers pushed them aside and began to bark orders to the airline staff. One, a petite Chinese woman, picked up the wall microphone. She issued her announcement first in Mandarin, then English.

"Ladies and gentlemen, we are about to begin boarding. As an extra security precaution, in addition to your boarding passes, we ask you to please produce your passports and present them for inspection. We appreciate your cooperation. Our first-class and business passengers are now welcome to board, as well as any other passengers who may require extra time or assistance."

Kyra, trying very hard not to take a deep breath, dug into her carry-on for her falsified passport. Hers and Jonathan's were economy seats. She didn't know which seating class Mitchell and Pioneer would be in. She looked through the crowd and picked out Jonathan thirty feet from her position, standing in the thoroughfare. She didn't make eye contact with him. He had nothing to worry about. He wasn't the one who had beaten an MSS officer in an alley or ditched several more during a run through the city with the most-wanted man in the People's Republic of China.

The MSS officers stood almost shoulder to shoulder, the first taking a passenger's passport and holding it over a printout the second held. They compared the travel document with the printed page, then held it to the passenger's face.

They waved the first passenger through.

They know he's loose. The MSS had almost certainly detained the

Zhous. But the large number of security officers and soldiers running past through the terminal meant they didn't know where Pioneer was.

Kyra approached the gate. An old Korean man standing at the head of the line moved forward, leaning on his cane, and he held his boarding pass and passport out to the security officers. The lead MSS officer took the passport, rifled through it until he found the visa stamp, and scrutinized it for several seconds. He turned to the inside cover and held the man's photograph next to the sheet his partner held. They jabbered on in Mandarin. The one not holding the passport spoke into a portable radio and waited until he received an answer. Kyra wished dearly that she could understand the language to get some feel for their level of anxiety.

The Korean stood calmly as the two Chinese security officers talked over his case. The one holding his passport leaned over and looked at his face for several seconds. The Korean pulled back, apparently uncomfortable with the close inspection, but otherwise held his ground.

The MSS officer frowned, closed the passport, handed it to its owner, and waved him through. The airline attendant gave him a traditional Mandarin greeting. He nodded and gave her his boarding pass. She ran it under the scanner and extended it to him, but the Korean was still trying to pocket his passport with shaky old hands, leaving Kyra to wait an eternity until he could move on. He finally managed to secure it inside his jacket, then took back his pass and awkwardly pushed himself forward through the door.

Several more passengers moved through, then Kyra stepped up to the gate and held out her passport. She focused on her hands to make sure there was no tremor in her fingers. She wanted to give no outward sign of discomfort. The MSS officer took the passport and studied the brunette with an ugly look for a long second before opening the fake document. She put her hands in her pockets and turned her attention to her breathing and her heart rate, which was faster than its usual pace but not enough to make her uncomfortable. The two officers spoke again and the officer holding the radio clicked the mic and spoke into it. It spat back an answer and the MSS officers frowned but said nothing. The one holding her passport looked to her again. Kyra gave them no expression. She wondered if they had studied Western faces enough to discern emotional states.

Just give me back the passport, she thought.

• • •

The Korean reached the end of the ramp and carefully stepped over the small gap onto the Boeing 767. A pretty young Korean attendant asked him in her native tongue if he would like help finding his seat. He didn't understand the language, but he nodded anyway. She took his boarding pass, directed him toward the first-class cabin, and then took his arm and helped him down the aisle. He shuffled between the seats, using them for support, until he reached his row. The attendant helped him settle into the seat, noted that he had no carry-on for the overhead bin, and asked if he would like a drink and a hot towel for his face. He demurred on the towel.

He had no idea what it would do to the prosthetics Monaghan had applied to his face.

The attendant left and Pioneer turned to the window. His face rigid, he stared unseeing at the city skyline in the distance. Beijing was lost to him. He realized that he didn't know what tears would do to the prosthetics either. Perhaps he should have asked for the towel after all.

He looked to the front and saw the attendants repeating the greeting ritual with another passenger who entered the cabin. Kyra Stryker nodded to the attendant and turned down the aisle. She didn't look at him.

The MSS officer returned the last passport to its owner, a teenage Canadian girl, and his partner shrugged and spoke into his handset. Their superior acknowledged and the PLA soldiers who stood to the side slung their rifles. They moved as a unit through the terminal toward another gate at the far end. Flights would be boarding all night. The entire Sixth Bureau was stretched very thin, they had been told, and no one could tell them when replacements would arrive.

The attendant closed the boarding ramp door, locked it, and tested the security panel. Her shift was over. Walking away from the gate, she reached into her pocket, pulled out a disposable cell phone, and pressed a button. She didn't know who she was calling or even what phone number had been preprogrammed into it.

"Hello," a woman answered in excellent Mandarin.

"Dinner is served, four courses, all cold," the attendant said.

"My thanks." The call disconnected from the other end. The attendant entered the nearest restroom, waited a few moments until the lone

visitor walked out, then removed the SIM card from the phone and flushed it down a toilet. She then dropped the phone into the garbage.

At Mitchell's now-empty desk, Monaghan replaced the telephone handset and put her hands over her face. *See you soon, boys and girls,* she thought. She suppressed the urge to walk to the window and make a rude gesture in the direction of Zhongnanhai.

Mitchell had prewritten two cables to Langley the night before. Now Monaghan could tell his former deputy, the newly promoted chief of station, which one to delete. The other would only take a few moments to transit the Pacific. There was no telling how long it would take the Ops Center staff to flag it for Barron after it arrived. The NCS Director would be impatient. Monaghan picked up a secure phone and dialed.

CIA DIRECTOR'S OFFICE

Cooke hadn't left her office on the seventh floor for two days. She took her meals in the director's dining room—the Agency provided her with a personal chef, who worked in a restaurant-quality kitchen—and stepped out into the hall only when she had to return to the Operations Center for short briefings on military developments in the South China Sea. When Barron had advised her to go home the day before, Cooke had dismissed the suggestion out of hand. She knew that it had hardly been sincere, made more out of duty than any belief she would act on it. Barron would never sincerely ask her to do something he wasn't doing himself. Still, the guilt from wanting to heed the man was sharp. Cooke *was* tired and even the coffee was losing its power to keep her going. The amount of caffeine required to keep her alert was making her hands shake. She told herself that going home was pointless, that she wouldn't be able to sleep because the thought of her people in the field would keep her awake. Cooke knew that was a lie and wouldn't admit it to herself, but finally she didn't have a choice. The couch looked to be a better pillow than her desk, and so she dismissed Barron, locked her office, and reclined on the couch. The director kept the lights on, the blinds open, and hoped that she had enough strength left to keep the rest short.

She knew she had failed when the knock came at the door. Her sense of time was gone and her mind was foggier than before. Her vision finally focused on the wall clock. Four hours had passed. She pulled herself up. The doorknob felt like lead in her hand.

It was Barron. Her body felt like a heavy sack of grain as it fell into the chair. "Give me some good news," she ordered.

Barron obeyed the order after he'd closed the door behind him. "He's in the air," he said without preamble. Cooke closed her eyes in relief. "Ninety minutes and he'll be on the ground in Seoul. The MSS overran the airport but they didn't ID him. Two feet away and they couldn't figure out who he was. Monaghan did some great work."

"What about the others?"

"Everyone's on the plane," Barron said. "They're all clear unless the PLA decides to send some MIGs after them."

"Make sure Stryker gets a promotion and a week's leave. Monaghan too. I take it you flew Pioneer in style?"

"You asked, he received," Barron said. "First-class seat and a charter flight to Dulles from Seoul. Mitchell is sitting nearby to keep him under control in case he gets panicky. That happens sometimes when people finally realize that they're not going home again. They'll be on the ground here by tomorrow afternoon. We'll change planes there and take him to the Farm."

"He deserves it. Stryker?"

"She and Burke got coach. We didn't want everyone sitting together in case somebody got picked up." He reached into his pocket and pulled out a cigar tube, a Davidoff Millennium. He offered it to Cooke and pulled out another for himself when she took it. "He's out of China. I think that's worth breaking a minor federal law."

Cooke extracted the pungent stick from its cylinder and drew it under her nose. "Expensive. I thought you gave these up."

"It's never too late to restart a bad habit."

"I have a better tradition in mind. And it'll save you from an argument with your wife." Cooke took Barron's cigar, pulled it from the cylinder, and put the brown stick in her mouth. She replaced the cigar he had given her in its tube. Then she fetched a Sharpie from her desk and scrawled *Pioneer 2016* on the side. The CIA director turned to the shelf behind her desk, opened the humidor sitting there, and dropped the cigar inside. Barron's addition to her collection made four.

INCHEON INTERNATIONAL AIRPORT
SEOUL, SOUTH KOREA

The handwritten sign read "KWON Moo-hyun."

Milo Sachs had no idea who Kwon Moo-hyun was but he doubted that Mr. Kwon was truly Korean. Sachs was the youngest case officer in Seoul, so he'd drawn the short straw for this duty. Chief of station Seoul gave him the name for the placard and an order not to ask questions. He was to stand with the other professional drivers, meet Mr. Kwon, and lead him to a private hangar near the edge of the field, then fly with him on the private Learjet back to Dulles Airport. He was under orders not to talk to Kwon except to direct his movements. Sachs was an escort, nothing more. He would get three days' leave in Northern Virginia as compensation, hardly enough to recover from the time lag, after which he would fly back to Seoul to resume his regular tour of duty.

The plane landed on schedule, the airline attendants opened the door, and the limousine service drivers took their places to the side of the exit. The first two people off saw his sign and walked to him. The Westerner was balding, salt-and-pepper hair in the places he still had it, with a sizable paunch at his waistline. The Korean man walked with a cane, but he appeared somewhat more spry than his age should have allowed.

"I am Kwon," the man said in Korean. It clearly was not true. His accent was so heavy that Sachs was sure the man had memorized the phrase. He probably didn't even know what he was saying.

"A pleasure," Sachs replied. "Come with me, I will take you to your next flight."

"Not yet," Mitchell said. "We need a private place where we can ask this gentleman a few questions first."

"You're Mitchell?" Sachs asked. Mitchell nodded. "We've got a charter flight waiting in a private hangar. Safest place to talk is probably on the plane."

"Works for me," Mitchell said. He hadn't taken his eyes off the door where the passengers were deplaning. Another pair of Westerners exited, looked around for a brief second, and then moved in their direction. The woman was quite pretty, Sachs thought. A short-haired brunette with glasses, she doubtless was a case officer. He wondered how old she really was. It was easier to make a younger person look older than to do the reverse.

"Time to talk?" Kyra asked Mitchell without preamble.

"Private hangar," Mitchell told her. "You get fifteen minutes. That enough?"

"We'll find out," Jonathan said.

Mitchell gestured everyone toward couches in the plane's aft section and they all took their places. Jonathan leaned forward and studied the Chinese man. He had extrapolated Pioneer's age from the biographical data in the files he'd finally gotten after badgering Barron for access. The Chinese asset had been in college during the Tiananmen Square Massacre, which meant that he would be middle-aged now, but the disguise obscured all traces of that. He'd only seen the man's true appearance for a short minute before Monaghan had gotten her hands on him. Pioneer had looked somewhat older than middle age, though Jonathan knew he had no baseline for comparison, but it didn't surprise him. Pioneer had been committing treason for over twenty years. Such a life could age a man well before his time.

"I'm Jonathan. This is Kyra," Jonathan said in English. "I want to ask you some questions about the Assassin's Mace program." Mitchell translated. If the senior officer disapproved of using real names, he said nothing. Jonathan caught the *shashoujian* term but recognized nothing else. It was a beautiful language. The tonals made it sound like singing and he doubted that he could ever master it. He spoke Romance languages only and found them difficult enough.

Pioneer nodded and replied. *"I wish that I had been able to access more information on the* shashoujian, *but much of it was compartmented beyond my reach. What do you want to know?"*

"We sorted through your reports. There wasn't any progress on the *shashoujian* until 1999. Correct?"

"Correct. Jiang Zemin started the program in 1996, but there was little worth reporting for three years. A few papers, a few efforts to steal some US weapons. Several senior military officers developed ideas for weapons, but the PLA lacked the expertise to make any of the designs work. It was all science fiction." Mitchell didn't bother trying to convey the venom he heard in Pioneer's voice. *"They were stupid old men dreaming of weapons that we won't be able to build for a hundred years. Anything they could dream of that could reach your carriers, the PLA couldn't build."*

"So what changed in 1999?" Kyra asked.

"I don't know," Pioneer admitted. *"If there was a breakthrough, it was*

compartmented and I couldn't access it. There was some new cooperation between the PLA and Xian Aircraft Design and Research Institute, but I reported on that."

Jonathan nodded. "I read that report. If there were no successes, were there any significant failures that you didn't report?"

"Why are you asking about failures?" Mitchell asked.

"Science is all about failure," Jonathan explained. "Test, fail, test again, until you have a breakthrough. If he can outline some major research failures after 1999, it might show us the direction that the PLA's research took."

"Fair enough," Mitchell said. He translated.

"The J-20 was a disappointment, useful mostly for trying to humiliate your visiting military officers, and we would never have enough to match your Raptors. And the Dongfeng missile was always suspect. Senior party leaders were losing faith in all of it, so they removed it from the shashoujian program," Pioneer answered.

"No successes, lots of failures," Jonathan said. "Something set them off. We're missing something."

"I agree, but I don't know what it would be. In fact, around that time, the MSS even wanted to shut the program down."

"Why?" Jonathan asked. That hadn't been in the reporting.

"Because the MSS feared that CIA had penetrated the program. It was true, as I had done that, but not like they thought."

"What do you mean?" Mitchell said.

"I was sure that the CIA did not have another penetration with better access than mine inside the shashoujian. I know that intelligence services like to confirm information from multiple sources, but my case officers were never asking me about the things the MSS was afraid you knew. I was the senior MSS archivist. I assumed that even if you had a more senior penetration, my case officers would still have asked me those questions. They never did. I tried to raise them sometimes, but the case officers never seemed interested. They liked me to respond to their questions. They did not like me to invent my own taskings. They said it was a risk."

"He's got your number cold," Jonathan told Mitchell.

"Yeah, well, it happens when the case officers aren't technical specialists in the subject they have to ask about," Mitchell said. "They stick to the questions that you analysts send them from headquarters. If you don't send the right questions, they never get asked."

"Chalk one up for the system," Kyra said.

"What triggered their fears that we had penetrated their program?" Jonathan asked.

Pioneer sat back and thought for a moment. *"It happened after you bombed our embassy in Serbia. I forget the exact date."*

Jonathan cocked his head. "Serbia . . . ," he said quietly, but Kyra overheard. "Did the MSS smuggle anything through that embassy related to the Assassin's Mace?"

"I know that the Guojia Anquan Bu Tenth Bureau purchased something of value from a senior Serb army officer in Belgrade and sent it to Beijing through the diplomatic pouch a few days before the bombing. The Tenth Bureau is responsible for stealing foreign technologies, so I assumed the Serbs had stolen some piece of equipment from NATO. When your Air Force blew up the embassy wing, the MSS was convinced that President Clinton had ordered the strike to keep the delivery out of their hands. That is why they refused to believe that the bombing was an accident. They still believe that." Mitchell translated. Jonathan leaned forward and put his head in his hands.

"You don't know what was in the package?" Mitchell asked Pioneer.

"I don't. I tried to find out, but the MSS kept the records compartmented. I could never access them, so I had nothing to report. I was not even sure that the technology had anything to do with the shashoujian. *The timing of the sale and the MSS worries about a penetration could have just been coincidence. I do know that after it came to Beijing, the MSS gave it to the PLA and from there it went to Chengdu. But they often buy stolen technology abroad. It is common."*

"I've been an idiot!" Jonathan hissed.

"What? What is it?" Kyra asked.

"It's been sitting there the entire time and I was too stupid to see it," Jonathan said. "We should have seen it when we did the timeline." He stood up and looked at Mitchell. "We're done. I've got what I need." Mitchell nodded and spoke to Pioneer in Mandarin, telling him the conversation was finished.

"What did we miss?" Kyra asked.

Jonathan took a deep breath. "You remember that the timeline showed no progress in the Assassin's Mace project until 1999?"

"Yeah," Kyra said. "We've been looking for an event that kick-started it."

"We've been looking for an event *in China*," Jonathan said. "That was stupid and narrow-minded. There was a kick-start event, but it didn't happen in China. It happened in Serbia."

"What happened in Serbia?"

He shook his head. "Stupid," he said, quiet but still intense. "We can break this thing open. He gave us the Assassin's Mace." His voice was calm. "He's had pieces that he didn't know belonged to the puzzle. So did we, for that matter. We could've figured it out without him if we'd been smart enough. I was an idiot not to see it," Jonathan said. It was an honest admission that stemmed more from exhaustion than humility. The sleep deprivation was finally degrading his ability to think, and the caffeine pills were now doing him more harm than good. He hoped Kyra was doing better, but she had been under more stress and alternating between coffee and alcohol.

Jonathan checked the clock and did the conversion of time zones in his mind. It was 0830 at Langley. He turned to Mitchell. "I need a secure cell phone and a laptop."

Sachs reached into his pocket and produced a mobile handset. A backpack from the plane's cockpit produced an iPad. "You can't keep those. I had to sign for them."

Jonathan shot the junior officer a withering look as he pulled the phone from his hand. "How long before we leave?" he asked Mitchell.

"By the schedule, thirty minutes. But we own this plane. You need us to wait?"

"If you would," he said. He handed the tablet computer to his partner. "I'm calling home. I need you to look someone up for me."

"Who?" she asked.

"Pyotr Ufimtsev. *P-Y-O-T-R. U-F-I-M-T-S-E-V.* Trust me, you'll know it when you see it." Kyra shrugged, pressed a button on the computer, and began typing. "We just need a little more," Jonathan said, as much to himself as anyone listening. "And we need to talk to the Navy."

"About what?" Mitchell said, exasperated.

"Have you ever heard of Noble Anvil?" Jonathan said.

Kyra looked up. He was as excited as she had ever seen him during their short time together. She sifted through her thoughts as she pressed the return button to start the Internet search on the name Jonathan had given her. She had a good memory for acronyms and code words. Developing memory skills was a standard part of case officer training, and life in government service demanded it anyway. "The US part of NATO's Allied Force operation in Yugoslavia back in ninety-nine," she said.

Jonathan nodded. He was more grateful that he wouldn't have to explain the reference than impressed with Kyra's knowledge of military history. "The Air Force bombed the Chinese embassy by accident. The Chinese believed there's no way we could have screwed up our targeting that badly, so somebody must have ordered it. And they think we ordered it because they had a piece of classified US technology in the building—something sensitive enough that the Chinese thought we might be willing to bomb their embassy to keep them from shipping it to Beijing."

"Wait . . . the F-117 Nighthawk?" She started swiping her finger across the computer's screen, looking through the search results.

Mitchell said nothing for a moment, searching his thoughts. "The one the Serbs shot down."

Jonathan nodded. "The only stealth plane we've ever lost to hostile fire. Six weeks later to the day it was shot down by the Serbs, we dropped a bomb on the Chinese embassy sixty miles away. But the PLA wasn't part of the shootdown, so we never had a reason to connect it with the Assassin's Mace program even when the Chinese thought we had."

"I thought the Nighthawk was destroyed on impact," Kyra said.

Jonathan shook his head. "There was more than enough intact for an intel service to reverse-engineer. Imagery shows that the plane wasn't vaporized."

"Why not?" Mitchell asked, curious. "Most planes that fall from a few miles up just leave a smoking crater."

"Nobody knows for sure," Jonathan said. "My guess is that the fly-by-wire computers kept trying to level the plane after the pilot bailed out. Nighthawks have the aerodynamic properties of a brick. The only way one stays up is if the computers can make adjustments to the control surfaces fast enough, so the pilot uses the stick to tell the computers where he wants to go, and they figure out how to adjust the airframe to make it happen. I think the SAMs exploded close enough for the shrapnel to shred the airframe and damage the control surfaces. The pilot bailed out, but the computers kept trying to fly. They leveled the plane out enough to keep it from turning into a fireball when it hit."

"That actually makes sense. You would think that the engineers could have come up with something that could glide in a pinch," Mitchell mused.

Kyra stared at the iPad screen. "I read about this. Computers in the seventies weren't powerful enough to calculate the radar cross sections of curved surfaces," Kyra said. "They could only crunch numbers for flat surfaces, but flat areas are perfect radar wave reflectors. Right angles are the real killers because they reflect virtually the entire radar wave back to the receiver. So Lockheed had to build a plane with flat surfaces and no right angles. Now you could do the math on one of these." She held the tablet computer up.

"The Air Force didn't bomb the crash site?" Mitchell asked.

"Serb civilians overran the site too quickly," Jonathan replied. "We've got pictures of little old Serb ladies dancing on wing sections still smoking from the impact. The idiots probably all died of cancer. And the Serbs don't have the industry to build fighters, stealth or not, so they likely went looking to sell the technology for money. The Chinese would be the perfect buyers. They've got money, our technology in the Gulf War freaked them out, and they were trying to modernize their military. The Assassin's Mace project was under way, and stealth bombers would be the perfect weapons to use against an aircraft carrier."

"You think they've got a working stealth bomber?" Mitchell was engrossed now.

"Yes," Kyra said. "Yes, they do." She pulled the phone out of Jonathan's hand.

CIA INFORMATION OPERATIONS CENTER

The STU-III's tiny display finally read "TS//SCI" and the secure voice button went red. Weaver had hoped that there were enough fiber optic lines between Beijing and Langley that the encrypted phones could make a connection quickly, but the wait had been painful. In truth, it probably had taken less than fifteen seconds.

The encryption stripped Stryker's voice of life, as expected. "I hope you've got something for me, Mr. Weaver," she said.

"Lunch, I think," Weaver said. "I finished reverse-engineering the CAD app's subroutine yesterday. I extracted the algorithm and converted it to standard mathematical notation. That took most of the night, but it's oh so pretty. The problem is that I can't match the equations to anything. I'm not good enough at math to know what I'm looking at," Weaver said. He had earned a C grade in the required course for his computer science degree, and that had been a gift from a merciful professor. Weaver had never seen the point. He'd been a programmer for more than a decade now and had never needed any math beyond what he had learned in high school.

"I might be able to save you the trouble," Kyra said.

"I'll buy you a beer if you can."

"You'll be buying me more than that. Take a copy of the equations and run over to—" There was a pause as Kyra asked someone a question that Weaver couldn't make out. The encryption stripped too much detail for him to understand quieter voices. "Run over to WINPAC."— the Weapons, Intelligence, Nonproliferation, and Arm Control center—"You need to find a senior analyst who works air defense issues. If you can, they should be able to lay hands on a copy of a Russian science paper that will explain the algorithms."

"It's not on the web?"

"Only in Russian," she explained. "You read Russian?"

"You have the title and author?"

"*Theory of Edge Diffraction of Electromagnetics.* Written by Pyotr Ufimtsev, 1966. The original Russian title is *Metod kraevykh voln v fizicheskoi teorii difraktsii.*" It sounded like Stryker was reading the titles off something. Weaver's ear for accents wasn't well trained, but he'd been sent to Russia on several occasions. Stryker's Russian pronunciation sounded flawless, the accent nearly pure Muscovite as far as he could discern.

"Give me a second, I don't have a Cyrillic keyboard," Weaver said. He winced and hoped that Kyra appreciated sarcasm, but she sounded too tired to care. The tech stole an engineer's graph pad from the next cubicle and hunted for a pencil. "Repeat the name." Kyra repeated the Russian words again. "What's the paper about?"

"Stealth."

"I thought Lockheed Martin invented stealth in the seventies," Weaver said.

"Ufimtsev worked out the math, but the Russians didn't realize what it could be used for. Lockheed Martin did. We think the algorithms you extracted are Ufimtsev's equations for calculating radar cross sections. He figured out that the size of the object reflecting the radar wave is irrelevant: all that matters is the shape. That's why that number on the CAD program only changed when you loaded a new shape. It was the radar cross section. The actual dimensions of the object were irrelevant."

"That's counterintuitive," Weaver said.

"The technology works."

"I guess," Weaver said. "If nobody in WINPAC has a copy of that paper, I'll have to see if the librarians can track it down."

"Whatever you have to do," Kyra conceded. She disconnected the phone.

CIA DIRECTOR'S OFFICE

The CIA director's secure phone rang. She enabled the encrypted connection. "Cooke."

"It's Burke. We're in Seoul."

"How were the potstickers?"

"Wish we'd had the chance to try some," Jonathan said. "I need a favor."

"Sure."

"This might be nothing, but I want to rule it out if there's no connection. Did the Taiwanese ever figure out what that chemical was that took down those SWAT officers in Taipei?"

"The Ops Center finally dropped that one on my desk yesterday, after you two started playing games with the Chinese," Cooke said. "The chemical was something called chlorofluorosulfonic acid. Finding out what that is took another call. The common use is to inhibit water vapor from condensing at near-freezing temperatures. It's used occasionally by DoD to break up contrails on aircraft so they can't be tracked visually from the ground. Is that helpful?"

"You have no idea."

"You going to tell me what this is about?" Cooke asked.

Jonathan told her. "Kyra and I need a flight to one of the carrier battle groups in the Strait," Jonathan said.

"Not a chance. I am not sending you two into an active war zone," Cooke declared.

"We know what the Assassin's Mace is. I can either explain it to an admiral in person, or I can explain it in a cable and we can pray that he bothers to read it and loves my Shakespearean prose."

"You're not the most charming analyst."

"Charming enough for you, I hope," Jon answered.

There was a very long pause and Jonathan found himself listening to the slight hissing static. "You're going to owe me whole barrels of whiskey when you get home," Cooke finally said.

"I'll be able to afford them with the performance bonus that you're going to give me," Jonathan said. "By the way, you should call Garr Weaver. He's an IOC analyst but he should be knocking around WINPAC in another hour or so. He's got something you'll want to see."

"I'll track him down," Cooke said. "Give me fifteen minutes to call the SecDef and see about getting you down to the *Lincoln*." It took her precisely that long to get back to him with the answer.

INCHEON INTERNATIONAL AIRPORT
SEOUL, SOUTH KOREA

Jonathan snapped the handset shut and tapped it lightly against his forehead.

"And?" Kyra asked.

Jonathan looked to Mitchell. "You're taking off without us," he said. He turned to Kyra.

"Where are we going?" she asked.

"The *Abraham Lincoln*." It was his turn to smile. "You never get to go if you don't ask."

Kyra grinned. "Oh, yeah." She leaned over to Mitchell. "I want to say good-bye to him." Mitchell nodded, then turned to Pioneer and spoke to him in Mandarin. The Chinese asset listened to Mitchell, focused on his face until the man stopped speaking.

Sachs watched as the old man turned to Kyra after a moment's silence. "Thank you," Pioneer said. The man spoke a bit of English after all. There was a strong undercurrent of gratitude in the words, stronger than he would have expected between an asset and his escort. Sachs wondered what the brunette had done to deserve it.

"You're welcome," Kyra said. Then she leaned in close and whispered to him in plain English. "You'll never be alone."

Sachs couldn't tell whether the man understood her. He seemed to grasp the emotion if not the words. Regardless, Pioneer gripped her hand with both of his own, bowed to her again, and then turned to Mitchell and said something in Mandarin.

"'I hope to see you soon,'" Mitchell translated. "We need to get in the air." Kyra looked at Pioneer and nodded.

"We're gone," Jonathan said.

The analysts climbed down the stairs and moved to a safe distance. Mitchell grabbed the rope and pulled the stairway up into the plane, then locked the hatch as the Learjet's engines began to spin up.

"They'll be at Dulles in eighteen hours," Kyra said. "Now what?"

"We meet our own escort," Jonathan said. "Have you ever been on an aircraft carrier?" he asked.

"No," she said.

Jonathan smiled. "Trust me, you'll love it."

"No, I won't," Kyra assured him. "I get seasick."

She made the analyst wait as she bought Dramamine at one of the airport shops.

USS *ABRAHAM LINCOLN*
482 KILOMETERS NORTHEAST OF TAIWAN

Captain Nagin eased back on the F-35's throttle and leveled the plane as he came out of his turn. Two fellow Bounty Hunters were behind him, one fifty meters off each wing, and another trio of his fellow Bounty Hunters ten miles behind. All six stealth planes were sharing data with feeds coming from *Lincoln*, an AWACS out of Guam, and a pair of E-2C Hawkeyes that had taken off from the carrier after Nagin's flight. For the moment, their own active electronically scanned array (AESA) radars were off and the F-35's four-panel cockpit screen still offered Nagin a fine view of the sky ahead. The horizon was dark with thunderclouds, and a lightning storm thirty miles ahead was giving a light show as good as any the *Lincoln* CAG had ever seen from a cockpit. It was a beautiful sight, as long as one kept a respectful distance, and one he wouldn't have minded lingering to watch.

The four Chinese Su-27 Flankers ahead marred the view.

The Flankers were in an echelon formation, each plane slightly to the rear and to the right of the one ahead, and all a thousand feet higher and two miles ahead of Nagin's flight. They were also on course to encroach on *Lincoln*'s defense zone unless they changed course in the next five minutes. Some things were not to be trifled with in Nagin's world, and the safety of home was one them. At the moment, home was the *Lincoln*—the landing strips on the flattop, not to put too fine a point on it.

"Think they know we're here?" asked one of Nagin's wingmen, a youngish lieutenant, call sign Squib. The other wingman was Cleetus.

"Nope," said Nagin. The Flankers' relatively weak radars almost certainly hadn't been able to get a return off the stealthy F-35s. And with the AESA systems off, there were no emissions for the Flankers to detect. "Think I'll go introduce myself."

Nagin pulled back on the stick and advanced the throttle ever so slightly, and his plane obediently rose in the sky, pulling ahead of the rest of his personal pack and pushing forward toward the Chinese fighters. He closed the distance gently until he was in position to join the formation, becoming the rearmost plane in the echelon line.

I love this part, he thought. He pushed the F-35 forward a few meters until he flanked the Chinese fighter in the rear position.

The PLA pilot took a moment to notice, obviously seeing the US Navy aircraft only out of his peripheral vision at first. Then his head swung full around. Nagin couldn't see his face through the darkened helmet visor, but the other pilot's body language told him everything. His head began to jerk wildly about and he started to slip switches in the cockpit with abandon. Doubtless he was yelling to his flight leader and wondering where the American had come from.

Nagin waved, then motioned hard for him to change course. The PLA pilot made no obvious response. Nagin gave the entire group several seconds to respond, but the line held steady on course.

Okay, Nagin thought. *Meet the boys.* "Gentlemen," he said over his radio, "time to open the coat."

The two Bounty Hunters to the rear both grinned behind their visors, reached forward to the four-panel computer screens above their knees, and pressed virtual buttons on the glass. The AESA radars in the F-35s both came alive in tandem and washed the Flankers in electromagnetic waves. The Su-27s began screaming threat warnings in their masters' ears. A second later, the F-35s' bay doors snapped open and their missile loads emerged, breaking the stealth profiles. The F-35s were suddenly visible to anyone with a radar.

The Flankers immediately began to break formation.

"Now where did they come from?" Nagin chuckled to himself. The sight of two F-35s appearing out of nothing on the Flankers' heads-up display must have been a brutal shock, which was the point.

The Flankers went in four different directions, all moving west at varying altitudes and headings. Nagin eased back on his throttle and pushed his stick forward to descend a thousand feet to rejoin his flight. "Close up and pull back," he radioed back to Squib and Cleetus. "No sense making them think we're too anxious to get rowdy." The two wingmen retracted their bay doors, restoring the stealth profiles, then killed the AESA radars, and all three F-35s disappeared off the Flankers' screens.

I wonder which one scares them more? Nagin asked himself. *Watching us just appear or seeing us go away?*

USS *ABRAHAM LINCOLN*
SOUTHEAST COAST OF TAIWAN

They came aboard the carrier in the middle of a squall. The flight from Seoul to Tokyo's Narita Airport had been turbulent but short. A Navy driver had delivered them to the US Naval Air Facility at Atsugi and led them to a waiting C-2A Greyhound on the tarmac. There had been no conversations with the crew, no talking at all except for the short safety briefing, which Jonathan had ignored. The ease with which he strapped himself in suggested that he'd had practice, but the turboprops were loud enough to discourage Kyra from asking him any questions. Once aloft, Jonathan slept and left Kyra to wish she could do the same. The float coat vests they were ordered to wear were not uncomfortable but the seats and the "Mickey Mouse" helmets with heavy ear protectors were. She might have made do, but the plane itself refused to sit still. She had never been aboard a propeller-driven aircraft. The Dramamine did nothing for her nerves. Every bit of wind and rough air made the Greyhound jump, leaving her edgy and awake. Alone in her thoughts, she wondered whether the aircraft could evade a MIG should the Chinese decide to take offense at their approach to the war zone. Probably not.

The seat belts performed as advertised when the plane hit the deck harder than Kyra thought possible for an aircraft to survive and then rushed to a stop in a distance too short to be natural. Unseen crewmen disconnected the tailhook from the wire and Kyra watched, too tired to be curious, as they folded up the wings. The plane taxied to a space forward of the carrier island to make room for a Hornet coming less than a minute behind them. The crew chained the Greyhound to the deck and only then did the passengers deplane.

Horizontal rain lashed the deck and everyone on it. Kyra was stunned to feel the deck pitching and rolling under her feet. She'd thought a carrier was too large to toss about, and she stumbled as the crew hurried them to a hatch into the island. A seaman from the Air Transport Office dropped their wet bags at their feet and gave them cursory directions to their quarters.

It was the night watch. The island decks were at full lighting but the spaces under the hardtop were visible only under the red flood-lights that preserved the crew's night vision. Their staterooms were on the O-2 level, a single deck removed from topside, where Kyra could still hear and feel aircraft launching and landing. The planes were hitting hard in the storm. She suspected that they could have berthed her several decks below and she still would have heard it. Jonathan had warned her during the drive to Atsugi that a carrier was not a quiet place.

The stateroom was smaller than a college dorm, all gray metal and blue carpet, but she had the space to herself, for which she was grateful. She had her choice of three racks stacked in a vertical bunk; she chose the middle. Entering the lowest would have required her to get on her knees, and the upper rack was even with her head. She was sure that trying to get out of it in the dark with the ship pitching about would have been a dangerous exercise.

There was a television mounted on the upper shelf of the metal desk, and Kyra found a live feed of the flight deck besides the DoD channels. She settled on CNN and tried to catch up on the war, but the news, the noise, and the rolling of the carrier in the restless sea together failed to keep her from wanting to collapse. The adrenaline that had surged through her during the Beijing operation had long since worn off. She hadn't slept in days and now she was more tired than she could ever remember.

She changed her clothing, pulled a Mini Maglite from her pack and turned it on, then killed the room light and crawled into the small bed. The rack barely gave her the space to roll onto her side, as her shoulder brushed the upper bunk. Kyra clenched the lit Maglite in her teeth as she locked the restraining curtain to keep herself from rolling out. A fall onto the metal desk next to the bed could kill her.

She turned off the flashlight and was surprised for a few moments at how complete the darkness was before she dropped into unconsciousness.

Reveille sounded at 0600, full lighting came on in the hallway and climbed under the door, breaking the blackness. The aircraft beating on the deck had never broken their rhythm throughout the night, and the morning shift now began pounding its way across the hallway's floors. None of it disturbed Kyra a bit until Jonathan's endless pounding on her door finally broke into her private oblivion.

CHAPTER 14

SATURDAY
DAY FOURTEEN

Grumbling by the enlisted notwithstanding, the Navy did not bestow flag rank on the gullible or the uncritical. Pollard was quite the opposite, perhaps too critical too often, or so he believed, but he made no apologies for applying stress to his intelligence officers. There was a difference between an error and an intelligence gap. He had suffered through intelligence briefings every morning at sea since his days as a carrier XO and could discern in less than a minute whether the briefer knew his subject. Pollard respected officers willing to confess uncertainty and had blocked the promotions of several who tried to fake their way past him. The admiral had no desire to humiliate any officer for no good reason, but Pollard had no patience for those who thought they could waste his time. Few tried it twice.

His standards were no different if the briefer was a civilian. His gut impression of the analysts sitting in his quarters was favorable. Burke gave no sign of being intimidated by rank. Pollard had come across few men who acted with such equanimity in his presence aboard this ship. It was rare and slightly annoying. He didn't consider himself a tyrant to be feared, but some display of intimidation would have shown a healthy respect for the experience and accomplishments underlying his senior rank.

The woman was harder to read. Stryker came across as an odd mix of confidence and inexperience, traits that were usually contradictory. She handled herself well enough around the officers but deferred most questions to Burke.

"If it had been my choice, I would have denied you permission to come aboard. You have some friends in high places," Pollard told them. The order had come from Showalter by way of a shore-to-ship call. "I don't like having civilians aboard in a possible war zone. Nothing personal."

"Understandable. But I promise, we can justify our presence," Jonathan replied.

"You've got five minutes to do it," Pollard said.

Jonathan nodded. "I assume you've heard of the Assassin's Mace project?"

"Of course."

"We believe the Chinese have deployed an Assassin's Mace weapon and the PLA might be setting either the *Lincoln* or the *Washington* up as the target of a weapons test," Jonathan said.

Pollard dropped his head and stared at the analyst over the top of his glasses. "You get right to the point, Mr. Burke," Pollard said.

"Socializing isn't his strong point," Kyra advised.

"Okay, forget the clock," Pollard ordered. "What's your evidence?"

"Director Cooke has given us approval to share some intel with you that came from a CIA asset who was the senior archivist inside Ministry of State Security headquarters in Beijing," Jonathan began. "He worked for us from 1991 until yesterday, when Ms. Stryker here exfiltrated him from the country." The officers turned their heads to Kyra and the admiral's eyebrows went up, but he remained silent. Kyra blushed a bit at the attention. "He's provided us with information that suggests the PLA has developed stealth technology. We can review the fine details if you have the time, but suffice it to say that we believe the PLA has at least one fully functional stealth aircraft."

Pollard lowered his head and stared at the analysts, then pulled off his glasses and dropped them on the coffee table that separated him from Burke. "Mr. Burke, the Chinese have been showing off a stealth plane for years. Every piece of intel I've read says it's a test bed piece of crap that can barely fly, much less fight. They just roll it out as a show-piece to embarrass the SecDef when he goes over for a visit. So please tell me you're not that far behind on current events."

"That's not the plane you need to worry about," Burke said. "The J-20 is, I suspect, used for misdirection, to make us think the Chinese are less advanced than they really are. The PLA has a stealth fighter that can most definitely fight."

"And what's your evidence that this thing is functional?" Pollard said.

"First, and most to the point, our asset told us point-blank that the J-20 is considered a disappointment by the PLA and was removed from the Assassin's Mace project years ago," Jonathan replied. "Then there's the bombing of the Kinmen power station. Everyone assumed that a Chinese fifth-column unit or sapper team took it out on the ground because the radar track didn't show anything inbound before the explosion. But the radar track wasn't entirely clean. There was a radar hit on a lower frequency above the target for a few seconds before the explosion. Stealth planes are detectable on low-band frequencies, but most modern radar systems don't use them because they pick up birds, clouds, and everything else."

"Yeah. The clutter gets bad on the scope, and the software doesn't always do a great job cleaning it up," Nagin agreed. He looked at his superior officer. "Would've taken a lot of explosives to dig that hole, but I can believe that the PLA had that much stored up on Kinmen."

"With plenty more on Penghu and Taiwan proper," Pollard added, skeptical.

"In the absence of our other intelligence, I would agree. But imagery analysis suggests that the blast pattern was consistent with an air-dropped munition," Jonathan said. "It certainly would have been far easier to deliver that quantity of explosives from the air, and it would have made a good first test of their current stealth technology. Then they took out the *Ma Kong*. She was a *Kidd*-class vessel, so she wasn't top-of-the-line by our standards, but her radar systems were still better than most of what the Chinese have sailing around the Strait, and she was a key component of Taiwan's air defense network. No sapper team did that, and I think it's unlikely the PLA Navy really got a submarine that close to a secured naval base and then back out again without being detected."

"Tough," Pollard agreed. "But not impossible. So where did they build this thing?" He didn't expect an answer.

Jonathan surprised him. He turned to Kyra and said nothing. It took her a second to realize he expected her to answer. It took another second to review the data in her head and extract the answer. "No idea," she said. "But they've been test-flying it at Chengdu."

"Very good," Jonathan muttered.

"Chengdu?" Pollard asked.

"It's the one air base not in the Nanjing Military Region where imagery showed significant activity once the fighting started," Kyra said. "And it's where the Chinese sent the F-117 wreckage that they bought from the Serbs."

"Okay, you're going to tell me that whole story later," Nagin advised her. "You think the Chinese have their own Area Fifty-One."

"Why not?" Kyra asked. "It worked for us."

"And why do you think this is all a weapons test?" Pollard asked.

"It's the dog that didn't bark," Jonathan replied.

"Excuse me?" Pollard asked, impatient.

Kyra grasped the reference immediately. "Admiral, did the PLA harass you during your approach to Taiwan?"

The admiral and his CAG exchanged short glances. "They certainly could have made life harder for us," Nagin finally answered for the pair. "We've chased off a few PLA fighters. Four or five planes at the most each time."

"No submarines tried to approach?" she asked. "No surface vessels?"

"No," Pollard admitted. "At least none that our ASW screen has reported."

"Any cyberattacks on TRANSCOM, NIPRNet, or any of the other critical military networks?" Kyra asked.

"Not that we've heard," Nagin said.

"And that, gentlemen, flies in the face of everything we know about Chinese doctrine for mounting an invasion of Taiwan," Jonathan concluded. "The plan is for the PLA to do everything it can to delay your entry into the Taiwan Strait while they're making their move, and they aren't following the plan. So there are two possibilities. Either they're planning to invade Taiwan and what we know about the plan is wrong, or they aren't planning on invading, in which case they don't need to follow the plan. And I can't believe the first one is right because no sensible OPLAN for invading Taiwan would ignore the presence of US carriers."

"And that means you're here because the Chinese want you here," Kyra finished. "We were playing China's game the minute the president ordered you into the Strait. It's the logical end to the theory. Your Aegis air defense systems are more advanced than anything the Chinese have and we've had decades to figure out how to beat the Ufimtsev equations. They don't have a test bed that can make sure their plane works against your systems, and they have to know that before they can attack Taiwan."

Pollard took his time coming up with an answer. "That would be a risky way to test the platform," Pollard said. "If it doesn't work, they've blown their black program open."

"If it does work, they change the entire balance of power along the Pacific Rim," Jonathan countered. "Consider it. The PLA takes the first small steps toward invasion to draw in some carriers. They test the plane. If it takes out the carrier and the president pulls the rest of the fleet back, they go full bore against Taiwan. If it takes out the carrier and the president doesn't pull back the fleet, they start taking out the fleet. And if it doesn't take out the carrier, they pull back and still own Kinmen, knowing that no president in his right mind will start a full-on war to take it back for the Taiwanese. The possible rewards outweigh the risk no matter how it plays out."

"Point taken," Pollard admitted.

"It's still just a theory," Nagin observed. "You don't have a smoking gun. You have a radar hit that could be a flock of birds and a pile of reports from a single source that possibly point at a stealth plane program, which could have produced that showpiece junker and not some mysterious second fighter."

"When do we ever have a smoking gun in this business?" Kyra replied.

"Assuming I believe you, how do we defend against a stealth bomber?" Pollard asked, ignoring the question,

"I think you have to draw it out into the open. Give it a target worth chasing," Jonathan said.

"You think I should take the battle group into the Strait," Pollard said. It wasn't a question.

"I think that if you don't pick the time and place, Tian Kai will."

Pollard lifted a coffee mug from the table sitting between himself and the CIA officers, took a long sip, and then set it down carefully in the exact spot from which he'd picked it up. "Mr. Burke, there are eighty-seven hundred sailors in this battle group," the admiral said. "Fifty-six hundred on this ship alone. Another three thousand on seven ships and three subs, and so far, President Liang hasn't showed me that he's got the stones to defend his own people, much less help me defend mine. And if I order us into the Strait and the Chinese really do want to rumble for Penghu, the PLA won't need a stealth fighter to kill a lot of my kids. So it shouldn't surprise you that I'm not going to even think about giving that order unless you can give me something better than a theory and a bird on a radar track."

"Give me a few hours—," Jonathan started.

"Mr. Burke, you can have all week as far as I'm concerned," Pollard replied. "I've got this battle group right where I want it and I'm not moving without a good reason."

• • •

"Any matches on the names?" Kyra asked. She crooked the phone between her head and shoulder, checked her watch, and tried to ignore the gaze of the Navy ensign who thought he never had enough female visitors in his comms shack.

"Barron put the screws to the Taiwanese. They finally coughed up enough information for us to get matches on all of them," Cooke said. "A few are unknowns, but that's to be expected. One of the MSS officers at the Taipei raid site where they recovered the acid was from the Tenth Bureau, a gentleman by the name of Han Song. We also have two reports of him taking trips to Chengdu. A shame he didn't get a lungful of the stuff. Makes me wonder why the Chinese can't figure out how to make it."

"I asked that too. Jonathan thinks they probably just wanted a sample of ours to reverse-engineer so they could compare it with their own recipe."

"That makes as much sense as anything else we've come up with," Cooke said. "Anything else you need?"

"Admiral Pollard isn't buying. We could use a little more material to persuade him."

"What are you asking for?" Cooke asked.

"It would help if you would declassify Pioneer's reporting," Kyra said. "He's out of country now, so there's no threat to him if we clear Pollard and a couple of members of his staff to read the good stuff."

Cooke frowned at the other end of the phone. "Barron won't like that, but we'll have a talk. Is that it?"

"For now."

"Then I've got someone else here who wants to talk." There was a pause while Cooke handed the phone over to someone else.

"It's Weaver." Kyra realized that her call to Cooke had been transferred to the WINPAC vault. The IOC analyst was at his desk and Kyra could hear several people chattering in the background. Weaver was hosting a small party in his office, it seemed. "I found your paper. Some crusty old gent in WINPAC had a hard copy. You should see his office. Looks like he never throws anything out. Paper everywhere. Anyway, the equations match. The CAD program definitely calculates radar cross sections. WINPAC is running some test objects now to check the accuracy, but it looks like the Chinese worked out their own coding for the algorithm," Weaver said. "By the way, there was serious bribery involved to make your deadline."

"I'll make sure Jonathan pays off the debt," she promised.

"He's not there, is he?" Weaver asked.

"Nope. So I get to be his pimp for once," Kyra replied.

"That will do nicely," Weaver said. "See you soon."

Kyra handed the phone back to the ensign and stepped out into the crowded passageway. She looked both ways and realized she had no idea how to get back to the admiral's quarters.

Pollard dropped the file folder on his desk. The Stryker woman had delivered it to his staff a few minutes before and then left for Wardroom 3 to grab breakfast. The admiral had always preferred to study intelligence reports in private before meeting with his J2 to ask questions and saw no reason to change that habit for the two civilians, no matter what they were selling.

After ten minutes of reading, he summoned Nagin to his quarters. "What do you think?" Pollard asked his subordinate. He kept his own counsel but he was not so arrogant as to think he was always the smartest man in the room.

Nagin was still searching through his own copy of the reports. "Well, the CAD program is a real kicker, isn't it?"

"Yes, it is," Pollard agreed. "Combine that with these reports from that Chinese asset, and Mr. Burke's theory suddenly looks a lot more reasonable." He tossed his glasses onto the file folder, then sat back and put his hands behind his head.

"If Burke and Stryker are right and the PLA moves on Penghu, we could end up with a big hole in the flight deck if we try to intervene. Even if we stay on this side of the island," Nagin said. "If the PLA does finally have a real stealth plane, once they know we've seen it, a withdrawal will look like we're retreating out of fear. They'll claim it deterred us."

"And they'd be right," Pollard said. "So either we bloody the PLA's nose now or they'll just get more aggressive and we'll catch it all later."

"*If* Burke and Stryker are right," Nagin added. "They still don't have a smoking gun."

"A smoking gun happens a lot less than people think," Pollard said. "Stryker was right. Everyone always wants that perfect piece of intel that tells you exactly what's going on *right now,* and you can almost never get it. Those two have given us intel that's as good as any we could really ask for and better than most of what we usually get." He leaned forward and rested his arms on his knees and covered his eyes with his hands. He felt very tired.

"So what do you want to do?" Nagin asked. "If we go charging in there and pick a fight with the Chinese, we might be starting a war. The president won't like that much."

"No, he won't," Pollard agreed. "We run, we lose. We stay, do nothing, and get hit, we lose and some of my kids probably get killed. So I want to go hit 'em. If they've really got a stealth plane up in our sky, we find a way to shoot it down. We make them think the whole project was a failure. We make them believe that this Assassin's Mace was a waste of time, money, and some pilot's life so we don't have to see it again."

"The Chinese won't abandon stealth," Nagin said. "They know what it's done for us. They'll keep at it until they make it work." The idea that he might have to share the sky with hostile stealth fighters did not sit well with him.

"Probably," Pollard admitted after a few seconds' thought. "Then the Pentagon had better perfect those unmanned fighter drones before we lose too many pilots." He hated the thought of robot fighter planes, and of losing pilots just a little more. He'd been a pilot too.

"So where do we start looking for the thing?" Nagin asked. Pollard just shook his head.

CHAPTER 15

SUNDAY
DAY FIFTEEN

The Navy called this particular version the Reaper, but Kyra still struggled to stop thinking of the drones by their more common name of Predators. The MQ-9 unmanned drone could carry arms for ground attack. Admiral Pollard wanted to make the Chinese nervous. The hunter/killers' trip from Kadena Air Force Base on Okinawa to the Chinese coast had taken four hours and had reached their second set of waypoints shortly after nightfall three hours before. A radar technician in the Combat Information Center told her they could stay up for twenty hours more before they would have to return to Kadena to refuel. Each Reaper was loaded out with Hellfire missiles that no one expected to use on this mission, though they could have carried a five-hundred-pound bomb if the Air Force so desired.

But the mission at the moment was not attack. NRO had retasked satellites to watch the coast, particularly the PLA nuclear missile forces, but the overlords in Chantilly were nervous that the Chinese might decide to take a shot at the orbiting cameras. The drones could provide near-constant coverage, which Pollard demanded, they were far cheaper to replace if destroyed, and spares could be brought along in hours. A damaged satellite network would take years and tens of billions of dollars to restore. NRO had assured the Department of Defense for years that its network could provide the wartime coverage the United States needed. There was less confidence in that assessment now and Pollard had no patience for it. His request to the Air Force for their Reapers had not been polite.

If there was an Assassin's Mace, it seemed likely to fly from one of six air bases within two hundred fifty miles of Taiwan, Jonathan had guessed. Navy Intelligence had designated three as prime candidates using some criteria they had not bothered to share with Kyra. She'd ignored the chance to catch up on the intelligence in favor of sleep, but Jonathan assured her that the deductions were sound and she trusted him. The Reapers had reached station near all three hours before. The first was circling off the Fuzhou coast. Its two brothers would need another half hour to arrive over Jinjiang and Longtian.

The PLA's combat air patrols had not challenged the drones during their approach over the open water. One MIG had made a quick pass, close enough to get a visual and see the missiles. The Reaper had sent back excellent video footage of the Chinese pilot ogling the drone, but the Reaper had been over international waters and the MIG had moved away. *Probably wondering what a Reaper's air-to-air capabilities are,* Kyra thought. It could carry Stinger missiles, the tech had informed her, and she wondered if the Chinese pilots knew that. They were probably calling home asking for data in case they had to engage, and the Central Military Commission and the Politburo were likely debating the issue. If Tian and his circle did decide to engage the Reapers, it would be a one-sided fight and the United States would lose several million dollars' worth of unmanned drones.

Light from the passageway leaked into the J2 office, briefly disturbing the red tinge cast by the overhead lamps. Kyra watched Pollard enter. She kept her place next to the door, and if the senior officer noticed her presence, he didn't acknowledge it. His focus went immediately to the Reapers' radar track on the master screen.

"Anything?" Pollard asked. It really was a moot question. The senior CIC officer on duty had standing orders to report anything more than a MIG flyby.

"No, sir," one of the officers reported, this one a lieutenant. Kyra knew how to read the ranks, yet another skill deemed important by the NCS. "The drones are outside Chinese airspace per your orders, with a five-mile cushion. AWACS are tracking multiple CAPs over the Strait, but they're giving the drones plenty of room."

"Not five miles, I bet," Pollard said. It was a rare joke from the senior officer aboard. The men laughed. Kyra did not, but she did allow herself a smile. "Let's make 'em nervous. Shift the tracks west, quarter mile every pass, until they're within a mile of the line." The drones could return video footage of the coast from much farther out than their current position of seventeen miles east. They did not need to move in closer, but surveillance was not their true mission. The Reapers would have gone into the Strait whether there was an Assassin's Mace or not, but now they would make for very expensive bait if the Chinese chose to see them as such.

"Aye, sir," the tech said.

Kyra looked at her watch: 2227 hours. International law dictated that a country's territorial waters and airspace extended twelve nautical miles out from its coastline. The Reapers were five miles beyond that line and started moving toward it. They would fly in circles, one round every fifteen minutes by her estimation, cameras aimed at their targets, moving closer by a nautical mile every hour toward an invisible line found only on maps. If the Chinese didn't interfere, the Reapers would be within one mile of their airspace, a whisker by any standard, in four hours. It would be a long, very slow night unless the Chinese made it interesting. Kyra thought about leaving, going to her cabin and trying to sleep, but she suspected sleep wouldn't come. The Navy prohibited alcohol on board, and she'd had enough men try to flirt with her that she didn't want to pass the time in a wardroom. She reached for an empty chair and pulled it against the rear wall where she could sit out of the way.

CHAPTER 16

MONDAY
DAY SIXTEEN

It happened at 0237. The Reaper targeting Fuzhou had just crossed the thirteen nautical mile marker drawn on the radar track. Without a sound, the infrared video feed turned to static.

"What happened?" a lieutenant asked. Kyra didn't know his name. "Camera malfunction?"

"No, sir," one of the techs answered. He couldn't have been more than twenty by Kyra's estimation. "Complete loss of all feeds. Sir, that one is down."

"Freeze the track shift on the other two," the lieutenant said. "Keep them outside the thirteen-mile limit. It looks like that's where the PLA drew its red line."

The Reaper had dropped all its feeds simultaneously. Kyra was no military analyst—*yet?*—but there weren't many possibilities worth considering. *Only one,* she thought. *The Chinese just destroyed a Reaper and nobody saw it coming.*

"The AWACs sent over their radar tracks and we compared ours with theirs," the J2—*Lincoln's* senior intelligence officer—said. "One of them caught a return that we didn't, which bugs me. It's a weak hit, but definitely a hit." The J2 cued up the track on one of the smaller screens. He walked the video forward one frame at a time. "Starting at kill minus five seconds, the screen is clear. Four . . . three . . . and there." Kyra watched, saw an icon, a red triangle, appear behind the position marking where the Reaper spent its final seconds. The J2 advanced the frame. "The bogey shows up for less than two seconds and then . . ." The red triangle disappeared in a single frame, with the Reaper icon clearing off the screen a second later. "We have a ghost."

"We should be so lucky," Nagin said.

"Your ghost has a temper and can dish out a hard kill," Kyra said.

"Is that your stealth plane, Mr. Burke?" Pollard asked.

"I believe so," Jonathan said. "I suspect that the Assassin's Mace has internal weapons bays to keep the stealth profile intact, like the F-35. I suggest that what you just saw on the radar track was the return signal from a stealth plane that opened its bay doors to fire an air-to-air missile. The plane closed up the doors, restored its stealth profile, and fell off the screen."

"That fits with what we expect the other man to see when we're flying F-35s against him," Nagin said. "Not quite a smoking gun but maybe as close as we're going to get."

"He took the fat piece of bait you left dangling for him. Doesn't that worry anyone here besides me?" Kyra asked.

"Never let them see you sweat, young lady." Pollard glared at her. "Yes, they took the bait. It means that either the Chinese are convinced we have no idea what's going on and that they can knock down a Reaper with impunity. Or they're confident enough in their design that they don't care whether we know," he reasoned. "The former is more likely, and this puts us in a good position. But in either case, at least we can make an educated guess which air base he's flying from. Are we getting anything from the other two?"

"Nothing we haven't already gotten from the birds in orbit," Nagin said. "Troops massing at the ports, enough to make a play for Penghu, but not nearly enough for a stab at Taiwan proper."

"No time like the present," Pollard said. He would have preferred to have Navy Intel take a long, hard look, preferably a few years' worth of looks, at Jonathan's theory and evidence before risking his ship, but Tian Kai seemed determined not to grant them the time. "J2, tell Kadena to recall the other two before the PLA decide to take a shot at them. No sense wasting the taxpayers' money." The admiral picked up the mic and called the bridge. "Helm, make your course one-nine-five, speed ten knots," Pollard said. He hated for *Lincoln* to run at anything less than full speed, but silence would be more important. F-22 Raptors from Kadena would provide additional air cover. They had launched two hours before and mated with a tanker that came over from Guam. The two AWACS birds that were circling several hundred miles to the northeast had come from Okinawa as well. The PLA would see those, but not the Raptors, which were stealth fighters. If the PLA Air Force decided to move on the airborne radar platforms, Chinese pilots would start dying in large numbers with no warning.

"All ahead full, course one-nine-five, aye," the bridge officer announced.

"We'll round the point in two hours," Pollard said to Nagin. "Send the Vikings and the Seahawks up just before then to begin ASW operations. They should have a free run for a couple of hours. We should pass east of Liu-ch'iu Yu before the storm clears." The rain pounding on the ocean surface would make it harder for *Lincoln's* submarine-hunting aircraft and helicopters to find the Chinese subs that were certainly holding station off the Taiwanese coast, but it would also mask the noise from the planes and choppers' engines from the Chinese fast-attack boat hiding under the waves. The storm would move past them to the east before *Lincoln* would reach the northern point the admiral had set as his private goal.

"A shame we have to hug the coastline so close," Nagin said. "I'd love to drive right up the middle of the Strait just to tell the Chinese what they can do with themselves."

"Makes me wish they'd try to approach us from starboard. I'd love to watch some Chinese subs get swamped in the silt plain," Pollard said. Much of Taiwan's coast was a mud flat, submerged only a few feet under the surface, which extended a half mile to the west. "And I'd bet real money that the PLA has sleepers on the beaches with binoculars watching for us, but they won't see us in this squall." The rain would see to that, as well as the fact that the entire carrier group had killed their running lights. GPS removed much of the danger of a collision between friendly ships, but night maneuvers in tight formation near a coastline were a risk even with help from satellites.

"Are you sure you won't want a JAG on the bridge for this?" Nagin asked.

"A good lawyer doesn't tell you what you can and can't do," Pollard advised his subordinate. "A good lawyer tells you how you can do what you want to do legally. But never ask them, if you can avoid it."

"Always better to ask forgiveness than permission?" Kyra asked. It was the rule to live by in the National Clandestine Service.

"POTUS gave me the green light. But I don't need anyone's permission to protect my carrier group," Pollard said.

CHAPTER 17

TUESDAY
DAY SEVENTEEN

the first launch had been overwhelming. Kyra was forced to scrounge a pair of ear protectors, these off a first lieutenant who was eager to spend five minutes talking to a woman.

She wasn't counting but was sure at least twenty or more Super Hornets had taken to the air in the last few minutes, and now F-35s were moving onto the flight deck. *Lincoln* was going to war. Kyra wondered why Pollard hadn't evacuated her and Jonathan to the mainland. Maybe the admiral didn't want to risk a departing helicopter or Greyhound giving away the carrier's position.

She felt a hand tap her shoulder and turned. Jonathan waved her inside. She followed him through the hatch, pulled the heavy metal door closed to seal out the sound, though some still penetrated the bulkheads, and pulled her ear protection down so she could hear the senior analyst.

"Nice trick, scrounging the muffs," he said. "I couldn't get anyone to loan me a pair."

"You don't have the same draw with men who've been at sea too long," Kyra said.

"No doubt," Jonathan said. "The admiral invited us to camp out in the Tactical Flag Command Center when the shooting starts."

"Safest place on the ship to keep two civvies from getting hurt during the fight?" Kyra asked. The TFCC was below the flight deck near Pollard's quarters, almost directly underneath catapult number one.

"If the Chinese start shooting at us, there won't be any safe place on the ship," Jonathan said. That shook her a bit, he saw, and it was understandable. Playing with the MSS on the Beijing streets had been dangerous, but her training had offered her a degree of control over events. She wouldn't get that if a Chinese antiship missile was inbound.

"You think we'll get hit?" she asked.

He shrugged. "Always a possibility. But attacking a drone is one thing. Attacking a carrier is quite something else. The public handles stories about downed Reapers better than pictures of ships with holes in them. We might just find out how committed the Chinese really are."

"If the Mace works and we can't prove the Chinese attacked us, wouldn't that be irrelevant? Isn't that what it's for?"

"If the Mace blows a hole in this ship, the president won't be send-

Kyra had Vulture's Row to herself. The open-air balcony gave her a broad view of *Lincoln's* flattop, from which F/A-18E/F Super Hornets were launching and landing at a steady clip. The rain had stopped and the sky was just light enough after the dawn that she could make out the contours of the other surface vessels in *Lincoln's* group. An experienced military analyst could tell a vessel's class by its shape. Kyra wished for a moment that she'd had that training and supposed that Jonathan could do it. She knew these naval officers could do it. Regret welled up, surprisingly strong and sudden, that she'd never served in the military. Kyra had considered it. She had even taken the military ASVAB exam after high school and managed a perfect score. Recruiters had called her at home for nine months after, but her father forbade her from entering the service. Peter Stryker was a high-minded liberal UVA political science professor with a religious streak who had protested the Vietnam War, still thought soldiers were baby-killers, and had threatened to disown her if she joined the military that he hated so much. He hadn't carried through on his threat when she had joined the CIA only because her cover status gave her a reason not to tell him, and she never would if she could avoid it. He'd wanted his daughter to become an activist lawyer but had at least made peace with her being an entry-level executive in a software company. Kyra was sure they would never talk again if she ever told him the truth. What she wasn't sure about was whether that would bother her. They talked little enough as it was.

A brief suspension of flight operations had given her a few hours of unbroken sleep until the first launches began without warning. Kyra had pulled herself from the bunk, piled her hair under a blue *Lincoln* ball cap she'd charmed off an ensign the day before, and made her way to Vulture's Row to watch. All four of the catapults were engaged. The carrier had already launched its support aircraft and was now sending up its fighter squadrons in short order. The noise generated by the multiple screaming Pratt & Whitney and Rolls-Royce jet engines during

ing carriers into Chinese waters anytime soon," Jonathan said. "*That's what the Mace is for.*"

The E-2C Hawkeyes were the first planes to go up. *Lincoln* only had four of the airborne early warning planes and they would not be straying far from the fleet. All four pushed immediately for higher altitudes, almost to their limit of thirty thousand feet, turned south, and spread into a quarter-arc formation with a fifty-mile spread. *Washington* sent four more aloft at nearly the same time. They mirrored the half arc to the north, forming a shallow half circle together with their *Lincoln* brothers that started west of Taiwan's midpoint and reached to the island's southern end. Together with the two AWACS aircraft from Kadena and Guam circling behind the airborne line, there were ten aircraft aloft whose raison d'être was radar tracking. Together, their connected radar network would have been overkill for managing the destruction of almost any air force in the world. On this day, they were looking for a single plane and the combined crews were left wondering if they were enough.

The S-3B Vikings left the carrier deck next. Their missions for the day were midair refueling. All carried buddy fuel tanks under their wings. They stopped their ascent at a mere five thousand feet and began slow orbits of their carriers, waiting for the next aircraft that would be leaving the decks.

The EA-6B Prowlers followed. Two had been aloft since before dawn, providing electronic cover for the carrier by jamming Chinese radars. They would be landing shortly to refuel and switch flight crews before going back up to join their brothers.

Lincoln's F-18 Hornets took their turns after the Prowlers. They all turned northwest from *Lincoln's* once they were in the air. *Washington's* own Hornets lined up on the deck with four waiting on the catapults. They would sit on the deck, their pilots antsy to fight but not launching until *Lincoln's* fighters engaged the enemy. Once *Lincoln's* planes began running low on fuel and ammunition, *Washington's* second wave would move in and cover their brothers' withdrawal.

The Bounty Hunters' F-35 Joint Strike Fighters went up last. They turned west as one and pulled away from the carrier fleet. They lowered their noses and did not level out until they had reached an altitude of one hundred feet above the waves of the Taiwan Strait.

Nagin was the last to go up. He flew in formation with the Bounty Hunters for two minutes, then rolled away, pulled back on his stick, and climbed for the sky.

Lincoln herself was hugging Taiwan's southwestern coast. The position gave the small fleet the maximum distance between itself and China's land-based forces and effectively prevented any PLA subs from sneaking up anywhere on *Lincoln's* starboard side. The American ships were under EMCON—emissions control, radio silence. That and the Prowlers' electronic jamming would make finding the fleet a hard job for the PLA Air Force, at least until Pollard wanted that situation to change.

THE TAIWAN STRAIT

"This is not a good idea." Lieutenant Sam Roselli and his EP-3 Aries crew had taken off from Kadena hours before. "Same schedule, same flight plan. We'll get the same MIGs off our wing and the same missile lock up our tail."

"Somebody has to be the bait," Lieutenant Julie Ford said. "Might as well be us." The radar track showed several MIG combat air patrols off the coast and eight E2-C Hawkeyes dispersed in a north-south arc with a pair of AWACS birds circling behind. Some commercial traffic was heading east away from Taiwan and in various directions from the Chinese coast. There were no US fighters even close to the EP-3's altitude.

"I'd feel better if I could see 'em." Stealth planes flying on the waves weren't easy for anyone to see, allies or enemies alike. The laws of physics didn't discriminate between American and Chinese radar receivers, especially when the Vikings were out there doing their electronic warfare voodoo.

"They're out here," Ford said. Unless the entire mission had gone totally FUBAR from the start. She hoped Admiral Pollard aboard the *Lincoln* would have the courtesy to let them know if that was the case.

The EP-3's HUD flashed a change. At least two dozen icons appeared in sequence over the Chinese coast on the radar track Ford and Roselli were sharing with the Hawkeyes. The icons formed up after several minutes in the air and began moving east. "I guess the PLA wants to see what's going on," Roselli said.

"Come to Mama," Ford said.

Three of the triangles broke away from the main group. "Three contacts inbound, bearing two-zero-seven, range thirty miles," one of the Hawkeyes reported. Ford stared at the HUD. The Su-27s were approaching too fast for comfort, using their afterburners for no good reason other than to intimidate the much slower EP-3. *You can't run* was the message.

All done running, she hoped.

It was a very short minute before three Su-27s rocketed past the Aries faster than the speed of sound. The sonic boom shook the EP-3, and the turbulence increased as the prop-driven plane passed through the roiled air. Roselli pushed forward on the stick until the aircraft reached calmer air a thousand feet below. The MIGs turned and reduced speed to match the US Navy plane's course.

"Tallyho. Weren't we just here?" Roselli muttered.

Two of the MIGs flanked the EP-3, one off each wing, with a third holding position behind. "Lead bandit is on our six," Ford announced. She looked to starboard. The Su-27 was close enough that she could see into the cockpit through the canopy. The PLA pilot waved at her, signaling for the EP-3 to change course. Ford shook her head. *We're in international airspace and you know it,* she thought.

The flight leader didn't disappoint. The EP-3's threat receiver lit up on schedule. "Bandit just lit us up!" Ford announced. This time Roselli didn't push the stick forward to dive for the waves. And he knew that this time his hand was shaking for certain.

"This is fun," he muttered.

"Break!" Nagin ordered. The PLA Air Force, already engaged in active hostilities against Taiwanese territories, had just threatened a US Navy aircraft over international waters. At least that would be the story recounted in the UN Security Council. The Chinese would deny that they intended to shoot the EP-3 down, but the positive radar lock and the ongoing war would make it difficult for the Chinese ambassador to argue against the USS *Abraham Lincoln* coming to the defense of an unarmed US aircraft under the circumstances.

Lincoln's unstealthy Hornets had held back over fifty miles to the rear, leading the Chinese pilots to think those were the closest American fighters. It was a bad assumption. The Bounty Hunters had held their F-35 Joint Strike Fighters at less than a hundred feet above the waves while flying in circles around the EP-3's course. The Su-27s' radar washed harmlessly off the Bounty Hunters, the energy deflected in every direction except back toward the Chinese planes. With the EP-3 now under threat of hostile fire, every US Navy fighter pilot in the area pulled back on the stick and the planes climbed for the sky in a wide sunburst formation that would have made the Blue Angels proud.

"There!" Ford yelled. An absurd number of icons appeared on the radar in a circle around their position almost simultaneously, and they were close. The fact that the radar returns on the new planes were holding steady meant that their missile bays were open.

It took less than a second for the Chinese pilots to prove they had seen the same on their HUDs, though she doubted the enemy pilots knew what they were up against. Every Su-27 was getting multiple threat warnings off their receivers, and the Chinese fighters began banking and rolling hard enough that Ford wondered whether the Chinese pilots weren't seeing spots from the g-forces pulling the blood away from their brains and down to their legs.

"That's our cue," Roselli said. He pushed forward on the stick and the nose dropped. "Elvis is leaving the building." There was no sense in giving the PLA another target. He suspected that the MIGs would be far too busy to go after his aircraft, but he was not a gambler at heart, even without the rest of his regular crew on board.

The F-35s were in near-vertical climbs. All of them found a missile lock on a dancing MIG and began maneuvering to keep the Chinese fighters within their firing envelope. One of the PLA pilots pulled his aircraft around toward the ascending stealth fighters and the lead F-35 roared past the Su-27's nose less than two hundred feet out. The Chinese aviator reacted on instinct and pulled the trigger on his gun for a half second before realizing what he'd done. The rounds missed, but the tracers were visible.

"We are taking fire!" someone announced over the comm.

"Weapons free," Nagin ordered.

The targeted F-35 pulled left, banked over, and rolled to wings level. The AMRAAM in his open bay dropped out and shot forward. The rocket motor burned for less than two seconds before the warhead struck the MIG's airframe and ripped the plane in half. The stealth

fighter's weapons bay snapped shut, restoring the plane's stealth pro-
file. The dead Su-27's wingman was maneuvering for a shot when the
F-35 suddenly dropped off his radar track. The Chinese pilot screamed
Mandarin curses into his microphone.

The Battle of the Taiwan Strait had begun. The Chinese had fired
first. The Americans had drawn first blood.

TACTICAL FLAG COMMAND CENTER
USS *ABRAHAM LINCOLN*

The TFCC was not designed for beauty. Exposed cables and pipes
ran through the ceilings and electronics were sticking out of the walls
in almost random fashion. Kyra couldn't find any logic or order to the
layout, but she was sure that the design made sense to somebody. And
it was *cold,* which did make sense when she thought about it. *Nuclear-
powered air conditioning*, she realized.

Pollard had left the line open to CIC. "Fire up the network."

Every vessel in the *Lincoln* fleet turned on its air-search radar
almost simultaneously and flooded the air with electromagnetic ra-
diation. The Hawkeye and AWACS rotodomes added their own radar
beams to the sweeps running across the battle zone.

The first waves reached the MIGs and struck every surface in direct line of sight of a radar transmitter. The flattened surfaces of the
Su-27s reflected huge amounts of energy back to their points of origin.
The radar energy traveled at light speed; every transmitter afloat and
in the air received solid hits from the Chinese planes in microseconds.
The MIGs' onboard computers screamed as they detected the energy
emissions and their pilots had a new problem to worry about.

The same radar waves reached the F-35s. The stealth planes' air-
frames absorbed much of the energy and the nonmetal composites
under the skin let more through unhindered to pass out the other side
and into space. The minimal energy that remained struck the carefully curved surfaces and rebounded in every direction possible away
from their transmitters. None of the ships and planes scanning the air
received more than an unmeasurable fraction of its own radar energy
back from the stealth fighters.

"This'll be the craziest furball the Chinese have ever seen," Pollard muttered. "A dogfight where you can only see half of the planes."

Lincoln could tell where its birds were only by interrogating their transponders. The F-35s reflected radar from *Lincoln* the same as it did from the Chinese. One of the techs in the TFCC filtered out the transponder returns for a few moments at Pollard's request so the admiral could see what the PLA would see, and it was bizarre. The carrier's receivers picked up occasional weak returns from the radars mounted aboard the Hawkeyes, the AWACS, other ships in the fleet, and even the F-35s themselves, but the signals were broken up, and so the CIC screens marked the F-35s sporadically, like fireflies sparkling in a dark field. *Washington's* F-18s moved through Taiwanese airspace, flying close to the deck, but Kyra could tell that they were holding their distance and holding down their speed to preserve fuel until they engaged, and she assumed that the second carrier's F-35s were close to the inbound Hornets. She was impressed by their radio discipline. The pilots were probably crawling out of their flight suits to join the fight.

"Why are they dropping in and out?" one of Pollard's aides asked, an ensign whose name Kyra hadn't bothered to learn. The icons marking the MIGs' positions were moving in arcs around the screen, steady, bright, and disappearing at a steady pace. More were moving east from the Chinese coast.

"Stealth works best when radar is monostatic, where transmitters and receivers are near the same location. But if the target sends enough of the radar wave in a different direction, the receivers don't see anything," Pollard said. "Putting the Hawkeyes and AWACS around the battle space in a circle to pick up those deflected waves breaks that model. It's a multistatic radar net. The F-35s are reflecting the beams in different directions, but we have receivers where the radar beams were going to end up instead of where they were created. But when an F-35 makes a course change, it sends radar waves off in different directions from where it was sending them the second before. So no receiver in the net gets a constant reflection off a stealth fighter when it's juking around. We need more airborne receivers. We've tried tuning some of the radars to the lower frequencies. Stealth doesn't disperse radar waves in the lower bands well, but that'll open the net up to more clutter—clouds and the like. We'll never get accurate fixed position returns, but we might get an idea of where to look. It beats waiting for a visual contact on this Chinese stealth plane, assuming they have one."

"And assuming they send it out," Kyra muttered.

"Sir," one of the techs called out to Pollard. "We have bandits taking off from the coast." Multiple icons were appearing on the scope.

"Keep your eye on Fuzhou," Pollard ordered. "Turn the Hornets loose."

THE TAIWAN STRAIT

Nagin's sense of duty alone kept him from pushing the stick forward and diving into the fight. The largest aerial battle since the Second World War had erupted three miles below him, and it made him sick that he had to stay above it. Navy aces were being made, the first since Vietnam, and he wouldn't be one of them. At most, he would shoot down one plane today. If there was no Assassin's Mace, the CAG likely would return to *Lincoln* as the only Bounty Hunter not to score at least a single kill, given the number of MIGs moving out from the coast. The PLA Air Force was offering his squadrons an embarrassment of targets and more were coming from the west.

He rolled his plane to port to get an expanded view of the aerial battle. A second MIG exploded as a Bounty Hunter AMRAAM penetrated the fuselage at supersonic speed and ignited the jet fuel and ordnance. Nagin saw no parachute and another icon disappeared from his helmet HUD. The MIGs couldn't even see half their enemies on their own radars, and to his practiced eye their maneuvers showed panic in their ranks. The Chinese pilots were trying to focus on the planes they could see, but the Hornets themselves were an even match in performance for the MIGs, the Hornet *pilots* more than a match, and the F-35s were a painful overmatch. Every time a Chinese fighter tried to maneuver behind one of the American planes they could see on radar, their wingmen began screaming about an F-35 lining up behind for a kill shot. It was turning into a one-sided slaughter. The Chinese were finding the stealth disadvantage was too great. Their only advantage was numbers. The Americans would start running out of missiles and fuel eventually, which forced the carriers to stagger the rate at which their forces joined the fight. The first wave would return to *Lincoln* as fighters from *Washington* moved in. The fight was taking place at the extreme edge of *Lincoln's* air defense umbrella, where the ships themselves would began shooting Chinese planes out of the sky if the MIGs came too far east.

Enough of that, Nagin thought. He had a different mission from his brothers and it would be a stupid death if this so-called Assassin's Mace shot him down while he was off watching the dogfight like a gawking plebe watching his first Army-Navy college football game. He started to roll wings-level when one of the Hornets pulled out of the fight into a high arc, pushing Mach 1, a MIG in close pursuit. The Hornet suddenly began dumping speed and pushing its nose higher. *J-turn,* Nagin realized. The American pilot—he couldn't tell who—was forcing his plane into a stall and then would use his flight surfaces to reverse the turn. It was an advanced maneuver, difficult in a Hornet, and one that Nagin wouldn't have tried in a large fight. *Don't get fancy, come around and let your wingman brush him off. Plenty of targets, you'll get yours.*

The MIG pilot was better trained than Nagin would have thought. The Chinese aviator recognized the J-turn and moved inside the curve to line up a kill shot. In a moment, the Hornet would be hanging in the air, as close to motionless as a Navy fighter ever got when it was off the ground, like a piñata waiting for a child to smack it with a bat. But the MIG was too close and the pilot overestimated the time he had to close the distance. The Hornet dropped more speed and the arc of his turn shallowed. The MIG pilot finally saw the danger and tried to pull away too late. The MIG-27 just missed the Hornet's fuselage and the two planes sheared off each other's wings instead.

Nagin held his breath, rolled and banked, and began a slow turn to keep eyes on the dead Hornet. Neither plane exploded on impact, but the Hornet was in a fast tumbling spin and the air around it was thick with burning jet fuel for the few moments before it began a death spiral down. The metal husk fell through its own flaming fuel, smoke now pouring from the burning skin of the fuselage.

Get out, Nagin thought. He hoped the other pilot was still conscious.

"Jumper is hit!" someone yelled over the comm.

Every alarm in the dying US fighter was screaming, and Jumper, rookie though he was, didn't need anyone to tell him it was time to leave. The Hornet pilot reached between his legs, pulled the handle, and then crossed his arms. Explosive bolts in the windscreen fired, blowing the windscreen away from the fuselage. The rocket motors under him fired, driving the Martin-Baker ACES II ejection seat up its rails and out of the plane. The rockets burned off their propellant, the seat fell away, and the chute opened automatically. He wondered if the Chinese ejection seats were as reliable. The answer, it seemed, was no.

"*Lincoln,* I confirm one chute," Nagin said like he was reading the newspaper. Another US naval aviator had just become a lifetime member of the Martin-Baker Fan Club, though the seat's rocket motors manufactured by that company had shortened the man's spine by a half inch. The downed pilot would not complain. The Chinese pilot was learning that the alternative was far worse.

COMBAT INFORMATION CENTER
USS *ABRAHAM LINCOLN*

"CSAR, go!" CIC ordered. One of the combat search-and-rescue Seahawk helicopters circling the carrier peeled away and rushed forward toward the fight. It would stay a hundred feet off the deck to avoid the Chinese radars as long as possible. They could have flown higher. The MIGs now had more pressing problems than trying to spot helicopters, but if not, the CSAR pilots wouldn't have been deterred anyway. No Americans would die in the waters of the Taiwan Strait if they could prevent it, and enemy fire was not going to stop them from at least making the attempt.

TACTICAL FLAG COMMAND CENTER
USS *ABRAHAM LINCOLN*

A pair of triangles on the master screen moved out of the fight and began arcing far too close to *Lincoln*'s position. "Two bandits inbound, bearing two-three-zero, range forty miles!" one of the junior officers yelled.

"They're going for the escorts. Probably trying to open a hole to the carrier," Jonathan told Kyra. "Came around the fight from the southwest. Must be riding close to the water." All of *Lincoln*'s fighters were out of position to intercept and none would be able to close the gap before the MIGs closed the distance for a missile shot.

"Worked for us," Pollard said. The radar return off the two planes was intermittent. *Shiloh* was closer to the inbound planes but off-axis from their approach vector. *Gettysburg* was in a direct line. Pollard didn't bother to radio out to the picket ship. Every captain in the battle group knew his primary job was to protect *Lincoln* even at the cost of his own vessel.

Two icons appeared, both moving away from the approaching MIGs and toward the carrier group. "Two vampires inbound on *Gettysburg*! Range thirty-five miles!"

"Helm, evasive. Fire control, stand by," Kyra heard someone from *Gettysburg* order over the comm. She supposed it was the captain. Seven miles ahead of *Lincoln*, *Gettysburg*'s four General Electric gas turbine engines surged to full power, using all eighty-thousand horsepower to drive the ship into a hard turn through the choppy waters of the Taiwan Strait.

"Range, twenty-five miles. *Shiloh* is firing," one of the *Lincoln*'s techs said. The cruiser was off angle from the inbound missiles but was three nautical miles closer to the missiles and had the first shot.

The antiship missiles were Yingji-82 Eagle Strikes. The solid rocket boosters pushed the missiles to their maximum speed, then fell away into the sea, and the Yingjis' turbojet engines kicked in. Both missiles settled at three meters above the Strait and pushed forward at just under Mach 1.

The two Jian-10B planes had dropped toward the sea once they broke away from the fight. They aimed for fifty feet above the waves, first hoping to get lost in the sea return to evade the AWACS and E-3A Sentry radars when they fired on *Gettysburg*, then to evade the picket ships' fire control radars. It didn't help. Both planes took direct hits from RIM-116 Rolling Airframe Missiles. The pilots died instantly as they and their aircraft were almost vaporized between the missile warheads and their own flaming jet fuel.

COMBAT INFORMATION CENTER
USS *ABRAHAM LINCOLN*

"Hit!" *Shiloh* had knocked down one of the Yingji with a Phalanx Close-In Weapons Systems gun, which cut the odds in half for *Gettsyburg*, but her sister ship now had to defend itself. "One vampire inbound on *Gettysburg*, range seventeen miles, Mach point nine. Sir, it's passed inside

Shiloh's firing envelope," the tech observed. "CIWS guns didn't have time to take the other one, and her RAMs won't be able to catch it."

"Deploy countermeasures." Kyra heard *Gettysburg*'s commanding officer give the order over the comm. The man sounded like he was announcing the weather. *Gettysburg*'s chaff launchers began firing clouds of aluminum strips in front of the carrier, hoping to confuse the Yingji's radars.

"Tracking," *Gettysburg*'s Fire Control tech said. "The Artoos will get 'em." The *Ticonderoga*-class cruiser's Phalanx guns looked like the famous robot but were far more lethal.

"Hope you're right," Kyra heard Jonathan mutter.

One of *Lincoln*'s radar watch cut into the conversation. "Sir, I have an intermittent radar contact, bearing three-four-five, altitude twenty thousand feet, distance thirty miles."

"Out of Fuzhou?" Pollard asked.

"That course is probable but not confirmed, sir."

"And not one of ours?" Pollard asked. This contact wasn't skimming the sea to get lost in the waves. The possible bogey was four miles above the Strait.

"No, sir," the junior officer answered. "I've seen him twice. Unless I'm seeing three different planes or flocks of birds on a parallel course, this bogey came around the fight from the northwest. Constant bearing, decreasing range, distance and time between contacts are consistent with a single fighter."

"You get that, Grizzly?" Pollard asked.

"Grizzly copies," Nagin said. "Moving to intercept." He pulled the stick right, rolled, and pointed his F-35 toward the northwest. He prayed that he would find seagulls.

TACTICAL FLAG COMMAND CENTER

"How many sailors on *Gettysburg*?" Kyra whispered to Jonathan.

"Four hundred, give or take."

"Range ten miles," someone said over the comm. "*Gettysburg* is firing."

No safe place on a carrier, Kyra thought.

Not safe.

Jonathan looked down at his arm as Kyra squeezed it hard. The woman was starting to hyperventilate.

Gettysburg's computers determined that the remaining Yingji was a threat without any help from the fire control technicians. Once its algorithms determined the Chinese missile was close enough, two rockets ignited and flew out of the deck launcher. They went supersonic, their infrared sensors locked onto the Yingji's engine, and they closed the distance within seconds. The first RIM-116 warhead exploded within a few meters of the Eagle Strike and scattered a fragment cloud in its target's path. The metal bits punctured the Chinese missile's nose cone and damaged the stabilizing wings. In a fraction of a second, it shuddered in flight, yawed, and the airflow threw it into a circular spin off its flight path. The second RIM-116 finished the job an instant later. Its shrapnel punctured the Yingji's engine and ignited the remaining fuel. The airframe tore itself apart. Chinese missile wreckage hit the Taiwan Strait at almost Mach 1, and bits of metal skipped across the waves for hundreds of yards.

"Lucky," Pollard muttered. "Won't get lucky forever." *Lincoln's* pilots were outnumbered and still eating the PLA alive anyway, but it wouldn't last. Pollard was surprised that the Chinese Air Force hadn't sent more aircraft after them, but that wouldn't last either if they stayed in the Strait long enough. Chinese submarines could well have been advancing, but his instincts told him that was not the case. The Chinese seemed content with an aerial fight, which gave Pollard a very sick feeling inside. There was nothing to be gained by throwing older fighters and inferior pilots against the US Navy's aviators and Tian knew it. The dogfight was holding the carrier in position to retrieve its planes, and now the radar network had picked up a possible hit.

"They're playing with us," he announced. "Maybe they wanted to try conventional arms before giving their science project a test run." He checked the wall chronometer. "We've got ten minutes. If the PLA wants to keep fighting after that, *Washington's* boys can have some fun."

"I've got to get out of here," Kyra muttered. She pushed past Jonathan and ran out into the passageway.

"Wait—," he started.

"Sir?" the tech spoke up. "That intermittent contact has altered

kept working on their own. She turned her head and only then saw that she wasn't alone. Another young woman, a seaman apprentice, was hanging on to the rail too. She looked at Kyra, her eyes wide with terror. The seaman was younger than she was, still a kid, she realized. Scared out of her teenage mind enough that the girl had abandoned her post, wherever that was. *We're at general quarters. Where's your station?* Kyra thought, suddenly rational. *They'll throw you in the brig.*

Kyra felt a hand on her shoulder and she grabbed it. *Jonathan,* she knew.

The strange plane dove for the water, rolling to one side. Nagin saw its bay doors open. A pair of missiles rolled down, and suddenly the Assassin's Mace was on his scope. Nagin swung his F-35 around as hard as the avionics allowed, but the Chinese stealth plane was arcing inside his turn.

One of the enemy plane's missiles flew off its rail with white smoke trailing behind and punched into a thundercloud ahead, where Nagin lost sight of it.

Fighter-BOMBER, he realized.

The bay doors snapped shut and the Assassin's Mace disappeared from Nagin's scope. His AMRAAM went blind and the PLA's stealth fighter rolled away from Nagin.

Nagin could see the plane with his eyes but his F-35 couldn't see it on radar.

So that's what it feels like, he thought. *Okay, a knife fight it is.*

The inbound Yingji missile was twenty-five miles out and moving at Mach 1.6.

The Tactical Flag Command Center and every radio on the carrier exploded with excited chatter. Pollard was proud that everyone wasn't diving for cover under their stations.

"You have to come inside!" Jonathan yelled.

"Can't," Kyra said. Her rapid breathing made it hard to speak. "I can't."

"It's not safe out here!"

"You said . . . you said 'no safe place on a carrier,'" she finally managed to answer.

"Some places are less dangerous than others."

Kyra heard the 1MC speaker switch on. "All hands, brace for shock!" Then the chaff launchers fired.

Lincoln was no destroyer or frigate but she was hardly defenseless. The *Nimitz*-class vessel, like her sisters, had been built to fight a Soviet navy and air force with hundreds of planes, so the designers had assumed that somewhere, someday, a bandit would get close enough to fire on a carrier. *Lincoln* carried her own countermeasures and point-defense weapons.

"Countermeasures." *Lincoln*'s captain in the CIC held his voice steady. The crew relied on his calm as much as anything to control their own fears.

On the flattop, the carrier began ejecting chaff into the air, port side. The Phalanx guns and Sea Sparrow missile launchers pivoted toward the inbound missile.

"Range nine miles and closing. Sea Sparrows firing."

Pollard stared at the screen, watching the incoming missile close on his carrier. If it was going to hit anywhere, he would lay money on it striking the carrier island. Right where he was standing.

"Inside, now!" Jonathan yelled. Kyra saw his gaze fixed at the horizon.

"What—?" She turned to look just in time to see *Lincoln* fire its missiles.

The RIM-7 Sea Sparrow launchers put two missiles into the air. The solid propellant motors fired and got the weapons to speed in less than two seconds. They closed the distance to the incoming Yingji in a fraction less than seven.

"Miss!" a tech announced. "Eagle Strike was just outside their kill radius. Distance two miles. Artoos tracking." The Yingji and Sparrows had closed on each other's positions at a relative speed of almost four thousand miles an hour, giving the Sparrows too little time to make course corrections before detonation. Each missile had a ninety-pound warhead that pushed shrapnel in a thirty-foot circle, but the Yingji slipped through.

"We do it the old-fashioned way now." Pollard's voice was hard steel, but the crew knew he was trying to sound optimistic. The Phalanx guns

were the last resort and considered less effective against high-speed missiles than the Sea Sparrows, which had just missed.

The chaff launchers kept punching aluminum strips into the air, trying to confuse the Yingji, which stubbornly held its course. The port-side Phalanx guns fore and aft spun on their mounts a bit, making a final targeting correction, and the 20 mm Gatlings fired together, sounding like the Devil's own chainsaw. Streams of lead erupted at the rate of four thousand rounds a minute.

Kyra heard the buzzing of the guns, surprisingly loud over the other deafening noise of the flight deck.

"Get down!" Jonathan grabbed her and pushed her down onto the deck behind the metal shield of the railing. He fell on top of her, then pushed himself up onto one foot to go for the seaman apprentice, who was still frozen in place.

The first gun missed by inches. The second hit the Yingji's nose cone just off center and ripped it to pieces at a distance of three-quarters of a mile from *Lincoln*. The antiship missile was torn apart by a combination of bullets, stress from the supersonic air ripping into its now-damaged frame, and, a moment later, impact with the Taiwan Strait at just under Mach 2 a half mile from the carrier. At that speed, hitting the water was like diving into a field of concrete. The missile shattered into thousands of pieces, bits skipping across the water like stones. Others flew through the air in a straight line toward the ship.

Kyra heard tiny bits of metal on metal clang on the hull, sharp sounds, like gunshots hitting a steel backstop at supersonic speed.

The seaman apprentice shrieked. Kyra twisted her head to look as she heard the other woman's body hit the deck plates. Jonathan scrambled over to her, and Kyra hauled herself to her feet. She heard *Shiloh* fire another missile miles away. Another Phalanx gun, probably *Gettysburg*, sounded in the distance.

The sailor was on her back and still conscious, a dark spot expanding on her blue coveralls over the left shoulder. Jonathan pulled the woman's uniform open and tore her shirt so he could get a look at the wound.

• • •

"Vampire down," the tech announced, his own voice quavering just a hair.

Lucky, Pollard thought. "We can't stay here all day." The admiral looked at the screen. "Sometime this week, Grizzly," he announced. The mic wasn't live. Nagin didn't need to hear the nagging to get on with his job.

Nagin rolled in the opposite direction and approached the other plane almost head-on, certainly inside the Chinese plane's radar cone, and the enemy fighter hadn't shot at him. Nagin's own plane hadn't detected a radar sweep from the other plane. Even with the help of the AWACS and the entire *Lincoln* battle group, the return was still weak when it did show up. Nagin took a chance, put the F-35's nose dead on the Mace, opened his missile bay, and switched on his active radar. The Slammers still refused to sound the tone that would have announced their willingness to shred the other plane into burning pieces.

Nagin had never shot at another plane with his guns. He had maybe three seconds' worth of gunfire, and dogfighting another stealth plane was not something any Navy pilot had ever trained for. In fact, he was pretty sure that the Lockheed engineers had never even studied the possibility.

The Mace pushed hard into a turn and went nose down. Nagin followed, opened up his throttle to keep the distance constant, and pulled the trigger. *I'm gonna pound your brains out.*

His gun flashed and the 25 mm rounds missed their moving target as the Chinese arrowhead rolled to the side and braked hard. Nagin cursed as the Mace curved behind.

"No, you don't," Nagin muttered again, still loud enough to be broadcast. Nagin lifted his nose and leveled out. The Mace followed and Nagin rolled a quarter turn and went for the sky. The black plane behind him started to follow, but gravity pulled hard as it tried to end its dive and it could not make its climb as steep. Nagin backed off on his thrust, arced over and dove. The Mace flashed across his path, leveled, and dove again for the water. It was a skilled maneuver, and Nagin had expected no less. It only made sense that one of the PLA's best pilots would be at the stick of their newest plane.

Jonathan reached underneath the woman's back and felt for blood. There was plenty. "Shrapnel, still in the shoulder. She's bleeding fast.

Might have nicked the subclavian artery," he said. He looked over his shoulder at Kyra. "Get down to the battle dressing station on the flight deck level. We need a corpsman—"

"I don't know where that is," Kyra protested.

Jonathan frowned, then pulled off his jacket and overshirt. He pressed the shirt against the girl's wound and she cried out in pain. He grabbed Kyra's arm with his free hand and pushed her hand down on his shirt. "Press here. Don't let up. I'll be back."

She shifted around Jonathan as he stood, lifting his hands off the sailor only when Kyra's hands were firmly on the girl's shoulder. "How do you know where it is?" Kyra asked.

"Not my first aircraft carrier," he said. Then he stepped through the hatch.

"They're in a rolling scissors," Pollard said. The other Navy officers grumbled in agreement. Both planes were looping around in a line, trying to get position behind each other. It also meant the Chinese pilot had some real training. Assuming the pilots' skills were an even match, the winner would be the man flying the better plane.

Nagin had dropped his airspeed too far for comfort and still couldn't stay behind the Mace. The Chinese plane was slower to accelerate despite its second engine but the larger wings gave it more control at slower speeds. *It's heavier than I am,* Nagin thought. Perhaps the Chinese hadn't figured out or stolen the methods for manufacturing all the lightweight composites that made up most of his own F-35. It was a question some engineer would have to figure out after the fact. Grizzly's immediate problem was that the hostile was crossing in behind him.

Tracers ripped by Nagin's cockpit. He rolled the plane hard while dropping altitude.

Time to bug out of this. If the Mace was more maneuverable at slow speeds, then the throttle would be the American's friend today. He pulled out of the roll and into a hard turn away from the Mace, the fighters moving in opposite directions. Nagin pulled back and climbed for the sun.

The Mace came around and started vertical toward the F-35. The hostile plane fired its guns again, the rounds going wide left. Nagin rolled over, turned into the Mace's path and the two planes rushed past each other close enough that the jet wash rocked both planes. Nagin lifted his fighter into an Immelmann turn, moving in a half circle until his direction was reversed and he rolled wings-level.

The Chinese pilot was reversing his turn through a wide circle, like a car making a U-turn, leaving his fighter near the same altitude as the F-35.

"Come on, get inside that guy's turn," Pollard muttered.

"Sir, our ten minutes are up. Our birds are gonna be getting close to bingo fuel," one of the junior officers announced.

"Any other bandits in positions to make a run on us?" Pollard asked.

"No, sir," the junior officer replied. "We've got them cordoned off."

"Contact *Washington*. Tell them it's their turn to play," Pollard ordered. "Once they're in position, recall our people."

"Aye, sir."

The seaman apprentice tried to move under Kyra's hands and screamed as the bit of shrapnel ground against her collarbone.

"Don't move," Kyra ordered her. "If you move—"

"I got shot?" It came out almost as a stutter.

She doesn't know what happened. Kyra had taken the Agency's course on trauma medicine, training for officers who were going to serve in war zones, where they might get pressed into service as first responders. Her thinking was suddenly clear and she recognized the symptoms of shock. The girl's breathing was rapid and shallow, and she was staring straight up at the blue sky, her pupils dilated. "Yeah, something like that."

"It hurts."

Kyra had to lean close to the girl's head to hear her. "I know," Kyra told her. *Distract her,* she thought. "What's your name?"

"Cassie."

Nagin eased back on his throttle the smallest bit and pulled inside the Mace's turn. The Chinese pilot saw it and throttled up his own plane. He began closing the distance between the two planes, trying to make the American overshoot or slow down again to avoid that error.

Nagin grinned and slammed his throttle full forward. The F-35 jumped forward and crossed the Mace's turn. He pulled hard right on the stick, rolled the plane, and came around in a tight circle that threatened to cross the Chinese plane's turn again.

Gotcha.

The distance between the planes was less than two miles and the Mace couldn't move any direction fast enough to escape the F-35's attack vector. Nagin kicked the afterburner, tracked the Mace's direction for a quarter second, and pulled the gun trigger.

The rounds tore into the Mace's airframe, shredding wing and stabilizer metal into jagged petals and ripping holes that began to spew fluids in dark contrails as the plane rolled into another corkscrew. Nagin held the gunsight on the black bird until his gun ran dry. He watched his tracers embed themselves in the black plane's airframe—

A solid red triangle appeared on the radar track. "There!" Pollard yelled. The cheers in the Tactical Flag Command Center were matched by the noise coming over the comm from the crew in the CIC. "Hard to hide from radar with a bunch of jagged holes in your wing."

"Sir, MIGs are moving to protect the Chinese plane," someone announced over the comm. "Our birds are in pursuit. Time to intercept, forty seconds."

"They won't get them all," Pollard said over the speaker. "Not enough missiles left to take them all out. *Washington's* fighters?"

"Two minutes out," someone said.

"Grizzly, you've got thirty seconds and then you'll have company," Pollard said.

Twenty more than I need. The Assassin's Mace was in a steep dive, trailing black smoke and juking like a nervous insect. The island of Penghu was filling the canopy. Nagin pushed his throttle forward, fired the afterburner, and broke the speed of sound. Everyone on Penghu would hear it. Grizzly ignored the ground and focused on his helmet HUD. The radar in the nose was trying to get enough data on the black fighter for a missile lock, but even wounded, the black diamond was making itself a hard target. The Mace jerked up its nose and leveled out more quickly than Nagin had thought possible. He deployed the airbrakes and pulled back on his own stick and felt his entire body push against his seat harness as gravity pulled hard on him. He came out of the dive a half mile below the Mace. The Chinese stealth plane banked and turned toward its approaching brothers as it tried to close the distance faster than Pollard's deadline.

Nagin got inside the Mace's turn and put the Joint Strike Fighter's nose directly on the Chinese fighter's underbelly. The HUD in his helmet sounded a tone.

"Fox three!" Nagin said, trying not to shout.

The weapons bays under the F-35 snapped open. One of the two AMRAAMs mounted on the doors dropped out. Its rocket motors ignited and the bay doors snapped shut in less than a second.

The missile closed the distance to the Assassin's Mace in four seconds. The Chinese pilot rolled hard left and deployed chaff and flares. The aluminum strips and pyrotechnics scattered behind did nothing to confuse the weapon tracking his ruptured airframe. The missile punched through the metal cloud and arced in toward its target.

The Assassin's Mace had a lifespan that could now be measured in single seconds. The pilot knew it and reached for the ejection handle.

The missile exploded ten feet off the Mace's right aileron, showering the rear quarter of the plane with shrapnel that tore into the prototype plane's nose and forward body. The shock wave tore off the port wing and ignited a ruptured fuel tank. The rear half of the stealth plane's airframe was shredded, with black smoke and flames leaking from every hole. The aircraft pinwheeled clockwise and the metal screamed as it began to tear itself apart.

Explosive bolts around the canopy fired. The plastic bubble tumbled away and the Chinese pilot's ejection seat rocketed out of the dying plane.

Nagin arced around the dead plane and watched as it tumbled through the gray sky, flames and smoke marking its path down toward Penghu.

"I'm thirsty," Cassie said. Her blood had soaked through Jonathan's shirt and Kyra's hands were covered with it. The average human body had five liters of blood. Kyra knew the girl had lost at least one, but it was easy to overestimate blood loss.

"They're coming," Kyra said. "They'll patch you up and you can have all the water you want." *Hurry up, Jon,* she thought.

Kyra saw the hatch open out of the corner of her eye. She twisted around and saw a corpsman step through carrying a duffel bag, then a second, and Jonathan behind.

"MIGs are bugging out!" one of the pilots announced. With nothing left to defend and fresh US fighters inbound, someone had given the order to retreat. The icons on the master screen showed the remaining Chinese planes turning west. *Lincoln's* CIC exploded in shouts and yells. It would have been a moment for hard drinks and tall beers if the Navy didn't ban alcohol aboard its vessels.

"Nothing left to protect," Pollard said. "Call *Washington*. Tell them no pursuit. They won't like that but I'll buy Admiral Leavitt a few rounds to smooth things over."

The staff could hardly understand him over the cheers coming through the 1MC.

CHAPTER 18

WEDNESDAY
DAY EIGHTEEN

The SH-60B Seahawk helicopter set down on a hill that offered Kyra a high view of the crash site. The artificial wind clawed at Kyra's eyes as the Navy airman slid the door aside and he yelled at her to keep her head down. Stepping out onto grass that whipped at her feet, she landed off balance. She almost fell onto her knees as the air pushed her from all sides. Kyra balanced herself, ran out from under the helicopter, and straightened up once she passed outside the rotor wash.

Taiwanese soldiers had roped off at least fifty acres of the valley expanse below the hill. The zone inside the rope line was overrun with Taiwanese and US Naval Intelligence officers and civilians from who-knew-where. It looked like an archeological dig with grids of stakes connected by twine to allow for mapping the precise locations of recovered pieces. Men in jumpsuits with gloves and masks were carefully bagging and tagging debris that was still lying about. Dozens of parts, twisted and charred with serrated and ragged edges, were sticking out of the dirt like steel plants in an alien garden ready for harvest. A portable hoist had one large piece—part of the plane's nose, she thought—suspended from a harness. Two men were guiding it onto a flatbed truck. There was a hangar somewhere at the Makung airport where those men would crate up the remains for reassembly at some US air base. No one would tell Kyra where. She suspected no one had made that decision yet. Usually a postcrash assembly was meant to determine the cause of a crash, but in this case that was known. This reconstruction would be a perverse kind of reverse engineering. Engineers would rebuild the metal corpse to see if they could discern its design and estimate its capabilities. It would take years. Doubtless, some CIA officers who'd played no part in the plane's discovery would make their careers on the project.

The still-smoldering crater was larger than she'd imagined on the flight over. The rough oval was two dozen yards long, half as wide, and deeper by at least ten feet than the tallest man in the hole. The fire had burned the nearby vegetation to its roots, and the surface was an odd mix of blackened rock and light-brown earth. It felt stiff. Only a few sections of the plane were still visible, all black, whether from the original RAM-absorbing topcoat paint or the heat of the fire now extinguished, she didn't know. Some of both, she supposed. The plane had hit the ground at a sharp angle and set off a wide-reaching fireball, judging by the burn radius. Kyra realized then that some of the pebbled detritus under her feet was shrapnel from the plane. Small wisps of smoke were still rising from the pit. She hoped it was not carcinogenic but knew chances were not good. The stiff wind carried most of it away as it came over the crater's lip, but the men inside had filter masks on their faces.

Jonathan was standing at the crater's edge staring down into the pit. She reached his position and stood next to him. He didn't turn. "Any word on the pilot?" he asked.

"Taiwanese Army picked him up in the woods outside Baisha Township. There was no sign of PLA search-and-rescue in the air over the Strait," Kyra said.

"Surprising," Jonathan said. "I would think they would want their test pilot back."

"I would," Kyra said. "They'll find a way to spin his detention in their favor."

"That seems likely," Jonathan agreed. "What about that seaman apprentice?"

"Her name's Cassie," Kyra said.

"Did a little sisterly bonding, did we?"

"A little," Kyra admitted. "Spent some time talking to her down in sickbay after surgery. Turns out she's from Virginia too. A place called Dillwyn in Buckingham County, not thirty miles from my parents' place. Anyway, they got the shrapnel out. It missed the artery but managed to cut up some muscles and other blood vessels. She'll be in rehab for a while. Probably get transferred to shore duty."

Jonathan nodded. "You called Cooke?"

"Yeah," she said. "There's a team on its way here to help the Taiwanese go over the wreckage. She's expecting us back tomorrow. The Navy is going to fly us to Pearl Harbor in a few hours and we'll catch a commercial flight to Dulles. I thought we were going to get a day in Honolulu to sleep off the jet lag, but I guess not."

"The president needs some answers sooner," he said. "He still has to talk Tian down."

"You don't think this is over?" Kyra asked.

"I suspect the shooting is finished, but there are always the diplomatic rituals to follow," Jonathan said.

"Do you think the PLA would have gone after Taiwan if that thing had crippled the *Lincoln*?" Kyra asked.

"Actually, I doubt they ever truly intended to take out a carrier when this all started. I suspect they just wanted to test the stealth against our radar systems, but Pollard's little furball caught them by surprise and suddenly they had more on their plate than they were ready to handle. Or maybe they did intend to fire on a carrier all along. If they'd hit *Lincoln*, and President Stuart had ordered the Navy to pull back, there'd be a really nasty power shift going on right now in this part of the world. Maybe Tian Kai really was gambling for high stakes."

"The Navy wouldn't have seen it coming if you hadn't told them to look for it."

"Our saving grace is that the Chinese don't know that," he said. "They might think Nagin and his boys got lucky. And I could have been wrong."

Kyra stared into the craters and watched as two men struggled to lift some twisted metal—part of the cockpit frame?—where others could secure it to another harness. "There's your smoking gun," Kyra said.

Jonathan shifted his feet and kicked a piece of metal a few inches toward the crater's rim. "Nagin said it was beautiful. It's a shame he had to tear it up."

"It tried to put a missile into the ship we were on. I'm not sorry," she said. "You sound surprised."

"I suppose I am," Jonathan said. "The Chinese have a wonderful sense of design in many specialties, but military hardware isn't one of them. The PLA has never paid much attention to the aesthetics. They've had a hard enough time making their homegrown gear work, much less make it pretty, not that we always do a great job of that either, I suppose. They didn't build this thing alone."

"You think the Russians helped?"

"They would be the most likely candidates." Jonathan nodded. "But the Chinese are trying to innovate. They've had to steal technology to get to the point where they could do that, and buy what they couldn't steal. But they're turning a corner. They're showing ingenuity."

Kyra shrugged and stared into the hole. "I'm sure we'll see another one of those."

"No doubt," Jonathan said. He paused to watch the portable crane deposit its load on the flatbed. The wing section scraped across the metal truck bed with a painful screech and the workers began to chain the debris down. "Still, by the time they've perfected it for manned fighters, we'll be coming at them with unmanned fighters."

"They'll try to steal those too," Kyra said. "Maybe we should be stealing more of their gear."

"You really were born to work for NCS, weren't you?" Jonathan asked. Kyra smiled and said nothing. He removed his hand from his coat pocket and put a small device in her hand. "Have a souvenir."

Kyra turned the unit over in her hand. It was a gauge with cracked glass over a sphere lined with horizontal markings and Chinese characters. "What is it?"

"The plane's attitude indicator, I think."

"The PLA still uses mechanical gauges in their planes?"

Jonathan shrugged. "For that one they did. I guess they haven't mastered the art of designing an all-glass cockpit."

"Won't they want this?" Kyra asked, nodding her head in the direction of the recovery team in the hole.

"Every plane in the world has one, so it wouldn't tell them anything about the plane's capabilities," Jonathan said. "When they don't find it, they'll just assume it was there."

"Isn't that stealing?" Kyra asked, smiling.

"I told you before, if you have to ask before you take something, you're working for the wrong agency."

"You missed your calling," Kyra said. "You should come work for us."

"Thank you, no," Jonathan said. "I assume that Seahawk is waiting for us?"

"Yeah."

"A shame," Jonathan said. "All we get to see of Taiwan is a smoking hole." He turned and began to climb the hill. Kyra followed and tried to keep her footing in the loose dirt and metal shavings.

ZHONGNANHAI, BEIJING

Dunne was not nervous about meeting with Tian. He'd been demarched too often in his life for that and even Tian couldn't rouse those feelings in him anymore. He was just tired of dealing with such men. They were pure political animals for whom every encounter with the US was a personal test, and Dunne was tired of the diplomatic bloodletting. Hearing too many lies and telling too many of his own had worn out his soul; he needed to go home and heal. It was time to let younger men with more fire in their soul for dealing with hypocrites and confrontations take his desk.

This meeting, though, he was looking forward to. It had been a long time since he'd felt that. This meeting would be different. For once, it would be about the truth. Diplomats got to talk to chiefs of state like this maybe once in a career.

"Ambassador Dunne, would you like some tea?" Tian asked. He was unmoved, as though the Battle of the Taiwan Strait had never occurred, much less gone against him.

"No, thank you, Mr. President."

Tian nodded. "Zeng, leave us," he ordered in Mandarin. "This meeting will be private."

Zeng bowed and left the room. Tian turned away from the counter and teapot and returned to the chair behind his desk. Dunne didn't sit. This wasn't the time for it.

"I would have Zeng stay to translate," Tian said, switching back to English, "but I believe this discussion will be less pleasant than our past meetings."

"I don't doubt that, Mr. President," Dunne said. "I'm sure your English will be more than suitable." If nothing else, Dunne was sure that Tian knew enough English curse words. Most of the foreigners he'd ever met did.

"Ambassador Dunne, your country has interfered in Chinese internal affairs," Tian announced. "It will not happen again."

"With respect, the United States will always stand by her allies," Dunne replied.

"And your commitment to the 'One China' policy?"

"Our commitment has never been absolute, sir," Dunne admitted. "We acceded to it to keep the peace in the hope that China and Taiwan could work out a peaceful settlement. If China is determined to go to war instead, President Stuart might have to reconsider his position on the issue." Dunne was perilously close to overstepping his bounds as a diplomat by talking about a president's future actions, but this was one time that he was willing to go to the edge.

Tian looked at the ambassador and Dunne saw a flash of rage behind

the man's eyes, but his face never moved. "There can be no other position now. The United States and Taiwan have lost. Surely you see it."

"Quite the contrary," Dunne told him, surprised. "From our point of
view, it is China that has lost . . . lost a great deal more than you realize, I think."

"Your blindness surprises me, Aidan. I have always considered you
to be an insightful person. I think it is very clear what we have gained,"
Tian said. "We control Kinmen. Its release will come at a steep price to
both of your countries. Part of that price will be the return of the traitor
your officers helped escape during these events."

"I have no knowledge of any such escape," Dunne said. It was not a
lie. He had tried very hard to stay out of Mitchell's affairs, but he had
to restrain a smile at the thought that the chief of station had found a
way to twist a knife in Tian's ribs.

"I believe you. But President Stuart surely knows about it, or will,
and I will make the same demand in a few days. If he concedes, we
will get our traitor back and his execution will be made public. Your
CIA will have shown itself to be feckless again. If not, and he refuses,
then Kinmen will remain under our control and Taiwan will blame
you for the loss. Your alliance with the island will be strained, and
they will be the weaker for it," Tian said. He sipped his tea and set
the cup on the desk. "It would be better to return him, but I don't
expect that President Stuart will do it. It has always been a failing
of your country that you will not sacrifice a few lives for the greater
good."

"You are quite wrong about that, Mr. President. The difference between us is that when we sacrifice a few for the many, those few have
volunteered themselves. We do not consider our people to be dispens-
able."

"Quite foolish of you, relying on people to make their own choices
in such matters," Tian said, almost dismissive. It was one of the few
times Dunne had seen true emotion break through the man's facade.
"The people do not know what is best."

"Only because you refuse to tell them the truth," Dunne countered.

"The truth is what we say it is," Tian said.

"That, sir, is foolish."

"It has served us very well in the past."

"It didn't serve you at Tiananmen Square," Dunne said. "At least not
as well as you think it has. I promise, your people haven't forgotten.

And the rest of the world certainly hasn't. Pretending it didn't happen doesn't make it so."

The rage flashed behind Tian's eyes a second time. "You judge us for trying to maintain order at home when the United States tries to impose its order on the world?"

"The United States does not turn its military against its own citizens, sir," Dunne explained. "A military exists to kill the enemy. When it is used to keep order among its own people, the people become the enemy. Just as you claim there is only one China but you see the Taiwanese as the enemy."

"They are Chinese!" Tian hit the desk with his hand. "There will be no independence for Taiwan! Their citizens have seen what we will do if they continue to press for separation. The next president they elect may not be a fool, but he will support reunification. We will press him and he will be weak because he will have seen the price of defiance!"

Dunne looked at Tian for a long moment, and then he smiled. "Sir, you have not gained nearly as much as you think," he said. "I doubt very much that the independence movement on Taiwan is dead. Quite the opposite, I'm sure. I suspect that you are correct about Liang. You have humiliated him, and we're not altogether sorry about that, but you might find that he was right about one fact. His people will support a leader willing to stand up to you. The next Taiwanese president may be more troublesome than Liang was, and the Politburo will have you to blame for it. You won't understand this, but people who have tasted freedom are loath to give it up to a bully. So, yes, you hold Kinmen, but the world has seen you for the bully you are. This will play like Tiananmen Square. It's too late to turn off the cameras. You have set back the world's view of your country by twenty years. There may be sanctions—"

"There will be no sanctions," Tian said, waving his hand in another dismissive gesture. "Your country cannot afford them. Our economy is almost as large as yours and Americans want our goods too much."

"President Tian, you are making the same mistake that every tyrant has ever made about the United States," Dunne said. "You equate our wealth with unwillingness to sacrifice for a just cause. You'll be surprised at what Americans are willing to support when their sense of justice has been offended." *And you offend us, sir.*

"America is weak," Tian said. The contempt was thick. The Chinese president was dropping all pretense of equanimity, whether intention-

ally or not Dunne couldn't tell. "You can't stand pictures of dead soldiers, expensive gasoline, or anything else that disrupts your easy lives.
Americans will not suffer that for Kinmen alone. We will see who is
right."

"I am," Dunne said without hesitation. "Read history, sir. A great
many leaders who believed that Americans are weak because they live
well has learned otherwise. And it won't be 'for Kinmen alone.' When
the American people hear that you shot down one of our pilots and
tried to sink one of our carriers, they will not sit still. There may not be
a war, but they will want to see you punished. And you still need our
markets more than we need your factories. Your government's political
survival depends on them. Ours doesn't."

"The PLA will maintain order, as it always has," Tian said.

"In the short run, I don't doubt it. But the more of your citizens you
kill, the more the free world will come to despise you. You have started
your country on a spiral down, and you, President Tian, aren't the man
to stop it. And if it doesn't stop, the Chinese century will be over before
it's even begun. You've threatened everything your country hopes to
do for the next fifty years, and all you have to show for it is Kinmen, a
wrecked stealth plane, dead pilots, and a terrible news story that Harry
Stuart or the next president will release at the moment of his choosing.
Eventually, the PLA and the party will see it."

"I will be here long after you and your president are gone," Tian
said.

"Both of us retire in a few months, so that's not saying much,"
Dunne said. In saying it, he suddenly felt more free and uncon-
strained than he had in years. "But you've guaranteed that President
Stuart's successor will follow his lead in dealing with you. Our foreign
policy toward China will be set in stone as long as you remain in
office, and I think you're going to find that Kinmen will weigh very
heavily on you."

"Your next president will not send your carriers here. We have finally
tested our military against yours. We have seen our weaknesses and
yours. We will correct ours. The next plane will succeed where this one
failed. We have your stealth technology, we have Kinmen, and we are
a step closer to Penghu. We will meet on more equal terms next time,"
Tian said.

"Mr. President, the United States Navy just destroyed the most advanced plane in your arsenal. Your navy has not proven itself capable of

taking on our carrier battle groups, and I have the president's personal assurance that you will be seeing more of them in the future. As for seeing more of our weapons, I remind you that your air force was just introduced to our *second*-best fighter plane. Heaven help your pilots when they meet our first."

"We held many weapons in reserve," Tian said. "Your carriers would not have survived."

"Perhaps not," Dunne admitted. "But if you ever do manage to destroy one, all of China will pay a very heavy price for it." Tian said nothing and Dunne let the silence hang for a good while. "President Tian," he finally said, "our countries don't have to be enemies."

"Perhaps not," Tian replied after a long moment. "But never friends as long as you help Taiwan defy us. The island must come home."

"Make home a place where Taiwan feels welcome, and it will come on its own," Dunne said. For that, Tian offered no reply, and Dunne let the silence hang in the air for a good long time. *Time to go home,* he finally told himself. "Do you have a message you would like me to pass to President Stuart?"

Tian looked up. "You may tell him that this is not over."

"No, sir, it surely is not," Dunne replied. "Good day, President Tian." He bowed, turned his back to the Chinese head of state, and walked out of the office for the last time.

CHAPTER 19

THURSDAY
DAY NINETEEN

The river was far larger than any Pioneer had ever seen. It was very wide and he wondered if it was the Potomac or maybe the James. A careless remark by a laborer at this plantation facility told him that he was in Virginia, but where exactly he didn't know. He had seen maps of Virginia. So much US history had its start in this state, and much of that came back to those two rivers. From its width he could tell that he surely was near the Atlantic Ocean, but whether he was near Washington or Richmond he didn't know. The west bank here—he had divined the direction from the sun's lazy arc through the cloudless sky—was frozen red clay, and the erosion suggested the river was large enough to suffer from visible tides. He had been watching bits of ice flow past him for several hours now and had tried to imagine that it was the Yangtze to comfort himself. That failed him. Reality weighed too much on his thoughts. Pioneer would not be going home again. China was denied territory now.

He never gave much thought to how the CIA might exfiltrate him from his homeland. It was an event that he'd never expected would happen, and the reality had proven frightening at the time and mundane in retrospect. The escape from his apartment had been sudden and terrifying. Until he walked off the gangway in Seoul, it had driven every thought from his mind except what he needed to survive at the moment. He'd been in the air a half hour after the interview in the private plane, and the release of tension that came with the realization of his safety had left him worn, more so than he could ever remember. He had slept for long hours and finally awakened over California. It was a blessing that saved him from the claustrophobia that could have set in on the cramped little jet that had stopped only for fuel during the flight to . . . here. An hour's drive in a car with blackened windows finished the trip to his new home, which was a small colonial-style house in a wooded area near the river.

They wouldn't tell him where "here" was. After all he had given them, the CIA still did not trust him enough to tell him where he would live out his first year in the United States. He imagined they had a logical reason for it, learned through harsh experience. He certainly was not the first defector they had brought to some rural piece of ground by a river like this one. Just as certainly, some of those other defectors had been double agents who found a way back home. So the CIA would not want Pioneer to know enough to compromise a location where they might bring other defectors from China someday.

The house was small, and temporary to be sure, but palatial by his standards. His Beijing apartment had been small by design and grubby by his habits. This home had two levels, bathrooms on each, and was furnished, with shelves full of books in English that he couldn't read, and decorated with paintings of cowboys that fascinated him. Pioneer wondered whether there were real cowboys, or were they another creation of movies like the ones that so exaggerated the excitement of life as a spy? He hoped for the former.

Pioneer wondered if the MSS had emptied his Beijing apartment of his possessions yet. He hadn't owned much, but what he had owned was precious to him. He had brought only his photographs of his mother and father. He wouldn't have to forget their faces. Had they been alive, he wondered if they would be proud or ashamed of what he had done. His father had never cared for the party and had even spoken hard words about Mao and Deng at times when such sentiments could bring down equally harsh reprisals on those who were too public with their thoughts. It was his mother who had taught him that every choice he made earned a consequence that he couldn't choose. Pioneer was standing on the bank of a foreign river now because of a single choice he had made more than two decades ago. He wondered whether he would have made the same choice if he could have seen the end from the beginning.

Daily he received visitors in his living room whom he was not free to turn away. He was no longer an active asset, but his mind still held many useful bits of information about the PLA, the Politburo, Tian Kai, MSS programs, and covert human assets, some of which were here in the United States. Picking his brain clean like a vulture over a rotted carcass doubtless would take years. After that, he didn't know what they would do with him. A man on the plane had promised him, in flawless Mandarin, that he would be given a home, a job, a stipend, and a new name. He didn't know whether they would let him decide where his new home would be. There were Chinatowns in most US cities of any size, though he didn't think it would be wise to live in such a neighborhood. Wouldn't the MSS expect him to hide among his own people? Would it make him easier for them to find? Would they even look for him? If they found him, what would they do? There were no reports from the MSS archives of kidnappings on US soil. Would he be the first?

Barron had promised him US citizenship if he wanted it. His lack of excitement for the offer surprised his old case officer. Pioneer had not committed treason for the United States. The CIA simply had been the conduit through which he could best hope to damage the party. He might have chosen the British or even the Russians had they been in a better position to realize his goals. He wondered if he could have built a new life for himself in Moscow.

Could he do it here? That was the true question. He closed his eyes and listened for God or the river to tell him.

There was no answer.

Barron and several others stood on the short hill behind him, waiting in the cold, including the woman who had pulled him out of his home. They had been there for more than an hour. They had said nothing that he could hear.

He turned his back on the water, sat down on the hard shore, and closed his eyes.

Kyra savored the smell of the Jack Daniels Old No. 7 whiskey and felt her throat aching for a taste but shook her head when Cooke offered her the glass. She wasn't sure that she wasn't an alcoholic, and three days dry aboard the *Lincoln* had taught her that the draw was a little too strong for her comfort. She had restrained herself on the flight home, but she doubted she would have the strength to go dry again if she indulged now.

Cooke shrugged and offered the tumbler to Jonathan. "You realize," he said, "that whiskey is an industrial-grade solvent flavored with charred creosote leached from oak barrels?"

"Absolutely," Barron said. He held up his glass. "And mellowed by letting it drip through ten feet of sugar maple charcoal. The end product of a chemical process so improbable it could only have been divinely inspired."

"I can't begin to guess how many brain cells that will kill," Jonathan said.

"Given the occasion, I consider it a worthy trade," Barron said.

"Amen," Cooke agreed. "And you should make an exception for once," she advised Jonathan. "You almost got yourself killed." There was plenty more she wanted to say about it to him, but not in present company.

"Far be it from me to question management," Jonathan said, amused. "But a ginger ale will do nicely."

"Aren't you just lucky?" Cooke told him. She reached into her shoulder satchel, pulled out a soda can, and handed it to him. "It's even cold." Jonathan cracked it open.

"How are the Zhous?" Kyra asked.

"Roland and Rebecca?" Barron replied. "They led the MSS on a merry chase for two hours before getting picked up. They spent an uncomfortable night under some bright lights, but the Ministry finally had to let them go. Their cover held up, and wearing a red backpack isn't strong evidence to build an espionage case, even in China." He drained his glass, then continued. "We'll leave them in place for another few months just for appearances and then bring them home. They'll get their pick of assignments after that."

"And what about Pioneer?" Kyra stared down at the Chinese agent sitting on the cold ground before the river.

"Well enough, I think," Barron told her. "We have him under a discreet suicide watch. The transition period is always rough. It's the oddest thing. A person can live under so much stress for so long, but it's after they come out from it that they break emotionally. Threat of death doesn't stop them, but take away their homeland forever and they consider killing themselves. Pioneer doesn't seem like the type, but he could use a friendly face if you'd like to help with the debrief."

"I would, thank you," Kyra said.

"I assume you want to go back to the NCS?" Cooke asked.

"To be honest, ma'am, I don't know if I want to stay at all," the younger woman replied.

"You should. You have a talent for the work," Cooke admitted. "We'd approve you for a post overseas, and Micheal Rhead will be gone by the time we sign the paperwork."

"It's not the work, ma'am. I don't know if I can stand the politics,"

Kyra said. "These politicians would run over their mothers to get in front of a camera, and we have to trust them to make decisions about whether our assets live or die?"

"Stuart made the right choice," Cooke said.

"The DNI didn't," Kyra said. "And Stuart picked him in the first place."

"Rhead is an aberration. And as presidents go, Stuart understands our business better than most," Barron said. "He told Rhead to resign for 'personal reasons.' That ought to tell you something about what he thinks about our business."

"What would you have done if Stuart had ordered you to leave Pioneer in place?" Kyra asked.

"I would have given the order to exfiltrate him anyway," Cooke said without hesitation. "And then I would have resigned and gone home and waited for the FBI to come arrest me. You haven't been in the business long enough to see that most assets are amoral. Rhead was right about that. They use us as much as we use them. They have their rewards and most of them aren't worth your loyalty. But Pioneer is a rare exception, and when you come across one of those, you take care of him."

"And you?" Kyra asked Barron. "What would you have done?"

He pointed at Cooke. "Same as her," he said. "Actually, I threatened to do it."

"He did," Cooke admitted. "There is a time to fall on your sword, but now isn't it, and if you quit, I think you'll regret it. Anyway, I hope this will help change your mind." Cooke handed her drink to Barron, opened the messenger bag she had slung over her shoulder, and extracted a pair of hinged cherrywood boxes. She opened the first, pulled a printed card from her pocket, and turned to Jonathan. "Jonathan Burke, for performance of outstanding services or for achievement of a distinctly exceptional nature in a duty or responsibility, I present you with the Distinguished Intelligence Medal." She put the card inside the case, closed it, and offered it to the analyst.

"Thank you," Jonathan said, taking the wooden box.

"Winning the award is more important, but you know there's money attached to that, right?" Cooke asked.

Jonathan smiled. "I do. And who says winning the award is more important?"

"Ah, the mercenary analyst. A dying breed," Cooke said. She opened the second box and read off the card inside. "Kyra Stryker, for a vol-

untary act of courage performed under hazardous conditions, for outstanding achievements and services rendered with distinction under
conditions of grave risk, I present you with the Intelligence Star." She
replaced the card and delivered the award to its owner. "There's another
one of those waiting for you back at headquarters. We couldn't give you
one for Venezuela as long as Rhead was around, but Clark here took
care of business after the resignation hit the president's desk."

"Thank you, sir," Kyra said, taking the cherrywood box. She opened
it. The bronze coin inside was stamped with an eagle's head in profile
atop a sunburst over a five-point star, with the words "Central Intelligence Agency" and "For Valor" written around the circumference. She
didn't say anything, instead running her fingers over the metal. Then
she closed her eyes. A warm feeling rose up inside her chest and she
felt tension drain out of her shoulders.

"You won't be able to tell anyone about that," Barron said. "Not until
Pioneer's file is declassified, anyway. You'll be an old woman when that
happens. Sorry about that."

"Nothing to be sorry about," Kyra said. She closed the box. "But we
just lost our best asset in Beijing. The Chinese are starting to test their
capabilities. It's a bad time to have intelligence gaps on their intentions."

"We have more assets. There are always more," Cooke told her.

Kyra looked down at Pioneer, sitting in the sand, eyes closed, and
wondered what he was thinking. "Not like him."

"Sure there are," Jonathan countered. "Plenty of people want to
change the world for all the right reasons. Just have to find them."

Cooke looked at Jonathan, surprised. "You're going soft."

"I didn't say I wanted to be the one who had to go looking for them."

"You were right," she said. "You really are an acquired taste."

"And yet, you still haven't fired me," he observed.

Smiling, Cooke leaned in close and nudged him hard. And Jonathan
finally smiled back.

Cooke turned Kyra. "No need to hide you anymore. Two Intelligence Stars in three months. I think with that on your record, you can
pick your assignment. What do you want to do?"

It took the younger woman a few moments to settle on her answer.
"I want to finish the mission," she said, nodding toward Pioneer. Kyra
stepped forward and walked down the sandy shore.

ACKNOWLEDGMENTS

My wife Janna, who decided that the Exceptional Performance Award money would be better spent on a laptop for writing than on paying down student loans and who played single mother far too many nights while I learned how to write a novel the hard way.

My parents, Carl and Lynne Henshaw, for their love and support; and my siblings Glen, Neal, and Susan (herself, a fine writer) for their patience with my incessant prattling about the book.

"Uncle" Paul, "Aunt" Sally, and Zach Stewart, who always believed that it could be done and that I could do it; and Amy Dunafin and Glenda Mora, who thought years ago that an awkward, skinny kid just might be able to write a book someday. Everyone should have such friends.

Flint Dille, Sam Sarkar, and Nick Brondo for taking my writing more seriously than I took it myself; and Ken Freimann and Jason Yarn, my literary agent, for putting all the wheels in motion.

The Touchstone Team—Lauren Spiegel, my editor, for her wise suggestions and guidance; Lisa Healy, my copy editor, who saved me from many an embarrassing gaffe; and Cherlynne Li and Ervin Serrano who created that marvelous cover for the book.

Keith Blount and his Literature & Latte Team, for creating Scrivener, the app that ended four years of pain trying to write a novel with a word processor. A writer who's trying to draft a novel without using Scrivener is probably a masochist.

The members of the CIA Red Cell who taught me the ropes, and who are some of the smartest people I've ever met in my life—Bob, Paul, Dave, Tom, Donna, Harry, and Vincent.

And the other Agency officers who I've worked with, honorable public servants and good people all, who are dedicated to protecting a nation and do a fine job of it—Tom, Steve, Ken, Rachel, Brad, Jennifer, Mike, Norm, Mali for helping with the Chinese language, and all the rest too numerous to list.